The Third Book of the Rune Blade Trilogy

BROKEN BLADE

Ann Marston

HarperPrism
An Imprint of HarperPaperbacks

HarperPaperbacks
A Division of HarperCollins*Publishers*
10 East 53rd Street, New York, N.Y. 10022-5299

This is a work of fiction. The characters, incidents, and
dialogues are products of the author's imagination and are not to
be construed as real. Any resemblance to actual events or
persons, living or dead, is entirely coincidental.

ISBN: 0-06-105627-8

HarperPrism is an imprint of HarperPaperbacks.

HarperCollins®, 📖 ®, HarperPaperbacks™, and
HarperPrism® are trademarks of HarperCollins*Publishers* Inc.

Cover illustration by Yvonne Gilbert
Maps by Barbara Galler-Smith

First printing: February 1997

Printed in the United States of America

Visit HarperPaperbacks on the World Wide Web at
http://www.harpercollins.com/paperbacks

❖ 10 9 8 7 6 5 4 3 2 1

For Tom and Laura Marston,
my parents,
who taught me how to fly
and left me free to do it

And for Laura and Dan Gyoba,
who also know how to fly free

The Royal Houses of Celi, Skai and Tyra

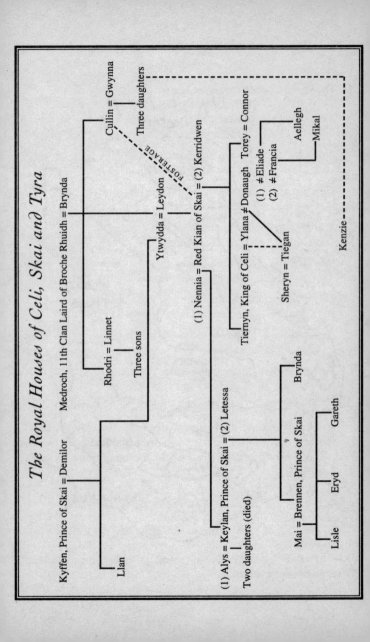

Notes

The year is divided into eight seasons:

Late Winter:	Imbolc to Vernal Equinox (February 1 to March 21)
Early Spring:	Vernal Equinox to Beltane (March 21 to May 1)
Late Spring:	Beltane to Midsummer Solstice (May 1 to June 21)
Early Summer:	Midsummer Solstice to Lammas (June 21 to August 1)
Late Summer:	Lammas to Autumnal Equinox (August 1 to September 21)
Early Autumn:	Autumnal Equinox to Samhain (September 21 to October 31)
Late Autumn:	Samhain to Midwinter Solstice October 31 to December 21)
Early Winter:	Midwinter Solstice to Imbolc (December 21 to February 1)

The four sun feasts are Midwinter Solstice, Vernal Equinox, Midsummer Solstice, and Autumnal Equinox.

The four fire feasts are Imbolc, Beltane, Lammas, and Samhain.

Pronunciation Guide

The "C" in Celi is the hard Celtic "C," so Celi is pronounced Kay-lee

The "dd" is the Welsh "th" sound, as in *the*n, thus Myrddin is pronounced "Myrthun."

Book Three of the
Rune Blade Trilogy

BROKEN
BLADE

PART

1

The Messenger

The formal ballroom of the palace of the Borlani Emperor felt like the inside of a sweat hut. Too many candles to count—thousands of them, it seemed—blazed and flared in the luxuriously decorated room, each adding its own contribution to the sweltering heat. In the brilliant light, gems and crystal sparked and flashed in a scintillating display of lavish wealth as formations of richly dressed courtiers broke and swirled throughout the room like eddies in a stream.

The candlelight did a good job of disguising the faded colors and worn edges of the once-opulent wall hangings and upholstery on the graceful couches. If one didn't look too closely, the chips in the crystal goblets and the small dents in the silver serving platters hardly showed at all.

Naturally, I looked. Of course, I said nothing, but smiled and dutifully pretended like everyone else not to notice. The display made by the courtiers almost made up for the dingy and poorly repaired mosaic on the ballroom floor.

The thickest concentration of elegant men and women clustered near the throne where my prince, Tiegan of Celi, stood speaking with the Borlani Emperor, a gilt-and-crystal goblet of wine held in his hand. Tiegan's dark gold hair gleamed in the candlelight. As always, he stood with casual grace, his body elegantly supple and lithe beside the portly Emperor and his equally portly Empress.

I stood beside an open window in the vain hope of catching a cool breeze coming off the sea. My ball gown, ells and ells of floating pale green tissue silk, might have been suitable for this stuffily overdressed function, but it did nothing to ease my discomfort. The sempstress had given me no room to breathe in it. The bodice bound so tightly to my ribs and waist, I could not draw a deep breath without the danger of splitting the dress right up the back. On the other hand, the neckline was cut low enough to make dangerous folly out of even *trying* to take a deep breath. And, of course, I could carry no sword while wearing it. Without her sword, any bheancoran is uncomfortable, and I was no exception. The presence of the jeweled stiletto in my garter above my right knee wasn't as comforting as it should have been. In order to get at it, I would have to fight my way through five layers of silk.

I sipped delicately at the iced wine I held and glanced around the room again. Not that I expected danger in this well-guarded ballroom, but I was sworn to protect Tiegan, and old habits die hard. None of the people I had met here seemed dangerous. Their talk was mostly court gossip—who was seen creeping from whose bedchamber, and who was vying for favor and influence. Harmless chatter, most of it—unless you happened to be the one being chivvied out of favor. Or, may-haps, married to someone skulking in someone else's bed-chamber.

The Borlani are an old culture. They conduct their intrigues and stylized political machinations with a skill and brittle for-mality that fascinated me. I had learned a lot in the two fort-nights we had been here. What I might do with the knowledge when I returned to Celi, I had no idea. Certainly the subtle weave of plot and counterplot would be nothing less than ridiculous and ludicrous at home.

Two men standing by the entrance of the room caught my eye. Both were dressed in dark clothing, one in unrelieved black and the other in drab brown. They appeared shockingly out of place among the peacock display of the rest of the men present. One of the men, the one in black, had hair so dark it seemed to absorb all light, giving back no shine to the candle glow. I was too far away to see the color of his eyes, but I thought they might be as black as his hair.

I was certain the man was Maedun.

Well, why not? The Maedun were not barred entry into Borlan. Borlan was not at war with Maedun. Not yet, at any rate, even though the Maedun had taken Laringras, which lay against the western border of Borlan. The Borlani may have lost their empire, but they still maintained a formidable army, and there were rumors that their magicians were a match to any blood magic sorcerers the Maedun could produce.

Both men seemed intent on the Emperor. Or perhaps it was Tiegan who held their rapt attention. It was no secret that Tiegan and I had come from King Tiernyn, Tiegan's father and my uncle, in Celi to speak with the Emperor about trade and mutual assistance in the event of an attack by the Maedun.

The man in black turned slightly and looked straight at me. For a moment, his face remained blank and unreadable. Then he smiled coldly and inclined his head in a brief, mocking acknowledgment of my presence. A cold chill rippled down my spine.

I glanced at the Emperor, who was still chatting with Tiegan, smiling and gesturing broadly with the hand holding his own goblet. He paid no attention to the two men at the door. When I looked back at the entrance of the ballroom, both men were gone.

A servant swept past with a tray held balanced in one hand. I deposited my empty goblet on the tray as he passed, then made my way slowly through the break and eddy of the courtiers until I stood beside Tiegan.

The Emperor held out his hand to me. "Lady Brynda," he said, smiling effusively. His Celae was fluent, but oddly accented. "How lovely you look tonight." The Borlani tongue has difficulty with our Celae "L" sound, and his words came out strangely pronounced, almost lisping. Between the childish pronunciation and his corpulent body, the Emperor might be mistaken for a comic figure. But he had come to the throne as a child of thirteen and had held Borlan strongly for the better part of fifty years. Several people had made the error of discounting the cold shrewdness in the porcine little eyes, and most of them lived barely long enough to regret the fatal error. Some of them, so the stories went, never realized exactly why they died. The Borlani Emperor smiled and beamed at his subjects, but those watery, ice-blue eyes missed nothing.

He turned to the Empress, who looked almost as hot and uncomfortable as I felt. Of course, she bore the weight of at least ten times as much jewelry as I did. "Doesn't she look lovely, my dear?"

The Empress smiled vaguely at me. "Very lovely," she murmured.

I dropped a small curtsy. "Thank you, Your Excellency. And thank you, too, my lady Empress."

"We must talk again," the Emperor said. "You will join us later for the meal, my lord Tiegan? You and this ravishing lady must sit next to me."

"Of course, Excellency," Tiegan said, bowing.

The Emperor still held my hand firmly captured in his. He raised it to his lips and nipped flirtatiously at the knuckle of my middle finger. Smiling blandly, he released my hand and turned away to speak with another courtier who stood politely waiting for attention on the other side of the Empress.

Tiegan glanced down at me. One of his eyebrows rose in query. The threads of the bond between us vibrated within my chest, and I knew he felt my uneasiness as well as I did. He took my arm and led me to a quiet alcove near a window.

"What is it?" he asked when he was sure we were alone and out of hearing of anyone.

"Two Maedun men were just here," I said. "I think they were watching you."

He looked around, but the two men were nowhere in sight. He nodded. "It's time we were out of here, anyway," he said. "I can't leave until after that cursed banquet, but there's no reason for you to stay here. Go back to the ship and make sure everything is ready to leave in the morning. I'll be along as soon as I can."

"Be careful," I said. "I don't trust those two Maedun. They could be up to anything."

"Knowing the Maedun, they probably are." Tiegan smiled,

but there was no humor in the expression. "I'm too valuable to the Emperor," he said. "He'll let me go nowhere without a whole contingent of guards armed to the teeth. Will you be all right?"

"I'll be in a carriage," I said. "And the Emperor always gives me two or three guards when I go abroad. Make my excuses to the Emperor. Tell him I felt faint or something. Or tell him the truth. If I try to eat anything wearing this ridiculous gown, I'll burst out of it and disgrace us both."

He laughed. "I'll do my best," he said. "The randy old goat will be highly disappointed that he won't be able to peer down the neckline of your gown during dinner."

I said something highly uncomplimentary and unregal about the Emperor.

Tiegan laughed again. "You're sure you'll be all right?"

"Of course." I made a distasteful face. "I'll be guarded. Don't worry about me."

"Very well. I wish I could go with you." He turned to speak with a courtier who bulled his way across the room to our alcove. I took the opportunity to slip away unnoticed.

An elegant carriage awaited me when I stepped out into the stultifying humidity of the Borlani night, relieved to escape the ponderously formal Imperial reception. Even the tissue-thin silk of my ball gown felt too heavy and restricting in the heat. I swore the first thing I'd do when I got back to the ship was change into my tunic and trews. They were heavier than the ball gown, woven of linen rather than silk, but they didn't bind so tightly to my body and gave at least the illusion of cool comfort.

The carriage footman, a wispy man resplendent in white-and-blue livery trimmed with a preponderance of gold braid, stepped forward and made me a stiff, formal bow.

"You are the lady Brynda al Keylan of Celi?" His accent was so thick as to be nearly unintelligible.

My Borlani was better than his Celae. "I am," I said. "You are to take me down to the quayside. Back to our ship, the *Skai Seeker*. Do you know where it is?"

One of his sleekly groomed eyebrows rose infinitesimally in disapproval. I had scandalized the poor man again. Borlani women did not, under any circumstance, venture out unescorted at night, or at any other time. It was my observation that even ladies creeping out for a clandestine meeting with their lovers were accompanied by no less than three armed guards and a lady's maid or two. How they managed to keep their assignations secret was beyond my understanding.

However, I was not Borlani; I was Celae, and Celae women came and went very much as they pleased. We are not known for our tractability or our submissiveness.

I drew myself up to my full height, which put my eyes on a level with his, and stared haughtily at him. I probably outweighed him by nearly a full stone. Bheancorans to the princes of Celi or Skai are not small, dainty women. I had started training with a sword when I was five. I had both the height and the weight to be a good swordswoman, and this footman had spent most of his life riding on an elegant coach, handing tiny, delicate Borlani women into or out of it. His color deepened even as his expression faded to perfect, bland neutrality, and he bowed again, then offered his hand to assist me into the carriage. I got a brief glimpse of the wide grin of one of the armed guards sitting above the door as I got in.

The interior of the coach was stiflingly warm. But not as hot as the palace ballroom. Trickles of sweat ran uncomfortably down my back and between my breasts beneath the silk of the gown, probably staining it beyond redemption. As the carriage began to move, I raised one of the window shades enough to let some air in, and blessed Tiegan for giving me the opportunity to escape early so that I could return to the ship to ensure that all was ready for our departure on the morning tide.

We had already left our departure from Borlan late. If we

hoped to elude the equinocal storms that ravaged the coasts of the Isle of Celi as autumn approached, we had to leave with the morning tide on the morrow, or risk long delays in a Falian or Isgardian port as we waited out high winds and violent seas. And any continental port was bound to be less than friendly to a Celae vessel.

I sat back and opened my fan, the one useful frippery carried by all Borlani women. The coach turned a corner, and I lost sight of the tarnished glory of the Imperial Palace. Nearly five hundred years ago, the Borlani Empire had spanned the continent. The Imperial Palace had been the showplace of the world back then. As the Borlani Empire slowly shrank back to encompass only Borlan itself and a handful of smaller vassal states to the east, the palace faded with the empire. The emperors, though, had lost none of their arrogance if the present one was a fair example, nor had they lost their taste for pomp and ceremony.

It was no wonder the Borlani had tried to take over the world, I thought irritably as I used the fan to try to force some cool air against my face. Had I lived in this steam bath, I'd be eager to find cooler climates, too.

We took another corner and entered a long, wide street lined with tall houses. The Borlani built their homes flush to the street—an outer shell of rooms built of thick stone around an open central courtyard to ensure air circulated throughout the whole structure. They were very different from the snug houses we built on Celi to keep out the chill of the winter winds. Ruins of houses built to the Borlani design still dotted the continent. The northern Isgardian winters must have been a terrible shock back then for the first Borlani lords to claim estates in those newly conquered lands.

Tiegan and I had come to Borlan at the invitation of the Emperor as emissaries from Tiegan's father, King Tiernyn of Celi. It seemed appropriate that two countries with a common enemy might discover they had much to discuss. The Maedun had conquered most of the continent, with the exception of the mountainous country of Tyra, the Isle of Celi, and what remained of the Borlani Empire. Laringras, on Borlan's western border, was ruled by a Maedun Lord Protector, who had taken the throne from the king of Laringras over forty years ago. The Borlani were understandably wary and suspicious of the Maedun, trusting them no more than we did on Celi. They had no more wish than we did to end up as a Maedun protectorate.

The Emperor had made Tiegan welcome. They had spent most of the two fortnights we had been here in conference, discussing everything from trade agreements to mutual assistance treaties against the Maedun. Even though I was Tiegan's bheancoran, and sworn to protect him, as a woman, I was excluded from the conferences. Women in Borlan definitely did not participate in any form of political negotiations, and any woman who so much as showed an interest in them was instantly suspected of a propensity for deviance. I fumed in tight silence, and every evening, Tiegan and I spoke in my chamber and made notes of what had gone on during the conferences. We were cautiously sure it had been a most successful mission, but both Tiegan and I were eager to return to Celi. We had laid the groundwork; the details could be left up to ambassadors, who were more fitted for this mind-numbing work.

The carriage drew to a halt. I glanced out the window with a vague idea that the trip to the quayside had been an extremely swift one. But all I saw through the narrow gap between the bottom of the window and the shade were crumbling warehouses. We were nowhere near the pier where our ship was docked.

I slipped the window shade up higher and leaned out. Nothing but the vague shapes of warehouses met my eye. No torches lit the street. Even the stars overhead were dark behind the clouds. "What's going on?" I demanded. "Where are we?"

But only silence replied. Then I heard running feet approach the carriage. Overhead, someone grunted. Instantly alert, I listened hard, reaching for the stiletto in my garter. Something heavy fell with a loud thud and clatter to the cobbles beside the coach behind me. I recognized the sound of a falling body when I heard it. Someone had overpowered the guards.

Before I could pull up all the layers of that thrice-cursed skirt to snatch at my dagger, the footman opened the door on the opposite side of the carriage from where I sat. Behind him, a shadowy figure said, "You're sure this is the one? The Celae woman?"

"I'm certain," said the footman.

He stepped aside. I was still trying to fight my way through to the hilt of the stiletto hidden in my garter as two men leapt into the coach. One of them held a blanket. He threw it over my head, entangling me in its musty folds. I managed to grasp the dagger. One of the men grabbed my wrist, twisting it painfully, and I dropped the dagger. I jabbed my left elbow viciously into the man scrambling into the carriage beside me and had the satisfaction of hearing the breath go out of his body in an agonized grunt.

The other man swore. I struggled with the smothering folds of the blanket and managed to get my head and one arm free. Snarling, I reached out clawed fingers at the second man's eyes. He sprang back, his reflexes better than they had any right to be.

I couldn't reach the stiletto on the floor of the coach, hampered as I was by both my gown and the evil-smelling blanket. Swearing, I drew my feet up to kick out at the second man, who was still trying to get into the carriage. He drew back his hand, then swung at me. I managed to snap my head back so that his hand missed me. But he held something that crashed into my head just behind my ear. My last impression was of the infuriatingly triumphant smirk of the weedy footman.

2

I awoke to utter darkness and the gentle creaking and rocking of a ship under way on a calm sea. The hissing rush of water sliding past a wooden hull came clearly through the bulkhead somewhere behind me. I lay curled on something hard and uncomfortable. And I was cold.

Odd. I couldn't remember Tiegan coming back to the ship. And I couldn't remember weighing anchor and leaving the harbor. . . .

I tried to sit up. Sudden pain exploding through my head sent nausea churning through my belly and squeezed all the breath from my lungs. I fell back onto something both gritty and slimy at the same time, something that sent the fetid stench of mold and decay swirling in the air around my head. I choked and gagged, but managed to expel nothing but a mouthful of bitter bile. Part of the stink around me was the reek of vomit.

Surely not my own. I never became ill aboard ship. Never . . .

Fragmented images flashed through the blinding pain in my head, snatches of memory that made no sense. And overlying it all, the incongruous impression of the smug, self-satisfied grin of a weedy little footman.

I sat staring stupidly into the darkness, trying to sort it out. I puzzled it out with slow, dogged determination and frustrating difficulty. The realization that I had been kidnapped was slow in dawning. How did it make sense to kidnap me when Tiegan was far more valuable as a hostage? While it was true I was the daughter of the Prince of Skai, Tiegan was the only son of the King of all Celi. If it came right down to it, I was expendable; Tiegan wasn't.

I raised my hand to my head, trying to ease some of the pounding agony behind my eyes, and lay back on the bed.

Bed? More like a pile of rotting sacks. The coarse fabric shredded between my fingers as I gripped it.

Whoever the two men were who had paid the footman—and probably the driver—of the coach to bring me to those warehouses, they had known who I was. I remembered one of them demanding confirmation that I was "the Celae woman."

But what did they want with me? Where were they taking me? And for what purpose?

There was no doubt that I was aboard ship, or that the ship was at sea. The creaking of the hull timbers and the murmur of water made it indisputably clear that we were no longer in the harbor, but on the open sea.

And where was Tiegan?

Oh, dear gods and goddesses. Tiegan . . .

I came to my knees in a rush and banged my forehead on a low beam above the filthy bed of sacking. I fell back onto my heels, cradling my head in my hands and making soft little mewling sounds of pain as tiny, bright points of light danced behind my closed eyelids. The blinding flash of renewed pain didn't make it any easier to think.

Questions I had no answers for tumbled through the confusion. Had they also taken Tiegan? He was my prince. I had sworn to protect him with my life if necessary. Was he safe? We were bonded. He would have known instantly that I was in trouble. Had he come looking for me? Had I unwittingly drawn him into a trap, too?

Careful not to jar my head, I sat back, then tried to clear my mind. Tiegan and I were linked by the unbreakable bond of bheancoran and prince. I had always been able to sense his presence as a soft, quiet thrumming under my heart.

But all signs of the link with Tiegan were gone completely.

Gone? Was Tiegan dead?

Quelling the panic that threatened to overwhelm me wasn't easy. I had to take several deep breaths, forcing myself to remain calm. Just because I could find no trace of Tiegan's presence through the bond that linked us did not mean he was dead. It might simply mean that the distance that separated us might be too great.

I remembered my grandmother Kerri telling me once of the time when she had thought my grandfather Kian dead, and how the apparent severing of the bond between them had left her feeling hollow and empty and barren. A great and echoing internal silence was how she described it, filled with bleak despair and grief. Even the memory of it, nearly fifty years later, paled her cheeks and set a haunted expression in her eyes.

Slowly, I tested my spirit. Pain was present there, as was anger. But no internal silence. A flood of relief washed through me, leaving me light-headed and giddy. Tiegan was all right.

But the relief was short-lived. A loud, scraping sound broke the silence of the darkness. Someone was unbarring the door, making ready to enter my prison.

I had barely time to fall back onto the pile of rotten sacking, feigning unconsciousness, before a shaft of light slanted across my feet and the tattered hem of my ruined ball gown.

"Faugh," a woman's voice said in disgust. "By the gods, it's foul in here."

A man's deeper voice rumbled something I couldn't catch.

"Never mind that," the woman said. "Bring the lantern here so I can look at her."

The light became suddenly brighter, closer. I caught a whiff of the heady scent of spicy, exotic perfume above the stench of the small cabin.

"Look at me, girl," the woman said.

Her voice was compelling beyond all measure. In spite of myself, I opened my eyes and stared up at her.

"I've been searching for you for a long time, girl," the woman said. "How convenient that you were in Silichia the same fortnight I came to speak with the Emperor."

She stood bent slightly forward under the low overhead, leaning over me, her face lit by the golden glow of the lantern, her midnight black hair blending with the shadows behind her. She was quite the most beautiful woman I had ever seen, her complexion smoothly pale and flawless, her eyes nearly as black as her hair.

Maedun! Only a Maedun had that unique combination of black hair and black eyes. And there had been two Maedun men in the palace ballroom. The one man had smiled at me as if he recognized me. But why would she want me? And what had happened to Tiegan?

The Maedun woman saw my recognition and nodded, but she didn't smile. She reached out. A thin, black mist trailed from the tips of her long, graceful fingers and wrapped itself around my head. Numbing cold seeped into my head as I breathed in the loathsome mist. It slid down my throat into my chest to wrap itself around my heart. Nearly choking, unable to speak, unable to think at all, I could only stare at her.

"Red hair," she murmured. "Well, well, well. Grigori was right, then. Have I snared one of the Tyr's get from Celae?"

"The Tyr?" the man behind her repeated.

She glanced at him over her shoulder. "Kian dav Leydon ti'Cullin." She made my grandfather's name sound like a curse. "Known as Red Kian of Skai. The man who killed my father."

I knew then who she must be. Francia, sister to Hakkar of Maedun, the sorcerer who had tried to invade Celi nearly fifteen years before I was born. Her name was legend in my family. She had seduced King Tiernyn and tried to enslave him with her blood magic. And she had borne a child to him, a child she had spirited away to Maedun when the Celae army repulsed the invasion.

But it was not possible that this could be the same woman. The Francia who had come to Celi all those years ago would have to be the same age as my father. This woman looked no older than I.

The man holding the lantern hawked and spit on the floor. All I could see of him was a full blond beard and an impression of untidy fair hair hanging to his shoulders. His eyes were only deep pools of darkness cast by the shadow of his brows under the upraised lantern. He might have been Saesnesi. The musty smell of stale wine and old sweat came strongly from him. "This one's worth something, is she?"

"Oh, yes," the woman said. "Your men did well in this, Captain." She turned back to look at me again. It was only then I realized there was something eerily strange about that flawless face—something dreadfully *wrong*. It held no expression. It was blank and characterless as the face of a statue cast in porcelain, and like fragile porcelain, it looked as if it might shatter if she smiled or frowned. She had used her sorcery to maintain her youth, but it had stolen all the life and mobility from her face, leaving it a brittle mask.

Francia reached out and put her hand to my head, her fingers tangling in my hair. "Too young to be the Tyr's daughter," she murmured. "Which of his sons is your father, girl?"

I had to bite down hard on my lower lip to prevent myself answering her. The salty tang of blood tasted sharp against my tongue. I tried to close my eyes, but couldn't against the compelling force of the black mist.

She bent lower and cupped my temples between both her hands. Those black, fathomless eyes stared into mine. "I know the Tyr is your grandfather, girl," she said softly. She stroked my hair almost lovingly, no expression on her youthful face. "And one of his sons is your father. But which one? The Enchanter, was it? The one who killed my brother Hakkar? Or was it one of his brothers?" She traced the line of my cheek with one carmine-tipped finger. "My brother is long dead now, but you must know his son lives. His son is now Hakkar of Maedun, and he has all of his father's power. My loving nephew will be pleased with you. He may not have the man who killed his father, but he has you." She cupped her hands around my temples again, peering straight into my eyes. "I'm sure you'll enjoy meeting your cousin, girl. My son Mikal. His father is King of Celi, you know. Perhaps we'll put him on the throne when we take Celi. Who is your father, girl?"

It was as if I stood on the edge of a yawning abyss, struggling against the empty void that threatened to suck me down into thick, swirling clouds of chilling emptiness. I gasped for breath, fighting to draw back from the brink of the precipice. The inexorable pressure continued unabated, sapping all my strength, all my vitality. I wanted to scream in terror, but my voice was frozen in my throat.

Then the crushing force was gone. I fell back, gasping for air, on the filthy sacks.

Francia laughed softly. "So you have some magic. Not much, but a little." She straightened and stepped back. "Oh what a prize you are, girl," she said, exultation thick in her voice. "Far, far more valuable than that magicless son of the King. I'll take you back to Maedun and let my nephew Hakkar see if he really has come up with a way to deal with the magic that accursed Enchanter raised to keep us out of Celi."

The light vanished as the door slammed shut behind them. The thud of the bar dropping into its slots on the outside of the door was loud in the sudden silence. I curled onto my side, huddled around the choking nausea that churned in my belly. Then I realized what the woman had said. It shocked me into startled alertness.

More than fifteen years before I was born, my uncle Donaugh, twin brother to King Tiernyn, had raised a curtain of magic around the Isle of Celi to keep the Maedun away from our shores. Because Celae magic was derived from gentle Tyadda magic, it could not be used to kill. It would not allow itself to be used to kill. When a Maedun ship, or a ship carrying Maedun, entered the curtain of magic, it emerged, not near the shore of Celi, but offshore where its journey had begun. Donaugh and his two apprentices, Llyr and Gwyn, kept the curtain strong.

But Francia had said that Hakkar of Maedun had discovered a way to overcome the curtain of magic. Neither Donaugh nor King Tiernyn had any knowledge of that discovery. Choking nausea rose in my throat as I thought of the green mountains and valleys of Skai overrun with Maedun Somber Riders. Tales of how they subdued the countries they had taken circulated everywhere, told in taverns in Celi in hushed and awed tones. The tales were filled with death and horror. The Somber Riders left great tracts of land behind them spoiled and burned, where nothing lived or survived. Whole villages slaughtered as warnings against insurrection were common.

My country . . . My people . . . I couldn't let that happen to them.

Somehow, I had to warn Tiernyn and Donaugh. Somehow, I had to get back to Celi and tell them the Maedun were planning another invasion—an invasion that might succeed this time.

The woman came again to see me on what I thought must be the following day. She touched my forehead, and that thick, foul mist engulfed me again. I have no memory of her leaving me.

Time lost all meaning. Occasionally, someone would enter the room and give me a bowl of gruel or thin stew, and I ate it. Fresh water appeared often in a fired clay flask by my head, stoppered with a hank of greasy rag. My head felt as if it didn't belong to me, pounding and throbbing with each beat of my pulse. When I tried to move, it was like fighting my way through a waist-deep pool of viscous pitch. A strange lassitude gripped my whole body, and I couldn't summon the strength to struggle farther from the stinking heap of sacking than the leathern slop bucket placed near the bulkhead by my feet.

Somewhere behind the morass of disoriented detachment smothering my mind, I knew I had to escape to warn Tiernyn and Donaugh. But where could I go aboard a ship at sea? Escape from this noisome cabin meant nothing if I could not leave the ship.

When I tried to reach the little magic I had been born with, I found nothing but a black, empty pit, devoid of even the smallest spark of magic. Despair flooded through me, but the sorcerous black mist tangled around my heart and in my head would not allow me even tears.

I have no idea how long I lay in a half stupor in the fetid little cabin. There were no portholes. I had not even the waxing and waning of light to mark the passing of the days. Occasionally voices broke into my daze, but the words they spoke made no sense. I lay in a vague lethargy, uncaring and lost in hopeless despair.

I dreamed, the images moving through my restless sleep like shadows in the sluggish waters of a slow-moving stream. Tiegan was there, sunlight glinting in his dark gold hair as he called to me, his hand outstretched. But I couldn't go to him. The blood sorcery snare held me too tightly.

We had bonded, Tiegan and I, with the unbreakable link of bheancoran and prince when I was eighteen. I had known since I was old enough to hold a practice sword that we would be so bound one day, as my mother Letessa was bound to my father, and Queen Ylana was bound to my uncle, King Tiernyn. I also knew that, even though my father had married his bheancoran, as had Tiernyn, Tiegan and I could never marry. He was my cousin, and the blood-kin relationship was too close.

Helpless within the web of Francia's sorcery, I watched Tiegan search for me through my dreams. His image was so vivid, so real, I felt I could have reached out to touch him, but I couldn't move. I wanted to call to him, to assure him I still lived, but my lips would not form the words. Tears of rage and frustration welled up in my eyes, but I hadn't even the strength to raise my hand and brush them away.

*   *   *

Something woke me. I opened my eyes to darkness and lay still, wondering what had awakened me. I sat up, listening intently. It came to me only gradually that my body no longer felt dragged down by lead weights, and my head no longer ached. Before I could wonder at this, I realized what had disturbed me.

The ship was quiet. I heard neither the groaning creak of a ship under way, nor the hissing of water along the hull. The ship rocked gently, but it was the subdued motion of a vessel at anchor, or secured to a pier. My heart leapt as understanding exploded in my mind. We had reached whatever destination the ship had been bound for, and the spell Francia had put me under had worn off.

I scrambled to my knees, mindful of the low ceiling, and crawled to the door. Pressing my ear to the rough wood, I listened carefully. Someone moved in the corridor beyond the door. It sounded like only one man, moving restlessly every once in a while. It made sense that they would post a guard, probably only one. They certainly had no reason to think that I would be in any condition to attempt an escape.

A memory of the babble of voices heard as if in a dream batted at my mind. Francia's voice, I thought, saying something about taking me to her nephew, and securing a carriage for the journey. If she were already gone from the ship, that might explain why the spell seemed to have worn off. But how long did I have before she returned to renew the spell?

The ship dipped sharply. Off-balance, I fell forward, thumping my forehead against the uneven, roughly planed wood of the door hard enough to send bright lights exploding behind my eyes. I swore vehemently and pushed myself erect. I was becoming heartily sick and tired of whacking my head against something hard. I'd had quite enough of it. Enough to last a few lifetimes.

Above me, the deck resounded to the hollow thump and scrape of cargo being moved. I crawled back to the pile of sacking, thinking furiously. I had to get out of here, and I had to do it before Francia returned. Should she have the chance to put that loathsome spell back in place, I would have no hope of escape at all. I had no illusions about my future once she had delivered me to Hakkar of Maedun.

Gnawing on my knuckle, I looked around me, but could see nothing in the darkness. I needed something to get me out of here. A weapon . . . But a weapon would do me no good unless I could coerce someone to open the cabin door to give me a chance to use it.

Cold, burning rage flared in my belly. By all the seven gods and goddesses, I would not let them use me against my kin or my land. If they thought I would be so complaisant a plaything, they had another thought coming. I cursed the Emperor of Borlan—the whole flaming Borlani Empire—for insisting I could not bring my sword to the palace. If I'd had Whisperer's burning blade in my hands now, I'd have no problem with that door, or any man on the other side of it either, come to that. I'd certainly have had no problem with those accursed kidnapping vermin in the first place. The image of the Rune Blade shimmered before my eyes, its blade flaming bright.

Flaming bright . . .

In a flash of inspiration, I reached out to grasp a fistful of the rotting sacking of my bed. Suddenly, I knew. What did sailors fear more than anything else in the world? I lifted the disintegrating fragments of sacking and smiled.

Fire, of course. Fire . . .

I had small magics. Certainly I had the magic to ignite a candle two tries out of four. Would it work to ignite the damp, rotting sacking?

Working feverishly, I gathered handsful of the sacking and heaped it in a pile by the bulkhead opposite the door. I tore strips from the tattered skirt of my petticoat to add to the pile. A shallow puddle of water splashed and slopped around my knees as I worked, but I ignored it. I sat back on my heels and concentrated.

But my magic wasn't there. Where it should have been

was nothing but a chilling void. Francia's spell was still at work.

I slammed my fist down on my knee. No! No, I wouldn't let her defeat me like this. I could break through that unclean darkness she had set into my mind and my soul. My magic was the earth and air magic of the Tyadda of Celi—light against the darkness of Maedun blood sorcery. I *could* break out of the blackness. Light banished darkness. Even the smallest flame defeated the deepest night.

But I couldn't find the spark. In despair, I sat back on my heels. The thick, foul air in the cabin threatened to choke me. Darkness wrapped around me like a blanket, heavy enough to cloud my night vision. Above me, the rumble of the men unloading the cargo pierced my aching head like shards of glass. The deck plunged and dipped sharply as the crew manhandled another bale or barrel down the gangplank. Another wave of queasy disquiet knotted in my belly with the motion. Again, the filthy water splashed up through the poorly joined decking boards and over the small heap of rags piled in front of my knees.

Tears stung my eyes, but I didn't know whether they were from the blazing fury or the helpless despair that warred in my chest. I cursed softly and lifted the rags to squeeze the water out of them, then flung the sodden mess against the door. It hit with a wet splat. I managed not to scream in frustration and rage, but only by biting my lip until it threatened to bleed.

This was hopeless. I couldn't find enough magic to kindle dry tinder. How could I make the ribbon of needfire to ignite damp rags?

I staggered back across the deck, grabbed an armful of the rotten sacking, and flung it to one side. Perhaps there was drier stuff beneath the slimy, gritty top layer. Clouds of dust and mold burst up from the sacking. I sneezed and turned my head away from the reeking fetor. Gods, I'd give anything for a bath and clean clothing. And a clean, dry place to sleep.

But first, I had to get off this thrice-cursed ship.

Shreds of the rotten sacking came away in my hand. It felt reasonably dry. Drier than the rags I'd been trying to use, at any rate. I tore away a double handful and went back to crouch by the hull bulkhead again. My hands shook as I spread my fingers over the little pile of rags and threads.

"Beodun, Father of Fires," I whispered. "Please. Just one little spark. Just enough magic for one little spark." But no trace of the quivering ripple of magic moved in my breast. I sank back on my heels, tears of frustration stinging my eyes again.

Suddenly, I realized that the ship was still and quiet, and had been for a while. I looked up at the ceiling, listening hard. The crew had finished unloading the cargo. That could mean that, except for a few guards, the crew was ashore, drinking in a nearby tavern. And it could mean I had very little time left before Francia returned to take me to her nephew.

Anger welled up in my chest, banishing some of the despair. I had inherited more than just my red hair from my grandfather through my father. I had more than my fair share of his nearly legendary stubbornness, too. I would not allow her, or her nephew, to turn what little magic I had against Celi. I *would not*!

Then I felt it—the pulsing tightness in my belly, then the tingle that ran down my arms like music vibrating a harp string. A single spark leapt from my fingertips into the heap of rags. A slender wisp of white smoke spiraled up. The tiny spark became an ember, then a small flame lapping at the rotten sacking. I fed a few more threads of sacking to it, hardly daring to breathe lest I extinguish the feeble flame.

Finally, I knew it would not go out. I threw more handsful of sacking onto it, then pressed myself to the bulkhead beside the door. Thick, acrid smoke swirled around me. I crouched, holding the hem of my ruined dress over my nose and mouth, and waited. Flame licked at the sacking, sullen red through the smoke.

Now was not a good time for it to occur to me that I was in

very real danger. I had forgotten to check to make sure the guard was still outside my door. What if nobody heard me when I yelled? What if nobody smelled the smoke? It wouldn't be the first time that my anger and stubborn obstinacy got me into trouble.

"Fire!" I shouted. "Help me! There's a fire in here!"

But the guard was still outside the door, and he heard me. He made a sharp exclamation of dismay. Seconds later, the heavy bar on the door scraped as he lifted it, and the door swung inward an inch or two. Damp, cool air flooded into the cabin, laden with the dank, fishy smell of a waterfront. The fire seized the fresh air and burst up to lap at the bulkhead and the ceiling.

A man's head appeared around the door. He swore as the smoke billowed up and swirled out the top of the doorway. Shouting for help, he pushed the door opened wider.

I put both my hands against the door and pushed hard, putting the full weight of my body and my anger behind it. It sounded as if I had shoved the door into a pile of sticks. The man went over backward in a clatter, his head hitting the decking in the narrow corridor with a thump like an overripe melon hitting stone. He'd have a headache to match mine when he woke up—if he ever did wake up. I sincerely hoped he wouldn't.

Gathering up my skirts, I leapt his sprawled body, wasted a precious half second to find the ladderway to the deck, and sprang for it. I came out on deck only steps away from the gangplank. Two seconds saw me onto the dock. Three more, and I was lost in the untidy warren of warehouses and shanty taverns lining the waterfront.

3

I leaned against the wall of a building deep in an alley, shivering and gasping for breath. Towering columns of flame from the burning ship lit the waterfront, casting eerie shadows along the narrow alley floor. Silhouetted against the glare, figures of men darted and leapt purposefully to remove the endangered cargo from the pier. Lights appeared on ships close to the fire as crews worked frantically to move them away. I pressed myself deeper into the shadows as a crowd of shouting men raced past in the darkness toward the dock. I recognized the lank blond hair and beard of the captain of the burning ship. My erstwhile captor. But there was no sign of Francia.

I reached for the dagger above my knee before I remembered that it was no longer there. For half a heartbeat, I hesitated, then moved deeper into the alley. I had no weapon. Exposing my hiding place was even more dangerous than lighting a fire to burn a ship down around my own ears. Not only perilous, it was downright stupid. I may have my moments when I'm angry, but most of the time I don't qualify as a half-wit.

My best course of action right now seemed to be putting as much distance as I could between me and that ship. Then I needed to find out where in the world I was, so I could start making my way back to Celi. It wasn't going to be easy. I had no weapon, no money. The combs holding my stringy, greasy hair back from my face were silver. They might fetch a few silvers if I could sell them, but certainly not enough to buy me passage to Celi from here—wherever *here* was.

First item of importance. I had to find out where I was.

I watched through the narrow opening of the alleyway. No more men pounded past toward the fire. The burning ship had seized the attention of every man in the area. I hoped none of them would spare me a second glance. I took a moment to gather my strength, then sprang toward the street.

And rammed full tilt into a man catapulting himself around the corner of the alley.

The force of the impact knocked me backward into the filth of the alley floor. The smell of it nearly made me gag. My feet tangled with his, and he fell forward on top of me. Every ounce of breath burst out of me, paralyzing me. His forehead met mine with a crack that sent bright flashes of light spinning before my eyes.

He clapped his hand across my mouth. But I couldn't have managed a mew like a kitten right then if my life depended on it. All I could do was struggle feebly to draw air into lungs that felt as if they'd never move again.

He rolled up against the wall of the building, burrowing into a heap of refuse. He still held me tightly to his chest, so perforce I went with him. Struggling and straining to find air, I had no strength to fight him. Mayhaps it was as well I couldn't breathe. The stench would have made me retch.

"Gods above," he muttered. "A woman."

My lungs began to work suddenly. I gulped in air, decided I was going to live for a few moments longer, and bit down hard on his hand. He swore and yanked it away from my mouth. I managed to draw in a long, rasping breath, then another.

"Don't scream," he said softly. He pressed his hand over my mouth again, more gently this time. A reminder more than an imperative. "There'll be a dozen irate Maedun freebooters come boiling around that corner if you do. Your chances with them will be no better than mine."

I looked up at him. He was little more than a shadow between me and the flickering light. The vague shape of a sword hilt rose above his left shoulder. I tried to reach for my magic, but I'd been too long exposed to that cursed blood magic of Francia's, and starting the fire had used up all the magic I'd been able to find. There was nothing but a bleak void where the magic should have been. But if the

Maedun were after him, too, I was ready to trust his word. I nodded, and he removed his hand.

Shouts and the cadence of running feet sounded beyond the alley mouth. He pulled deeper into the pile of refuse and ducked his head so that his face pressed against my shoulder. The stench that rose up around us overpowered even the foul air of the waterfront. His body spasmed as he gagged, and I had to swallow several times before I was certain I wouldn't retch. In moments, the men had gone past, and he looked up, supporting his weight on one elbow.

He rubbed his forehead. "You're a dangerous woman," he said. "And a hardheaded one, at that."

I became aware that something warm and wet soaked into my hip, which was pressed tight against his side.

"You're hurt," I whispered, as the clamor died in the distance.

"Aye, well, one of them caught me from behind and got a wee bit lucky with his sword." He rolled away from me and struggled into a sitting position against the wall, one hand pressed to his side. He tipped his head back, letting it rest against the dirty stone. "If it hadn't been for that ship going up like a pine torch, I'd be a dead man for sure. It distracted their attention quite handily."

I brushed slimy chunks of refuse out of my hair, trying hard not to think about what they might be, and sat beside him. "You're welcome," I said.

He looked at me, one eyebrow raised quizzically. "You did that?" he asked, surprise in his voice.

"Yes. And I'd do it again in a minute if I could. They had me captive in a filthy little cabin. The Maedun woman planned to take me to her nephew. A new toy."

The gleam of his teeth flashed white in the flickering darkness. He laughed softly. "So you set fire to their ship and ran."

"Yes. And I wish I'd killed every last man on that ship. But they were ashore."

"A dangerous woman, indeed." He got to his feet, pushing

himself up the wall with his hands. For a moment, he stood,
head bowed, breathing shallowly. He was taller than I had first
thought. Even slumped as he was, I barely came up to his
shoulder, and I'm no small woman. He wore a kilt and a white,
wide-sleeved shirt, open at the throat. A plaid pinned at the
shoulder by a plain, round brooch fell across his left arm and
down his back to just above his ankles. A dark stain spread
across his shirt above right hip.

"You're a Tyr," I said. It was only then I realized we were
speaking Tyran. The language comes as easily to me as Celae.
I grew up spending one season every year or so with my
grandparents in Tyra. It's related to Celae, and not a difficult
language to learn.

"Aye," he muttered, pressing his hand again to the wound
in his side. "Clever of you to notice."

I swore under my breath and pulled up the tattered skirts of
my gown to get at my petticoat. It was almost as dirty as the
alleyway, but I had nothing better. I tore a wide strip from the
hem and folded it into a thick pad.

"Move your hand," I said. I pressed the pad against the
wound. "Hold that." I tore another strip off the petticoat and
bound it quickly around him, reaching around behind his back
to knot the strip firmly into place. "You need a Healer."

He tried to grin at me, but grimaced in pain instead. "If ye
could manage to produce one as handily as ye produced that
fire, I'd be grateful," he said. "As it is . . ." He took a step. His
knees buckled beneath him, and he nearly fell. I thrust my
shoulder into his armpit and grabbed him around the waist. He
was heavy, but I held him.

"I've a room in an inn not far from here," he said, his voice
rasping. "If you could help me a wee bit, I could rest there."

The inn he guided us to was a poor one, lacking all amenities,
except mayhaps a touch of token cleanliness. Obviously, the
Tyr was not a rich man, but he had a tiny room to himself in

the eaves above the kitchen. A narrow cot with a lumpy straw mattress, and a small chest of drawers left barely enough room for two people to stand on the small, ragged woven mat.

A ewer in a cracked bowl sat beside a candle on the chest, the ewer filled with water that looked fresh and clean. A sliver of yellow soap lay on a threadbare towel beside the bowl. I didn't think either belonged to the innkeeper.

The Tyr collapsed on the bed as I lit the single candle on the chest. The light gleamed on his hair, red-gold as freshly minted copper. My father had hair like that. A kick of homesickness thumped against my chest, and I turned away quickly to hide the sudden tears in my eyes.

Thinking longingly of a tub filled with hot water, I poured water from the ewer into the bowl and dipped the towel into it. I knelt on the floor beside the cot and pulled the Tyr's shirt out of the waistband of his kilt. My breath caught in my throat when I saw the wound. The sword blade had bitten deep into the web of muscle laid neat and flat across his hip and belly. It was a grievous wound, deep in the flesh above his hip, but it looked fairly clean. I bent forward and sniffed, but I could detect no stench of excrement. Perhaps his gut hadn't been perforated. If so, he was lucky.

"You need a Healer," I said.

"Aye," he said, his voice faint. "Likely I do. But there seems to be a distinct shortage of them around here."

"Let me help you get that sword harness off," I said.

He raised himself as I fumbled with the buckles, but was too weak to be much help. When I finally freed him of the sword—heavier than any sword I could ever wield—he fell back again, his mouth drawn thin with pain.

I bit my lip and sat back on my heels. My gift of magic was a poor one, at best. I had magic enough to resonate with the Skai Rune Blade I carried—the sword that was still aboard the *Skai Seeker* with Tiegan. My ability to call the fire from the dark couldn't match the gift of my uncle Donaugh, brother to King Tiernyn, and the most powerful enchanter on the Isle of Celi. And my Gift for Healing was certainly nowhere near that of my aunt Torey. A feeble thing at best, even when I could make it work. I had found only an empty, black void back in the alleyway when I tried to reach for my magic. Could I find the Healing power? And could I control it if I did? The Tyr might well die if I couldn't help him.

I wanted badly to help him. My grandfather Kian was Tyran. The blood of the Clan Lairds of Broche Rhuidh in Tyra ran in my own veins, somewhat thinned by two generations of Celae. But it was there, and this man mayhaps was the next best thing to a kinsman.

I closed my eyes for a moment, concentrating. A faint, welcome resonance thrummed in my chest. Putting my hand to the Tyr's forehead, I stared directly into his eyes. Green eyes. Green as the emerald that swung on a fine chain from his left ear beside the single thick braid of red-gold hair.

"Sleep," I said softly.

His eyes closed, and he slumped down onto the bed. I placed my hand to the wound and reached for the threads of magic that should have been throbbing in the air around me, and in the earth beneath me. But there were none. This wasn't Celi. I had no idea where we were, but it was a land devoid of intrinsic magic. Or at least, barren of magic I could work with.

I took a deep breath, closed my eyes, and drew the strength from deep within myself. The power ran through my veins and sinews like music runs along a harp string. It flowed from me, deep into him, drawing my energy along with it. I couldn't heal the wound completely, but I had power enough to bring the raw edges together, to stop the bleeding, to start the natural healing his strong, healthy body could complete.

When I finally drew my hand away and opened my eyes, I was exhausted. But the gaping edges of the wound had closed, showing an angry red scar. It still looked raw and sore, but I could do no more. He would be in no shape for a few days to wield that greatsword of his, but at least now he would not bleed to death before my eyes.

I staggered to my feet and looked at the wet towel I still held, then at the bowl of water and the soap. I had no illusions about how I must look and smell after only the gods knew how long in that filthy cabin, then rolling about in the muck in the alley. I stripped out of the ruined ball gown and washed as best I could. The water was cold and the soap smelled strongly of lye, but it was clean, and as close to paradise as I could come at this moment.

My clothing lay in a stinking heap near the door by a saddle pack. I went to my knees and opened the pack. Inside were two clean, white shirts like the one he wore. Surely he wouldn't mind if I borrowed one. I glanced over my shoulder. He lay in sound sleep on the cot. I pulled one shirt out of the pack and slipped it over my head. The hem fell well past my knees, and the cuffs hung down several inches below my fingertips. He was a big man, that Tyr.

There was no place for me to sleep but on the floor. The bed held only one blanket. I unpinned the Tyr's plaid and gently removed it from around him. Then I struggled for a moment to get him under the blanket. As I tucked it around his shoulders, he murmured something in his sleep, and the corner of his mouth curled in a hint of a smile. I looked down at him for a moment. Now that sleep had erased the lines etched around his eyes and mouth by the pain, he looked much younger. Certainly not yet thirty, and probably closer to twenty-five. Cleaned up with his hair brushed and neat, he would be a very good-looking man.

The plaid was made of good, oiled Tyran wool. I scrambled up onto the end of the bed, opened the window, and shook it vigorously. Most of the filth clinging to it snapped away into the dark. When I pulled it back inside, it looked relatively clean and presentable.

Wrapping the plaid around me, I kicked my filthy clothing into the corner, then curled down onto the floor. After the dank, rotten sacking in the cabin of the ship, the warm plaid and the reed matting were extravagant comfort indeed. And the plaid smelled pleasantly of the Tyr—clean male sweat, warm wool, and the faint tang of woodsmoke. It reminded me of being a child and being wrapped warm and safe in my father's arms.

I slept.

I awoke to find myself curled on the cot, the blanket tucked around me. I sat up quickly, spilling the blanket to the floor. Both the Tyr and his plaid were gone, but his saddle pack still lay on the floor near the door. Before I could wonder where he went, the door opened and he entered, carrying a tray laden with fresh bread, dried fruit, and cheese. If the wound still pained him, he gave no sign of it. He moved briskly, with lithe grace.

"I bid ye good morning," he said cheerfully, smiling.

"Good morning yourself," I said. "Is it still morning?"

He laughed. "Oh, aye. But barely. I've brought ye food for the fast-breaking."

I scooted over on the cot so he could sit beside me. His hair, even brighter red in the morning sun streaming through the narrow window, was clean and brushed. It hung free to his shoulders except for that single thick braid by his left temple. My grandfather wore a braid like that. A Tyran clansman's braid is his strength; he gives it up only in death. Below the thick, red-gold eyebrows, his eyes were the same clear green as the emerald in his left ear. The unadorned hilt of the sword rose above his left shoulder. His kilt, a faded blue-and-green tartan, was frayed and worn around the hem, but was of good quality wool and finely woven. He had found a fuller because both kilt and plaid were clean and freshly pressed.

He put the tray down on the bed between us. "Are you Celae?" he asked. He handed me his knife for the cheese.

I broke off a piece of the bread and cut a thick slice of cheese. The bread was warm and fresh; the golden cheese was not. It tasted like something worthy of the gods and goddesses.

"Yes," I said around a mouthful of cheese and bread. "Celae. How did you know?"

He touched his side. "You Healed me," he said. "As far as I know, only the Celae have that power."

"Well, I'm not much of a Healer."

He grinned. "Aye, well, ye did fine enough wi' me. Ye dinna exactly look Celae with that hair. It's almost Tyran, it is. A bit too pale, though."

I touched the snarled mass of pale apricot-gold hair that hung in strings around my face. On my brother Brennen, the color looked magnificent. On me, it just looked washed-out. "I got left out in the rain too long and bleached out," I said shortly.

He raised one eyebrow in acknowledgment of my ill-tempered reply, then ignored it. "Your eyes are Celae, though." He looked directly into them. "Brown-gold. Aye, definitely Celae. You're a long way from home."

I concentrated on the food. Nothing had ever tasted so good before. The dried fruit—apricots and dates and figs—were delicious, too. "So are you," I said. "A long way from home, that is." I paused, a dried fig poised halfway to my mouth. "Where are we, anyway?"

He helped himself to more cheese and bread. "Banhapetsut," he said. "In Laringras."

I knew a little about Laringras from the geography lessons I'd struggled through when I was a child, and from the wondrous maps hanging in my father's study at home. Banhapetsut was a small seaport city, not very important, about forty leagues southwest of the capital, Matchetluk. But the main merchant trail from the west bypassed Banhapetsut, and even the trading vessels made port there only to reprovision before they journeyed to Matchetluk at the head of navigation on Laringras's great River Maun. I was a long way from Celi.

"Where did the Maedun take you?" he asked.

"In Borlan. Silichia." I offered no explanation of what I was doing in Borlan. I didn't know him well enough yet to admit to who and what I was.

He raised one eyebrow quizzically. "Borlan?"

I glanced at him, certain he was going to ask how I came to be there. But he only raised the eyebrow again, then turned his attention back to the tray of food. He cut himself a slice of cheese and broke off a chunk of bread, giving them his full attention.

A most unusual man, this Tyr. A respecter of privacy.

The sleeves of the shirt I wore kept falling down over my hands and getting in the way. I pushed up the flapping cuffs in a futile effort to keep my hands free to eat. No sooner did I get one sleeve pushed up than the other slipped down over my hand. He watched me struggle for a moment, amusement glinting in his eyes. Then, when I was ready to rip the sleeve off in exasperation, he leaned forward and, in solemn silence, tied the cuff laces around my wrists.

"Thank you," I said ungraciously.

He inclined his head. "You're most welcome, my lady." He reached for a handful of dates, then cut another thick slice of cheese. "You might give me your name," he said. "Who do I thank for this?" He gestured toward his hip and the strip of bandage that showed through his open shirt.

"I'm called Brynda al Keylan," I said. "I assume you have a name, too?"

"Kenzie." He grinned crookedly. "Just Kenzie. Some call me Kenzie Catfoot. The sword, ye ken. They say I have some small talent with it."

I glanced at the breadth of his shoulders and the webs of muscle under the smooth skin of his chest. More than some skill, I'd say.

His face had gone blank, waiting for me to ask the obvious question. But he had respected my privacy; the least I could do was respect his in return. I would not press for reasons why he would not, or could not, give me a name for his father. I nodded and went back to the meal.

He leaned back against the wall, his long legs stretched out before him. "I suppose," he said, "that our next step should be getting the both of us out of here alive. You back to Celae, and me back to my work in Isgard and Falinor."

"Work?" I asked.

He shrugged. "I'm a merchant train guard. The Maedun may own half the continent, but they're not fools. Trade goods still move from one country to the next, and even the Maedun can't get rid of the bandits that prey on them. There's always work for men like me. The Maedun leave me alone."

"They didn't leave you alone last night."

"Aye, well, I saw something I shouldn't have, and those freebooters were annoyed with me. That's why I believe the wisest course would be to take myself out of their way for a while."

"I have no gold," I said. "But if you help me get back to Celi, I can promise you more wealth than you could make in a year as a merchant train guard."

He grinned. "I had thought of that," he said. "We'll have to do something about your clothing. Ye surely canna go out in public in that shirt of mine, nor can ye wear that expensive rag in yon corner. But dinna worrit yerself, lass. I've an idea . . ."

4

Kenzie left again shortly after we finished our meal. He wouldn't
tell me where he was going, but assured me he would be back
as soon as he could. A few minutes later, someone knocked
softly on the door. I opened it to find a young serving girl in
the hall, holding a large jug of steaming water. She smiled
nervously and thrust the jug into my hands. She said something I couldn't understand, but a gift is a gift in any language.
I thanked her, using my rudimentary Laringorn. She bobbed
an abbreviated curtsy, then turned to go. She nearly tripped
over the ruined ball gown I had thrown onto the floor.

She bent to pick it up and made an expression of distaste as
she saw how filthy it was. Bits of dirt and dried flakes of
garbage fell to the floor as she brushed the fabric experimentally. She shook out the dress and held it out at arm's length
before her, assessing the damage, then looked at me, her eyebrows raised in question.

"Take it," I said, hugging the jug of hot water to my chest
like the treasure it was.

She nodded, bobbed another curtsy, and left, closing the
door gently behind her.

Not much of Kenzie's sliver of soap remained. I used it all
as I scrubbed myself head to foot. I ran out of hot water as I
rinsed the soap out of my hair and had to complete the job
with what was left of the cold water in the ewer, but I wasn't
about to quibble over small details. I could not remember a
bath ever before feeling so luxurious. Living in the palace at
Dun Camus in Celi, where hot water and large tubs were plentiful and popular, one tended to become spoiled. Never again,
I vowed, would I take bathing for granted.

Kenzie's thoughtfulness in sending up the girl with the hot
water touched me. I made a note to thank him when he returned.

My hair is long and fine, and it tends to curl. When wet, it tangles badly. It was clean enough to squeak between my fingers as I sat on the bed, letting it dry in the slight breeze blowing in off the courtyard. I had nothing but the ornamental silver combs to work out the tangles, but they'd have to serve. It might take a while, but I had nothing else to do while I waited for Kenzie to return.

He was gone long enough to start me worrying. When midafternoon passed with no sign of him, I passed beyond worry to anger and back to worry again. The room had one small window, but it looked out over the back courtyard, the midden heap, and the stables. I didn't want to take a chance of being seen dressed only in Kenzie's shirt, so I didn't dare try to find a place where I could watch the entrance off the street.

By the time the sun had traversed most of the way through the afternoon sky, I had gone through the worry-anger-worry cycle several more times, and ended up with anger at his inconsiderate thoughtlessness in leaving me here to worry about him. Had those Maedun freebooters he'd run into the night before caught up with him again? His wound had certainly not healed enough to allow him to swing that greatsword of his with his former strength and agility. Was he even now lying dead in some filthy gutter? Or had he simply deserted me?

There was precious little space in the tiny room to pace. Two steps toward the door. Turn. Two paces back to the cot.

A knock on the door sent me diving across the room to open it. I yanked the door inward, expecting to see Kenzie, and simply stared at the young serving girl who stood there, smiling nervously. She held a frothy bundle of pale green silk in her hands. My ball gown.

I stepped back and opened the door wider, beckoning her into the room. She came in, then shook out the dress and laid it on the bed. A small miracle had occurred. The dress was clean and mended, and looked, if not like new, then at least respectable again. I bent and examined the tiny stitches darning a long rent in the overskirt.

"You did this?" I asked, turning to her in wonder.

She smiled shyly and nodded, a tinge of pride lighting her face. As well it should. She had certainly done as well or better than any professional sempstress could have done repairing the dress. If she created clothing as well as she mended it, she could have made herself a comfortable living at it.

I looked at the ball gown again, then at her. She wore a plain homespun skirt in a dark brown wool, and a plain, long-sleeved white blouse gathered simply at the neck by a lace. Over it was draped a loose tunic that fell nearly to her knees in a paler brown than the skirt. She was nearly as tall as I, but my shoulders were broader. The dress would certainly fit her. And if the dress fitted her, then her clothing might fit me. On impulse, I picked up the dress and held it against her.

She stepped back, startled. I smiled and nodded, holding the dress against her again. She took the dress from me and smoothed the fabric down against her hips and thighs. Then she shook her head and tried to give the dress back.

"No," I said. "It's yours."

She had no Celae or Tyran, and I spoke little Laringorn. But eventually, through signs and repeated use of the few words I did know, she realized I was asking to trade. She shook her head, then turned and ran from the room.

Frustrated, I flung the ball gown onto the bed and threw myself down beside it. A moment later, the serving girl knocked lightly on the door and entered, carrying a bundle of clothing. She shook out the garments one by one, smiling as she held them up for my approval. A skirt similar to the one she wore, but in a dark forest green, a pale yellow blouse, and a lighter green overtunic, all of it coarsely woven, but clean and completely suitable.

I took them from her and laughed in delight. "Yes!" I cried. "Wonderful. They're perfect."

She turned to the ball gown on the bed, then very carefully

picked it up and held it reverently against herself. Smoothing the silk with a loving hand, she looked up at me, her eyes shining. I don't know where she might ever have the opportunity to wear such a frivolous garment, but she would obviously be much happier than I wearing it. It was a dress far beyond her means ordinarily, but if she could use it, she was more than welcome to it. I certainly couldn't wear it traveling from Laringras back to Celi. The clothing she had brought me was perhaps not as comfortable and utilitarian as the tunic and trews I normally wore, but it was certainly more serviceable than that gown.

She left with her prize, and I scrambled into the skirt, blouse, and tunic. Everything fitted reasonably well, although the skirt was mayhaps a bit short. It barely covered my ankles. I had no shoes, but the serving girl had been barefoot. Mayhaps no one would notice my lack of footwear.

Moments later, my hair plaited and tied with a string unraveled from the blanket, I slipped out of the room, down the stairs, and out onto the street.

Banhapetsut in daylight looked much better than it did at night. The inn was well away from the warehouse district surrounding the waterfront. I didn't think anyone from Francia's ship would be in this district. Shops belonging to craftsmen of all descriptions lined the street to either side. The tavern on the inn's lower floor enjoyed a good business as craftsmen crowded in to have a mug of ale and catch up on the news. The people I passed on the street looked like solid, sober citizens, none of them rich, but all of them respectable.

Most of the people on the street were men. I saw only two women, one of them obviously a servant. Both were accompanied by men, the first—someone's goodwife by her dress— attended by three armed men. Only one man escorted the serving girl. He looked as if he, too, were a servant, but he was well armed. Both women wore shawls which completely covered their hair.

As I hurried down the street, I became aware that everyone

was staring at me in disapproval. The goodwife with her armed escort sniffed and turned up her nose in contempt as she passed me. One of her escort gave me a definite leer. Even the servant girl covered her mouth with her hand and turned away rather than look at me, her face going pink with either embarrassment or amusement.

Mayhaps I should have asked for shoes. And something to cover my head.

It came to me slowly that I was the only unescorted female on the streets. And there had been no mistaking the contempt on the face of the goodwife, or the meaning behind the leers of the men. I had mayhaps made a sore error in venturing out alone in a city I knew nothing about.

I thought it might be prudent to make my way back to the inn as quickly as possible. I certainly couldn't afford trouble. Not here. Not with Francia and what would certainly amount to a troop of Maedun soldiers looking for me.

Someone stepped into my path, a big man wearing a uniform with an ornate badge on his left shoulder. He wore a sword hanging in a scabbard from his belt and a badge on the sleeve of his shirt. City guard, I thought. Not Maedun, by his coloring. I jumped back and nearly stumbled on the uneven cobbles. He reached out and put one hand to my hair, grinning. He said something, and pulled me forward.

I leapt backward and spun around to run, and ran headlong into another man wearing the same uniform. He grabbed me and tried to pull me into his arms. The stale smell of sour ale on him was nearly overpowering. He bent his head and tried to kiss me, but I managed to turn away, and he slobbered on my cheek and the side of my throat. The first man said something that made the man who held me laugh.

My captor was strong. He held me in a bear hug, his arms wrapped around me, pinning my own arms to my sides. I could gain no leverage to fight him. He laughed again and tried once more to kiss me. I bent my head to keep out of the way of his mouth. Then as his grip loosened a bit, I snapped my head up. The crown of my head met his jaw. His mouth snapped shut with a crack that surely fractured a tooth or two. At the same time, I raised my left foot and brought my heel down as hard as I could on his instep. He howled with pain and rage, and let me go. But even as I spun away from him, the other man seized my braid and nearly yanked me off my feet. Involuntarily, I screamed.

The man whose teeth I had cracked advanced on me, his face twisted with rage. Before I could do anything, he drew back his hand and slapped my cheek hard enough to knock me back into the man who still held my braid. My vision blurred, and the whole side of my head felt numb. He stepped forward, obviously meaning to strike me again.

The muted susurration of drawn steel made both men turn, dragging me along with them. Through the haze before my eyes, I barely made out Kenzie leaning negligently against the side of a building, his naked sword in one hand. His eyes were narrowed, and he was grinning, but it wasn't a grin I'd want him to direct at me. Not if he meant it. Sunlight gleamed off his red-gold hair and sent green sparks from the emerald in his ear flashing against the skin of his throat. In spite of his casual posture, he held his body tensed and ready, his weight balanced on the balls of his feet. He reminded me of a mountain cat, coiled and eager to strike, and he looked completely and unutterably dangerous, a mad barbarian Tyr out of the misty hills of legend.

He gestured toward me with his chin. "That," he said, enunciating slowly and deliberately, "is mine."

The guard with the broken teeth snarled out a few words I couldn't understand. Probably just as well. They sounded as if they might be an uncomplimentary description of both my lineage and Kenzie's. Kenzie stepped away from the wall, still smiling, and raised his sword. He said something. All I caught was the word for bitch hound. The guard turned white. His hand made a convulsive movement toward the sword at his side.

The other guard glanced speculatively at Kenzie's naked blade, then reached out and stayed his partner's hand, shaking his head.

"I said that's mine," Kenzie said. He took another step forward, raising his sword slightly. The smile never left his face. A light of pure, eager anticipation sparked in his green eyes.

The second guard loosened his grip on my braid and let it fall. He said something placating and gave me a none-too-gentle push toward Kenzie. I stumbled, but recovered before I bumped into him, then ducked behind him, out of the way. The guard shrugged philosophically, as if the diversion had been worth the try, but it wasn't a terrible disappointment that it hadn't worked. He grabbed his partner's arm and pulled him with him as he turned and moved off down the street.

Kenzie watched them until they rounded a corner out of sight, then turned to me, sheathing the sword as he turned.

I straightened and brushed the hair from my face. "Thank you," I said. My puffy lip and cheek made it difficult to speak.

He didn't answer. He merely regarded me with an expression of exasperation and mild annoyance on his face.

We had gathered quite a crowd. He looked around, still alert and ready for trouble. But the onlookers weren't about to give any. One by one, they began moving away, intent once again upon their own business. Kenzie stepped forward, picked me up, and slung me over his shoulder as if I were nothing more than a sack of meal.

"Put me down!" I cried. "Put me down this instant—"

"Keep quiet," he said. "If you make any fuss, we'll have a dozen or so Maedun soldiers down our throats in a minute, and I want that as little as you do." The tone of his voice brooked no argument.

The scabbard on his back fetched me a good clout on the side of the head, and the uncomfortable, head-down posture didn't do my aching face any good at all. But I shut up. One thing I really didn't want at all was a troop of Maedun soldiers investigating a disturbance with me at its center.

He said nothing during the brisk hike back to the inn. He was not overly careful of me as he mounted the stairs to our little room over the kitchen. Once my head cracked painfully against the wall, and once it was my ankle. I bit down on my lip to keep myself from crying out, and imagined myself slowly peeling the hide from his body in retaliation.

The door to the room swung shut behind me. Kenzie dumped me unceremoniously on the bed. I bounced once, then surged to my feet, hands on hips to confront him. But even as I was drawing a breath to begin yelling, he beat me to it.

"If ye weren't already battered and beaten, lass," he roared, "I'd take ye over my knee and paddle your bottom for you! Just what in the name of all that's dear and good do you think you were doing? Do you know what you nearly did? Have you any idea at all?"

The force of his anger drove me back a pace. "Don't you dare yell at me!" I shouted. "Just who do you think you are?"

"I'm the man who's trying to get your precious hide out of Laringras intact and unsullied. That's who I think I am."

"I was out looking for you." I clenched a fist and shook it under his nose. "What do you mean, running off all day like that and leaving me here all by myself? I was worried sick about you. And what makes you think I need your help anyway to get back to Celi?"

He stabbed a finger in the direction of my cheek. But I noticed he was careful not to touch it. "That makes me think it. I told you I'd be back when I could." A deadly calm settled over him. It was worse than his anger. He raised one finger and pointed it right under my nose. "Ye might have got us both killed out there, lass," he said. "D'ye realize that?"

"How?" I demanded. "Get us both killed? Just by walking out into the street to look for you?"

"This is Laringras," he said as if that explained everything.

"So?" A child's word. Defiant and insolent. Mayhaps even sulky. I hated how it made me sound, but, at the moment, I could think of nothing else to reply.

"So several things," he said. "First, women in Laringras are one of two things. They're either some man's chattel—their father's, their husband's, their lover's, their son's, or their master's. If they don't belong to some man, they're—let's say women of easy virtue who receive coin for certain favors to men."

"That's barbaric."

"Barbaric it may well be, but that's how things are in Laringras. The Maedun approve of the situation, so it's not likely to change in the foreseeable future. And it's certain not to change between now and the time we leave here."

"I refuse to be any man's chattel—"

"No doubt you do. But those two city guards were well within their rights when they accosted you, at least according to their lights. The only reason I got you away without a real fight is that they thought you were my woman—my wife or my mistress or my sister, it matters little. If they had thought you were merely a woman I had paid for the evening, I would have had to kill one of them, or both, to get you away. Think how far we'd get on our journey to the Western Sea if I ended up on the executioner's block, and you landed up in a brothel. Or dead along with me."

Appalled, I stared at him, unable for a moment to speak. Finally, I wet my lips with my tongue. "I didn't know," I whispered.

"Aye, well, you should have," he said, with more than just a trace of asperity in his voice. "That's why I told you to stay here and wait for me."

"You might have told me why," I said, and hated the petulance in my voice.

"I thought ye'd know," he said in exasperation. "By the horns of Cernos, lass, how could you *not* know how things are here?"

"How could I know? I've never been to Laringras before."

He made a disgusted sound with teeth and tongue. "Tcha-a-a." Then he sighed. "Aye, well. Ye know now." He stepped forward and put a surprisingly gentle hand to my bruised cheek. "Let's see if we can't get that cleaned up a bit for you."

5

We went down together to the common room of the inn for our evening meal. Like any modest Laringorn woman, I wore a shawl that covered my hair and shrouded most of my face in shadow. Just before we entered the room, Kenzie settled his plaid firmly on his shoulders and straightened. He seemed to change before my eyes. Even in his frayed and faded kilt and plaid, he attained an elegant and regal bearing. He put me in mind of my father again, and more, of my grandfather Kian as he must have looked as a young man. He might have belonged in the Great Hall of Broche Rhuidh, standing beside my grandfather's kinsman Brychan, Thirteenth Laird of Glen Borden and First Laird of the Council of Clans. There was, I decided thoughtfully, much more to this man who called himself Kenzie Catfoot than a simple merchant train guard.

He offered me his left arm. "To show them that I honor you," he murmured. "They won't bother you."

I glanced around the room. Most of the patrons were men. Two or three women sat at tables, appropriately covered and protectively surrounded by armed men. I put my right hand delicately on his elbow and used my other hand to pick up the rough, homespun skirt as if it were made of finest silk. Kenzie gave me the ghost of a wink, then we swept into the room.

The landlord hurried forward to seat us, and shortly we had steaming bowls of savory stew and mugs of cold ale on the table in front of us. I caught a few men glancing speculatively, first at my bruised face, then at Kenzie with a knowing smile.

Amusement glinted in Kenzie's eyes. "They think I had to put your in your place," he whispered.

I stiffened. "I *know* what they're thinking," I said acidly. "I can't say I'm overly fond of playing the part of a woman who needs putting in her place."

He shrugged and went back to his meal. We finished eating in silence. He offered me his arm again as we left the common room to return to the tiny room over the kitchen.

He picked up his sword from the bed and strapped it onto his back. "I'll have to be leaving you again for a while," he said, adjusting the harness more comfortably around him. "I take it you know better than to wander off by yourself now?"

"Where are you going?" I asked.

"Man's business," he said.

I'd had more than enough of being treated as if I were a sweet but none-too-bright child. I couldn't help it. I put my fists on my hips and went off around his ears like a batch of chestnuts popping on a hearth.

"Man's business, is it?" I cried. "Confound you, Kenzie Catfoot, you've spent too much time on this side of the Laringras Alps. Don't you *dare* speak to me as if I were a woman with the vapors, you idiot!"

He gave me a blank look and blinked once. Without a word, he turned and walked out of the room. The door slammed behind him hard enough to rattle the ewer in the crockery bowl on the chest.

Never in my life had anybody been so rude to me. Never! How dare he walk out on me. Shocked nearly to speechlessness, I stood there for a moment before the realization struck me that he might not come back again. I leapt to the door, yanked it open, and caught a glimpse of the green and blue of his fluttering plaid disappearing around the corner into the narrow stairwell.

"Kenzie!" I shouted. "Don't leave me here!"

His footsteps on the wooden stair treads paused. A moment later, he appeared at the head of the stairs in the hallway. He stood watching me silently, his mouth making a grim and level line.

I took a deep breath and pushed back the hair that had fallen across my forehead into my eyes. "Please come back," I said more quietly.

He didn't move. "I dinna ken if I fancy the idea of spending the distance between here and the Western Sea with a fish-wife," he said.

"You could at least tell me where you're going and how long you'll be," I said with all the dignity I could muster. That probably wasn't much, considering the sorry state of my face. "So I won't worry." I smoothed my skirt with the backs of my hands. "I realize you're under no obligation to me, but I'd like to think we have at least friendship between us."

He stood for a moment longer, then adjusted the set of his plaid on his shoulder and came back to the door. "Aye, well, ye did save my life," he said, touching his hip. "I owe you thanks and help for that."

"You saved my life, too, so we're even," I said.

He grinned. "I saved perhaps your virtue," he said. "Not quite the same thing."

I bit down on the acidic reply that tried to rise to my lips. Instead I merely smiled. "Perhaps not. But I'm grateful."

"I've business with some men," he said. "I don't know how long it will take, but dinna worrit yourself. I'll return as soon as I can. You might want to get some sleep."

"I can't go with you?"

His mouth firmed again. "This is Laringras, Brynda," he said.

I said a rude word, then caught a glint of amusement in his eyes. "Laringorn women could use a few lessons in how to assert themselves," I muttered.

He grinned. "Given time, my lady Brynda," he said, "I'm sure you'd prove to be a fine teacher." He turned and walked back down the corridor to the stairwell. Just before he disappeared, he gave me a broad smile and a wave.

There was nothing else for it. I went into the tiny room and closed the door behind me.

I dreamed that night. My sleep was filled with wild images of hunted things fleeing in terror through the forest, pursued by vague, dark shapes I couldn't see. At first I thought it was a herd of roe deer trailed by a pack of hounds that were black as the night itself. But the deer were people, crying out in fear as they plunged through tangles of bramble and thickets of blackthorn. I thought I saw the silver gleam of my uncle Donaugh's hair, and the dark red-gold glint of my brother Brennen's as I fled with the hunted. But my heart hammered in my chest, and my breath came in gasping sobs, and I had no time to pay attention to who or what ran with me. All I knew was that we must get away from what pursued.

We burst out of the forest onto a wide, grassy meadow running along the top of a steep cliff. Below, the breaking waves pounded against the dark rocks, sounding like the beating of a huge heart. The horizon painted a misty line between gray sea and gray sky. Nothing wavered out there. Where there should have been the silvery shimmer of the curtain of enchantment my uncle Donaugh had raised against the Maedun, there was nothing. No trace remained of it but isolated curls of black smoke. Above the sea, ravens like flecks of soot hovered, waiting to feast on the carcasses of the dead. Their raucous cries sounded harsh and voracious as they circled endlessly.

Then I was alone, running in blind terror through a shaw of hollies. The branches tangled around me and threw me to the dank ground. The terror behind me drew closer as I struggled to find my feet. I couldn't free myself; I was trapped by the hollies. I rolled over and stared in horror as an amorphous black shape hovered over me. Even as I opened my mouth to scream, a face formed vaguely in the blackness.

He looked down at me as I lay at his feet. It was my uncle Donaugh, turned once again back to a youth, and he glared at me with venomous hatred blazing in his eyes. But they weren't Donaugh's brown-gold eyes. They were black and empty as the night itself, and the pupils flared sullen red, like flame twisting through black, oily smoke.

I screamed.

*   *   *

I came surging out of sleep, the echo of my own cry still ringing in the room. Even as I stared around me, looking for the black horror, the dream faded until it was nothing but shreds and tatters of fear. In moments, all that was left was the rapid beating of my heart to remind me of the terror of the dream.

The ragged cadence of my breathing gradually slowed. My mouth was dry, my throat raw from my hoarse cry. I swallowed several times, thinking with longing of the flask of wine left over from the evening meal. But I didn't get out of bed. I didn't think my knees would hold me.

A voice came softly out of the dark, startling me. "Are ye all right, lass?"

I hadn't heard Kenzie come back to the room. "Yes," I said. My voice sounded as rough as my throat felt. "Yes, I'm all right. Just a bad dream."

"Dreams can have verra sharp edges," he said, his voice warm and comforting in the dark. "You're sure you're all right?"

"Yes, thank you. Just fine."

I heard him turn over and the rustle of fabric as he drew his plaid closer around him. "Then I'll bid ye good night."

I burrowed down under the blanket on the lumpy mattress and prepared myself again for sleep. But it was a long time before it came to me.

Dawn was barely more than a paling of the eastern sky when Kenzie rose from his pallet by the door, waking me instantly. He picked up a bundle from the floor near the chest and tossed it onto the bed. "For you," he said.

I lit our stub of a candle and opened the bundle. It contained a tunic and trews in a dark brown, woven from good, fine wool, and a white shirt similar to the one he wore, but very much smaller. A cloak in a warm, russet brown wrapped a pair of soft leather boots that looked as if they should fit.

The wide leather belt that had secured the whole bundle looked as if it, too, would fit nicely.

I turned to him. "Thank you," I said gravely. "Why did you buy these things?"

He produced another bundle. This one contained cold, roast meat, cheese, bread, and apples, and a flask of wine. He spread the food on the bed and sat down. I hastily pushed the clothing aside and sat down beside him.

"I was listening in taverns most of last night," he said. He offered me his knife to cut the food. "They're out looking for you."

I nearly dropped the bread. I turned and stared at him. "They're out looking for me?" I repeated. "*Who's* out looking for me?"

"The Maedun." He took the knife from my hand and cut slices of the meat. "The soldiers. The whole city garrison. They're combing the city for you. At least I assume it's you. A Celae woman with reddish hair."

My hand began to tremble. I closed it into a fist. "Francia," I said. "It has to be Francia."

"Who's this Francia?"

"Have you heard of a sorcerer named Hakkar?"

He grimaced distastefully. "Oh, aye," he said. "He's well-known enough in Tyra. A most unpleasant man."

"Most unpleasant, indeed," I said. "Francia is his aunt. She's the woman who was on the ship I was captive in."

He gave me a decidedly speculative look, then nodded. "I see," he said slowly. "Then it's as well you're here rather than still on the ship." He nodded to the pile of clothing on the bed. "I decided that, since these disagreeable and ill-mannered Maedun are seeking a lass, why then, you'd needs must be a young lad. Besides, as a lad, you'll not be so conspicuous out on the streets by yourself. Finish your meal. We'll leave when you're ready."

*   *   *

When we were finished eating, he politely stood with his back to the room, one shoulder leaning against the wall, while I changed. Everything fitted reasonably well. The trews, tunic, and shirt were a little big, but the belt took care of the extra fullness around my waist. Even the boots fitted well enough. When I asked him how he had managed to find boots the right size, he turned back to me, grinning.

"I measured your foot while ye slept," he said. "The length of my spread hand less a thumblength. It's dainty wee feet ye have."

I looked at the size of his hands. He had *very* big hands—hands that matched the rest of him. I couldn't decide whether the remark was a compliment or an insult, so I refrained from comment. It was enough that the boots fitted, and I probably wouldn't get blisters walking or riding in them. I merely said, "Thank you." I pulled my hair to the front of my shoulder and began separating it into strands for braiding.

Kenzie looked at me critically. "Better," he said. "But shouldn't you do something about . . . er . . ." He gestured toward the front of my tunic. "Boys aren't exactly shaped like that."

I glanced down. My bosom isn't overly generous, but it's there. Kenzie had a valid point. "Do you have a scarf or something?"

He rummaged in his saddle pack and pulled out the long strip of white silk I had used as a shawl the previous evening. "Will this do?"

"Perfect. Now, if you'll turn your back again?"

The scarf, tightly wrapped and secured, took care of most of the problem. It wasn't the most comfortable thing in the world, but it worked reasonably well. When I had finished dressing again, Kenzie turned and studied me critically.

"Well, ye look a lot less like a lady now," he said. "But ye won't pass as a lad yet." He drew his dagger. "Let me see your hair." He took a step toward me.

I jumped back. The bed caught me just below the knees,

and I fell onto it, thumping the back of my head against the wall behind me. "What are you going to do with my hair?" I demanded.

"It wants cutting," he said calmly. "No lad would dast wear hair that long. Especially here in Laringras."

My hand went defensively to the unfinished braid. "You are *not* going to cut my hair!"

He loomed over me as I scrabbled back on the bed as far as I could go. The uneven planking and plaster of the wall dug into my back between my shoulders, and I could move no farther away. The dagger blade in his hand sent wicked glints of reflected sunlight flashing onto the drab blanket, red with the dawn light.

"D'ye want to get home, lass?" he asked.

"Don't be ridiculous. Of course I do. But what's that got to do with cutting my hair?"

"This is Laringras," he said patiently.

"You keep saying that," I said in exasperation. "I *know* it's Laringras." This was my hair we were discussing. I may complain about the color and the unruliness of it, but it was mine, and it had never been cut. I wasn't about to submit to my first haircut without protest. Especially a haircut administered by a hulking Tyr wielding a dagger.

"Aye, well, then ye'll know several things about it," he said. He didn't put the dagger away, nor did he step back. "First, women in Laringras don't dress in men's clothing. It's cause for imprisonment. Mayhaps even execution in some cases. And if ye look like a woman, ye must dress like a woman."

"I'm Celae," I said, not taking my eye off that dagger. "In Celi, women dress like this all the time."

"Aye, they probably do," he said, still patient. A parent trying to reason with a recalcitrant child. "But in Celi, a woman is her own person, is she not?"

"Yes, of course."

"But this is Laringras. Here a woman is—"

"A chattel or a whore," I said. "I know. You keep telling me. It's barbaric."

"Aye, so ye've said. Barbaric it may well be, but that's how things are here, as you've already discovered the hard way." He sat on the bed, trapping me neatly between him and the wall. "Ye canna appear on the streets dressed as a man with your hair nearly down to your knees."

"But if I'm to be a Celae boy—"

"Brynda, my own hair is long for here. If I weren't big enough, and good enough with this sword, to prove my manhood, things would not go easily here for me. Your hair is too long, and it must needs be cut."

"I can hide my hair," I cried.

"And how d'ye propose to do that?"

"I'll wear a hat," I said desperately.

He gestured around the room. "D'ye see a hat here? I didna purchase a hat, if ye'll notice."

"Then you'll just have to go out and get one," I said, trying to sound authoritative.

"No." He reached out and seized my braid. "What's it to be? A lad or a lass?"

"You can't cut my hair!"

"My lady Brynda, no woman in Laringras goes into the street without an escort. Not unless she's willing to risk arrest or being treated like a common whore. And no woman in Laringras would ride a horse across country with only one Tyran barbarian as escort. It's either be a lad, with shorn hair, or ye'll simply have to stay here until you can find an escort of Laringorn soldiers to take you through the mountains into Isgard. And I fancy ye'll find Isgard little different now that the Maedun hold it."

The prospect of being left to make my own way back home was even more appalling than the thought of losing my hair. I stared at Kenzie. He looked back, his expression grave. But there was a definite glint of amusement in those cat-green eyes. Amusement and implacability. He meant what he said. I had to make my choice, and I had to make it now. Either I let him cut my hair so he would accompany me back to Celi, or I kept my hair long and tried to get through Laringras, Falinor, and Isgard on my own. Not a pleasant prospect.

"What's it to be, lass?" he asked softly.

Well, if I had to make the best of a bad bargain, the least I could do was take it in reasonably good grace. I dropped my hand and turned so that the back of my head was toward him. I squeezed my eyes tight shut.

"Then cut it. Do it quickly. Just cut it."

All I felt was a single tug as he slid the blade between the back of my neck and my braid and jerked the blade toward him. Seconds later, he handed me the plait, long as my arm. I clutched it in both hands and turned to look at him. My misery must have been plain in my face, because he put his hand tenderly to my cheek.

"I'm sorry, Brynda," he said gently. "But it had to be done."

"Yes, I suppose it did." I coiled the braid and looked around for something to put it in. He handed me a leather pouch. I tucked the braid into it, then buckled the pouch at my waist. I stood up. "If I'm to be a boy, may I then have a sword?"

"A sword?" he repeated incredulously. "A woman with a sword? In Laringras?"

"Will you for the love of mercy *stop* reminding me this is Laringras?"

He had the grace to look contrite. "I apologize," he said. "But a sword?"

"I can use one," I said heatedly. "And I'm not a woman, remember? I'm a man."

Amusement filled his eyes and spilled over into laughter. "Well, mayhaps not a man," he said. "But certainly a lad. Here, let me even up that hair a bit so it looks less as if it were just hacked off." His expression softened. "I'm sorry, my lady. But it had to be done."

I nodded, then turned away to let him work. The back of my neck felt cold and uncomfortably vulnerable. But he was right. It had to be done. I took a deep breath. "You had best stop calling me *my lady*," I said. "My brother used to call me Bryn. In Celi, it's a man's name."

The cold edge of the dagger moved against the back of my neck. "Bryn it is, then," Kenzie said briskly. "We'll say you're my young brother." He stood up and put away his dagger. "There. That looks better. Ye'll have all the lasses sighing over these curls."

"How wonderful," I said sourly.

6

The stableboy led two horses out into the courtyard as we left the inn. The big bay gelding was obviously Kenzie's horse. It whickered in greeting and pawed impatiently at the ground as he approached. The other horse, a dark roan mare with a white blaze down her face, stood quietly, ears pricked forward alertly.

My uncle Connor, Duke of Wenydd, breeds the finest horses on the Island of Celi, or on the continent, too, for that matter. Over the years, I've picked up a fairly good general knowledge of horses from him. I'm not an expert, but I knew enough to recognize a beautifully appointed horse when I saw it. The mare looked dainty and delicate, high-spirited and high-stepping, but she had the depth and breadth of chest that spoke of endurance and strength, and the long, sleek muscles beneath the glowing hide that promised speed. An elegant and expensive horse, and not one a man who wore a threadbare kilt might be expected to own.

The stableboy handed me the reins, waited for a moment until Kenzie flipped him a copper coin, then vanished back into the stables. I reached up to stroke the mare's glossy neck.

"She's a beauty, Kenzie," I said, then frowned at him as my suspicion grew. Kenzie Catfoot was not a man with enough chiming silver in his purse to afford to buy a horse like this. "You didn't steal her, did you?"

He turned to me, one eyebrow raised, and placed his spread hand on his breast. "Ah, dear wee brother, Bryn, ye wound me to the heart!" he said in mock horror. He laughed, and swung himself up into the bay's saddle. "Aye, well, the man who used to own her might say I stole her. But she's mine fair and square. I won her in a dice game. She's the reason I was so late in getting back here last night. The game was a long one and verra serious, ye ken."

"You won her—"

"Oh, aye. I did that."

I looked at the mare again, then at him. "What on earth did you use to wager against him with?"

He reached forward and patted the bay's neck. "Why, the fine wee lad here, of course," he said. "The man who owned the mare had a lust to own him, fine example of horse that he is. Had I lost, we'd both be walking to Honandun, you and I." He sounded inordinately cheerful for a man who had wagered almost everything he owned on the fall of the dice. "But I didna lose. And she's a braw wee lass, is she not?"

"A fine wee lass, indeed," I said weakly. I swung up into the saddle. The mare danced beneath me, then settled nicely as I gathered in the reins.

Kenzie grinned. "She suits you well," he said. "It might be best if we took ourselves away before her former owner rids himself of the fog of wine sickness and convinces himself he was robbed rather than the victim of mere ill luck."

Banhapetsut was just beginning to waken as we rode out of the courtyard of the inn. Only two or three people were on the street, none of them looking too wide-awake. Kenzie turned right, away from the rising sun, as we entered the street, and urged the horse to a brisk walk. The mare fell naturally into place at his left side.

I felt horribly conspicuous with my shorn hair, but we aroused no comment as we moved swiftly along the street. I kept my head down, diffidently letting the mare find her own pace beside Kenzie's horse, and expecting someone at any moment to point at me and shout out his suspicions that I was not what I seemed to be. I wanted no repeat of the scene with the two city guards. Once was enough to last me more than a lifetime. We had to move out of the way of a heavily laden wagon, and the driver gave us a cheerful wave as he passed. He gave me no more than an incurious glance.

I felt naked without my sword on my back. My two silver combs were tucked into my belt pouch. They might be worth three or four silvers apiece. I wondered if that would be enough so that, given a chance, I might purchase a sword. It wouldn't be a Rune Blade, but any sword at this point was better than none at all.

The opportunity came sooner than I expected. We turned a corner and entered a large, open market square filled with stalls crowded cheek by jowl into every available inch of space. The vendors were just beginning to set out their wares for sale. Along all four sides of the square, merchants' shops stood with their fronts open as the merchants arranged their merchandise to show it off to best advantage. The smell of freshly baked bread hung thickly over the square, and my mouth watered with it.

A few early-rising shoppers wandered among the stalls, baskets hung over their arms. Most of them were women, all accompanied by the requisite complement of two or three guards. I noticed that most of the guards didn't appear too happy to be wandering the market at this hour. But the women moved from stall to stall, carefully examining the wares on the tables, the guards dutifully trailing along in their wakes.

Merchandise of every description lay piled high on the tables. Fruits and vegetables, flour and meal, fish and poultry, both live and dressed, jewelry, fabrics ranging from glossy silks to serviceable woolens in a riot of colors ranging from vivid to soft and muted, cooking vessels, clothing, flowers, shoes and boots, needles and pins, and children's toys. Vendors were already moving through the thin crowd crying their wares of sweetmeats, wine and ale, and small, succulent meat pies. The air was thick with the scents of perfume, spices, cooked food, human sweat, and horse dung.

The mare shied at the assault of noise and smell. I had a small argument with her before she settled again. She stepped fastidiously among the filth littering the cobbles as we skirted the market. We were nearly past the crowded square when I spotted the weapons merchant's stall by itself a few paces beyond the crush.

I called to Kenzie, then dismounted and led the mare to the stall. A variety of edged weapons lay on a cloth on the table, ranging from an array of jeweled daggers to half a dozen swords. One sword caught my eye. The hilt was barely long enough for a man to use two-handed, but my hands were smaller than most men's. The hilt was made of some black wood, with a straight crosspiece handguard that matched the metal of the blade. The whole sword was plain and unadorned except for a fine tracery of silver wire in an intricate interlocked pattern along the hilt. The blade itself was as long as my arm, and fairly narrow, although it appeared sturdy and serviceable. It wasn't a Celae Rune Blade by any means, but if it was properly balanced and tempered, it might serve me well enough.

The merchant behind the table smiled broadly in welcome as I approached, displaying a mouthful of huge teeth, yellowed from years of chewing tobbo leaf. By the lack of breadth to his shoulders and the delicacy of his wrists, I took him to be a mere merchant of other men's craftsmanship rather than the weaponsmith himself. But if the sword were well made, it might be worth purchasing.

Kenzie caught my arm. "Where do you think you're going?" he demanded. He had left his gelding beside the mare a few paces back. Both horses, their reins trailing on the cobbles, stood patiently waiting, showing no signs of moving away.

I gestured toward the stall. "I want a sword," I said.

He looked at the merchant, who stood beaming behind the table, then shook his head. "Not here," he said. "There are other places where we can find better weapons much cheaper."

"Not so, Excellence," the merchant cried. His Tyran was thickly accented but fluent enough. "I have here the finest weapons in the city, if not in the whole of Laringras. Let the boy look. I have something to suit his strength and his reach."

He hefted an ornate sword that looked more like a fashion accessory than a weapon. "Look at this. See the craftsmanship? Is this not a fine weapon? Just the thing for a boy such as your young brother."

The jewels on the hilt looked more like glass than real jewels, and not very good glass at that. I ran my fingernail along the blade. It left a streak in the silvery surface. That probably meant a particularly poor job of metal plating. When I looked carefully, it became apparent that the silver veneer was bubbly, indicating poor quality steel or iron beneath. I pushed it away.

"This would chip or break the first time it was used," I said. "What about that one?" I pointed at the sword that had first caught my eye. "How much?"

The merchant carefully laid the first sword back on the cloth and picked up the smaller one. "This one?" he asked. "Ah, this one is one of the finest swords ever made. It will take and keep an edge forever. And look at the hilt. Finest ebony and silver." He thrust it at me. "Feel the balance. And for only nine silver."

"Nine silver?" My heart sank. My combs might have been worth eight silver at most. Certainly not nine. And I had nothing else I could barter with.

"And cheap at the price," the merchant said, smiling broadly. He held out the sword again. "Try it out, young Excellence. You'll see."

I put out my hand for the sword, but before I could take it, Kenzie's hand closed around the hilt and snatched it out of my reach. He stepped back and swung the sword experimentally for a moment, then dropped it unceremoniously back onto the table.

"Rubbish," he said scornfully. "Not worth one silver, let alone nine."

The merchant picked up the sword again and rubbed the hilt on his sleeve, outrage and disbelief on his face. "You call my finest weapon rubbish?" he cried. "Excellence, this blade is made of the best steel on the continent."

"It's rubbish," Kenzie said again. "But seeing as the lad wants it, we'll give you two silver for it."

"Two silver!" The merchant went red in the face. He put the sword down and placed one hand over his heart. "How can I feed my family on only two silver? Eight silver, then. Eight, and it's yours."

I picked up the sword and stepped away from the stall. Behind me, Kenzie and the weaponsmith continued their haggling. I stopped listening and turned my attention to the sword.

It was heavier than I had first thought, but it fitted my hand reasonably well. The undecorated blade was honest steel, grayed rather than silvered, and polished to a satiny sheen. The edge felt keen enough beneath the ball of my thumb. I swung the sword one-handed in a swift figure-of-eight pattern. My wrist complained of the unaccustomed weight. When I tried it two-handed, it felt better. The balance was not as precise as my own sword's, but it wasn't bad. With some practice, I could learn to compensate for the difference.

Kenzie and the merchant stopped wrangling. Kenzie reached around from behind me and took the sword. "Let's go," he said. "We can find something better at a more reasonable price at another market." He tossed the sword carelessly onto the table and walked away, pulling me with him by the arm.

"You want to steal it from me," the merchant cried after us. "Five silver, then. Five silver, and it's yours."

I pulled my arm out of Kenzie's grip and turned back to the merchant. If the merchant would take five silver, he might take four. My silver combs were certainly worth four silver. And I wanted that sword. I was pulling the combs out of the pouch when I heard angry shouts and the swift, hissing whisper of drawn steel. I glanced quickly over my shoulder to see five armed men closing in on Kenzie. They were Maedun by their black hair and clothing, but not soldiers—not the Lord Protector's men. Kenzie held his greatsword in both hands as he stepped back, trying to watch all five men at the same time.

"We meet again, Tyr," one of the Maedun said, grinning widely in anticipation.

"So we do, Robard," Kenzie replied politely. "Always a pleasure to see you."

"Mayhaps I will open your other side this day."

"You may certainly try," Kenzie said. "But ye'd best not set your heart on succeeding."

I snatched up the sword from the merchant's table. Even as I turned, the sword raised and ready, Kenzie twisted out of the way of a wild flurry of sword blades as all five of the Maedun rushed him at once. His face contorted in pain as his posture pulled at the half-healed wound above his hip, but he moved deftly enough. His blade bit into the right arm of the lead attacker, nearly severing it.

Leaping forward, I swung my own sword, catching one of the Maedun by surprise. The blade of the sword caught him across the spine, just above the small of his back. He screamed and went down. I jumped over his twitching body, placing myself firmly on Kenzie's left. He spared me a brief glance and a hard, fierce grin, then turned back to face the three remaining freebooters.

They backed off warily. Odds of five to one they were comfortable with. Odds of three to two weren't quite so certain.

The one Kenzie had called Robard spoke tersely to his men. I had learned Maedun when I was young, but he spoke too quickly in a slurred idiom, and I caught very little of what he said. He sneered at me, then laughed and made an obscene gesture, dismissing me as a negligible obstacle, an untried boy. I grinned back at him. Better men than he had been unpleasantly surprised by the bheancoran of Skai.

"I'll take the ugly one," I said to Kenzie, nodding toward Robard.

Kenzie didn't take his eyes off the three freebooters. "Aye, well," he said. "Be careful, then. His looks alone are enough to tie that blade into knots."

"Aye," I said. "He's almost as ugly as you—"

The three freebooters all surged forward together. I swung around to place myself between Kenzie and Robard. He was not that much taller than I, but his sword was longer and heavier. It had been a long time since I practiced, and the unfamiliar weight of the new sword in my hand made me clumsy. I very nearly didn't survive the first seconds of the encounter. Only sheer good luck got me out of the way of the first energetic and deadly swing of Robard's dark sword. I nearly stumbled as I gave ground, but then conditioned reflex and years of training took over. I lost myself in the exacting rhythms of the dance.

I was as aware of Kenzie's whereabouts as I would have been of Tiegan's. Without conscious effort, I moved with him so that I remained in place to guard his left. The sword in my hands didn't sing as my own sword did, but it served me well enough. My lack of practice and the unaccustomed balance of the sword caused me to make too many missteps, but I was fortunate in that my opponent had obviously had little formal training with the sword. He relied on brute strength alone.

The Laringorn sword proved its mettle as I blocked the vicious cuts Robard aimed at me. Steel rang against tempered steel, and the force of his blows sent shocks all the way up my arms into my chest. For the first moment or two, all I could do was parry the rain of blows. I had no chance to attack. But I studied Robard's form and style, coldly analyzing his strengths and weaknesses as Fiala had trained me to do. The man had little grace and no finesse, but his strength and speed almost made up for it. I was forced to give ground, but I did so knowing I drew the Maedun farther from Kenzie.

"I will make dog meat out of you, whelp," he grunted.

"You will find I choke you if you try to devour me," I replied.

The man used his sword as if it were a cudgel or an ax. He was fast, and he was strong, and these traits had obviously served him well enough in the past. I doubted he had ever come up against a Celae-trained swordbearer before. And on top of this, to add to his confidence, he thought me to be an untried boy.

That was a bad mistake.

Robard surged forward, swinging his sword like an ax. I spun out of the way, ducking under the whistling arc of the blade. He had overbalanced. Even as he hopped to one side to steady himself, I thrust out with my sword and buried the point deep into his groin.

He staggered back, bleeding profusely, almost yanking the sword from my grip. As he fell to the ground, I managed to free my sword, then looked up to see a squad of Maedun soldiers, their faces grim and angry, running down the narrow street toward us. At the same time, Kenzie swung his sword and the blade slashed deep into the belly of the last freebooter.

"Here come more," I shouted.

Kenzie swore, then he grabbed my arm and nearly hauled me off my feet as he leapt for the horses. I pulled free and spun back toward the weapons merchant's table. He was nowhere in sight. A man with a healthy respect for caution, that merchant. I snatched the two silver combs from my belt pouch and slammed them down onto the table.

"For the sword," I shouted. I turned to find Kenzie beside me, mounted on his bay. He had looped his reins over the pommel of his saddle, and held his sword in one hand, the reins of the mare in the other, guiding the bay by knee pressure alone.

"As much as I admire your honesty," he said gravely, "it's high time we were gone from here." He looked across the market square. The Maedun soldiers were halfway across the square, plowing through the crowd toward us, knocking people out of their way. He glanced down at the combs on the table, and shook his head. "Whisht, Bryn, ye've badly overpaid him." He tossed me the mare's reins, then leaned sideways in his saddle and scooped up a plain leather scabbard that hung on a peg behind the table. "This should fit, and I'm sure the merchant will deem it a good bargain for the combs."

The merchant in question huddled under the table. He glared up at Kenzie, then at me, but he said nothing. He reached up and snatched the two combs off the table. They disappeared into some deep pocket within his robes.

Mayhaps I *had* overpaid him.

I vaulted into the mare's saddle and grabbed the reins. Kenzie put his heels to the bay's flanks and bent low over the saddle as the horse sprang forward. I was less than half a second behind him, the sword still clutched in my hand.

It was a wild ride we had through the city, the horses' iron-shod hooves striking sparks off the cobbles of the pavement. The mare, neatfooted and deft, never faltered, but once Kenzie's horse put a foot wrong and nearly went down.

My heart in my mouth, I watched helplessly as the big bay slipped, fully expecting to see Kenzie thrown to the cobbles and the horse break its leg. But it recovered, and Kenzie kept his seat.

Moments later, we were in sight of the city gates. Glancing back over his shoulder, Kenzie drew his horse down to a more decorous pace. I drew up alongside him.

"We seem to have lost them," he said breathlessly. He held his hand pressed tightly against his hip, over the wound, and he looked paler than he should have. "It's best if we act as if nothing's wrong as we pass the gate guards."

I nodded, unable to speak.

"Give me that sword," he said. I handed it to him, and he thrust it into the scabbard and handed it back to me. He grinned at me. "I've changed my mind. It's certainly a fine idea indeed that ye carry a sword, Bryn. Ye seem to know how to use it well enough. I thank ye for the help back there."

"It was my turn," I told him grimly, and he laughed.

I had no way of securing the scabbard to my back, so I hastily undid my belt and threaded the leather through the loop on the scabbard. Not the most comfortable way to carry a sword while riding. When it was secure, I looked up at Kenzie. "I'm bheancoran," I said shortly. "I was brought up with a sword in my hand."

He raised one red-gold eyebrow. "Bheancoran, is it?" He grinned. "Aye, well, it's no wonder you handle a sword well."

"I was clumsy," I said. "I'm out of practice."

He laughed. "Oh, aye. We'll certainly have to see to it that ye get plenty of practice from now on."

The guards at the gate barely gave us a second glance. They were more concerned with a huge wagon loaded down with kegs of ale. One wheel had become stuck in a rut, half-blocking the gate. The teamster cracked his whip, shouting and swearing at the team of straining oxen. There was barely enough room for the horses to slip between the tall sides of the wagon and the stone wall of the gate. I had to pull my feet up out of the way or lose some skin off my legs.

We came out of the city onto a vast, flat plain covered with dry, brown grass. To the east, behind the city, the land rolled endlessly flat toward the border of Borlan. To the west, the tops of the Laringras Alps, blue with distance, blended into the hazy horizon. South, to our left, lay a vast salt marsh and the sea. We set out northwestward along the road at a decorous brisk walk.

"Did you hurt yourself back there?" I asked. "How's your wound?"

"I pulled it a bit," he said. "But it'll do well enough until we can stop for a while." He pointed toward the mountains. "We go that way," he said. "We can pick up the merchant trail through the pass. With luck, we'll be in Isgard in less than a season. We'll have to hurry, though. Snow closes the passes shortly after Samhain. I've no wish to be caught in the mountains in a blizzard."

"How far to Honandun after we get through the mountains?"

"Another half season mayhaps, if we meet good weather," he said. "It'll be tricky finding a ship's master willing to tackle the voyage from Honandun to Celi that close to Midwinter, but you'll be safe in Honandun until ye can take ship home."

Home . . . Tiegan would be waiting. I closed my eyes briefly, then straightened in the saddle.

"Then let's not waste time here talking," I said. "It's time we were off." The sooner King Tiernyn knew of the new Maedun threat to Celi, the better. I had a long and difficult journey ahead of me. I hoped it would not be too long, or that my warning would not be too late.

7

I checked Kenzie's wound the first time we stopped to rest the horses. The exertion of the fight had opened it, and he had bled a little into the bandage padding. I tightened the bandage around him. I could do nothing else right now. There were no flows of earth and air magic around me in this dry, sere land, nothing I could reach for to give me strength enough to Heal it. I'd have to use my own strength and vitality, but I couldn't do it here. It would have to wait until we stopped for the night, and I could sleep to replenish the strength I poured into him.

"I *told* you not to go about doing silly things and opening that wound," I said as I reapplied the bandage. "My Gift isn't strong enough to Heal it completely."

He raised one eyebrow. "Next time, I'll tell the horde of angry Maedun that I canna fight them until I heal," he said gravely. "I'm sure they'll show understanding."

I pulled the bandage a little tighter than I had to. He sucked in his breath sharply, but said nothing.

"Do that," I said.

"I had little choice in the matter, you'll notice," he said, rubbing his hip. "That feels better now. I'll have no trouble riding with it bound tight like that."

"I'll Heal it tonight, after we've camped."

"No need." He swung back up onto the bay. "Are we ready to go again?"

We rode hard for the first three days, swiftly leaving behind the humid salt marsh along the river delta by the sea. We stopped during the day only to rest the horses. At night, we found sheltered places among the tall grass and scrub thornbushes to snatch a few hours sleep. The track, hard-packed and reasonably well traveled, plunged almost immediately into the vast, semiarid prairie of dry, brown grass only sparsely watered by a random spring or a thin thread of stream. Occasional clumps of twisted pine marked the watercourses. I saw no alder or oak or ash. None of the familiar trees of home. Even the pines looked half-dead, dry brown and green, and choked with dust.

The track angled steeply northwest. Kenzie had told me that the main merchant trail lay farther north. We might expect to reach it about a fortnight out from Banhapetsut.

The sun beat down during the day, making wearing a cloak uncomfortably warm. But at night, frost rimed the grass, turning it stiff and gray. Even wrapped in my cloak and a blanket, I shivered in my sleep as the cold ate into my flesh and bones.

Gradually, the last glimpses of the sea to our left fell away as we worked our way north and west along the track. I noticed the land changing around us. More and more, the dry grass had given way to patches of flat, spiny growth, all dusty gray-green and green-brown. When I accidentally trod on one patch as we were resting the horses, a sharp spine pierced the soft leather of my boots and lodged in the flesh of my foot. It stung like fire. I managed to extract it, muttering harsh and unkind words about Laringorn vegetation, but my foot still hurt as if the thorn and its poison were still embedded in it.

"Cactus," Kenzie said by way of casual and completely unsympathetic explanation. "They get bigger as we approach the Ghadi Desert." He glanced down at my boot, still stained with blood. "Aye, and more vicious, too."

"They're worse than stickle thorns at home," I complained. "This surely is miserable country."

"It's harsh country," he said. "Even the plants have to defend themselves more vigorously than in softer climes."

In the next hour, I watched in dismay as my foot swelled painfully until I had to remove the boot. The swelling and the pain lasted for the rest of the day. After that, I exercised a lot more caution when dismounted, and I tried to steer the mare away from the growths.

I wasn't the best of company for the first three days. Francia's words about a new magic to overcome Donaugh's curtain of enchantment filled my mind, swirling around in my head like a dog chasing its own tail.

Fifteen years before I was born, the Maedun had attempted to invade the Isle of Celi. They had already taken all of the continent except for mountainous Tyra and Borlan. King Tiernyn with the army of Celi behind him met the invaders on the shore and nearly fell to Maedun blood sorcery. Donaugh the Enchanter, Tiernyn's twin brother, had called upon his gentle Tyadda magic to engage the black sorcerer, Hakkar of Maedun, in a magical battle. It cost Donaugh his right hand, but he defeated and killed Hakkar, and the invasion failed.

Hakkar's sister, Francia, had used the confusion of the invasion to steal away with the child she had borne by trickery and treachery to Tiernyn. Here, though, there was some confusion. Some of the stories made Donaugh the father of Francia's child. Neither Tiernyn nor Donaugh had ever said anything to clear up the confusion, and the story became just another of the hundreds of legends that had grown up around the beginning of Tiernyn's reign.

Donaugh himself set the curtain of enchantment in place early in the summer following the invasion. I had grown up knowing it was there, knowing we were safe from the Maedun as long as it was in place. Mayhaps all of us born after the invasion had grown complacent about our safety. I can't recall even once wondering what might happen should the curtain of enchantment disappear or be destroyed. Donaugh himself, along with two apprentices, kept the curtain in place. He had promised Tiernyn that Celi would be safe as long as he, Donaugh, lived, and as long as his successors after him lived. While Donaugh was obviously no longer a young man, he certainly wasn't ancient, and was in no danger of death by old age in the immediate future. And his apprentices, Llyr and Gwyn, were still young. Gwyn was barely into his teens.

The sorcerers of Maedun are a strange lot, nearly legend

both on the continent and in Celi. The magic and the name of the father are passed down to the eldest son when the father dies. The Hakkar of Maedun who was Francia's nephew and the present black sorcerer of Lake Vayle in Maedun, was son to the man who had led the invasion on Celi nearly forty years ago, and grandson to the man my grandfather Kian had defeated when my father was only a child of three or four. All of them were named Hakkar, and sometimes in the stories, they tended to become confused. The stories say that the father's magic passed to the son, the present Hakkar of Maedun, aboard the flagship anchored offshore in Celi as Donaugh slew the father. The son was but a child of perhaps ten at the time, but already had magic of his own. That he had never given up his father's ambition to subjugate Celi was common knowledge. Only Donaugh's curtain of enchantment held back another invading force.

But Francia had told me that Hakkar might have found a way to defeat that enchantment—a way involving the use of Celae magic itself. I shivered as I remembered the triumph in her voice as she spoke to me in that dingy, filthy little cabin.

Not so much as a rumor of this had reached Celi. Tiernyn had a network of spies on the continent, and he was in constant touch with my grandfather Kian in Tyra, who maintained his own network of spies and informers. My grandfather had an innate talent for putting together bits and snippets of information and coming to surprisingly accurate conclusions. But even he had no knowledge of this new discovery.

I had to get back to Celi, and I had to do it quickly. There was no telling if Hakkar and Francia had managed to get their hands on another Celae who had some magic. We don't hide away on our little protected island. Celae trade ships ply the seas. We have strong ties with Tyra, and visit there. I had been taken far too easily. How easily might some other man or woman be taken?

This journey would be long and arduous. But might it be too long? Cold fear clutched at my belly as I pondered what might happen in Celi should a Maedun invasion be successful.

I *had* to make it back to Celi in time to warn Tiernyn and Donaugh. I *had* to!

On the third night, a northwest wind blew down out of the mountains as we drew the horses off the track into a low copse of scrubby thornbush. The air was already growing colder, and frost had begun to settle onto the grass. Around the small, silty spring, a thin crust of ice stiffened the sodden mud. I set to making a fire while Kenzie took his bow and disappeared into the gathering dark.

We had left Banhapetsut with scant thought to provisioning ourselves for a long journey. I had thought there would be little problem, envisioning a string of inns and taverns along a track as well traveled as the merchant trail surely must be. But we had seen no signs of human habitation since leaving Banhapetsut. Most of the people of Laringras lived either in the cities, Kenzie informed me, or on farms strung out along the three main rivers, which lay mostly to the north and east of the Ghadi Desert. The inhospitable country we traversed was mostly uninhabited. Only a few tribes of wandering herders lived in it, and they tended to stay close to water.

In Celi, traveling and living off the land would have been no problem. Game was plentiful there, everything from deer to rabbits to game birds, and anyone handy with a bow could have meat roasting over his campfire at every meal. Edible roots, wild herbs, and fruits abounded, too. I had blithely assumed Laringras couldn't be much different from Celi.

I was wrong. But then, being wrong about Laringras and all things Laringorn was a habit I was, unfortunately, becoming used to.

Kenzie returned to the small campfire with two animals that looked somewhat akin to rabbits, but with much shorter ears, and long, pointed noses. Almost like rats. I looked at them for a moment, considering their origin, then decided I wouldn't ask what they were. They smelled like roasting rabbits as they spit and sizzled on sticks over the fire of blazing thornwood. When well cooked, the flesh was succulent and tasty. That was good enough for me. I didn't see the need of knowing exactly what they were. I'd probably feel much better in blissful ignorance.

Frost lay thick on the grass and the bare thornbushes by the time we finished eating. The dry, resin-filled thornwood made for a hot fire, but the wood burned quickly and needed replenishing often. I wrapped the blanket around my shoulders over my cloak, shivering as the cold air ate into my flesh. It couldn't have been much more than a fortnight past Autumnal Equinox, but it felt as cold as Midwinter in Celi.

A strange country, Laringras. A land of violent contrasts.

Above, the stars blazed fiercely in the black sky, so bright they looked as if they could be plucked right out of the night and used as candles. I had never seen stars that dazzlingly bright. Watching them, I nearly forgot about the urgency of my message for Tiernyn and Donaugh.

Kenzie tilted his head back and looked up at the dazzle of stars. "It's the desert air," he said.

His accurate divining of my thoughts startled me. I stared at him. "Are you practicing magic now?" I asked. "Or do you just walk through minds?"

He laughed. "No," he said. "Everyone who sees those skies for the first time is fascinated by them. I didna think you'd be any exception. It's the air, ye ken. It's so clear it's as if it's not there between you and the stars." His breath plumed whitely, like smoke, from his mouth and nose as he spoke. He settled his plaid closer around himself. "And it holds little heat at night when the sun goes down, even in the summer."

"It's cold enough now," I said.

"Aye, well, it'll get colder yet," he said. "This is just the beginning." He leaned forward to throw another chunk of thornwood onto the fire. A small constellation of sparks spiraled up into the night like a swirl of lost stars. He turned to me, the firelight glinting in his hair and limning half his face in rosy light. "Why are you in such a dither to get back to Celi?"

I hesitated, then told him of my fears. He listened without interruption, his gaze never leaving my face. When I finished, he nodded and considered in continuing silence what I had said.

Finally, he said, "Aye, I can see why ye might want to take that news back, and quickly. D'ye think there's real danger of invasion?"

I laughed bitterly with no trace of humor. "Who can say? Knowing the Maedun, I'd say yes. The danger is very real indeed."

"The Maedun are nothing to take lightly," he said. "Ever." He looked at me, his face intense in the flickering, fire-shot night. "Who are ye, Brynda?"

I withdrew into my cloak and blanket. "Just a misplaced Celae woman," I said, trying to make light of it.

"And bheancoran," he said. "Bheancoran to whom? Ye're surely too young to be bheancoran to the Prince of Skai."

In spite of myself, I jumped, startled again. "How do you know of the Prince of Skai?"

He chuckled softly. "I'm of Clan Broche Rhiudh of Tyra," he said. "Born in Glen Borden in the shadow of the Clanhold."

"I know," I said. "I recognized your tartan."

"I thought you had. I grew up not far from the Clanhold, in a glen a few leagues to the north. I'm well familiar with the stories about Red Kian of Skai and his wife, the lady Kerridwen. I know his son Keylan is Prince of Skai now, and ye're surely not his bheancoran."

I traced an idle pattern on my thigh, thinking. Kenzie Catfoot gave every appearance of being an honest and trustworthy man. Finally, I looked up at him. "Red Kian is my grandfather," I said. "My father is Prince Keylan of Skai. I'm bheancoran to my cousin, Prince Tiegan of Celi, the son of King Tiernyn."

"First King of a united Celi," he said, as if he spoke to himself rather than to me. "A strange thing, being king of a land like Celi. They were like the Tyrs for so many years, divided into their separate clans—"

"Provinces," I said, correcting him automatically. "Not clans in Celi."

"Provinces, then," he said. He laughed softly. "No man has ever managed to bring all the clans of Tyra together under one king. The closest we've come is the First Laird of the Council of Clans. Brychan of Broche Rhuidh, it is now, kin to your grandfather." He raised an eyebrow at me. "I've often wondered how your father would feel about being liegeman to his younger brother."

"My father is Prince of Skai," I said indignantly. "And he supported Tiernyn strongly all those years ago when Tiernyn was made King. Tiernyn carried Kingmaker, the sword my grandfather brought back to Celi from the continent. The sword proclaimed him King, and my father was the first prince to pledge his sword and his service. Besides, being Prince of Skai is no small thing in itself."

"Aye, apparently not. And now his daughter is bheancoran to his brother's son."

"Tiegan will be King of Celi some day."

"And you'll be bheancoran to a king."

I nodded. "If I can warn Tiernyn and Donaugh of the danger," I said.

He looked up at me. The firelight limned the lines of cheek and brow and threw deep shadows across his eyes. I couldn't see the fierce green of them, but I could almost feel the intensity of his gaze on my skin. "Have ye considered the possibility that it might have been the Emperor himself who betrayed you to the Maedun?"

Startled, I stared at him. "The Emperor? Surely not—"

He shrugged. "He's a wily old fox," he said. "And he knows what the Maedun want as well as any man on the continent. The Maedun want Borlan, aye, but they want Celi, too.

Indeed, Hakkar wants Celi more than he ever wanted Borlan. The Emperor might be more than willing to trade you and your magic for immunity for Borlan."

It made sense. But Tiegan and I had been so sure of an alliance. "But the Emperor agreed—"

"Did ye have anything in writing? Anything with the Imperial Seal affixed to it?"

"Well, no. Not yet. But—"

He shrugged again. "Then there's Francia herself," he said. "Did she no tell you she'd come to see the Emperor?"

More than just the chill of the Laringras night made me shiver. "Yes, she did say that."

"And did ye no wonder what business she might have with the Emperor?"

He filled his mug from the battered pot of khaf tea, then held out the pot to me. Absently, still deep in thought, I held out my mug, and he poured the last of the khaf tea into it. The brew tasted somewhat brackish because of the water, but I hardly noticed.

"You may want to warn your King Tiernyn that the Emperor's word may not be all that it seems," Kenzie said.

He had given me a lot more to think about. What he said made sense. I had never really trusted the Emperor. I roused myself and drained the khaf tea from my mug.

"You're right," I said. "I must warn Tiernyn. And pray the warning comes in time."

"We'll just have to see that it does," he said.

I looked at him. Wrapped in his plaid, his hair gleaming bright red-gold with the fire behind it, he could easily have been my grandfather as a young man. Or just about any other Tyr of Broche Rhuidh, for that matter. He was certainly well versed in the intrigues of politics. More astute than I, at any rate. I had not made the connection between Francia's presence and any false dealings on the part of the Emperor.

"Who *are* you, Kenzie Catfoot?" I asked softly.

He laughed and shook his head. "Just what you see, my

lady," he said, amusement bubbling though his voice. "A merchant train guard without a merchant train to guard at the moment."

"There's more to you than that, Kenzie," I said. "You say you grew up around the Clanhold at Broche Rhuidh. I'm wondering if you grew up *in* it, and I'm trying to remember if I ever saw you there when I was visiting." I looked at him. In the firelight, his hair glowed softly, and shadow filled his eyes and the hollows of his cheeks. Most of the Tyran clansmen I knew were tall and redheaded, and most of them were extremely good with their swords. But there was something about Kenzie that persistently reminded me of my grandfather, or his kinsman Brychan of Broche Rhuidh. A certain tilt to his chin at times, perhaps. Or the way he held his body so alert and ready when he hefted his sword. "Are you the Beltane child of one of the lords of Broche Rhuidh?"

He laughed again. "I'm no Beltane child," he said. "I was born closer to Midwinter Solstice than Imbolc."

"But you can't, or won't, name your father?"

The light of laughter died in his eyes, and a sour twist curved his mouth downward. "Aye, well, as for that," he said quietly, "my father, bless his immovably stubborn heart, has long since disowned me. Fatherless I am, and fatherless I shall remain." He pulled his plaid around himself and got to his feet. "I'll take the first watch. You'd better get some sleep. I'll waken you at midnight."

That ended the conversation as finally as if it had been cut by the blade of that Tyran greatsword of his. I watched him as he strode out to check on the horses, out into the darkness beyond the circle of light cast by the small fire. He held himself stiffly, straight as the blade of a sword. Mayhaps it was the trace of the Healer's Gift in me, but I thought I sensed a deep and abiding hurt in him, one that no Healer, even one as Gifted as my aunt Torey, could ever Heal.

I tucked the blanket around myself and curled down beside the fire to sleep.

8

Kenzie didn't waken me for my turn at guard duty until three
hours before dawn, then brushed away my protestations that
he had let me sleep too long. While I sat yawning and stretching, he wrapped himself warmly in his plaid and blanket and
lay on the other side of the fire with his back to me. I don't
think he slept much, and what sleep he did manage to get was
restless and fitful. With the first paling of the eastern sky
toward dawn, he was on his feet, giving a reasonable imitation
of a man refreshed and ready for a new day.

He said little as we broke our fast on the remains of our
evening meal and khaf tea made with muddy springwater. The
sun rose as we finished eating, making the frost-grayed grass
sparkle. He was unusually quiet as we saddled the horses in
preparation for resuming our journey, and a faint line drew the
heavy eyebrows together above the bridge of his nose. He
gave all the signs of a man deep in thought.

As the day progressed, the sun warmed the air. By midmorning, it was too hot to wear my cloak. I shed it gratefully
and tucked it into the saddle pack. Still, Kenzie maintained his
thoughtful, introspective silence. It wasn't at all like him to be
so quiet for so long. Had I known my remarks were going to
disturb him like this, I certainly wouldn't have said anything
last night. I watched him covertly, trying not to let him see me
watching him, and I wondered if I should be worried about
him.

To either side of the track, deep gullies seamed the land,
their sides pleated into fantastic shapes, carved by wind and
water into pillars and folds like the columns of a shrine back
in Celi. In the brilliant sunshine, they gleamed gold and
bronze and copper, glittering here and there with some min-
eral that sparkled like gemstones. No water flowed over the

stones at the bottom of the ravines, and the twisted skeletons of dead, dry bushes and stunted trees drooped dispiritedly above the empty watercourses. Somewhere insects droned lazily, and the clumps of tall, brown grasses whispered in the slight breeze.

Finally, I could stand the silence no longer. I had been letting the mare follow behind Kenzie's horse. I urged it to a trot so that I could ride beside him.

"Kenzie?"

He looked at me, his expression still abstracted.

"Kenzie, would you tell me why your father disowned you?"

He rode easily beside me, one hand on his thigh, his back sword-straight. For a moment, I thought he would ignore the question. As I suppose he had every right to. It was horribly intrusive, and the reason was none of my business in the first place. I suppose I had the idea that if he spoke about it, it might cease gnawing at him so badly.

He looked up, gazing intensely at the mountains, all hazed with blue and gray by distance. The heat of the sun lay across my shoulders, tangible as a cloak. The soft, hypnotic clop of the horses' hooves broke the heavy morning silence. Small puffs of powdery dust squirted from beneath the bay's hooves and shimmered like gold around its legs in the strong sunlight.

Finally, Kenzie sighed. "He disowned me because I struck him in anger," he said softly.

I stared at him. "You struck him? Your father?"

Sour amusement quirked the corner of his mouth. "Aye, I struck him. And in great anger. At the time, I thought I had cause."

I thought of my own father and my brother. Brennen and our father were both famously—or infamously—obstinate. They came by it honestly. My grandmother Kerri called my grandfather the stubbornest mule to walk on two legs like a man. It was a family trait, like the red hair, passed from one generation to the next. Over the years, that had led to more

than one confrontation with Brennen and Father standing nose
to nose and toe-to-toe arguing with enough volume to rattle
the windows. But neither had ever struck the other, and within
an hour after the argument, both acted as if it had never happened. I was used to explosive dissension, but in my family, at
least, it had never led to long-term bitterness, nor to violence
between father and son.

"He disowned you because you struck him?" I asked.

That bitter little downturning smile caught at the corner of
Kenzie's mouth again. "Aye, well, I thought at the time that he
might be somewhat overannoyed because I laid him in his bed
for half a fortnight." He shook his head. "It was only the cul-
mination of years of strife between us, ye ken. It seemed we
couldna agree on which side of the mountains the sun went
down on for years before that."

I glanced down at my hands to hide my smile. "Both of you
stubborn as rocks," I said.

"Aye, you might say that." He shrugged. "Well, it's a common trait in all Tyrs, they tell me."

"In many Celae, too, I think," I said.

"I was fifteen when it happened, nearly sixteen, grown almost
as tall as I am now and thinking myself a man. My father wished
me to marry a young woman from the neighboring glen."

I looked at him. His gaze was still fixed on the far mountains, but from the expression on his face, he was seeing neither the mountains nor the sere landscape around us. "You
didn't want to marry her?" I said.

He shrugged again. "No," he said. "And the young woman
in question didna particularly want to marry me. She was in
love with another, ye ken." His expression softened. "Aye, and
so was I, for that matter."

I said nothing. For a few minutes, we traveled in silence,
Kenzie lost in memories of the past. Finally, I looked over at
him.

"What happened?" I asked. Then I shook my head. "No,
I'm sorry. I have no business asking that."

"Well, it's true I dinna speak of it much," he said quietly. "It isna something I wish to remember verra often." He was silent for a moment. "My father wished me to wed a young woman called Serinal dal Methwyn. He thought the union would bring him advantage, ye ken. Serinal had other ideas, and so did I. She loved a young man who was with the army on duty near the Isgard border. Daffit dav Sion, his name was. A friend of mine."

"And your love?" I asked. "Who was she?"

He smiled. "Kethryn dal Bogarth," he said softly. "She was one of the lady Alysda's ladies—Brychan's wife. Her father was a nobody. He had few lands, no wealth. A very minor laird in a small glen north of the Clanhold. An officer in Brychan's army—and a good one. But Kethryn . . . She was lovely, and I loved her. After my father decreed I must wed Serinal, the three of us plotted together, and we spirited Serinal away to the border. She and Daffit wed there. By the time our parents caught up with us, she was with child by Daffit. That pretty well put paid to the idea of her wedding me."

I had to smile. "So far, it sounds like one of those romances the bards are always singing."

"Aye, it does," he said. He didn't smile. "We thought my father would accept the fact that Serinal was now beyond me, and settle down. But he flew into a rage and prevailed upon Laird Brychan and the lady Alysda to send Kethryn home to her parents. It was shortly after Samhain, and the new snow was already falling deep in the high passes. Kethryn and her escort were caught in the pass by a blizzard. They died there, all of them."

"Oh, Kenzie, no . . ."

He glanced at me, a wry expression twisting his mouth. "I blamed my father, of course," he said. "I all but called him a murderer, and in a rage of grief, I struck him. Struck him hard enough to lay him in his bed for half a fortnight with his jaw bound in a bandage to heal it where I'd broken it for him. It was then he disowned me. He said he'd have no such undutiful and rebellious ingrate as a son. I left Tyra that night and rode to Honandun, where I joined a band of merchant train guards." He straightened his shoulders and shook himself slightly, like a man shrugging off an uncomfortable cloak. "Aye, well, it was ten years and more ago. I've managed well enough without a father all these years."

There was little I could say, so I wisely chose to say nothing. We rode for a while in silence in the heat of the midmorning sun. After a long time, he pulled his water bottle from the peg on his saddle and handed it to me. I took a sip of the tepid water and gave the bottle back to him. He took a drink and replaced the bottle on its peg.

"I think I know where we are," he said, looking around. "If I'm right, there's an inn a league or two ahead. The trail divides there. One branch goes east to Matchetluk, and the other goes west to join the main merchant trail. The inn is the only one along this branch of the track. We'll reach it too early to stay the night, but Rachnal should have a good meal to give us."

"An inn," I repeated. "A bath . . ."

Kenzie grinned. "No baths at Rachnal's inn," he said. "Not unless you're willing to part with a couple of silvers to pay for it. Water's dear in the desert. Rachnal's inn is less than half a league from the river, but it's half a league nearly straight down."

Regretfully, I let go of the vision of water and soap and clean, ungritty skin. It had been a nice dream for the short while I'd been able to hold it. After a while, I said, "Do you still blame your father for Kethryn's death?"

For a moment, I thought he wouldn't answer, but presently, he shook his head. "No," he said. "Not any longer. It took me years to realize he wasn't responsible. It was an accident. It should have been safe enough to negotiate even the high passes at that time of year. The blizzard was unseasonable, something nobody could have predicted."

"Have you ever tried to tell that to your father?"

"Oh, aye," he said, sounding a little more cheerful. "I did. A few years ago, I sent a messenger to Tyra to tell my father when I'd be in Honandun, and asked if he might meet me there, or send a messenger so that I might give him a letter to carry back."

"And did he come?"

He shook his head. "I was in Honandun nearly two fortnights. My father never came, nor did he send a messenger." That wry smile tugged at the corner of his mouth again. "But I heard through others that he still had me outlawed for the horse I took from him when I left. It was his best horse I took, after all. So if he'll no come to me, I canna go to him, or risk imprisonment."

"Imprisonment!" I stared at him, appalled. "Your father would imprison you?"

He laughed without humor. "He's a proud and stubborn man, is my father. In a way, I suppose it's comforting to know he's not changed over the years. I'd worry about him becoming old and going into his dotage had he changed his mind. He finds it as difficult as I to forgive, and, even when he knows he was wrong, he's far too stubborn to admit it." One eyebrow twitched ruefully. "Aye, as I suppose I am." He glanced at me. "Ye're looking at a broken man, Bryn. Fatherless and clanless now to boot. An outlaw."

I studied his face. He was only half jesting. "But still with all a clansman's pride," I said quietly.

He laughed. "Oh, aye. Still plenty of that."

"Are you sure he received the message? Your father, I mean."

"There was no reason why he shouldna. The messenger was a reliable man. He—" He broke off and lifted his head, an intense, listening expression on his face. "Off the road," he said tersely. "Now."

I started to protest, but he gave me a glance that would have withered the grass, were it not already sere and burnt.

Then I heard it, too—the muted thunder of approaching horses. Kenzie reined the big bay around, and they slithered and slid down the steep side of the ravine beside the track. I followed with the mare, somewhat more cautiously, but the surefooted little roan had no difficulty with the descent. Kenzie had dismounted at the bottom and pulled the bay into the shelter of a weathered overhang formed by the wind that had carved the clay-and-sandstone sides of the gully. He motioned me in with him. I slid off the mare's back and pulled her into the shaded cleft.

"What is it?" I asked.

"Maedun soldiers, I think," he said. "I can't think of anyone else who'd be hurrying horses along this track in this heat. Stay quiet now."

Dust billowed up from the track above us as the troop of mounted men rode past. The rattle and clink of their bridle metal and the creak of leather made musical overtones to the rumble of hooves on packed earth. Kenzie's bay paid no attention to the passing horses, but the mare tossed her head, ready to greet them. I quickly muffled her nose with my hand, and she quieted.

"Maedun," Kenzie said by way of confirmation. "And in somewhat of a hurry, too, I'd say."

A cold chill rippled down my spine. "After me?"

He shrugged. "Mayhaps," he said. "You did tell me that woman was determined to take you to her nephew."

I shuddered again, then hunched as small as possible against the mare's withers. The last of the troop of horsemen clattered out of hearing beyond us.

"They'll be stopping at the inn, no doubt," Kenzie said.

"What are we going to do?"

"Do?" He raised an eyebrow quizzically. "Why, nothing. Not right now. We'll simply wait until we're sure they've gone, then we'll ask the innkeeper which way they went, and we'll go the other."

"And if they've taken the track westward?"

"Aye, well, I've an idea about that, too."

*   *   *

About an hour after noontide, we came upon the inn Kenzie
had spoken of. It sat in the apex of the wedge where the trail
split, facing down the tail of the "Y." To the east of the inn,
the trail edged along the steep, sandy cliff above the river.
The inn itself was a squat, sprawling structure, surrounded by
a man-high wall built of mud bricks. Bright green foliage
behind the walls spoke of a good, year-round supply of water.
I hadn't realized how thoroughly sick I was of the dusty gray-
green of the sparse desert vegetation until I saw those green
trees. An iron-grille gate stood partially open, casting black
shadows across the swept dust of the outer courtyard.
Hoofprints marred the silky-smooth dust around the gate, but
as far as I could tell, the same number of horses had left as
had entered.

"Is it safe to go in?" I asked.

Kenzie studied the prints on the ground, then nodded. "I
believe so. I know the innkeeper. I won't call him a good
friend, but we've known each other for most of the years I've
been traveling with the merchant trains."

As we entered the courtyard, a young boy came running
from the stables arranged along the left wall. He waited as we
dismounted, then gathered in the reins of both the bay and the
mare to take them to the stables. Kenzie gave orders to water
them and give them a good feed, then beckoned me to follow
him into the inn itself.

I paused before entering, looking at the orange trees in the
courtyard. "Water enough for oranges," I said.

"Aye," Kenzie said. "But Rachnal sells them dear, too."

The room we entered was large and cool, and dimly lit by
small windows cut into the thick mud brick walls. The beaten
earth floor had been sprinkled with water to keep the dust
down, and the tables looked clean although the smell of old
cooking and stale beer and ale hung thick in the cool air. There
was nobody in the room but an immense man wearing a white
apron, who stood behind the long counter. Behind him,

stacked kegs of ale and beer jostled for space with two huge, gracefully curved wine jars.

The innkeeper came out from behind the counter and advanced upon us. He was nearly as tall as Kenzie, and appeared to be almost as wide as he was tall, his white apron tied by a thong around his middle where he should have had a waist, but didn't. His round face split in a wide grin of welcome.

"Why, by the beard of the sun, it be Kenzie Catfoot," he cried. Startled, I realized he was speaking the Isgardian common tongue rather than Laringorn. "We heared ye was dead, lad, and long confined to the pits of Hellas."

"I've been in Banhapetsut," Kenzie replied. "It could be construed as being the next worst thing to the pits of Hellas."

The innkeeper made a face. "It be a mean and poor city indeed," he said. His gaze lit on me, and he raised both eyebrows in surprise. "And who be this with you, lad?"

Without turning a hair, Kenzie said, "You've not met my young brother, Bryn, have ye, Rachnal. I've been teaching him the vagaries of the life of a merchant train guard."

Rachnal reached out and slapped me on the back affably, with enough force to send me staggering forward a step or two. "Young brother, be he?" he said, laughing. "It's too young you be, boy, to take up the wicked ways of your brother."

There was enough subtle emphasis on the last word to assure me that Rachnal didn't for a moment believe a word Kenzie had told him, but I was reasonably sure that he didn't realize I was not a boy. Had he suspected I was a woman, his reaction to me would have been different. In the first place, I doubt he would have walloped me so firmly on the shoulder. No Celae man would have, and the more I learned about Laringorn men, the more I was certain no Laringorn man would have, either, but for different reasons. In Laringras, any man who touched another man's woman was in very real danger of losing his hand at the least, and his life at most. So far, my disguise seemed to be working rather well, but I had the uncomfortable suspicion that four days without adequate washing facilities may have helped considerably. My hair, like Kenzie's, was nearly gray-brown with road dust, and my face felt gritty, and was likely as smudged with sweat-streaked dirt as Kenzie's.

Rachnal stretched out one massive arm to indicate the tables. "Sit," he said cheerfully. "Sit, my friends. You be wanting food and, no doubt, ale to be washing the road dust from your throats."

"No doubt you'll wish to join us and hear our news," Kenzie said.

Rachnal laughed. "Of course, of course," he said. "Although what news be coming out of Banhapetsut, I hardly know."

He herded us to a table near the long counter and bustled around behind the counter, drawing three flagons of ale. As he placed them on the table, a woman came out of a door behind the counter carrying a tray laden with bowls of thin, savory stew and platters of bread and fruit. I hadn't realized how heartily sick I was of eating only those little rabbitlike creatures Kenzie caught until I saw the food Rachnal's wife placed before me. I fell to eating and left the talking to Kenzie. The ale was sour, but refreshing. It did the job of washing the dust of travel from my throat. And the food was as good as it looked and smelled.

When he had finished with his meager store of news from Banhapetsut, Kenzie leaned back in his chair, his flagon of ale in his hand, and grinned at Rachnal. "What did that troop of Maedun soldiers want this morning?" he asked.

Rachnal made round, innocent eyes. "What troop of Maedun?" he asked.

Kenzie grinned again. "Bryn and I saw them heading this way," he said. "We took ourselves out of their way, naturally enough. Who were they looking for?"

"Oh, *that* troop of Maedun." Rachnal grinned back at him.

"They say they be seeking some highborn woman from Celi. A woman with red hair. I wondered at that. Surely with red hair, she'd be Tyran, no?"

Kenzie shrugged elaborately. "I know too few Celae to be able to tell you," he said.

Rachnal snorted derisively. "I told them I be seeing no such woman come through here. Imagine a woman traveling alone in this country. If she tried to get out of Banhapetsut on her own, she'd never be making it. Some man would have scooped her up right off the street and had her hidden in his bed before she be taking ten steps."

"Aye, more likely," Kenzie said. "They'd do better looking in the bordellos than inns this far from Banhapetsut."

Rachnal took a deep draught from his flagon and wiped the foam from his mouth with the back of his hand. "I seldom see you without a merchant train," he said. "Where be you bound?"

Kenzie reached for the last orange. Luxuries back in Celi, they were as common here as apples were at home. He took out his dagger and carefully began paring the thick rind from the fruit. It made a long, curling spiral of golden orange trailing from the bright blade.

"We're to meet with my men later." He casually sectioned the orange and bit into one golden wedge. Juice spurted through the thin skin and ran down his chin. He blotted it with his sleeve. "Bryn and I were delayed in Banhapetsut when the merchant train set out from Matchetluk. I told Rhys we'd meet him at Black Rock."

Rachnal nodded sagely. "Well, I thought you be looking ill equipped to cross the desert by yourselves. Only two horses and no pack mules for carrying water." He stood up and gathered the bowls and platters, now empty of everything save crumbs and parings. "You'll not be staying the night, then?"

Kenzie shook his head. "No. We told Rhys we'd be joining him by early tomorrow morning. We're already late. We don't want the merchants becoming nervous about further delay."

"Ye'll be wanting supplies?" Rachnal asked. "Grain for the horses and provisions for yourself?"

Kenzie grinned. "If you've some to spare," he said. "And provided that you don't try to steal me blind by overcharging me."

"Overcharge you?" Rachnal looked scandalized. I couldn't tell whether the expression was genuine. Perhaps it was, but he was scandalized by the fact that Kenzie had so easily seen right through him.

"Grain for two horses for a fortnight," Kenzie said. "And a little meal flour and khaf tea for us."

Rachnal nodded. "I'll have Wilm bring your horses around for you while I put together what I can spare. Good journey to you, Kenzie. And to you, young Bryn. Be giving my regards to Rhys and tell him he still owes me a chance to win back my silvers."

Kenzie got to his feet and laughed. "By now, Rachnal, I'd think ye knew better than to dice with Rhys."

Rachnal's eyebrows rose. "Be ye saying to me that he cheats?"

Kenzie shook his head, still laughing. "No, but he has a way with dice. I believe he might even be something of a hatchling sorcerer." He dropped a handful of coppers on the table. "My regards to your goodwife Lina."

"Kenzie . . . "

Kenzie turned, one eyebrow raised in query.

Rachnal set the empty flagons carefully on the bar counter. "The Maedun also be asking after a big Tyr carrying a whacking great sword, and possibly traveling with a young boy. Apparently these despicable Tyrs unlawfully and without cause killed three of the Lord Protector's men, and badly wounded two more."

"Doesn't say much for the skill of the Lord Protector's men, does it, that two Tyrs could overpower five of them."

"Well, the Lord Protector's men become arrogant and careless with it occasionally. Of course, I told them I'd not seen hide nor hair of anyone like that."

Kenzie laughed. "Of course you did," he said. "Thank you, Rachnal." He paused. "Oh, they weren't the Lord Protector's men. Only freebooters. Robard and his pack of dogs."

Rachnal spit onto the packed-dirt floor. "I see. Well-done then. Good speed on your journey, lad."

9

After the cool of the inn's common room, walking out into the courtyard was akin to walking into an oven. The sun beat down like a hammer on my head. The same young boy brought our horses from the stable. Kenzie flipped the child a copper and was rewarded by a gap-toothed grin as the boy snatched the spinning coin out of the air and made it vanish into some hidden recess of his clothing.

We lashed the sacks of trail food for us and grain for the horses behind the saddles. Rachnal hadn't had a lot to sell, but then, we hadn't a lot of silver to purchase with, either. Kenzie calculated there would be enough grain to see the horses through the worst of the desert until we reached the higher foothills, where there was more forage for them. The meal flour, khaf tea, and dried fruit for us would have to be carefully rationed, but Kenzie assured me there were plenty of the little desert hoppers, so we shouldn't get too hungry.

We mounted in silence and rode out of the courtyard side by side. I was about to turn west, but Kenzie, who was on my right, reined his horse to the left and eastward. The bay's shoulder nudged against the mare's, and turned it, too.

"Northeast," he said firmly. "Toward Black Rock and Matchetluk."

I was about to protest, but Kenzie gave me a sharp look, then glanced back over his shoulder. I looked back to see Rachnal standing in the doorway of the inn, his arms folded above his ample belly. Kenzie gave him a cheerful wave, but he made no motion to wave back. He simply watched us leave. Moments later, the wall around the inn cut him off from my sight.

"But we wanted to go northwest," I said.

"Aye, we do," he said equably. "But I told Rachnal we'd be joining Rhys at Black Rock."

"Then we'll be joining a merchant train?"

"No. But Rachnal will tell the Maedun what I said about joining a merchant train near Black Rock. He'll tell them he saw us turn northeast when we left the inn."

I stared at him, aghast. Laringras and the Laringorn had an infinite capacity to startle me. "He'd betray you to the Maedun? But I thought he was your friend."

"He is." He sounded remarkably unconcerned. "In his fashion."

I couldn't help the note of censure that crept into my voice. "Where I come from, friends don't betray friends."

"Bryn—"

I knew that expression on his face by now and had no trouble predicting what was coming. "I know," I said. "I know. This is Laringras."

"Aye, it is." He shrugged. "Rachnal has to live here. He's Isgardian and is here on sufferance only. You can't blame him for doing what he has to do in order to survive." He grinned. "That's why he was verra careful to watch us leave, ye ken. He'll be able to swear with a clear conscience we turned northeast. The Maedun warlocks have ways of knowing when a man is lying. And I've been told lying to them is quite painful." He gestured ahead at a twisted and stunted pine. "About a furlong beyond that tree, there's a little trail that leads back to the northwest track. We'll take that. It won't add more than an hour or two to our journey time."

I looked at him. His expression was calm and serene. The corners of my mouth began to twitch.

"Kenzie Catfoot, you're a shameless liar."

He glanced at me, deadpan. "Aye," he agreed. "I'm that. And perfectly dreadful it is, isn't it?"

The journey from Banhapetsut to Rachnal's inn had taken us four days. The distance between the inn and the place where the track joined the main merchant trail deep in the foothills was only half again as long, but it took us better than eight days to travel. We had to stop often to rest the horses, and there was little water to be had.

Gradually, the foothills rose around us. The seamed and weathered landscape climbed more steeply, and the hills closed in around the track. The thornbushes disappeared, replaced by twisted and stunted pines. Eventually, clumps of scrawny, leafless aspen appeared among the pines. The spiny clumps of cactus gave way to hummocks of coarse, tough brown grass.

As the track climbed, the nights remained cold and clear, and the days grew colder, too, so that we eventually needed our cloaks even when the midday sun shone fiercely in the hard and endless blue of the sky. Then one day, we rounded the flank of a rocky hill, and there was suddenly a river plunging and boiling through a steep-sided canyon beside the trail. The water hurled itself over broken rocks and swept off into a narrow valley to our left. The track followed the river upstream.

It was as if we had turned a corner and entered a different world. The grass bordering the track was still dry and lifeless, but it was plentiful. The trees were thicker along the hills bordering the river, and looked healthier. I was not at all unhappy to see the last of the desert and its choking dust fall behind us.

Later that afternoon, we came out of the constricted pass into a broad, curving valley. A wide, well-defined track followed the precipitous bank of the river, leading deep into mountains soaring like jagged teeth of granite into the sky. Snow blanketed the peaks, extending in places down into the tree line, but remaining a good distance above the track.

Something inside me loosened, some knot of tension I hadn't realized was there. These were not the mountains of Skai, but they were mountains. The trees were mostly pine, aspen, and clumped alder, not the oak and maple and ash I was used to, but just being among mountains again lifted my spirit and made me feel unaccountably safer. For the first time since waking up in that filthy little cabin on the ship, I felt I really would see Skai again.

The river to our left flowed through a deep, narrow gorge, tumbling over broken rocks, sending spume drifting high into the air. At times, it hung like mist above the track. Toward evening, we passed a place where the water fell steeply over the lip of a cliff into a deep, turbulent pool. The thunder of its precipitous tumble made it impossible to hear each other speak.

Nearly a furlong above the falls, we stopped for the night a little earlier than usual. We found a place some hundred paces from the track, where a small stream tumbled down the side of the mountain in its hurry to join the river. A small grove of trees made a good shelter for the horses, and muffled the tumultuous sound of the river. Two ponderous leaning slabs of rock provided a warm place out of the wind to spread our bedrolls. It was my turn to build the fire while Kenzie saw to the horses.

He came back to the fire and slung one of the bedrolls around his shoulder, then rummaged through his saddle pack until he found the soap we'd had little chance to use since leaving Banhapetsut. When water is so scarce as to be more precious than gold, it can't be wasted for washing, and leaving a scum of soap in water for someone else to drink is the worst sin in the desert.

"I've a surprise for you," he said.

"A surprise? What sort of surprise."

"You'll see. Come with me."

He led me upward along the course of the tumbling little stream. It was a steep climb, and we did most of it on all fours, clambering and scrambling over huge tumbles of broken rock. At one point, I turned and looked back. It seemed an incredibly long distance nearly straight down to the little grove where the horses stood, all that was visible of our campsite. I looked up again just in time to see Kenzie disappear into a narrow crevice.

The crack between the rocks was hardly wide enough for my shoulders. Kenzie had to turn sideways and squeeze to get through it. Halfway through, I suddenly became aware of an odd stench floating in the air. It smelled for all the world like eggs rotting in a barnyard.

I popped out of the crevice like a cork coming out of a bottle, then simply stood and stared. We were in a small, bowl-shaped cavern, worn smooth by the water, partly open to the sky. The stink of sulfur hung heavy in the air, thick enough to choke me. A pool of steaming water, clear as air, lay placidly at my feet. The overflow poured out over the lip of the bowl, obviously the source of the little stream we had been following.

"If ye can stand the stink," Kenzie said, grinning at me, "I thought ye might appreciate a hot bath."

We'd had water enough for washing since leaving the desert, but it was barely above the temperature of the ice and snow in the mountains it came from. It took someone hardier and braver than I to immerse his body in it for more than a second or two at a time. I stared at the pool, and the choking fumes of sulfur hardly seemed to matter anymore. I was suddenly painfully aware that I itched all over. My clothes were stiff with sweat and dirt, and my hair hung in draggled strings around my face. The pleasures of Annwn couldn't have looked better to a home-coming warrior than that pool looked to me.

"I'll leave ye for an hour," Kenzie said, still grinning. "Mind ye leave some soap for me." He dropped the bedroll to the smooth stone. "I know ye prefer to dress as ye are, but I brought a change of clothing for you. Ye might want to wash the things you're wearing. Do that at the end of the pool, near the overflow."

I was tearing at the fastenings of my tunic and shirt before he had fairly disappeared through the crevice.

The small pool was hot enough to turn my skin pink. I

counted a bath well worth the scrambling trip up the precipitous path above our campsite. Even the stench of sulfur was no discouragement. I made merciless use of our small bar of soap and emerged deliciously warm and clean. Even my hair squeaked with cleanliness when I ran my fingers through it. It was still shockingly short, but I could tell it had grown a little since Kenzie had hacked it off back in Banhapetsut.

I wrapped myself in my blanket and rubbed myself dry until my skin glowed. I dressed quickly in the skirt and tunic I had bartered from the serving girl in Banhapetsut, then washed my trews, tunic, and shirt. The sun lay low above the western mountains as I finished. Carrying the wet garments, I began the scramble back down the cliff. By the time I climbed back to where Kenzie had the fire burning cheerfully, my hair was beginning to dry.

Kenzie had not been idle while I bathed. He knelt by the tiny streamlet, cleaning the last of two trout, each nearly as long as my forearm. I spread my clothing on bushes near the fire to dry and sat by the fire, finger-combing my hair.

Kenzie laid the fish on a flat rock near the fire, then went to his saddle pack and pulled out a clean shirt. He picked up his blanket, then grinned and shook his head in amused resignation as I handed him the sadly depleted cake of yellow soap. Chuckling softly to himself, he made his way upward and disappeared.

I set to work making flat cakes to eat with the fish. We were almost out of meal flour. I hoped we might find a farmstead or another inn in the next few days or so to purchase more. I laid the flat cakes to baking on the slab of rock by the fire and sat, watching them so they wouldn't burn, and waited for Kenzie to return.

Twilight had fallen when he appeared around the corner of the leaning slabs of rock, dressed only in a shirt that nearly reached his knees, and carrying the wet bundle of kilt and plaid. He spread them on the bushes near my trews and tunic, then wrapped the blanket around his waist and came to sit by the fire.

The fish was done and ready to eat, and I hadn't scorched the flat cakes this time. He took his share and settled down with his back against the rock wall to eat.

The hot water had made me sleepy with contentment. After the meal, I sat half-drowsing by the fire with my arms wrapped around my upraised knees, watching the play of light and shadow across the coals. For the first time since leaving Banhapetsut, I allowed myself to think about Tiegan and home. I had no doubts that he was safely there now. I wondered if he knew I, too, was reasonably safe now.

As I watched the fire, I could almost see Tiegan before me, and the family around him. Sharp spears of light radiated out from the coals of the fire, caused by the sudden rush of tears to my eyes. I missed them. I missed them all—my brother Brennen, his wife Mai and their children; Brennen's bheancoran, Fiala, who had trained me; my parents, my uncles, and my aunt Torey. And even Sheryn, Tiegan's wife. Unlike my kinsister Mai and Fiala, Brennen's bheancoran, Sheryn and I did not get on very well together. We never had, not since we were children.

Sheryn was Tyadda, one of the strange, fey race who had inhabited the Isle of Celi even before the Celae came to the island. Oddly enough, she was kinswoman to me even before she married my cousin Tiegan, the King's only son. Her grandmother and mine on my mother's side were sisters, and while my grandmother had fallen in love with and married Morfyn of Dun Llewen Landhold, hers had stayed in the Tyadda steading and married a Tyadda man.

Sheryn and I had not met until we were both fourteen, when she had come for a visit to Dun Eidon, my home in Skai. We hadn't become friends. She let me know in no uncertain terms that she considered any woman who took up the sword instead of the more *womanly* pursuits of needlework, weaving, and learning to govern a household, not to mention flirting, to be crass and unfeminine. I was already nearly a head taller than she then, and outweighed her by nearly two stone. She made me feel like a cow beside a delicate roe deer. I could easily have hated her then, had I not been completely caught up in gaining mastery over the sword. My own contempt for her, as a fragile little clinging vine with no mind of her own, was certainly equal to hers for me.

She had met Tiegan at Dun Eidon on that first visit. Tiegan, a worldly-wise twenty-six, had come to discuss things of the realm with my father, Prince Keylan of Skai. While he had nothing but casual affection for me, and the knowledge that one day I would be his bheancoran, he couldn't help but notice Sheryn's beauty, which even then was far above average, even for a Tyadda woman.

Until Tiegan's arrival at Dun Eidon, Sheryn had whiled away her time flirting outrageously with Brennen, who was just about to be married to Mai. Without turning a hair, she transferred all that devastating charm and attention to Tiegan. Tiegan went down before it like a steer to the poleax. I was, of course, perfectly disgusted with the whole dismal matter. Somehow, after that, Tiegan always managed to time his visits to Dun Eidon to coincide with Sheryn's. Last year, nine years after their first meeting, he married her. We got along little better now than we had when we were both fourteen, and for much the same reasons.

Out here in the wilds of the Laringras Alps, I could think about it calmly, and could almost feel amused that Sheryn should feel that way. Nobody knows for certain exactly when the tradition began that the Prince of Skai should be served by a bheancoran, a warrior-maid who acts as companion, confidante, and personal guard, but that same tradition says that the first bheancoran to the Prince of Skai was a Tyadda woman. My mother, Letessa al Morfyn, was bheancoran to my father, as his mother was bheancoran to his father. Bheancoran do not usually marry their princes, although it seemed for a while that a new tradition had started with Kyffen, who married Demilor. I don't believe the idea ever seriously occurred to either Tiegan or me that we might marry. We were cousins, after all, and the blood tie was too close. The bond of bheancoran and prince drew us closer in some respects than the bonds of marriage. I sometimes believed that Sheryn resented the strength of that bond, something she could not share.

A log popped in the fire, sending a spray of sparks dangerously near the hem of my skirt. I drew my feet farther back out of the way. Outside our sheltered enclosure, full night had fallen, and stars blazed in the black arch of the sky. I had been fire-dreaming for a long time.

Kenzie had been quiet for a long time, too. I looked up to catch him watching me, the oddest expression on his face. Firelight flickered across the line of cheek and brow, glinting in the soft growth of new beard. He looked at me as if I were a stranger, someone he'd never seen before. The startled look disappeared so quickly, I began to wonder if I had really seen it.

"I had almost forgotten you were a woman," he said softly.

"It was hard to see under all that dirt," I said.

"Ye're a lovely woman now," he said, his voice oddly hoarse. Then his face stiffened and he drew away. "I bid ye good night, Bryn." He wrapped himself in his blanket and lay down, his back to me. But I thought I heard him mutter something. It sounded very much like, "And a woman not for a broken man . . ."

10

I dreamed again that night. Once again, hunter and hunted fled mindlessly through forest and meadow. Only the vague shapes of terror churned through my nightmare. I saw nothing recognizable, but the knowledge of evil, of terrible hatred, followed me, slicing viciously at my soul with the teeth and claws of a snarling Veniani badgercat. Branches tore at my hair and skin as I ran, but I ignored them and ran as if my life depended upon it. Behind me, the black, formless terror followed hard on my trail. His laughter crackled in the air between the trees. "You can't get away from me, little cousin," he called after me. "I'll find you wherever you hide." The crash of pursuit through the forest echoed from the hidden face of rocks and cliffs around me.

I came breathlessly out of sleep, the dream still swirling in my mind. Half-convinced I still dreamed, I listened intently, unsure whether the noise I had heard was real, or just part of the dream. Framed in the inverted "V" of the enclosure, the sky to the east had just begun to take on the deep royal blue that indicated approaching dawn. The fire had died to smoldering coals, but it was still reasonably warm inside the sheltered space.

Kenzie sat with his back against the wall near the entrance to the enclosure, a darker shadow against the brightening sky outside. He turned his head as I sat up, watching me as I sat there, breathing in deep gulps of air while my heart raced in my chest.

"What is it?" he whispered.

"I don't know. I think I heard something."

"Someone approaching?"

"I don't know. A noise. Something."

I had been sleeping in just my tunic and shirt. I got up and went to the bushes where my clothes were spread to dry. The trews were nearly dry. I slipped them on, then crept back into the enclosure to strap on my sword. Kenzie reached up and slipped his sword in its scabbard, making sure it would move easily if he needed it. No sound disturbed the quiet of the waning night—not even birdsong.

"Kenzie? Listen . . . "

He rose slowly to his feet. "The birds," he said softly. "They're usually calling by this time." He stepped out of the shelter of the leaning slabs of stone, out into the small shelf of turf above the little stream. I fell in beside him, taking up a position to his left, just as if he were Tiegan. Even had it been light enough to see anything clearly, nearly a hundred paces thick with trees and bushes separated us from the track.

The muted clank of metal against stone sounded loud in the stillness. A shod hoof against the rock of the track? Kenzie reached up for the sword behind his left shoulder, but dropped his hand without drawing the blade. There was too little space between the trees to use a sword easily. He moved forward, slipping from the shadow of one pine trunk to the next, quiet as a shadow himself. I moved with him, placing my feet carefully without conscious thought. The soft, musical jangle of bridle metal, quickly muffled, came from somewhere ahead of us. Whoever was out there seemed to be still on the track.

As we crept closer to the track, the muted thunder of the river tumbling through the narrow gorge got louder. Kenzie darted into the shadow of a tree standing at the edge of the track. I slipped along in his wake.

The track appeared to be empty in both directions. Nothing moved in that narrow space between the trees and the precipitous bank of the river. It was wide enough here for three horses to travel abreast, but it was empty. Kenzie relaxed a little, but still did not step out onto the track.

Behind us, something crashed through the trees. I spun around, reaching for the hilt of my sword.

They came at us through the trees, men in black mounted on dark horses, swords drawn and raised. My heart nearly stopped. This was so exactly like my dream, I cried out in shock and dismay. But crying out was a waste of breath, and there was no time to spare for that.

Kenzie ducked one way behind the trunk of the pine; I ducked the other. Together, we stumbled out onto the track, where we would at least have room to swing our swords.

But we had no chance to draw them before the dark riders were upon us. I sensed rather than saw the blade of a sword slicing at my head as a rider swept past me. I threw myself to one side and caromed off the flank of another horse. Kenzie disappeared behind a third horse as he ducked a viciously sweeping sword blade.

The horsemen could see no better than we could in the semidarkness on the track. The horses swirled past, turned, and milled around, jostling each other, as the riders sought Kenzie and me. In the confusion, Kenzie dodged around a questing horseman and fought his way to my side.

There were too many riders and not enough room on the track. We were in their midst, and they couldn't get a clear swing at us with their swords, but they gave us no room to draw and use our own swords.

I looked up to see another rider bearing down on me. Brightening dawn gave barely enough light so that I could make out his face as a pale oval beneath midnight black hair. And his eyes . . . His eyes were black holes in his face, and I thought I saw a faint, red gleam in them. For an instant, I froze.

"There you are." His voice was soft, but I heard him clearly, even over the tumult of hooves against stone and the rushing water of the river.

"Bryn, look out!" Kenzie cried.

Those dark eyes mesmerized me. The rider laughed in triumph as he raised his sword. I couldn't move. Then Kenzie caught me around the waist, his arm pulling me tight against his belly and chest. He stumbled backward, and then, quite deliberately, leapt over the edge of the gorge, pulling me with him.

It was nearly two manheights down to the river. I had barely time to draw in a deep gulp of air before we hit the water. It closed over my head, cold enough to take my breath away. I gasped, choked, coughed, and gasped again, spewing water. Kenzie still held me tight against him. He coughed and choked, spitting river water, then kicked out strongly as the current swept us down the cataract toward the falls nearly a furlong downriver.

"Relax," he shouted in my ear. "Don't struggle. Keep your head above the water and relax."

I tried to answer, swallowed a pint of river water instead, then let myself go limp against him. The current swirled us about, and the steep sides of the gorge spun dizzily around me. The shadow of a huge, jagged rock loomed before us. I closed my eyes, but the current parted around the rock, sweeping us with it to one side of the rock. Water slapped against my face, and I concentrated on trying to breathe.

We were at the falls before I realized it. Kenzie shouted something, but I couldn't hear what he said. It was enough that his arm was still strong around my waist, meaning we were both still alive. But I wasn't at all sure we'd survive the plunge over the falls.

I didn't have time to worry about it. It was as if the world dropped out from beneath me. The force of the current shot us clear of the water, and we fell together for what seemed an eternity. Still, Kenzie held tight to me.

Again, we hit water. Kenzie's legs kicked against mine, thrusting us up to the surface of the pool beneath the falls.

"Kick with me," he shouted, his free arm pulling strongly against the water. "We have to get out of the current."

I kicked. I don't know if I was of any use, but I felt the tug of the water ease, and suddenly, there was a broken-rock shelf right beside us. I reached for it, clinging like a tree frog to bark. I think we were on the same side of the river as the trail, but I had completely lost any sense of direction.

"Hang on there for a moment," he said, his mouth near my ear. Even then, his voice was barely audible over the thunder of the falls. He clambered out of the water onto the narrow shelf, then turned and reached down for my hand. I seized the offered hand, my feet scrabbling for purchase on the slippery, broken rock as he pulled me out of the water.

It was light enough to see now. I looked numbly up at Kenzie, who stood with his back against the rock, gasping for breath. His sopping hair hung plastered against his forehead and streaming into his eyes, and his face was pale as chalk except for a huge bruise just now turning blue and purple along his left cheekbone. He raised a hand that trembled with fatigue and stripped the hair back from his eyes.

"Are you all right?" he asked.

I had no breath to speak. I nodded. When I found enough strength, I said, "Thank you. You saved my life."

"Aye, well, as to that, it was my turn, I think."

He reached up behind his left shoulder and grasped the hilt of his sword. Relief swept briefly across his face. Startled, I put up my hand. My fingers closed around the hilt of my own sword. As least we still had our weapons, although only the seven gods and goddesses knew what would happen to the things we had left in our camp, or to the horses.

"This way," he said, taking my hand. "There's a small cave behind the falls, but that'll be the first place they look if they come down here searching for us."

I looked up. The wall of the gorge wasn't as high here as it had been by our campsite—merely a handspan or two beyond Kenzie's head. Below our feet, the water in the pool swirled and bubbled in deep eddies and small whirlpools.

"He knew who I was," I said, still gasping for breath. "The leader of those men . . . He knew who I was." I shivered with more than just the chill of wet clothes and cold water. "He found me in my dream, Kenzie. I know he did. He'll be able to find me wherever we go."

"Aye, well, that's as may be, but I'd rather he found us

up there," Kenzie said, nodding toward the lip of the gorge. "We'd be pitifully easy targets down here for any bowmen."

I nodded. At least in the clear, we might have a chance to use our swords, now that we could see what we were doing. But the riders would be able to see clearly, too.

There was no sign of the riders on the track as we clambered up over the lip of the gorge. Kenzie grasped my hand, and we ran into the trees on the opposite side of the track. Keeping deep in the trees, we moved cautiously back up the track, toward our campsite.

The thunder of the falls drowned out any noise the riders made. They were nearly upon us before we heard them. I dived down into a tangled thicket of aspen, pulling Kenzie with me.

We could barely see the troop of horsemen through the tight weaving of narrow stems and dead undergrowth. But the leader stopped, his head up. He reminded me of a hound sniffing the air. In the brightening morning light, I thought I saw a thin, tenuous black mist swirling around his head. Faint as it was, the mist blurred the man's features. It was impossible to tell what he looked like, except that he was obviously Maedun, with the coal black hair that absorbed all light, and the black eyes to match.

That black mist was Maedun blood sorcery, deadly and dangerous even here in the skirts of the mountains.

I remembered the blood magic Francia had used on me. Nausea clutched at my belly. I froze again, like a sparrow before a snake.

Kenzie reached up for the sword hilt at his left shoulder.

"No," I whispered. "Don't move."

The leader hadn't moved, and the darkness around his head had not dissipated.

Blood magic. Magic formed of blood and pain and terror. Powerful and terrifying. Black as the deepest night, choking as oily water. Soul-destroying magic.

But darkness and night are banished by light. Celae magic—Tyadda magic—was magic of earth and air, bright and clean and shining as a crystal reflecting a candle flame. It was gentle magic, magic that would not allow itself to be used to kill. But it could hide us. If I had the strength to draw on it. If my meager Gift of magic were strong enough.

Banhapetsut and the desert beyond it held no threads of magic flowing through earth or air. But these were mountains. Celae magic, Tyadda magic, was born of the high and verdant mountains in Skai. These weren't Celae mountains; they weren't yrSkai mountains. But they *were* mountains, and all high places were sacred to the seven gods and goddesses.

"What are you doing?" Kenzie murmured.

"I need to try magic. A masking spell. Just don't move. No matter what happens, don't move."

Desperately, I reached out. Thin, tenuous threads of power fluttered around me, faint and weak, but perhaps usable. The spell I needed didn't draw a lot of power, but there wasn't a lot available, either within me, or in the flows around me. I didn't know if there would be enough, but it was the only chance we had right now.

The frigid water of the river had sapped most of my strength. I leaned back against Kenzie and reached out for the fragile stream of magic in the air around me, in the ground beneath my feet. Slowly, painfully I built a masking spell. The air around us sparked gently, like dust motes in a sunbeam, and tingled against my skin.

I gasped, then concentrated harder. This spell was so simple for my grandmother, or my aunt Torey. When they did it, no trace of effort showed on their faces, but I had to draw on every ounce of strength I had.

The leader of the Maedun riders on the trail still sat motionless in his saddle, questing around like a hunting dog on the scent of a roe deer. Perhaps he could sense my use of magic.

But I've been told that a masking spell is all but undetectable outside the spell itself, because the magic is all directed inward. I closed my eyes and focused on making Kenzie and me look like a shapeless rock among the clump of stripped, lifeless aspen.

My hands were freezing. I could hardly feel my feet, and my teeth wanted to chatter in my trembling jaw. But I clung to the frail threads of natural power and poured all of my own strength into the spell.

"They're not moving," Kenzie whispered.

I couldn't spare the strength to nod. But the air still fizzed around us. The spell held firm.

Finally, I felt Kenzie relax. "They're going on," he said softly. "Downriver. They're going to search the pool by the falls."

I nodded, but didn't open my eyes, didn't let go of the spell. I crouched close against him, shivering. He let go of me. I opened my eyes for a moment to see him unpinning his plaid. He swung it around us both, then drew me tightly to him again. Even wet, wool will hold in heat, and his plaid was of good, tightly woven wool.

"How long can you hold that spell?" he asked.

I could hardly speak. "I don't know. Long enough, I hope." I devoutly wished I had thought of it earlier, back when we were still warm and safe in the shelter of those great slabs of rock.

Gradually, the combined heat of our two bodies collected inside the plaid and I stopped shivering. I don't know how long I huddled there, gathered close against Kenzie's chest, held in the shelter of his arms, my eyes closed, every ounce of concentration I had focused on holding the spell. Presently, Kenzie stirred and raised his head.

"They're coming back this way," he whispered. "Probably heading back to see if they can find our camp."

I sent a small, fervent prayer up to Rhianna of the Air, giver of the gift of magic. *Please. Let me hold this spell. Just a while longer . . .* Laringras and Isgard were not Rhianna's countries. But mountains were her special places, and the yrSkai flattered themselves that they were special in her eyes. Perhaps she might hear me and, if she were so disposed, help.

Kenzie stirred against me. I opened my eyes, startled to see the long shadows of the mountains stretching eastward as the sun sank behind the shoulder of the soaring crag to the west. I had barely the strength to lift my head. The masking spell dissipated in a rush, and the released filaments of power stung like sleet against my skin as they snapped back into place.

"Are they gone?" I asked.

He nodded wearily. "I think so. They went downriver about an hour ago, and I haven't seen anything of them since."

"They'll have taken our horses . . . "

He chuckled, a warm, pleasant sound in the fading light. "They'd not get verra close to the bay," he said. "He's a stubborn beggar, verra much like me, and he'll not let anyone else take his reins. No, nor try to herd him anywhere he doesna want to go." He got stiffly to his feet and reached down for my hand to draw me up. "Can ye walk, Bryn?"

"I don't know. I think so."

I could, but barely. It was nearly full dark when we reached the place where we had been camped. The area was thoroughly trampled, and the horses were no longer in the little grove of aspen beyond the thin strip of turf outside the enclosure.

The Laringorn serving maid's dark green skirt lay ground down into the churned turf, torn and ruined. The kettle we had used to make khaf tea sat in the midst of the scattered ashes of the fire, one side caved in as if it had been stepped on by a horse. Nothing remained of our saddle packs but tattered strips of leather, the buckles vanished into the dirt, or taken away by the Maedun. The blankets lay in a heap near the back of the enclosure. I picked them up and shook the dirt out of them. They were torn and filthy, one of them with a large, charred hole in it. But they might still be usable.

Kenzie picked up his tin cup. Someone had stabbed the blade of a dagger through the bottom. What remained of our khaf tea and meal flour was strewn all over the sand that formed the floor of the enclosure.

"Charming people," Kenzie murmured as he examined the cup. He dropped the cup and went out onto the ruined strip of turf. He put his fingers between his teeth and whistled shrilly.

Not many horses will come when called like that. My uncle Connor had trained less than half a dozen to respond to a whistle. I was skeptical that it would work with the bay.

But Kenzie knew his horse far better than I did. The bay came to him. And what's more, it brought the mare with it.

I collapsed onto the filthy blankets, caught between laughter and tears. The strain of fighting the cold water of the river, then holding the masking spell for what had seemed an eternity caught up with me. We had no food, and nothing to eat it with even if we'd had it, but we had horses that acted as if they belonged in the ballads of the bards and traveling singers. What more could anyone ask?

11

We crossed the divide and rode into Isgard. We were lucky. We encountered no blizzards, no snow at all. The weather remained cold but clear as we threaded our way through the high, narrow passes. The deeper we moved into the mountains, the more streams of power I discovered woven into the ground and swirling in the air around me. As a precaution, I tried to keep a mild masking spell around us all the time, especially as we slept.

The Isgardian mountains were thick with cedar and ash, birch and silverleaf maple. The leaves of the maples flared brilliant crimson amid the burning gold of the birch leaves, and the ash berries hung in bright scarlet clusters among the saffron and sienna leaves of the ash trees. The crystal nights were chilly, but not as numbingly cold as on the east side of the mountains, and the days were cooler. Traveling became more comfortable.

We stopped for the night in a hollow protected by a tumble of glacial rock on one side and a tall stand of cedars on the other. Thick, dark green moss covered the ancient fallen trunks of cedars and the rocks around the torn-up roots. We cleared the moss down to the bare face of the rock beneath to make our fire.

Kenzie sat cross-legged before the fire, his sword across his knees. He worked quickly and deftly with the whetting stone and the oily rag to sharpen and clean the blade while we waited for the water to boil in our battered kettle.

"Another fortnight should see us to Honandun," he said without looking up. "I dinna think we'll have any difficulty finding a Tyran vessel in port. Not at this time of year. They won't be far from home now. Winter gales are too close."

I peered into the kettle. The water had just begun to bubble, so I dropped a handful of chalery leaf into it. It made for bitter tea, but it was refreshing after a skimpy meal of rabbit and bulb-root stew.

"I feel as if we've been traveling for years," I said wearily. "But at least we've haven't met any Maedun patrols."

He looked up at me, one eyebrow raised, the whetstone in his hand poised above the blade of his sword. "No more dreams?"

I shook my head. "Mayhaps the leader of that patrol thinks we're dead. He might not bother to search further for us."

He shrugged. "Mayhaps," he said.

"You don't sound certain."

"I'm not. With the Maedun, it never pays to be certain they'll do one thing or another." He smoothed the stone across the edge of the blade for a few strokes, then wiped the gleaming metal with the oily cloth. "He didna exactly seem like the type to give up easily."

"It could be the masking spell is working."

He shrugged again. "I hope so."

I lifted the kettle off the fire and set it to cool on the flat rock between us we were using as a makeshift table. "It seems to be easier to hold the masking spell here," I told him. "Mayhaps it's the mountains."

He gave the blade a final polishing and slipped the sword into its scabbard. For a moment, he busied himself putting away his stone and cloth, wrapping the stone carefully in the cloth before tucking it into his belt pouch. He got to his feet and stretched mightily, arms extended high above his head.

"Is that tea cool enough to drink yet?" he asked.

I touched the side of the kettle, scorched my finger, and shook my head. "Not quite."

He pulled out the only cup we had between us. "I shan't forgive that beggar easily for this," he said, frowning down at the cup. "One cup for two people. Ridiculous."

I laughed. "At least we have a cup."

He glanced at me, still frowning. "You're the one who's

traveling light, Lady Brynda," he said quietly. "Everything I own is right here before you." He reached for the kettle and poured some of the tea into the cup. "Whose turn is it to use the cup?"

"Yours, I think. Go ahead. I'm tired. I think I'll sleep now anyway."

As if speaking of him invoked his presence, the Hunter stalked my sleep that night. But now there was no frantic chase through the tangled forest. No prey ran terrified before the menacing pursuit. The Hunter had lost the spoor of his quarry. He moved with light-footed caution through the night, his footfalls cushioned and silenced by the carpet of old leaves on the forest floor.

I watched him, safe behind a curtain of bracken and ivy, following his movements as he ranged back and forth across the ground. He moved lightly and gracefully, like a dancer, blending with the night around him. I knew this time he could not see me, nor could he sense my presence through the masking spell.

His face, shrouded in shadow, held intense concentration, and the black eyebrows were drawn into a thick line, divided by the furrow between his eyes. As I watched him, I thought he became more insubstantial in the night, and I caught glimpses of another image behind him.

Curious and intrigued, I stepped forward. As if the Hunter were no more than an effigy painted on an ethereal veil of smoke, I drifted right through it and found myself standing in a space closed in on all sides by rough-cut stone. In the center of the room stood a low table holding a copper bowl. The only light came from two candles in tall candlesticks placed to either side of the bowl. Two people knelt on the stone floor, bent over the bowl, peering intently into the reflective surface of the water in it. A man and a woman. I stood directly behind the woman, facing the man across the wide, shallow bowl.

I saw only the line of the woman's cheek and brow half-hidden behind the ebony spill of her hair, but I knew her by the porcelain perfection of her skin. For a moment, startled and frightened, I tried to turn and run, but I was held there, unable to move.

Francia didn't turn, didn't look at me. She remained kneeling quietly, staring into the water.

The man's hair fell forward across his forehead, throwing his face into deep shadow. I saw only the clean, firm line of his jaw, and the finely modeled, sensual shape of his mouth. His hands on the sides of the bowl were black with blood, the stains splashed up his arms past his elbows, thick and crusted.

"Where are you, little vixen?" he murmured. "I know you're there somewhere. Show yourself."

I drew back, but he didn't look up. The candles flared, and the long shadows shimmered and danced across the stone floor. For the first time, I saw what lay behind him.

Bodies. Corpses of men and women, all of them with their bellies ripped and gaping. All of them with the fine, dark gold hair of Celae.

I cried out in fear and revulsion. The man looked up, and for a moment, our eyes met.

"Where are you?" he demanded harshly.

I leapt back, stumbling in my haste to get away from him. Then the shadows rushed in, and he vanished, along with the bowl, the woman, and the corpses.

I woke to find myself still sobbing with fear and horror, crouching deep in the little mossy hollow I had chosen for my bed. Kenzie knelt before me, grasping both my hands in his.

"It's all right, Brynda," he was saying. "You're safe. You're here with me. It's all right."

I thought he had said the same thing over and over again, but I couldn't be sure. My breath came in gasping sobs, the vision of those mutilated corpses hanging vivid and clear before my eyes.

"Were you dreaming true again?" Kenzie asked. He still held both my hands in his. They were warm and infinitely comforting around mine.

Unable to speak, I nodded. The image of the torn bodies began to fade, shredding like wisps of smoke in the wind. Then they were gone, and I had nothing but the residual taste of fear in the back of my throat.

"The same man?" he asked.

Again I nodded. "They're scrying for us." My mouth was too dry to speak properly. "He and Francia. They're scrying for us."

"Have they found us?"

"No." I took a deep breath. My heart stopped trying to tear itself loose from its moorings. I managed to relax. A sharp point of rock bit deeply into the small of my back. I shifted to a more comfortable position, and Kenzie let go of my hands.

"No," I said again. "I don't think so. The masking spell must be working."

He nodded. "Then we're safe for as long as you can hold it."

I nodded. "I think so." I looked at him. The firelight behind him turned his hair to flame. His shoulders looked solid and firm, and I felt safer just being with him. The reaction startled me. I had never felt that way about a man's presence before. It had always been my duty and privilege to make sure Tiegan felt safer because of *my* presence. How very odd . . .

"Can ye sleep, d'ye think?" he asked. "It's late, and we've a long way to ride in the morning."

I moved carefully away from him. "Thank you," I said a little stiffly. "I think I can sleep now. Thank you."

For a moment, I thought he would reach out to touch my hair, but his hand stilled, then fell to his side. "I bid you good night then," he said quietly.

*   *   *

We resumed our journey in the morning. Presently, the mountains fell away before us, and we rode out onto the wide grasslands of the Isgardian central plain. We left the track and set off cross-country, through fields and widely spaced woods. At night, we camped in the shelter of haystacks or in hidden spaces in the forests, avoiding the farmsteads and villages whenever we could. I dreamed no more of Hunter or hunted.

Eventually, we came to Honandun, Isgard's greatest port city, as dusk settled over the river delta behind us. On a high bluff overlooking the waterfront, the white stone elegance of what had once been the Ephir's palace stood in graceful splendor. It now housed the Maedun Lord Protector of Isgard, and the streets were filled with Maedun soldiers. But we were merely two more bedraggled travelers in a city full of strangers.

Our luck held, even in Honandun. A Tyran ship, as Kenzie had predicted, lay at anchor in the harbor. We found her master in a dingy little waterfront tavern that was tucked into a cranny amid the warren of narrow, crooked little streets. He was skeptical of my ability to pay for passage and had no compunctions about showing it.

I can be regal enough when I want to be. I drew myself up to my full height and stared at him.

"I am Brynda al Keylan, daughter of the Prince of Skai and bheancoran to the Prince of Celi," I said. "My father will guarantee my passage. If you'd rather, my uncle the King will see to it you're paid well."

Some of the skepticism melted. I knew what he saw as he looked at me—a dirty, ragged boy carrying a sword in the Celae fashion. But if my words melted some of the master's doubt, Kenzie shattered the rest of it when he performed the same transformation I had first seen in the little tavern in Banhapetsut. The ragged Tyran merchant train guard vanished and a dignified, if travel-stained, Tyran laird stood in his place, radiating nobility like heat from a flame.

"The lady's word is good," he said.

The master glanced from him to me, then to him again. Finally, he nodded. "Ye're lucky," he said. "We sail with the evening tide, and we'll be the last ship in port here this winter. Be on the pier at flood tide, or we'll leave without ye."

We had time to find a quick meal. Then Kenzie saw me to the pier. We stood for a while, looking at the sleek vessel. The tide was just about to turn, and the crew were preparing to sail. Already men swarmed in the rigging, making ready the great, square sails. I turned to Kenzie.

"Thank you," I said. The lump in my throat made it difficult to speak. "I really can't thank you enough. I'll make sure my father sends you gold . . . "

Two men stepped out onto the stone jetty. Both wore the kilt and plaid of Tyran clansmen. One of them put a hand to Kenzie's shoulder.

"We've been looking for you, Kenzie called Catfoot," he said quietly. "If ye'll be so kind as to come with us—"

Kenzie closed his eyes briefly, and for a moment, his shoulders slumped in defeat. But he straightened and shook off the restraining hand. "I'd sooner not," he said calmly.

"I believe ye have little choice in the matter," the clansman said. He moved his free hand out of the folds of his kilt. The fading sunlight flashed on the blade of a wicked-looking dagger. "Ye're wanted back in Tyra, lad. Ye'd best come wi' us now. Ye'd be far more comfortable than with irons at your feet."

"You can't take him," I cried. "He saved my life, and he deserves his freedom for that."

The second clansman regarded me with a grave stare. "And who might ye be, lad?"

"I'm Brynda al Keylan, granddaughter to Red Kian of Skai—Kian dav Leydon ti'Cullin of Broche Rhuidh."

A small, amused smile curled the corner of the clansman's mouth. "Aye?" he said. "Well, so you say."

Anger churned in my belly. I drew myself up to my full height. "Aye, I am," I said. "And I'll thank you to unhand Kenzie—"

"He's to come with us," the clansman said.

Angrily, I put up my hand for the hilt of my sword. Kenzie reached out and grasped my wrist. "Ye'll not be slicing up any good Tyran clansmen, Bryn," he said quietly. "And neither will I. Outlaw I may be, but I'm no murderer, and neither are you." He put his hand against my cheek. "Never mind, lass. I thought this might happen. It's all right. You have to hurry. You don't want the ship to leave without you." He bent forward quickly and pressed his lips to mine. His mouth was warm and soft on mine, the kiss more tender and welcome than it had any right to be. For a moment, I thought the air around us fizzed gently, and something odd happened to my breathing. When he raised his head again, I could only stare up at him, unable to speak. He touched my cheek gently, almost tenderly, tracing the line between eyebrow and jaw with two fingers. Then he turned away. "Shall we go, gentlemen?"

They walked away, Kenzie between the two guarding clansmen. Kenzie didn't look back. I had to run to get up the gangplank before the sailors pulled it aboard the ship. When I reached the deck and looked back, they had disappeared. My lips still retained the warmth of his kiss. I touched my mouth, tracing the outline with my fingertips, and wondered if the shape of his mouth might be indelibly imprinted on mine.

PART

2

The Bheancoran

12

I didn't mean to eavesdrop on the discussion between the King and the Enchanter, but by the time I realized what was happening, it was too late to come out of my inadvertent hiding place and slip away unnoticed. Had the day been brighter or drier, I would have been out on the practice field and well away from the solar when King Tiernyn and Donaugh came into the room. But I had been in a wretched frame of mind ever since awakening that morning after dreaming of Kenzie in chains in a Tyran prison. I had taken my lute to the solar to see if I could lose my sour mood in the music. Sometimes it worked. More often, during this past winter, it hadn't. But it was something to try when all else had failed.

The deep-cut windows with their padded benches between the heavy draperies and the glass made a comfortable place to practice the intricate arpeggios that Lloghar the Bard made look so easy. Eventually, my fingers became sore from plucking and fingering the strings, and I lost interest in the chords. I was staring morosely through the rain-smeared glass, my knees drawn up, arms wrapped around my legs and my chin resting on my knees when the door opened and both my uncles came in, already in the midst of a discussion that bordered on argument.

"You know why he's coming here, Donaugh," the King said, exasperation plain in his voice. "And you know the answer I must give him."

"Would it be such a hardship to send part of the army to Tyra?" Donaugh asked, his voice mild. I had never once heard him angry. He's always so much in command of himself, I doubt there's anything in the world that could rouse him to real rage. "The men spend their time gaming in taverns, and when they're not gaming, they're brawling.

They're contentious and belligerent when not on duty, and on the brink of insubordination when they are."

"What would you have me do?" Tiernyn demanded. "They train every day, but it's been thirty-seven years since we defeated the Maedun at Morgath's Bay. They know we're safe behind the curtain of enchantment you raised."

"But are we? What if Brynda is right? What if Hakkar *has* discovered some way to defeat that magic?"

"All the more reason to keep the army here," Tiernyn said.

"I'd think it was all the more reason to send several companies back to Tyra to fight them there. The more of the Maedun army fighting on Isgardian soil, or even in the foothills of Tyra, the less of it we're likely to see here on our own shores."

"And what do we do if the Maedun decide they'll invade while we've less of *our* army here?" The clink and gurgle of wine splashing into goblets came through the draperies clearly. "I trust your enchantment, Donaugh," the King went on. "But I don't trust that sorcerer Hakkar. His magic is as powerful as his father's was, I'm told, and his father nearly defeated you."

"And *his* father nearly defeated our father," Donaugh said. "But Father won, and so did I."

"It cost you your hand."

"Aye, it did. And now I'm a legend with one hand." Donaugh moved toward the window. I held my breath, my face burning as I anticipated discovery, but he turned away before reaching the window. His robe rustled softly as he settled into a chair not far from the window. "That was nearly forty years ago. The men who fought with us are growing old, and the young men don't remember."

"We're growing old, too, Donaugh." A tinge of wistfulness whispered through Tiernyn's words. Then his voice firmed. "There are even those who say I should step aside and make way for Tiegan. They want a younger king."

"Young men are always impatient. Remember how we were?"

"Aye, I do. It seems so long ago."

"When the Tyran ambassador arrives, give him the companies he asks for to take back with him. Let them learn what real fighting is. The army will be better for it. And so will we."

"And if half of them die over there?" The King began pacing, his footsteps falling lightly on the scattered rugs on the polished wooden floor. "I can't send men to die for a country not their own. They wouldn't stand for it."

"Tiernyn, *you* are still King. *They* will do as they're told." A soft chiming indicated a goblet being set down on a small table. "They grow soft, my lord King, and the Maedun grow restive. If Brynda is right—"

"If," Tiernyn repeated. "There's no guarantee she is."

"She said she heard it from the lips of Francia herself. Even if you've forgotten Francia, Tiernyn, I certainly haven't."

Tiernyn was quiet for a moment. "I wish I could forget her," he said softly. "Both her and that bastard she bore."

Donaugh didn't reply.

"Hakkar's father waited half a lifetime to invade Celi," Tiernyn went on. "The son waits, too. If we offer him an opportunity such as an army weakened by sending a third of it away, we'll have him on our doorstep. I've no doubt that he's working on magics to nullify your curtain of enchantment. If Brynda is right, then that's only a stronger argument for keeping the men home."

"That's as may be," Donaugh said. "But offer him an opportunity such as an army fighting among itself, and he'll be here all the sooner."

Tiernyn laughed, a rueful overtone in it. "Thirty-seven years," he said again. "And you're still taking me to task, Donaugh. Does the sword—does Kingmaker advise you in this?"

"No. But I watch this land, Tiernyn. I see the rot beginning in its core. Fighting men with no real enemy to fight grow stale and jaded. And discontented. They find their own battles."

"Let me think on it. Tiegan and Brennen will go to meet the ambassador. Let me think on it until they bring him back here."

"I'd advise you to think well."

I held my breath behind the draperies as footsteps crossed the room. Moments later the door closed, and I let out a long sigh of relief. But I didn't move. Not yet. Before I made my break for freedom, I had to make certain they had enough time to be well away before I slipped out into the corridor.

Donaugh spoke quietly, startling me so badly, I nearly leapt through the window. "You can come out now, Brynda. He's gone."

My heart made a creditable effort to burst right out of my chest. Heat burning in my cheeks, I reached out to pull the draperies aside, and swung my feet to the floor.

Donaugh stood in the middle of the room, his arms folded across his chest, the amusement in his eyes brimming over into a faint smile. His hair, once a rich, dark gold, now flared silver-white around his face like a cloud lit from behind by the sun. The gold cuff covering his right wrist gleamed in the wan light, but he had tucked it under his left arm so that it was not possible to tell that the hand itself was missing. He was tall, and the plain robe he wore, the color of dry leaves in autumn, emphasized his slenderness. The gaunt planes and hollows of his face could be forbidding, but the smile transformed his expression to amused tolerance and made him appear approachable.

He and Tiernyn are twins, my father's younger brothers. Tiernyn is the elder by some twenty minutes. I'm told that in their youth, it was difficult to tell them apart. But not now. Tiernyn's body had thickened with his years, and his face was fuller. Oh, he was still graceful and deft on the practice field when he sparred with the Swordmaster with that great Rune Blade of his. Kingmaker, the sword was named. Both he and the sword are legend, the subject of many of the songs and stories sung by the bards even now. While the bards sing of Tiernyn's prowess in battle against the enemies of Celi, they also sing of Donaugh's mastery of the flows of magical energy that web this island.

Both King Tiernyn and Donaugh wore an aura of power, but where Tiernyn's power is the physical power of command, of Kingship, Donaugh's is the more ephemeral power of spiritual strength, of magic. He wears it like a cloak, an entirely different sort of power from Tiernyn's. And, of course, Tiernyn has both his hands.

Donaugh hadn't lived at Dun Camus, Tiernyn's capital, since the army repelled the Maedun invasion all those years ago. He usually dwelt in a small lodge in the mountains of Skai, high up in the Spine of Celi. It surprised me to see him here at Dun Camus.

"You knew I was here all along," I said.

He nodded. "Yes, I knew."

"Yet you said nothing."

"You're not a serving girl to chatter secrets all over the palace, Brynda," he said gravely. "You're the daughter of the Prince of Skai, and bheancoran to the man who will someday be King of Celi. Should I not trust you with secrets?"

The heat rose in my cheeks again. I set the lute aside and let the drapery fall into place behind me. "But how did you know it was me?"

Donaugh seldom laughs, but he did now. "How not?" he said lightly. "I am, after all, an enchanter."

"You believe my message of danger from the Maedun, don't you."

"I do believe you. And I'm afraid Francia told you the truth." His expression grew bleak. "Child, we will always be in danger from the Maedun," he said. "Until the day that they are beaten back and destroyed, as their very own prophecy predicts."

I knew the tale, of course. Our family is tangled tightly in that prophecy. A Maedun seer long ago said an enchanter would arise from my grandfather's line, an enchanter who would destroy the Maedun. Donaugh wasn't that enchanter, or so he claimed. He had been instrumental in keeping the Maedun away from the shores of Celi, but he hadn't destroyed them.

"Will Tiernyn send the army to Tyra?" I asked.

"I hope so," Donaugh said. He glanced out the window at the drizzling rain. "The seas are still too stormy to send a ship across the Cold Sea. By the time a ship can cross in safety, Tiernyn will have made his decision."

And by the time a ship could cross in safety, the letter he had written to his kinsman, Brychan, Laird of Broche Rhuidh in Tyra, could go back with the ship. It pained me to think that Kenzie might have spent the winter imprisoned for the *crime* of taking one of his father's horses. Surely Tiernyn had it in his power to request and secure from Brychan a complete pardon for the man who had saved my life and seen to it that I arrived safely back in Celi.

The ship that brought me to Celi was the last ship to make port here from the continent before winter closed in. No sane ship's master would risk his ship in the gales that tore at the coasts during winter. And the storms this winter had been particularly violent. Only once had a ship come across the Cold Sea, and that was the swift little six-man courier ship which came to deliver the message that a new Tyran ambassador would come with the spring. The little ship left again within an hour of making port in Clendonan, hardly taking enough time to reprovision, as its master took advantage of a short break in the storms. It had come and gone so quickly, there had been no chance to give the letter addressed to Brychan to the master for delivery.

Donaugh reached out and touched my cheek. "Never fear, Brynda," he said softly. "Both Tiernyn and I will do our best for your big Tyr."

It didn't even startle me. Donaugh knew me well enough to read my thoughts through the expression on my face.

"Now," he went on more cheerfully, "you might want to go and greet your brother. Both he and Fiala have come from Dun Eidon with me."

"Brennen is here?" I grinned in delight. I hadn't seen him all winter, not since I'd come back from the continent. "Are Mai and the children with him?"

Donaugh shook his head. "No. They stayed in Dun Eidon. Brennen and Fiala are to go to Clendonan with you and Tiegan to greet the Tyran ambassador when he arrives. It's been a long time since you and your brother were together. I'm sure you'll have much to say to each other."

I recognized a dismissal when I heard one. I sketched a bow to him and hurried out of the room. It was only later that I realized I'd forgotten the lute. But it didn't matter now. My mood was considerably better. Brennen was in Dun Camus, and the message to Brychan could be delivered in perhaps as short a time as a fortnight or two.

I nearly ran right into Tiegan's wife Sheryn as I hurried down the corridor toward the guest wing. She was, as always, flawlessly groomed and coiffed, not a dark gold hair out of place, the folds of her gown falling in precise and perfect lines to her feet, as if they had been carved from some lustrous wood. Her hair was wound into a coronet braid around her head, and pearls gleamed in the shining coils, matching the pearls sewn into the neckline and cuffs of her gown. She was trueborn Tyadda, one of the strange, fey race who inhabited the Isle of Celi long before the Celae came and made it ours, back when the island was called Nemeara. Now the name survives only in the Dance of Nemeara, the huge, triple-ringed henge of stone in the north of the Province of Skai. Built in the shadow of Cloudbearer, the highest peak on the island, the Dance's origins were now lost in legend.

When the Celae first came to the island, the Tyadda were a fading race, their once-strong magic slowly dying away. Intermarriage between the Tyadda and the Celae strengthened the magic, but it would never be as strong as it once had been, even in an enchanter such as my uncle Donaugh.

I've heard it said that the Celae didn't conquer the Tyadda; they married them. It was a gentle conquest in that regard. There were very few trueborn Tyadda left now, and those few for the most part lived in hidden steadings deep in the mountains of Skai. Their dark gold hair and startlingly dark brown eyes tended to show up in the descendants of the Celae who intermarried with them. Both Brennen and I had inherited our brown eyes from our Tyadda grandmother, our mother's mother. But we had both inherited our red-gold hair from our Tyran grandfather, who was still known as Red Kian of Skai from the time when he had served as Regent for our father.

They were a beautiful race, the Tyadda, and Sheryn was a perfect example. She was small and slender, almost to the point of fragility. There was an ethereal quality to the bone structure of her face that would allow her to retain her beauty even into her ninth decade and beyond. Her skin was a delicate golden tan that I could only envy.

She wore a worried little frown now, but even the frown couldn't mar her beauty. As I passed, meaning only to nod politely at her, she reached out and caught my arm.

"Have you seen Tiegan this morning?" she asked.

"Not since breakfast," I said.

She arched one perfect eyebrow. "One would think that a bheancoran would keep better track of her prince," she said frostily.

I smiled politely, gritting my teeth so hard behind it, my jaw ached. "One might think the same of a wife with her husband," I said. That got to her. A spark of anger, quickly suppressed, flashed in her eyes. "Tiegan and I are bonded," I said mildly enough. "I serve him; I don't live in his sleeve. Nor he in mine, come to that."

She looked at me, opened her mouth to make a sharp retort, then changed her mind and frowned. She even frowned prettily. "He arose earlier than I this morning," she said. "He said something about consulting with the King, and I haven't seen him since. I need him now. There's something I must tell him."

"He might be on the practice field," I said. "Or he might be with his father."

She shook her head. Light glinted in the gleaming coils of hair. "No," she said. "I just saw King Tiernyn. He was alone."

I was anxious to see Brennen. I gently pulled my arm away from her delicate little jeweled fingers. "He'll show up," I said callously. "It's not as if he's vanished. He's probably just busy. But you might try the practice field."

She glanced out of one the tall corridor windows at the rain. "No, I don't think I care to go outdoors right now," she said.

I refrained from commenting on how the rain might adversely affect her hair or her clothing. "He'll be in the solar for the midday meal, I should think," I said. "You can catch him then." I nodded to her and made good my escape. So much for my improved mood.

I found Fiala before I found Brennen. She was just leaving the guest chambers as I came around the corner. She wore her trews and tunic, her great hand-and-a-half sword strapped across her back, and a long-suffering expression. Her hair, black enough to send blue glints back into sunlight, was bound in a heavy plait over her shoulder, leaving the angular planes and hollows of her face stark and unadorned. Her deep blue eyes were pure Celae under the heavy black eyebrows. She's taller than I—but not quite as tall as Brennen—and strong enough to wield a sword nearly as heavy as the sword Brennen carries. She had never married, claiming a bheancoran can't be bothered with a husband when she had a prince to worry about, too. Mind you, she always disappears with one certain captain on Fire Feasts such as Beltane and Lammas. It's difficult to tell how old she is. When I was fourteen and training with her, she looked about twenty-five. She still does.

She grinned when she saw me. "Don't go in there yet, Brynda," she said. "Tiegan is with Brennen, and they're already up to their eyebrows in a chess game. I was just going out to the practice field until they'd had a chance to sort out which of them is still undisputed champion." She cocked her head and regarded me gravely. "Bit on a lemon this morning, did you?"

"I met Sheryn in the corridor back there."

"Ah," she said. "I see."

She and Mai, Brennen's wife, had a wonderful relationship. The way Mai described it, she and Fiala were partners in keeping my stubborn brother in the correct frame of mind. Even had I wished the same sort of relationship with Sheryn, Sheryn herself would never allow it.

"Well, come with me," Fiala said. "You can work off your frustration practicing a fourth-level dance with me."

So we went to the practice field.

The sword in my hands sang softly, its intrinsic power whispering along the bonds that connected us, Rune Blade and bheancoran. Holding my own blade again, the sword I had received from the hands of my grandmother Kerri, was a joy in itself. As I moved through the intricate steps of the sequence, my patterns mirroring Fiala's, the blade gleamed in the gray light, the runes spilling along the blade glittering. Each movement, each step of the exercise demanded all my attention. My feet danced in precise patterns across the wet grass of the practice field and the blades, mine and Fiala's, cut exact designs through the drizzle floating in the air around us. Lost in the demanding precision of the dance, I could let go of all the problems of the last winter, at least for the moment.

13

I dreamed that night of a campfire in the high, clear reaches of the western mountains of Skai under the brilliance of a star-scattered sky. Someone sat beside me, a darker shadow against the night. I couldn't make out anything of his features or his shape, but his presence was comforting, solid, reliable. I felt safe and contented sitting beside him.

Around the circle of light cast by the fire sat the people I loved. My brother Brennen sat with his arm around the shoulders of his wife Mai, their children Lisle, Eryd, and Gareth at their feet. As always, Fiala was in her place at Brennen's left, her sword glinting in the light, her dark hair melding with the shadows behind her. Tiegan sat with Sheryn curled into the shelter of his arm, his cloak about both of them, protecting them from the chill of the night. The bond between the prince and me throbbed faintly in my chest just beneath my heart, familiar and reassuring.

My parents, Prince Keylan and the lady Letessa, were there, and my uncle Donaugh. Next to him sat my uncle Tiernyn, King of all Celi, and his wife, Queen Ylana. Tiernyn held his sword, the fabled Rune Blade Kingmaker, once lost, then found by my grandfather Kian and brought home to Celi. The runes cut deeply into the blade flashed and sparked in the firelight like facets of gems, collecting the light and sending it back into the shadows in glittering sparks of color. The black scar near the hilt looked like a rip in the fabric of the night, swallowing all light, giving nothing back to the fire.

No one spoke as we sat there, each of us absorbed in our own thoughts. But there seemed to be an attitude of waiting in the tense bodies and still faces around me. I found myself listening closely to the silence of the night. But no sounds disturbed the stillness. No night birds sang. No crickets called from the deep grass.

The flames of the campfire leapt and danced, then suddenly flared up brightly, sending hot, shadowed color lashing through the night. It ran, first gold, then red, around the circle, and stained the faces of my family livid red. As if they were bathed in blood . . .

Then, even as I watched, skin and flesh and muscle turned to ash and flaked away, leaving pallid white skulls grinning in the harsh glare of the fire. I looked down at my own hands on my knees before me, and saw only polished white bone . . .

I came leaping and gasping out of sleep, my body spasming like a gaffed silver salmon, my heart thundering as if it were bent on tearing itself loose from my chest. For a moment, I sat staring into the fire-shot darkness of a room lit only by a small brazier near the bed, trying to remember where I was. Gradually, the quivering surge of fear-energy abated, and I breathed more easily. I was safe in my own bed at Dun Camus, surrounded by familiar, comfortable things.

Slowly, I lifted my hands and studied them. I had to look for a long time before I managed to satisfy myself that what I saw was true. Bone, yes, but padded with muscle and tendon, and sheathed firmly and neatly in sun-browned skin.

A dream. It was only a dream.

I swung my legs over the side of the bed and sat with the bare soles of my feet pressed to the cold tile of the floor. The chill helped to convince me that I was real, and the dream was not. Outside the window, the first slackening of the dark heralded the approach of dawn.

I have always had vivid dreams, ever since I was a child. And some of them . . . Some of them were Seeings, visions of the future. But most of them were not. The problem was that I never knew which was which until *after* the event of the dream happened. And the clarity of the dreams had little or nothing to do with the reality of which were true Seeings and which were nothing but nightmare.

It came of having only a little magic. The thread of magic runs strongly through my family, but my gifts are scant and meager. They always have been. I have enough magic to resonate with the intrinsic magic of my Rune Blade, inherited from my grandmother. But this is something common in all bheancoran. I am certainly not unique there.

When I was twelve, my parents took me away from my training as bheancoran and sent me to Donaugh to see if he could strengthen and train my gifts. He took me to the Dance of Nemeara, but I felt nothing there but the faint thrumming vibration of the inherent magic of the brooding stones. I was with Donaugh a year, then he sent me home. My gifts, he told me gently, would always be small ones. In a way, it relieved me. It left me free to become bheancoran, as I had always known I must. I had magic enough to hear the music in my sword, to feel the power in the Dance, but little else. It was enough.

No, the small magics, my meager gifts, never bothered me much. It was only the dreams that could do that. They had not often proved to be Seeings. It had happened only seven times in my life—just often enough to verify that some of them were. Not knowing how to tell the difference between a Seeing and a nightmare both frightened and frustrated me.

I looked again at my hands. My whole, completely familiar hands. Of course, the circumstances of the dream were ludicrous. Why would my family be grouped around a campfire in the middle of the mountains of Skai in the first place? Only once or twice a year were we all in the same place at the same time, and that was here, at Dun Camus, for the meetings of the King's Council. And Dun Camus was in the middle of the Mercian downslands, not in the mountains of Skai.

Only a dream. Most certainly a dream brought on by the odd conversation I had overheard between Tiernyn and Donaugh yesterday morning. And perhaps influenced by memories of the journey across the continent with Kenzie.

I crawled back into the warmth and comfort of the bed, pulled the quilts up around my chin, and settled myself for sleep.

Only a dream.

The ties between Tyra on the continent and our Isle of Celi are strong. My grandfather, Kian dav Leydon ti'Cullin, was born in Tyra. His mother, daughter to Prince Kyffen of Skai, had married the son of the Clan Laird of Broche Rhuidh in Tyra. Kian became Kyffen's heir when Kyffen's only son Llan died without children. But my grandfather was never Prince of Skai. He held the throne as Regent only for my father, and when my father was crowned prince, my grandfather returned to Tyra with my grandmother and my aunt Torey.

Since shortly after Tiernyn's ascension to the throne of Celi as High King, there has been a Tyran ambassador in the Court of Celi. The last of these had suddenly taken ill with lung fever and died shortly after Samhain last autumn. He had been properly seen home to his Clanhold by his two aides, sailing across the Cold Sea in one of the swift little six-man courier ships that brave all but the fiercest storms the Cold Sea had to offer. But even they travel the sea only when the need is greatest. It's said that a courier ship will pitch and roll on wet grass—not the most comfortable method of plying the seas, winter or summer. Thus, it was a great surprise when another ship arrived shortly after Imbolc, when the winter storms were at their height, to bring word that another ambassador would be coming as soon as he could take ship from Tyra.

Vernal Equinox was four days behind us now. It was time to ride to Clendonan on the Tiderace to await the arrival of the ship from Tyra.

Early in the morning of the day after Brennen and Donaugh had arrived from Skai, four of us set out with a troop of twenty men. To Tiegan's left rode my brother Brennen, Fiala beside him. I had given up my usual place at Tiegan's left to

Brennen, and rode now at Tiegan's right. In my saddle pack, ready to be given to the ship's master, was Tiernyn's letter to Brychan of Broche Rhuidh.

We rode through a steady drizzle that could not quite make up its mind to become rain, but never quite stopped. It continued unabated for the full time we were on the road. Normally, the trip from Dun Camus to Clendonan takes only two days. We spent three days slipping and sliding through the slick, greasy mud of the road. When we finally reached Clendonan and were made welcome by Gwilyadd, Duke of Dorian, I had begun to wonder bleakly if I would ever be warm and dry again.

The weather could never be allowed to interfere with sword practice. Cold and wet as it was, Tiegan and I were out on the practice field behind the massive bulk of Gwilyadd's palace the morning after our arrival, seemingly eagerly bent on rending each other limb from limb. He is, of course, far taller and stronger than I and, under normal circumstances, could chop me into chunks of stewing meat with little or no trouble. But Fiala had taught me well. Lacking his strength, I used my smaller size and quicker reflexes to simply move myself out of the way of his massive sword. Gadfly technique, Fiala called it. Usually, I could wear down an opponent, keeping him leaping around trying to pin me down, until he quite literally ran out of breath.

The sword in my hands sang sweetly as I swung it through the precise, complicated sequence. I flowed across the wet grass, driving Tiegan back in a series of thrusts and slices. Lost in the rhythms and patterns of the dance, I moved automatically, one movement sweeping into the next with a perfection I don't often achieve. Tiegan's face paled with concentration. It pleased me to see beads of sweat break out on his forehead and upper lip. He was working harder than usual to fend me off. But in a moment or two, I'd have him, my blade pressing to his throat.

That moment never came. The sound of hoofbeats approaching at the gallop broke into my concentration. Tiegan looked over his shoulder at the rider and slipped in the rain-slick grass, falling to one knee. I stumbled as I tried to stop the swing of my sword in mid-arc. Tiegan regained his feet and leapt back out of the way of my quivering blade.

The rider drew his horse to a tumultuous halt and half slid from the saddle to drop to one knee in the grass in one fluid motion. He wore the Red Hart badge on the shoulder of his tunic, indicating he came from Dun Camus and from the King, Tiegan's father. His cloak hung sodden from his thin shoulders, snagged and tattered from the forest, his boots and trews splashed and spattered with mud. He had come in a hurry. He must have set out soon after we ourselves had left the palace.

Tiegan sheathed his sword, the motions deliberate and exact. I knew him well enough to see the effort he made to compose his face to hide his worry. "What is it, lad?" he asked, his voice carefully neutral.

"My lord Prince," the boy said, gasping for breath. "I am sent from Dun Camus to tell you your lady wife lies ill and has need of you."

The skin around Tiegan's mouth tightened, and sudden worry etched lines around his eyes. "I'll come at once," he said quietly.

I sheathed my sword in the scabbard on my back. "We're supposed to meet the Tyran ambassador tomorrow or the next day," I said. "Your father sent us specifically."

He barely glanced at me. "Sheryn's ill. I must go to her."

The messenger still knelt in the grass, his head bent while he caught his breath. "What's wrong with the lady Sheryn?" I asked.

"A flux of the chest, my lady Brynda," the messenger said. "Prince Tiegan is to come at once."

I shut my teeth on my bitter and scathing remark. There was no sense in it. All I would succeed in doing was making

Tiegan angry with me. All I said was, "We should leave at once, then."

Tiegan put his hand on my arm. "No," he said. "You'd best stay here and meet the ambassador with Brennen. If I can't be here to meet him, it's best at least two members of the royal house are here. We owe him that much honor."

"We owe him the honor of your presence," I said, then quickly wished I hadn't. Tiegan frowned at me. He's very much like his father when he does that. Very royal and infinitely short of patience with anything that even vaguely resembles a fit of pique.

"My wife deserves my presence, too," he said quietly.

I dipped my head in acquiescence. There was nothing to be gained by argument, and too much to be lost. "I'll convey your apologies to the ambassador, my lord Prince," I said, trying to keep my voice neutral. From the sharp look I received, I don't think I quite succeeded.

Rain. More cursed rain.

I looked up at the clouds, blue-black as bruises, hanging over the city of Clendonan. Broad, dark curtains of precipitation swept down out of the clouds, drifting across the restless gray water of the Tiderace, dappling the surface with streaks and stipples of light and dark. Beyond the Tiderace, barely visible through the heavy drifts of rain, stretched the flat reaches of the Summer Run, vaguely pale green in the murky light.

The palace of Gwilyadd, Duke of Dorian, was built on a low bluff above the city. The terrace where I stood faced out over the city, overlooking the foam-flecked waters of the Tiderace just below the palace where the River Lachlan emptied its muddy waters into the brackish sea. Behind me, the guest chambers offered dry warmth and shelter from the rain, but I had no wish to leave the terrace. Right now, I preferred the stark bleakness of the rain and gray sea.

The weather suited my mood perfectly. All the seven gods

and goddesses know I have a long way to go before I reach the level of wisdom a bheancoran is supposed to possess. I have barely learned to control my anger, not to vent it on people who have nothing whatsoever to do with the cause of my ill temper. I had retired to my chambers shortly after the midday meal, achingly aware that Tiegan was gone, well on his way now back to Dun Camus.

Sheryn had lost her child only a season before Tiegan and I left Celi for Borlan. She had not been strong enough to accompany Tiegan then, and I know she resented me because I went with him. It was uncharitable of me, mayhaps, but I couldn't help thinking that this sudden illness of hers might be little more than revenge to bring him to her side, leaving me to meet the ambassador without him.

What surprised me was the hurt that washed through me. The feeling of personal betrayal. When I admitted the feeling to myself, it shamed me. He had hurt my pride, leaving me behind. I have never considered myself to be the type of woman who sulks because her feelings have been hurt, but that was exactly what I was doing.

I am Brynda al Keylan, and I carry my grandmother's Rune Blade. I'm the daughter of the Prince of Skai, and I'm bheancoran to the man who will one day be King of all Celi. Surely I should be wiser and more forgiving than I am.

I'm bheancoran, as was my mother Letessa and my grandmother Kerridwen before me. We have a lot of pride. Some translate that word to mean obstinacy, but I can't help that. I come by the stubbornness honestly, too, come to that. My grandfather is possibly the most stubborn man in the world, if what my grandmother says is true. It probably is. She's lived with him for more than twice my lifetime. She ought to know.

Footsteps on the wet tile behind me made me turn. My brother Brennen, his cloak pulled tightly around him against the rain, came to the low wall and placed his hands on the stone. He leaned forward, looking out through the mist at the blurred green of the Summer Run across the water. He said nothing, but I could almost tell what he was thinking. He masked his disapproval of my brooding sullenness adroitly, but I knew my brother well. On the other hand, he knew me very well, too.

Brennen is five years older than I. He's a big man, and looks a lot like our father, and like our father, he's quick as a cat and graceful as a dancer. Or a born swordsman. He had inherited our father's build as well as the copper gold hair, and his eyes are a deep, golden brown, like mine. He would not look out of place in the kilt and plaid of a Tyran clansman.

Brennen chose to ignore my foul and sour mood. "We've just received word that the ship from Tyra entered the Tiderace about midday," he said. "She should be docking in the harbor shortly after dawn on the morrow."

Water dripped down my face from my sodden hair. I brushed it aside and shrugged. "Let's hope the ambassador doesn't mind being met by second-choice envoys."

He looked at me, his expression maddeningly placid. "We are, after all, nephew and niece to the King," he said. "Not exactly what I'd deem second choice."

"Tiegan should be here."

"You're still upset about that, are you?"

I swung around to face him. "I'm furious, Brennen," I cried in frustration. "I know I shouldn't let that woman bother me, but sometimes I just can't help it."

Brennen raised one eyebrow. "That *woman*, as you call her, is our kinswoman, Brynda. And she's Tiegan's wife."

I made an impatient gesture. "I know. I know. But I hate how she always tries to keep him beside her, as if he were a little lapdog." I turned back to the parapet and slammed my fist down onto the stone. That was a stupid mistake. It hurt! It hurt enough to bring tears to my eyes. I flexed the fingers, blinking rapidly to dispel the tears. The pain was probably a good thing. It prevented me from saying aloud what I was thinking. "*What kind of a bheancoran can be proud of serving a lapdog?"* Even I could recognize that as sheer, unadulterated selfishness on my part.

He touched my shoulder, drew me around to face him. For the first time, a hint of concern touched his face, drawing a faint line between his eyebrows. "He loves her, Brynda," he said softly. "And he's worried about her. Did you know she's with child again? He's worried that she might lose this one the same way she lost the last."

I turned away. Sheryn had nearly died when she miscarried her first child last year. My aunt Torey, who's a strongly gifted Healer, said that the child was ill conceived and could never have been brought to term. Had she not fortuitously been visiting Dun Camus with her husband, Connor, Duke of Wenydd, Sheryn would surely have died because no one could stop her bleeding. Torey's Healing powers had saved her life.

"He loves her," Brennen said again.

I looked up at him. He knows about love, Brennen does. He loves his wife Mai to distraction, and she returns his love fivefold. Perhaps I don't understand that sort of love. I'm unmarried and likely to remain so unless I meet a man who can command my love and respect as Brennen commands Mai's. Or, I thought sourly, as Sheryn commands Tiegan's. But in twenty-four years, I've yet to meet one.

I sighed. "I've a lot yet to learn," I said. "Duality grant that Tiegan doesn't run out of patience with me before I learn some. Or understanding."

Brennen grinned. "That's a good start right there," he said.

The ship arrived two hours after sunrise the next morning. It was tall-masted and sleek, built in Tyra by men who knew the sea and knew ships. It glided through the choppy water and lost all momentum, neatly and precisely, just as it reached the docks. The half-furled sails still glimmered softly with the remnants of magic left over when the ship had passed through the curtain of enchantment.

I stood with Brennen and Fiala on the pier as the sailors secured the ship to the stone jetty and manhandled the gangplank into place. The ship lay low in the water, heavy with cargo. Maedun may hold most of the continent under thrall, but the lands bordering the Great Salt Sea far to the east were free, and trade was brisk between the Easterners and Celae.

There was no mistaking our ambassador as he disembarked. He came unattended by servants, a tall, broad-shouldered man, dressed in a kilt and plaid of blue-and-green tartan, his red-gold hair falling to his shoulders except for a single braid by his lef temple. He was taller even than Brennen, taller than my father. He moved with a sense of latent power and grace, a regal bearing in his stride. He reminded me of the mountain cats of Skai. And he was young for an ambassador, probably around Brennen's age, or somewhat younger. The hilt of a two-handed greatsword rose above his right shoulder, leather-wrapped and plain but for a shimmering stone set into the pommel. An emerald on a fine gold chain dangled from his left ear. As he came closer, I saw that the color of the emerald matched his eyes perfectly.

With a shock, I realized I knew him. The new Tyran ambassador was Kenzie Catfoot.

14

Startled shock held me dumbfounded. I became aware that my mouth hung open, so I closed it. No matter how many times I blinked the sun out of my eyes, the Tyr striding down the gangplank did not change. It was Kenzie. The same Kenzie I'd worried and fretted about for the whole of the winter. Except now he was dressed in spotless, impeccably pressed kilt and plaid, and his shirt looked to be of finest lawn. It occurred to me that I'd seen that noble and regal bearing about him before, though, when he had escorted me into the dining room of the little Banhapetsut inn and, again, talking to the ship's master in Honandun. It would appear now that he came by that poise quite naturally.

Brennen stepped forward to meet him as he strode out onto the stone jetty. They stood for a moment facing each other, two strong men, each silently gauging the strength of the other. Brennen smiled.

"You are Kenzie dav Aidan?" he asked.

The corners of Kenzie's mouth curled in the smile I was so familiar with. "Aye," he replied gravely. "I am he."

"I am Brennen ap Keylan, kinsman to King Tiernyn of Celi, who sends me to make you welcome and escort you to Dun Camus."

Kenzie had represented himself to me as a broken man—fatherless, clanless, bereft of kith and kin. Now he said, "Then we two are also kinsmen. My grandmother was Wynn dan Cullin dav Medroch, foster sister and cousin to your grandfather. We are well met, Brennen ap Keylan."

Brennen made a graceful gesture toward me. "May I present my sister, Brynda al Keylan, who is bheancoran to Tiegan, Prince of Celi."

I stepped forward. Kenzie turned to me, and his smile faded.

"We've already met, I believe, my lord Ambassador," I said drily. "It would seem that your difference of opinion with your father has been settled."

"It has," he said gravely. "With thanks to your grandfather." He took both my hands in his and bowed, pressing the backs of my hands lightly to his forehead. "I'll explain later," he said as he straightened. He kept his voice low enough so that only I heard him.

"Please do," I said most politely.

As Brennen presented Fiala, I caught a glimpse over Kenzie's shoulder of another man leaving the ship. He was tall and black-haired, and slender as a willow branch, like many Celae. He hurried down the gangplank, hesitated slightly as he stepped onto the worn stone of the jetty, then turned toward the warren of waterfront streets. As he passed, he glanced incuriously at us. His eyes were as blue as mountain lakes under an autumn sky, almost too blue to be human, and he was far and away one of the most handsome men I'd ever seen.

Intrigued, I watched him. He moved quickly into a narrow street between the buildings and a trick of the light threw a deep shadow around him, making him look as if he were cloaked in darkness. A frisson of dread whispered down my spine. But when I looked again, the shadow was gone, and a moment later, so was he, swallowed by the busy crowd.

"Kenzie, who was that?" I asked, still looking in the direction where the stranger had disappeared.

"Pardon, my lady Brynda?"

"That man who just left the ship," I said. "Dark hair, very blue eyes. Was he a passenger?"

"I was the only passenger on this voyage, my lady," Kenzie said.

"Then were there any crew answering that description?"

Kenzie shook his head. "All the crew are Tyran," he said. "Why?"

That ripple of chill shivered down my spine again. "Nothing,"

I said. "I just thought I saw someone I recognized. I must have been mistaken."

Gwilyadd simply would not hear of us leaving Clendonan that day. He insisted on feasting the Tyran ambassador, and did an excellent job of monopolizing Kenzie during most of the day and the evening. That was mayhaps a good thing, for I had certainly not yet sorted out how I felt about speaking with Kenzie.

Ever since leaving the waterfront, a restive uneasiness had overwhelmed me, manifesting itself as an inability to concentrate, or even sit still. I interpreted it as anger and disappointment that Kenzie, whom I had trusted with my life, had lied to me. Well, perhaps not lied to me, but not told me the complete truth. He had certainly known from the moment I told him who I was that we were kin—distant kin, mayhaps, but still kin.

I could eat nothing during dinner, and excused myself early. The restlessness would not let me sit still. I took my sword and went out to the practice field. I had it to myself in the misty drizzle.

I drew my sword. "Dance with me," I murmured to it.

Whisperer sang again in my hands. In the wan, gray light, the runes along the blade shimmered like watered silk. *I am the Voice of Celi.* My grandmother's sword, and her father's before her. A Rune Blade handed down generation to generation for hundreds of years. No one knew for certain when the first Rune Blades had come to the Celae, but legend has it they were all created by Wyfydd the Smith, each sword crafted for only one person. There were few Rune Blades, and each was a treasure to be guarded. The greatest of them, Kingmaker, belonged to Tiernyn, and had brought him to the throne of the High King.

But Whisperer was mine, and we moved together as a team. Lost in the intricate movements of the dance, I could let go of the quivering uneasiness that had plagued me all day.

But for a moment only. Unbidden, unwanted, the restlessness bubbled up in my chest once more. It made me clumsy, and my foot slipped in the wet grass. Angry with myself, I held the sword before me and tried to clear my mind. Usually, I'm quick and nimble enough. But right now, I was more tanglefooted than the rawest beginner.

"I'd say that demon you're battling is in no immediate danger."

Fiala's voice behind me startled me. I spun around, automatically bringing the sword into a guard position. Fiala stood with her feet planted wide in the wet grass, arms folded across her chest, her own sword still sheathed on her back. I lowered Whisperer.

"It's a demon I've been battling all my life," I said. "We're well accustomed to each other, my temper and I."

"Would this have anything to do with a certain newly arrived ambassador?" she asked.

I didn't have to answer. She read it in my face. She nodded, unsmiling.

"I see. And I would imagine it's no coincidence that his name is Kenzie."

"No coincidence at all," I said.

She nodded again. "I thought I had taught you better than to let petty annoyances—"

"Petty?" I repeated hotly. "Do you call his deceit—"

She hardly missed a beat at my interruption. "—Petty annoyances clutter your mind while you danced with the sword." She regarded me quietly, her face devoid of expression. "Mayhaps you need more learning." She unsheathed her sword and brought it up. "Guard yourself."

I took a deep breath, knowing she was right. I raised Whisperer and braced myself for her attack.

I slept poorly that night, and woke suddenly with tendrils of a forgotten nightmare tangled around my heart. The terror had no shape or substance, just a formless dread that accentuated the restless uneasiness I'd been battling all day.

Further sleep was impossible. I flung back the bedclothes and reached for my houserobe. Belting it around me, I went out onto the terrace beyond my windows.

A west wind had come up sometime during the night and blown away the clouds. The moon, a thin crescent in the last quarter, lay just above the horizon, tossing amid a scud of left-over clouds and pursued by the cold, clear blaze of the Huntress Star. I placed my hands on the chill stone of the parapet and watched as the Huntress slanted down in her eternal quest after the moon. The air smelled fresh and sweet, redolent of the sea and of the young, green shoots thrusting through the warming soil. The cool wind lifted my hair from the back of my neck, drying the nightmare sweat. My hair was still not long enough to bind back in a braid, but it had grown a little over the long winter.

Soft footsteps behind me made me turn slowly and unhurriedly. Kenzie's presence in the shadowed dark of the terrace didn't surprise me. He had been trying most of the day to catch me alone to speak with me, I think. I had just as assiduously tried to avoid him, fleeing first to the practice field, then to my bed.

He stood before me, fully dressed, his plaid flung about his shoulders. "Before ye fly away from me again, will ye do me the courtesy of listening to me?" he asked quietly.

With no light but the waning moon, he was little more than a darker shadow against the pale stone of the palace wall. I could not read the expression on his face. The faint light gleamed on the silver brooch at his shoulder, a richer ornament by far than any he had worn on our long trek across the continent. I leaned back against the parapet, my hands braced beside my hips.

"Mayhaps I owe you that courtesy," I said.

"I would hope ye did," he said. "You'll be wanting to know why I didna tell you in Laringras that we were kin."

"That would be a fair assumption," I said. "You must have known the instant I told you who I was."

"Aye, I did."

He moved so that he stood beside me, one shoulder leaning against the tall merlon. So close, he was a looming presence in the night, smelling faintly of soap, and woodsmoke, and damp wool. I had a sudden flash of how that plaid had felt snugged around me in the little inn in Banhapetsut, and later, when he held me close against him in the mountains while I tried desperately to hold the masking spell to hide us from the Maedun. Something swelled in my throat, and I had to blink back sudden tears, thankful that he couldn't see them in the darkness.

"But I told you that I was a broken man," he said. "It was true then. I had no kith or kin, and could not claim kinship with you, or anyone else for that matter. I had no rights to your regard as a kinsman."

"You could have told me who you were," I said. "Or did that damnable stubborn Tyran pride of yours get in the way?"

He didn't answer for a moment. His face was in shadow, but I got the impression he was smiling ruefully. "Aye," he said at last. "I suppose it did. You are the daughter of the Prince of Skai, niece to the High King of Celi, and bheancoran to the man who will one day be King. I was clanless and fatherless. I didna want your pity as a lost kinsman."

"You're hardly a man to inspire pity, Kenzie Catfoot," I said drily. "Even if you were a broken man."

"I didna lie to ye, Bryn," he said softly. "I told you no untruths."

"No," I replied. "But neither did you tell me the whole truth."

He paused again. "My father is Aidan dav Clintock, Laird of Glen Garragh. I was raised there. I spent only my fifteenth and sixteenth year at the Clanhold at Broch Rhuidh, training with the Swordmaster there. I met Kethryn there. You know what happened after that."

"And now you've reconciled with your father."

"Aye." He chuckled faintly. "Your grandfather had a good hand in that. They were his men on the pier there in Honandun, did ye know that?"

I hadn't. It had never occurred to me to ask whose men they were. I had, of course, assumed they were sent by Kenzie's father.

"Your grandfather is still an imposing man, despite his years," Kenzie said. "I have no idea what he said to my father, but whatever it was, it caused my father to reconsider his disowning of me."

I had to smile. He was right. My grandfather could be extremely persuasive.

"While I'm confessing my sins of omission, I should tell ye now that it was through your grandfather's wishes that I was in Banhapetsut when you escaped from the Maedun ship."

I stared at him. "What?"

He shifted uneasily and settled his plaid more firmly on his shoulder. "I'd been working with him since shortly after I left Broche Rhuidh," he said. "Collecting information, ye ken. Kian dav Leydon ti'Cullin has a wide network of men like me. Since I'd made myself so damnably noticeable to the Maedun by getting you out of Banhapetsut, I wasna much use to him anymore as a spy. I suppose he felt he owed it to me to bring my father and me together again."

I pushed myself away from the wall and turned to look at him. "How did he know that?" I asked sharply. "His men met you in Honandun to take you back to Tyra. How did he know I was with you?"

"I told him," he said simply.

"You *told* him?"

"Aye. I sent a message to him the day after I met you, while you were at the inn there in Banhapetsut. It was just before I rescued you from those two city guards." He shrugged helplessly. "You were on that Maedun ship for nearly ten days, but Prince Tiegan knew within hours after you were taken that you had to be on it. Your grandfather had men in every port between Silichia and Honandun looking for that Maedun ship. I was on my way to look at it—and look for you—the first time I ran into Robard and his freebooters. We'd had dealings before, and he recognized me."

I stared at him, hardly knowing what to think. "Are you telling me that you were looking for me specifically down there on the waterfront?"

"Aye, I was. But as it turned out, you hardly needed my help to get away from that ship."

"And you didn't *tell* me this?"

He spread his hands. "How could I tell you?" he said. "Men like me—men who work in the shadows—Aye, well, let's just say the fewer people who know who we are, the better our chances of living to report what we know."

"You didn't *trust* me not to give you away?" This was even a worse betrayal than his withholding the truth from me. Did he think I'd give him away to the Maedun? Did he think so little of me as to think I'd betray anyone who helped me as he had? He towered nearly a full head over me, but I wanted to grab him by the shoulders and shake him until his teeth rattled.

He reached out and caught my hand. "It isna what you think, Bryn," he said softly. "Ye've never run up against a Maedun warlock. Ye've never seen what happens when they question someone. They can sense a lie, and they have ways of prying the truth out of people. If we were taken by some mischance . . . If ye didna know what I was, you couldna lie about it. Those warlocks wouldna put you to the question."

"Thank you very much for your kind and thoughtful consideration for my safety, my lord Ambassador," I said coldly. "I'm fascinated by the way you've managed to turn this about so that your perfidy and deceit were all to protect me. I can do very well without that sort of protection, thank you." I tried to pull my hand away, but he held fast to it. "You left me to worry about you for the whole of the winter. Do you realize how many sleepless nights I spent because I was envisioning you in a prison somewhere? You might at least have spared me that."

"I'm sorry. It never occurred to me that you might worry."

"It never occurred to you? Are you mad? You saved my life. You risked your life to help me across the continent, and it never occurred to you that I might worry about you?" I tried again to free my hand, but he wouldn't let it go. "Kenzie Catfoot—Kenzie dav Aiden—whatever you call yourself, you're an idiot. A plain and simple idiot!"

He stepped closer and put one hand to my face, gentle fingers tracing a line from my brow, down my cheek to my chin. "Bryn," he said, his voice sounding rusty and hoarse, as if he hadn't used it for a long time. "Brynda, I have to—"

I had a sudden premonition. I knew what he was about to say, and I didn't want to hear it. I yanked my hand away from him and took a quick step backward. The rough stone of the embrasure caught me just above the hips, and I could move no farther back. He put one hand to the merlon beside my head, and reached toward me with the other. I twisted away, ducked under his arm, and fled back to my room. He was still there by the wall, a dark shadow against the sky between the merlons, when I slammed the door of my room.

15

Morning brought sunshine and an achingly blue springtime sky.
The wind was warm enough but blew strongly. We rode with
our heads bent into it, cloaks pulled tightly around us to prevent them flapping like sheets hung to dry behind a laundry
shed. Brennen and Kenzie tried to speak with each other, but
conversation was all but impossible. The wind tore the words
away as soon as they were spoken. After a while, they gave up
and we rode in silence. Kenzie spoke to me once, but I shook
my head, indicating I couldn't hear him above the wind. I
didn't particularly want to speak with him. I had too much to
think about.

But I didn't really want to think about it now, either.

Fortunately, it wasn't difficult to let my attention wander.
All around us, signs of burgeoning spring rioted across the
wet countryside. Along the verge of the road, the young
bracken sprang delicately green, already nearly belly high to
the horses. Buds, red and swollen, hung ready to burst into
leaf from every branch, and soft gray furred the willow trees
tangled thickly between the taller elms, oaks, and maples.
Once I saw the creamy white of dogwood blossoms gleaming
through the darker green of holly and pine. Here and there, the
bright pink or white of early wildflowers starred the lush
green of new grasses thrusting up through the carpet of old
leaves. The air smelled fresh and clean, full of the fragrance
of growing things.

I missed the mountains of Skai in the spring. The downslands are beautiful this time of year, but there is no music in
the air made by the exuberant splash and gurgle of rushing
water as the snow melts and fills the rivers and streams. The
rivers are quieter here, even swollen with melted snow, sliding with oiled grace toward the Cold Sea to the east. And

there is no perfume from any towering cedar trees to enliven
the scent of wildflowers and young bracken.

By midday, the wind had died to a stiff breeze. About the
same time as the wind died, I noticed an odd thing happening.
Kenzie had been riding to Brennen's right, while Fiala rode as
usual to Brennen's left. I was to Kenzie's right, paying as little
attention as possible to him. My attention came back to him
suddenly when he fell slightly behind, and seemed to be edg-
ing his horse to the outside of the track, to my right. For a
moment, we performed an awkward little dance before he
moved back into place between Brennen and me, giving me a
puzzled look as he did. I realized this wasn't the first time it
had happened.

Then I caught Fiala's eye. She held her face carefully neutral, but laughter flashed in her eyes and threatened the corners
of her mouth, and I knew what Kenzie was doing. Like an
anxious sheepdog with a straying lamb, he was trying to get
me between himself and Brennen, in a position to be protected. I, of course, was trying to keep myself in position to
guard *him* much as I would guard Tiegan, were he there
instead.

A bubble of irritation prickled in my belly. This *wasn't*
Laringras. I needed no protection here.

When it happened again, I stopped my horse and gestured.
"Please, my lord Ambassador," I said. "It's best you ride
beside Brennen." I smiled tightly. "This is my country. I'm not
likely to transgress any rules here."

He stiffened. "Of course," he said, then inclined his head
graciously. "Forgive me, my lady Brynda." Amusement filled
his eyes and spilled over into a smile. "I'm obviously only a
barbarian Tyr with no knowledge of Celi's fabled bheancoran.
I willna trouble you longer with my recalcitrance." He moved
back into place beside Brennen and slanted a glance at him.
"She tends to bristle somewhat like an outraged wee hedge-
hog, does she not?"

I pretended not to hear the remark, but it earned him a

laugh from Brennen. "I've no doubt you'll learn quickly, my lord Ambassador," Brennen said. He studiously avoided looking at me, his laughter still tugging at the corners of his mouth. "And you've described my sister as accurately as I've heard for a while."

Heat climbed in my cheeks. Pulling my dignity about me like a tattered cloak, I guided my horse to Kenzie's right and looked straight ahead as we got under way again.

With both the sun and the wind drying the track, we made better time on the journey back to Dun Camus. As we drew closer to home, the bond I shared with Tiegan quivered strongly under my heart.

Something was wrong.

Something was wrong, but I couldn't tell what it might be. It wasn't Sheryn. If anything had happened to her, I would have felt Tiegan's grief sharply enough to knock me to my knees. The sensation tingling along the threads of our bond was not grief, nor was it fear or pain. Not exactly. Tiegan was in turmoil and the echo of it sent shards of troubled uncertainty through my own heart and spirit. Something troubled him deeply, and it made me afraid although I could not put a name to my fear. Nor could I identify the source.

Tiegan did not come to the steps of the Great Hall to greet us as we rode into the courtyard. Nor was Donaugh there. I found out later that he had left for his lodge in the mountains after we had started out for Clendonan. A solitary man, my uncle Donaugh.

King Tiernyn was there, though, and, beside him, Queen Ylana held the guest cup. As Kenzie mounted the steps beside Brennen and Fiala, Ylana stepped forward to offer him the cup. The Queen's health had been failing gradually over the last four or five years. She was now thin and pale as a winter-bleached reed, but she was still graceful and regal, despite her years and her silvered hair.

Kenzie drank deeply of the cup, then went to one knee and bent low over her hand, murmuring something I didn't catch.

He rose and turned to Tiernyn. The King extended both his hands, and Kenzie took them, bowing low and raising Tiernyn's hands to his forehead in the Tyran manner of respect.

As they went through the formality of greeting, I glanced up at the windows of the family quarters above the Great Hall. Tiegan was up there. Apprehension closed in a tight, cold fist around my heart. It wasn't quite sorrow that filled him and resonated along the threads of the bond, but whatever it was, it made my breath too shallow in my tightened chest. I knew I was in his thoughts just as surely as he was in mine. And it was my image in his mind that caused the unarticulated distress washing through him. My heart raced in sudden terror.

Had Sheryn convinced him to contemplate sending me away?

No bheancoran had ever been dismissed by her prince. Never once since the first Prince of Skai bonded with his Tyadda warrior-maid. Tiegan could not possibly be seriously considering sending me away. Could he? How could I live with the shame if he did? How could I live with the vast, terrifying emptiness that severing our bond would leave within me?

I found him alone in the solar, staring down into the fire on the hearth. He stood leaning one shoulder against the solid stone of the chimney, his arms folded across his chest, a troubled frown drawing his dark gold brows together above his shadowed eyes as he gazed down at the play of light and shadow across the coals. I stood for a moment watching him. Tiernyn's features were imprinted upon Tiegan just as surely as Father's are stamped on Brennen's face. But now, something about Tiegan reminded me more of Donaugh than Tiernyn—something about his posture, mayhaps, or the abstracted expression on his face.

Was this the cause of my uneasiness of the last several days?

He knew I was there, of course, but he didn't move; he didn't turn to greet me. He couldn't help being as conscious of my presence as I was of his. And, I thought, it was a wonder he could not hear the rapid hammering of my heart as cold despair filled me. At my sides, my hands had curled of their own accord into tight fists.

We had bonded right after I finished my training at eighteen. The bonding had already begun, of course, years before, when we both realized that I was destined to become his bheancoran, but the final threads had been woven in the shrine in Dun Eidon on my eighteenth name day. Even now, the delicate scent of smoldering racha leaf brings back the memory of bright flowers and ribbons cascading down the pristine white walls of the shrine, and the swelling burst of joy as Tiegan's hand and mine closed together on the hilt of my grandmother's Rune Blade Whisperer. I swore before all the seven gods and goddesses, and before the Duality, to serve him, to protect him with my life if need be, and he accepted my service with the same joy and sense of fitness and belonging that filled me to overflowing. Until the day he married Sheryn, nothing had disturbed the solidity of that bond.

I took a step forward, then faltered, suddenly aware of a spark of anger. Never before had I been hesitant in approaching him. We were bonded. We belonged together. This awkwardness, this strain between us now, was Sheryn's doing. The strength of the resentment that bubbled up in me shocked me. I wished she had never left that Tyadda steading to attend Brennen's wedding. I wished she had—

Oh, gods help me, no! I didn't really wish she had died when she miscarried Tiegan's child. Never that! Shame crept hot and thick up my throat and into my cheeks.

I took another step. "Tiegan?"

For a moment, I thought he would not look at me, would not even acknowledge my presence. Then he straightened and turned. His eyes were a dark, turbulent brown, and his mouth formed a tight and level line. He looked weary to the point of exhaustion. Finally, he held out his hand to me.

"Come here, Brynda," he said quietly.

I stayed where I was. "How is Sheryn?"

"Sheryn is all right. It was only a passing chill and a slight cough. She was better when I arrived home."

"And the child?"

He raised one eyebrow. "You know about the child?"

"Brennen told me in Clendonan."

He nodded. "I see. The child is in no danger. Sheryn says she feels quite well now."

I looked down at the polished wooden floor beneath my feet.

"Sheryn didn't call me back," he said. "She was surprised to see me when I arrived. She was upset that I had come home rather than stay to meet the ambassador. One of her women sent the messenger."

Sheryn is many things, but a liar isn't among them. Nor is Tiegan. I believed him.

He held out his hand again. "Come here."

I went to him as a child expecting chastisement might go to a loving father who was regretful that he must mete out deserved punishment, but determined that he would. He reached up and put his hand gently to the side of my head, cupping my face gently in the palm of his hand. It was a tender, loving gesture, and it startled me.

"What am I to do with the pair of you?" he asked softly. He ran his fingers down my cheek then dropped his hand to his side. "I love you, Brynda. You're not only my bheancoran, you're the little sister I never had and never stopped wishing for. But I love Sheryn, too. She's my wife, and she'll be the mother of my child."

I gathered my courage and met his eyes. "You're going to send me away, aren't you?"

He blinked in shock. "Send you away?" he repeated. "Whyever would I do that? You're my bheancoran."

Relief made my knees suddenly weak. I found a chair and collapsed into it, staring at him. "I thought you were going to send me away because Sheryn and I quarreled all the time," I said, aware that relief made me babble. "I thought you thought you had to choose between us and you chose her because . . ." My voice trailed off. My throat was too dry. I couldn't speak. I tried to moisten my lips with a tongue that was even drier.

Tiegan's wry smile turned down at the corners. "Oddly enough, Sheryn thought exactly the same thing when I spoke with her," he said. "She thought I would send her away because you two set off sparks against each other."

I stared at him. "Send her away? But you couldn't do that. She's your wife."

He gave a harsh and humorless bark of laughter. "It's to your credit that you see that," he said. "Just as it's to Sheryn's credit that she saw that I couldn't send you away because of what you are to me." He slanted a glance across at me. "So what would you suggest we do about this untenable situation."

I took a deep breath to steady myself. If the cause of my uneasiness and my bad dreams wasn't the threat of Tiegan sending me away, then it had to be something else. And I had neither the experience nor the wisdom to interpret it. I needed someone else to help me. Perhaps Donaugh . . .

"I'll try to get along with her better," I said. "No, really, Tiegan. Half the sparks that fly between us come from me. It's as much my fault as hers."

He smiled, real amusement in his eyes this time. "She said much the same thing."

I looked up at him in surprise. "Did she?"

"She did." He hesitated, and an odd, faraway expression came to his eyes. "Brynda, it's important that you and Sheryn get along together. Not just for my sake, but for your own sakes, and for the sake of Celi itself. There will come a time . . ." His voice trailed off into silence, and his eyes looked all blurred and black, only a thin ring of golden brown iris left. A frisson of fear rippled down my spine.

"There will come a time that *what* happens?" I asked softly. He didn't reply. I touched his arm, and he jumped as if startled. "Tiegan? What will happen?"

He frowned at me, puzzled. "I—don't quite know . . ." Slowly, the fey look in his eyes faded. His face cleared and he smiled. "There will come a time when you and Sheryn will team up to keep me under as tight control as Mai and Fiala keep Brennen," he said lightly.

I watched his face, but the odd expression had gone, and did not return. He merely stood smiling faintly at me. That shiver of apprehension crawled down my spine again, then it, too, was gone. Finally, I shook my head. "I doubt that would ever happen," I said. I nibbled on my thumbnail for a moment. "Tiegan, I'm going to go away for a while."

"Go away? But—"

"I've been having nightmares for the last fortnight or two," I said. "I thought it might have been because of this trouble with Sheryn, but now I know it's not. I want to go to Donaugh for a fortnight."

He nodded. "I see," he said.

I glanced up at him. I wondered if he really did. I wondered if he'd guess that mayhaps half my reason for wanting to go to Donaugh was my confusion about Kenzie's arrival as ambassador. But I had to find out about the nightmares. I looked down at my hands. A sudden image from my dream flashed through my mind. *White, bloodless bone* . . . I shook it off and looked at him again. "It will do me good to see Donaugh again. With your leave, I'll go tomorrow morning."

I dreamed again that night. Once again, firelight flared around the circle, flashing on gleaming white bone. It brought me out of sleep gasping for breath, and I couldn't relax into sleep again. I got out of bed, reaching for my bedgown, and again went out onto the terrace.

It seemed to me that lately I was spending more of my

nights on a terrace, contemplating nightmares, than I was spending in my bed. But Donaugh would be able to help me with this. If he couldn't help, then no one could.

A moon one night away from dark hung near the horizon. A scud of cloud hid the Huntress Star, but I knew she was there, relentlessly pursuing the moon. Tall pots of ornamental trees stood silvered in the faint moonlight, their budding leaves quivering gently in the soft breeze. I went to the wall and placed my hands on the cold stones, leaning far out over the wall, letting the cool breeze lift my hair and dry the sweat on my forehead and cheeks.

Someone moved across the dew-wet tiles toward me. I turned quickly, expecting Kenzie. But it was Sheryn, wrapped in a long, pale bedgown.

"Sheryn," I said. "You shouldn't be out here at this time of night. You'll catch a chill—"

She shook her head. "I'm warm enough in this," she said, brushing the back of her hand along the heavy folds of her bedgown. "I couldn't sleep. I was watching out the window and saw you come out here."

I smiled ruefully. "I couldn't sleep, either."

She bent her head and was quiet for a moment. "Do you think we might try to get along better?" She put out her hand to touch my arm. "Brynda, we may never become friends, but I truly hope that we might cease being enemies."

I laughed in wry amusement. "It would certainly be easier on all of us if we can manage that," I said. "Sheryn, I—I'm really pleased to hear about the child. I wish you a healthy child and all the joys of motherhood."

She stood for a moment, looking up at me, her eyes dark shadows in the moonlight. Then she smiled. "Thank you," she said. She turned and made her way back across the terrace to the chamber she shared with Tiegan.

I sighed, then went back to my own room. It was only an hour past midnight. I needed all the sleep I could get before I set out on my journey to Skai.

16

Donaugh's lodge nestled in a hanging valley high in the Spine of Celi. Behind it, towering crags of granite, snowcapped even in high summer, soared into the endless blue of the sky. The track I followed approached the lodge through a narrow pass between the shoulders of two mountains behind it. As I crested the rise, the lodge lay below me, trees crowded against the wall to the north, and a small checkerboard of garden fields hugged close to the south wall. In front of it, the valley plunged steeply down to the river below. Blossoms rioted on the fruit trees planted in a long row along the western edge of the garden, where they'd get the most sun. A man worked with a hoe in the garden, but I was too far away and couldn't make out who it was. Too young and supple to be Donaugh. It was either Llyr or Gwyn, but I couldn't tell which.

Donaugh had no servants at the lodge, save only Llyr and Gwyn, who weren't really servants. At one time, he'd had an old couple who looked after him and the lodge, but they had died many years ago, before I went to him for that year when I was twelve. Donaugh had lived alone until Llyr and Gwyn joined him. Unlike Tiernyn, he had never married. While Tiernyn was joyfully and thoroughly married to Ylana, Donaugh had always remained single. My mother said it was because the only woman he had ever loved died nearly twenty years before I was born. When I was young, I found it difficult to believe that a man as austere as Donaugh could ever love a woman so strongly and so deeply that he would never want another in her place. But since I grew up, and learned to know him better, I knew it was true.

As I got closer, I saw that it was Gwyn in the garden. He straightened and leaned on his hoe, shading his eyes with one hand as he watched me ride down the narrow track toward the house. He waved. I dismounted and led the mare carefully along the path, mindful of the young shoots thrusting out of the dark soil. Gwyn was fifteen, freckle-faced and apple-cheeked, his dark hair flying around his head in a tangle of unruly curls. He had grown since last I saw him, and his weight had not yet caught up with the spurt of growth, making him look whip-thin, almost gangly. His knobby wrists hung too far out of the cuffs of his shirt, but his grin lit his face the same way a lantern lights a window. Donaugh had more than once said that Gwyn's magic had the potential to be as strong as his own, but the boy was still learning how to use it properly. Well, he couldn't ask for a better tutor than Donaugh.

"Lady Brynda," he said, bowing slightly. "You are well come here. My lord Donaugh said you might be visiting today."

There was no sense in asking how Donaugh had known I was coming. Donaugh simply *knew* these things.

Gwyn dropped his hoe and reached for the reins. "Let me take care of your horse, Lady Brynda," he said. "My lord Donaugh is in the house. In the stillroom. He said for you to go right in."

The interior of the house was cool and fragrant with the scents of the herbs and medicinal plants hanging to dry from the beams in the ceiling. My eyes took a moment to adjust to the dimness after the brilliance of the sun outside, then I made my way through the main room and down the short hall to the small room across from the kitchen.

Donaugh stood at a table in the middle of the spotlessly clean room, pouring a dark, oily-looking liquid from a kettle into small bottles. He didn't turn as I entered.

"Bring me that basket of corks over there on the shelf under the window," he said, not missing a beat as he filled the bottles. "This has to be bottled and corked before it cools, or it might spoil."

I found the basket filled with tiny corks and brought it to the table. He poured the last of the liquid into the last bottle.

The final drop just filled the little bottle exactly. I could never tell if he used his magic to make things work out as precisely as that, but with him, it never failed.

"What is it?" I asked.

He pulled the basket toward him and tightly corked the first bottle. "Nothing special." He smiled at me, working quickly. "Just a tincture to ease a sore throat and tightness in the chest." He corked the last bottle and wiped his hand against his thigh, leaving a small dark stain on the pale fabric of his robe. "Now, suppose we find the ale Llyr placed in the spring to cool, and sit somewhere comfortable so we can talk, and you can tell me what's troubling you that brought you all this way."

So we talked. I told him about the nightmares that had disturbed my sleep for the past fortnight. He said nothing, but listened intently, a small frown creasing his forehead between his silvered eyebrows. When I told him about the dreams I'd had in Laringras, and how they seemed to resonate with the leader of the Maedun patrol leader that day in the mountains, the skin around his mouth paled and tightened, but still he said nothing. When I finally finished, he rose from his chair and went to the window.

Beyond the window, the mountain fell away steeply to the river valley below. He stood there, his left hand clasping his right wrist behind him, his head bowed. I don't think he was seeing the vast panorama of mountains and trees spread out below him.

Still without speaking, he turned and came back to stand in front of the chair where I sat. He placed two fingers gently on my temple and looked deep into my eyes. I have no idea what he saw there, but whatever it was, it caused him to nod slowly. He dropped his hand, and sat in his chair again.

"I believe you dreamed true," he said quietly. "Your Gift for the Sight seems to have strengthened since you were a child."

"The Sight?" I shuddered. "But what do the dreams mean,

Donaugh? The fleeing through the forest pursued by darkness? And the campfire consuming all but the bones of all of us?"

He shook his head. "I'm no more certain of the meaning than you right now," he said. "I'll have to think on it."

"Donaugh, I don't want this Gift. I don't *want* it!" I looked down at my hands, clenched into tight fists in my lap. "Can you take it away?"

Sympathy and understanding mixed with implacability in the planes and hollows of his face. "No, child, I can't," he said gently. "I can no more take it away than you can refuse it. You've been touched by Rhianna's hand, child. If she's with me, she'll tell me sooner or later what the dreams mean. Or she'll tell you. All we can really know now is that they mean that we have trouble ahead."

I shuddered again. "With the Maedun?"

"Who else would give us so much grief?" He looked out the window again at the expanse of mountains and sky. "But I think we shall survive them yet, Brynda," he said softly. "Many years ago, when I was younger than you are now, the *darlai* made me a promise at the Dance of Nemeara." A faraway expression crept into his eyes, and his voice became little more than a whisper, like the rustle of leaves in the wind. "*Three sons for you, Donaugh Secondborn. One son your bitterest enemy, one your staunchest ally, and one—*" He broke off abruptly and shook his head.

"And one son to do what?" I asked.

"It hardly matters now, child," he said briskly. "But sufficient to say that I was promised a line of kings to go forward until the stones of the Dance crumbled back into dust."

It was hardly a secret in the family that Aellegh, Celwalda of the Saesnesi in the Summer Run, was Donaugh's son by his love, Eliade. And it was no great leap of logic to place him as the staunch ally Donaugh had just mentioned. But I had never heard anyone speak of two more sons.

"Who are the other sons, Donaugh?" I asked.

"You've heard all the rumors about Mikal, Francia's son," Donaugh said.

I nodded.

He sat in the chair opposite me and looked around the comfortable room. "He was born right here, in this lodge," he said. "And he is my son, not Tiernyn's. We never confirmed or denied any of the stories. We thought it better that way. Francia thought she was seducing Tiernyn by magic when it was in reality me. We never bothered to disabuse her of the notion."

Hearing him speak so calmly of it sent a chill down my spine. Always before, Mikal had been nearly legend, not real. Suddenly now, he was very real indeed. ". . . Your bitterest enemy," I said softly.

"Aye, I'm afraid so."

"Why are you telling me this?"

He looked at me, his eyes wide and blurred, as if he were in a trance, unconscious of where he was, and who I was. "Because I believe you need to know this."

"And the third son, Donaugh?"

He shook himself like a man shrugging off a cloak. "I think I've spilled enough of my secrets into your lap for one day," he said. "It hardly matters, to be honest." He smiled again and got to his feet. "Now, as for your young Tyr, I believe you will simply have to get used to the idea that he's in love with you. Whether or not you accept his love and decide to return it is entirely up to you. But you must remember, being bheancoran certainly doesn't bar you from marrying, should you wish it."

"Marry him?" I stared up at him in shock. "After the way he deceived me?"

"In his mind, he was perfectly right," he said. "You think about that while I think about your dreams." He got to his feet. "Now, it's nearly dinnertime. Shall we see if we can coerce Llyr into preparing a meal for us? I'd hate to poison you with my own cooking."

*   *   *

If I dreamed that night, I didn't remember it on waking. Shortly after fast-breaking, I went out onto the mountainside carrying a basket and a small knife, with orders from Donaugh to collect as much snowberry root as I could find. The plants bloomed as the last of the snow melted around them, and by the time the new grass began to spring up, the flowers were gone. The tough, fibrous root was good for medicinal decoctions only after the pale flowers had withered and the small, bitter green berries had formed. If left until the berries had turned brown, the root could be poisonous.

I found a patch of snowberries in a small glade high above the lodge and set to digging out the roots. There seemed to be no hurry as I carefully stripped the berries from the plants and dropped them into the holes I'd made to dig out the roots. In the brilliance of the sun, the mist rising from the river swirled in ever-changing rainbows in the deep cleft of the valley below the lodge.

Far below me, on the track between the trees, something moved. I frowned and shaded my eyes with my hand, trying to see better. Donaugh didn't discourage visitors here, but he seldom had any, and no one except family would visit him without the courtesy of sending a messenger first to ask if a visit might be convenient.

I was too far away to see clearly, but I didn't think the rider on the track below wore the livery of a messenger. Then he passed out of the shadows of the trees into the open meadow above the lodge and drew his horse to a stop. He sat there, nearly motionless, looking out over the lodge and its gardens, a tiny dark figure against the green of the new leaves and grass. He seemed to be watching, waiting for something. It wasn't the way a courier or a visitor should act. He was too still, too watchful. That frisson of uneasiness shivered again along my spine.

He remained still for a moment or two, then shed his cloak and carefully folded it across his saddle. A dark shadow fell over him, shrouding him in sudden darkness. I looked up.

There were no clouds in the sky to block the sun. When he slipped the sword in the scabbard at his side and urged his horse forward, a spasm of cold dread closed around my heart. No Celae horseman wears a sword at his hip. It's too awkward, and the sword can tangle in the trees and undergrowth along the narrow tracks. I began to run.

I lost sight of him as I entered the forest above the lodge. Branches snagged at my hair and clothing as I ran through the trees. My foot caught on a protruding root, and I tumbled headlong into the damp carpet of last year's leaves, but I managed to bounce to my feet and run again. I thought my heart would tear itself loose from its moorings, and my breath came in harsh, gasping sobs. The trees hid the lodge; I couldn't see where the stranger was.

The north wall of the lodge enclosure loomed up through the trees ahead of me. I couldn't waste time running around it to the gate on the other side. I flung myself at the wall and scrambled up the rough stones. It was a drop of nearly two manheights to the ground on the other side into the soft, carefully cultivated soil of the herb garden. Between me and the house stretched a wide lawn, broken by plots of Donaugh's roses and a tangled grape arbor. There was no sign of the stranger.

I ran down the lawn. The sudden shade of the arbor blinded me for a moment, and I tripped over something lying on the lawn—something soft and yielding. The fall threw me to my hands and knees. I turned slowly to see what I had tripped over, not wanting to look, dreading what I would see.

Llyr lay facedown on the grass, his head pillowed on his crooked arm, as if he slept. Bright red stained the green of the lawn around his head, and I knew without touching him that he was quite dead. His throat had been cut so violently, the gaping wound was visible even as he lay on his belly. Llyr never carried a weapon. He'd had no chance to defend himself from the attack. This was brutal murder.

Oh gods. Donaugh . . . The stranger was after Donaugh.

I scrambled to my feet, my chest heaving as I tried to catch my breath. I had no weapon save the small knife I had been using to dig out the snowberry roots. My sword and my dagger were in the small chamber Donaugh had given me as a bedroom.

I found Gwyn a moment later, crumpled into a heap by the firewood he had been chopping when the stranger caught him. He still gripped the ax he had been using, but had obviously had no chance to use it as a weapon. His throat, too, had been cut.

The door to the kitchen stood open to the mild spring warmth. I drew the little knife from my belt and crept toward it. The kitchen was empty, but the quiet murmur of voices came from the main room down the short corridor. I pressed myself against the wall and moved silently down the corridor.

Donaugh lay on the floor beside the hearth, blood staining the back of his robe. For a moment, I thought he was dead, but he groaned, and pushed himself into a sitting position, his back propped against the stones of the fireplace wall. He held his face, pale as chalk, neutrally impassive, but I could see that he was in great pain. There was so much blood on his robe . . . The wound was a bad one, mayhaps even mortal.

The stranger knelt above him, a bloody dagger in his hand. I recognized him instantly. It was the same man I had seen disembarking from the ship that brought Kenzie to Clendonan. Only now, his eyes were a deep, flat black, not startling blue. Dark as his hair. And he was the same man who had led the troop of Maedun who had nearly killed Kenzie and me in the mountains of Laringras.

He was Maedun.

But how could it be? How could a Maedun be here in Celi? How could he have got through the curtain of enchantment?

Then I knew who he must be. Mikal, Francia's son by Donaugh through treachery. My cousin.

I had no weapon but the small dagger. But I had surprise acting for me. Mikal did not know I was there.

But Donaugh did. He glanced up and looked straight at me where I stood frozen in the hallway. His face gave away nothing, but before I could take a step, the air around me fizzed gently, and my skin tingled as Donaugh's magic folded itself around me in a masking spell.

No! He mustn't do this! He hadn't enough strength to protect me, and himself, too. I tried to move, but something held me fast. More of his magic. I struggled, but to no avail. Donaugh's spell held me frozen in place. I could do nothing but watch and listen helplessly.

Mikal knelt beside Donaugh, the dagger in his hand still red with blood—Llyr's blood and Gwyn's blood. And Donaugh's blood, too. He pressed the point to Donaugh's throat. A tiny bead of blood like a ruby swelled against the pallor of Donaugh's skin. Donaugh turned his head away, and Mikal laughed.

"My mother sent me to redress old wrongs, Enchanter," he said. "She bade me convey to you her greetings and her desire that you know we will kill all of you. And I will sit on the throne of Celi in my father's place."

Donaugh looked up at Mikal—at his son. "She would condemn you to a kinslayer's fate, would she?" he asked calmly.

"You are no kin to me," Mikal snarled. "I forswore my accursed Celae blood long ago."

"I am closer kin to you than you imagine," Donaugh said. "You may have forsworn your Celae blood, but you cannot deny it's there."

"It was good for getting me through your enchantment," Mikal said. "After my cousin showed me how to steal Celae magic. I regret that it wasn't your niece I took the magic from. I had thought her dead, but now I know she isn't, I'll take her magic later."

He drew back the dagger, then thrust it deep into Donaugh's chest. Donaugh slumped against the stones and the spell holding me faltered, then strengthened again. Mikal leapt to his feet and ran for the door. I would have cried out, but the spell held me silent.

I fought against the magic, struggling desperately to free myself from its constraints. Outside, the thunder of a horse galloping away from the lodge sounded loud in the stillness.

Quite suddenly, the spell dissolved. The magic snapping back into the flows of power in the earth and air around me stung my skin like nettles. The dagger was still in my hand, but Mikal was gone.

But Donaugh . . . Oh, gods. *Donaugh!*

I flung myself to my knees beside him, heedless of the bruising stones. Tears blurred my vision. I could hardly see as I reached out to him. Blood stained his robe, turning the pale brown fabric a ghastly crimson. More blood bubbled, bright red and frothy, around his lips.

Even I could feel all the empty numbness of a mortal wound within him as I pressed my hand to his chest. He opened his eyes, the vivid brown-gold clouded by pain as his life ebbed through the wound in his chest.

Helplessly, I held him against me as if by the strength of my arms alone I could hold his spirit in his body. "You shouldn't have protected me," I cried. "You needed your strength for yourself. You shouldn't have put the spell over me. Oh, gods, Donaugh . . . "

My heart hammered in my chest. Grief tore at my throat like the teeth of a northern silver wolf. His head settled against my shoulder, and he tried to lift his hand. I gripped it in mine. It was already cold, the fingernails taking on a bluish cast.

"Llyr and Gwyn?" he whispered.

"Dead," I said bitterly. "Mikal killed them."

"He has some Celae magic," he murmured. "I thought he was Llyr when he came in. A simple masking spell, and it fooled me. *Me*! How could I be so careless?" Pain flickered across his face—pain that had nothing to do with the great wound in his chest. "I couldn't let him see you. He wouldn't have killed you, Brynda. He'd have taken you to his bed, and only the gods know what your child by him might have been. I couldn't let that happen."

I shivered. "I wouldn't have let him take me," I said softly.

"You would have had little choice in the matter." He coughed, and a bubble of bright blood formed on his lips. "Brynda, you must warn Tiernyn." His voice sounded like the whisper of wind in dry grasses.

"Don't die," I pleaded. I was shaking so hard, I could hardly speak. "Oh, please, Donaugh. Don't die. We need you—I need you."

His fingers moved in mine, as if he were trying to grip my hand more firmly. But his strength—all the dazzling, brilliant flame of him—was nearly spent. "Brynda, child, you must warn Tiernyn," he repeated. Even with my ear close to his lips, I hardly heard him. "Without me, or Llyr and Gwyn, the curtain of enchantment will fall. The Maedun will come again."

"No," I sobbed. "I won't leave you. Please, Donaugh—Oh, please."

"You must go. Deity grant you will be in time." His weight against me seemed heavier, as if the last dregs of his resilience had drained from him. His head slipped forward until his brow pressed against the side of my throat. For a moment, I thought he was gone. I could no longer feel his breath fluttering against my skin.

Then he lifted his head and opened his eyes. And smiled. A radiant, joyous smile that lit his face and glowed in his eyes.

"Beloved," he murmured. The weight of his years lifted from him, and, for an instant, he appeared little older than I.

But he wasn't looking at me. He gazed intently at something or someone who stood behind me. He eased his hand out of mine and reached out.

"Beloved," he said again. "My Eliade—I've waited so long for you to come."

Startled, I looked behind me. There was no one there. Donaugh's hand fell back limply onto his knee. His body in my arms was suddenly lighter, almost buoyant. A long, shuddering breath quivered from his body and trembled against my throat. I felt his spirit leave him in a swift rush, as if he leapt eagerly to join what—or who—awaited him.

There was time only for a brief farewell to Donaugh, and to Llyr and Gwyn. I brought Llyr and Gwyn into the lodge and laid them beside Donaugh, covering all three of them with blankets taken from their beds. They looked so uncomfortable lying on the bare slate floor, but there was nothing more I could do for them. I knelt by Donaugh's shoulder and smoothed back the silver hair from his forehead, then bent to kiss him for the last time.

I left them there, all three of them, in the shelter of the main room of the lodge, the door tightly barred against predators. It was all I could do for them. I could not spare the time to bury them with proper honor, or to raise a cairn above their graves. But I wove three hoops for them and hung them on the door, the hoop for Donaugh decorated with a narrow braid of my own hair.

Tears blurring my vision, I found my horse and set out eastward, down out of the mountains, toward Dun Camus.

17

I hardly remember the wild ride down out of the mountains of Skai and across the downslands of Mercia. I stopped only to change horses at the army garrison posts along the road, each time leaving behind a horse half-dead from exhaustion. Night and day blurred together as I fled with my dire news to Dun Camus, and only the memory of Donaugh's brilliant smile at the end kept me from madness in my grief.

The gates of Dun Camus stood flung wide open in the early-spring sunshine as the horse stumbled through. The courtyard was alive with soldiers rushing purposefully between the barracks and the armory, their faces grim and taut with tension. A messenger spurred his horse away from the stables. My horse was too tired to get out of the way quickly, and he nearly ran us down. Someone hurried out to take the reins from me as I slipped out of the saddle to the cobble-stones. For a moment, I didn't think my knees would hold my weight, but strength came from somewhere, and I ran up the wide stone steps to the Great Hall.

The Great Hall was full of people. Tiernyn's five captains stood together by the hearth, talking urgently in low tones, but neither Tiernyn nor Tiegan was there. I ran past the captains and up the stairs to the second floor. Tiernyn's workroom was just above the Great Hall. The door was ajar. I burst in without knocking.

Tiernyn was alone in the workroom. He sat on a padded bench by the window, the greatsword Kingmaker across his lap. He stroked the blade absently as he stared out the window. When I entered, gasping for breath, he turned slowly to look at me. His face was contorted into lines of torment and distress. For the first time, I saw that he was old and tired. And afraid. His years weighed heavily on him as they never had before. I had never noticed the stoop in his shoulders before. Carefully, he laid the sword on the cushion and got painfully to his feet. The scar on the blade stood out glaringly black in the late-morning sun flooding through the window.

I had to hold on to the back of a chair to prevent myself from collapsing onto the polished wooden floor. "You know, don't you?" I said.

"That Donaugh is dead?" Sorrow wrenched his mouth into a twisted line. He glanced over his shoulder at the sword. "Yes, I know. Kingmaker told me." He looked at me again, his eyes bright with unshed tears. "How did it happen, Brynda?"

"Mikal," I said. "He killed Gwyn and Llyr, too."

"How did he manage to get through the curtain of enchantment? He's Maedun . . ."

I lifted one shoulder helplessly. "He's half-Celae. Donaugh's blood . . . Your blood. He learned how to steal Celae magic and work a masking spell with it. It fooled Donaugh's curtain of enchantment, and it fooled Donaugh, too."

He picked up Kingmaker and ran his finger along the runes engraved on the blade. "I told him we should have put that woman to death," he whispered. "Both her and that bastard she carried." He closed his eyes in pain. "But what kind of a king could order the death of a child? That would surely have shattered this sword." He traced the outline of the scar, his head bent so that his silver hair fell forward to hide his face. "He told me once that holding this kingdom together would cost me my life. I said then that a king's life was a small price to pay for a kingdom. I didn't realize that it would cost Donaugh his life, too. A high price . . ." He turned back to face me, his eyes bleak as lost hope. "My impulsive arrogance has come to haunt me, as he said it would."

I could not bear to watch his pain, resonating so closely as it did with my own. I closed my eyes and clung to the chair back, light-headed and giddy. I wanted to cry, but I was too exhausted. When finally I opened my eyes again, he had lowered the sword and stood watching me.

"The curtain of enchantment?" I asked.

"Down," he said. "Down and gone as if it had never been." He straightened his shoulders. The lines of his mouth firmed and once again he became the King I was familiar with, confident and certain in his power. "Even now, the Maedun fleet sails across the Cold Sea. We're preparing to meet them, as you will have already seen." He crossed the room to hang Kingmaker on its peg behind his worktable, then came to me and put his hand gently to my cheek. "You're exhausted, child," he said. "Go to your room and rest. Get some sleep. There's still time. You'll need your strength for what's to come."

I wanted to throw myself into his arms and weep like a baby. I had thought I had no more tears left in me, but the backs of my eyes stung. I blinked rapidly to dispel the tears and scrubbed my hands across my eyes. "Tiernyn?"

He raised one eyebrow.

"At the last . . . When Donaugh died . . . She came for him." I looked at him in wonder. Love that could reach from beyond Annwn like that was truly a miracle, and Donaugh had been truly blessed. "Eliade came for him. He went to her so joyously. And there was no pain. I felt no pain in him at all at the end. He was happy. Happy . . ." My voice broke, and I turned away so he could not see my tears.

"She has always been with him, I think," he said quietly. He put his hands to my shoulders and drew me around, holding me against his chest. He stroked my hair and murmured words that had no meaning, but soothed and eased the hurt. We stood like that for a long time, both of us near to drowning in our grief. Finally, I stepped away.

"I need to prepare," I said, my voice hoarse. "By your leave, my lord King."

Fiala came to my bedchamber shortly before midnight. I awoke to find her sitting on the edge of my bed, the shadow of her sword hilt rising abruptly behind her left shoulder. The faint glow from the brazier in the corner by the window limned the line of her cheek and brow with gold and red. Her eyes were only pools of darkness below her brows, and her mouth made a thin line of shadow above her chin. When she saw I was awake, she rose to her feet.

"Get dressed and come with me," she said quietly.

I flung back the bedclothes and sat up. "Where are we going?" I reached for my clothing.

"You'll see. Bring your sword. We'll need Whisperer for this."

She waited silently as I made haste to dress. I picked up Whisperer, and she led the way out into the corridor. Light spilled onto the polished wooden floor from under the door to Tiernyn's workroom. No light showed from Tiegan's workroom—the room that once was Donaugh's. As we passed, a young messenger darted down the corridor from the staircase and disappeared into Tiernyn's workroom. The murmur of many voices cut off sharply as the door closed behind him.

Fiala beckoned me to follow her. We dodged around officers and messengers on the wide staircase and made our way through the Great Hall. It was full of soldiers and officers. Young men in couriers' livery came and went swiftly, youthful faces grave and solemn with the enormity of the situation and the responsibilities of their tasks. The low and urgent murmur of voices ebbed and flowed throughout the room.

Dun Camus must have looked like this before the war with the Saesnesi was finally settled. Or the last time a Maedun invasion threatened Celi's shores. I shivered. Thirty-seven years ago. A whole generation had grown up since then not knowing what war was. Were there enough warriors left who remembered? Enough to lead us to victory? The only time I had used my sword in earnest was in Laringras, and that had been a shocking experience. How many of our soldiers had actually killed a man?

The courtyard was as crowded as the Great Hall. Torches

and candlelight flared brightly in the infirmary, where the Healers made ready to care for the inevitable burden of wounded. The doors to the main armory stood wide open, and men in farmers' dress came out carrying swords, shields, and bows. In houses all over Celi, women would be placing hoops of ivy in corner shrines and praying for the safety of sons, lovers, husbands, and brothers.

I shivered, even though the night air was warm and my cloak was of finest wool.

We went to the stables. One of the stableboys led out my mare and Fiala's gelding. We mounted, and Fiala led the way out of the palace gates and through the town.

The town was wide-awake, too. Lights gleamed in windows of all the houses we passed, and the open tavern doors blared music and frenetic laughter out into the night. We turned by the loom maker's shop and took the road leading down to a small gate in the town walls by the river.

The shrine of the Duality stood on a small headland a furlong beyond the gate. Twelve tall oaks surrounded it, transplanted from the forests along the foothills to the west. Ivy hung from the branches of the trees, making a softly swaying curtain. During daylight, the ivy threw ever-changing patterns of light and shadow against the pristine white walls of the shrine. Tonight, no moon shone, and the ivy whispered secrets in the gentle breeze.

We dismounted. Somewhere in the darkness beyond the oaks, a horse stamped and snorted.

"Why are we here?" I asked.

Without speaking, Fiala took the reins of my horse and led it away with hers. When she returned, she gestured to the door of the shrine. Puzzled now, I followed her up the path.

Inside the shrine, two torches burned on the altar, one to either side of the hoop of ivy representing the Unbroken Circle of birth, life, death, and rebirth. A stone bowl of water sat in the center of the altar, its smooth surface reflecting the torchlight in silky glimmers across the walls. Someone had placed a small bunch of hyacinth on the altar beside the hoop, and its sweet perfume filled the air. I looked at Fiala in question. But she said nothing.

Tiegan stepped out of the shadows beside the altar. Brennen stood behind him, cloaked in shadow. I recognized Kenzie beside him only because of his kilt and plaid.

"What is it?" I asked.

Tiegan held out his hand. "Come here, Brynda," he said.

I stepped forward. He took both my hands in his and bent down to kiss my cheek.

"We swore our oaths to one another as prince and bheancoran in a shrine like this one in Dun Eidon, in Skai," he said. "Tonight, we are on the brink of war, and I need you to swear me another oath."

I stiffened. "Tiegan, if you're thinking to release me from that oath—"

He laughed. "No," he said. "I could no sooner make you accept that than I could cause that river out there to flow uphill. Besides, I don't think this bond is breakable like that, do you?"

"No. I know it isn't."

He raised my hands to his lips and kissed first one, then the other. "We ride out to meet the Maedun soon," he said. "There's a very good chance that neither my father nor I will come back to Dun Camus when it's finished."

A lump of cold dread knotted beneath my heart. It was something I had refused to consider.

"I wish my father would stay here," Tiegan said. "He's getting close to seventy. Too old to be going to war. But trying to keep him home would be like trying to keep you from accompanying me." He smiled ruefully. "All of our family, stubborn as rocks."

I looked up and met his eyes steadily. "What do you want of me, Tiegan?"

"If I fall to the Maedun, and my father falls, the child Sheryn carries will be King of Celi." His grip on my hands tightened to forestall my protest. "I know a bheancoran seldom survives her prince if he dies in battle. I know that, and I know how you feel about your oath and our bond. But you must swear to me, Brynda, that if I fall, you'll not try to avenge me. For your sake, I would not have you follow me to Annwn— and for the sake of my father's kingdom."

I felt cold all over. The thought of his death—of the breaking of the bond—terrified me. "No, Tiegan," I whispered.

"Someone has to protect Sheryn," he said, his voice strained. "Someone has to protect the child and see that he's safe. It has to be you, Brynda. There is no one else I can trust with this task. You must see that she gets safely back to her people in Skai. The Tyadda will protect her there. And they'll see the child is properly raised."

I shook my head vehemently. "No, Tiegan. I won't leave you."

"I won't ask that you leave me while I live," he said. "But if I fall—"

"You won't! I'll be there, and so will Brennen and Fiala—" My face felt cold and sweaty in the night air. "Tiegan, I couldn't bear it if you died."

"Nor could I bear it if you died," he said. "But I'm asking you to bear the pain to see that my wife and my son are safe. It would be the last task I ask of you." He pulled my hands against his chest. The beating of his heart was strong and regular beneath the palms of my hands, vibrant and so very alive. "We may all survive this coming battle," he said softly. "We beat back the Maedun once before. Who's to say we can't do it again." But he knew, and I knew, that we'd had Donaugh's magic to help us then, and now Donaugh lay cold and still within the walls of his lodge high in the Spine of Celi. "Will you swear this for me, Brynda? It will make my going out to war all the easier for me if I know at least this is assured."

I looked up at him. He smiled at me, and the bond between us throbbed in my chest like the beating of my heart. "I'll swear," I whispered.

He let go of my hands and turned toward the altar. He drew his sword and laid it on the polished stone, then nodded at me. I loosed Whisperer from its sheath and placed it beside Tiegan's sword, Whisperer's tip against the hilt of his sword.

"Brynda al Keylan," Tiegan said clearly, "will you swear to me as bheancoran to the Prince of Celi that you will see my wife and unborn child safely to her kin should I fall in battle with the Maedun? Will you swear this before all the seven gods and goddesses, and before the Duality, and before these three witnesses, Brennen ap Keylan, Kenzie dav Aidan, and Fiala al Lluddor?"

I held out my right hand to him. He drew his dagger from his belt and nicked my palm just below my little finger. I stepped forward and let seven drops of blood fall on the altar by the ivy hoop, then held my hand over the bowl of water to let one more drop fall.

"I so swear before all the seven gods and goddesses, and before the Duality, and before these witnesses, and by the sword Whisperer." I reached out and picked up my sword. My blood smeared the hilt as I held the sword before me. I bent to kiss the cold stone of the altar, then turned to Tiegan. "I will protect your child with my life, Tiegan ap Tiernyn."

He put his hand over mine on Whisperer's hilt. "I accept your oath, Brynda al Keylan," he said softly. He let his hand drop to his side. "And I thank you."

Brennen stepped forward and put his hand over mine. "I stand witness to this vow," he said softly.

Fiala put her hand over mine. "I stand witness to this vow," she said. "And as bheancoran, I know the cost to you."

Then Kenzie came forward. His hand engulfed mine completely, warm and dry. "I stand witness to this vow," he said. I looked up at him, startled, and saw that he, too, knew how much this vow had cost me. He kept his hand over mine for a heartbeat longer than he should have. And when he removed his hand from mine, I felt the loss.

* * *

Shortly after dawn two days later, the Maedun came ashore on the south coast of Dorian. Even before messengers from Duke Gwilyadd of Dorian arrived at Dun Camus, our own lookouts reported the black smoke from the watchtowers smudging the southeastern sky. Before midday, Tiernyn's army rode out to meet the Maedun.

For the first time since they had bonded as prince and bheancoran, Queen Ylana did not ride to Tiernyn's left as the army marched to a battle. Tiernyn had flatly forbidden her to come because of her failing health. Ylana had not acquiesced without an argument, Tiegan told me, but finally gave in when she admitted that the fragility of her bones would never allow her to wield her sword properly, and it would distract Tiernyn to have to protect her. She bade him swift and safe return with tears in her eyes, and his own eyes had been suspiciously bright and wet.

Tiegan rode to his father's left under the Red Hart banner, and I rode to Tiegan's left. Behind us, Brennen and Fiala rode at the head of a column of yrSkai soldiers, Kenzie riding to Brennen's right. It hadn't surprised me when Kenzie insisted on accompanying us. He was perfectly correct when he commented laconically that every extra sword in the battle was an extra asset. I had seen him use that sword, and was glad that his skill and strength were on our side.

The army stretched out behind us in broad columns of mounted men, all carrying spears, swords and shields, or the wicked, deadly little recurved bows of the Veniani. It was an impressive sight. Vast billows of dust rose in a haze like smoke around thousands of mounted soldiers. Sunlight glinted on armor and bridle metal, swords and shields.

Men of every province filled the ranks of the army—men out of the mountains of Skai and Wenydd, men from the lush pastures of Dorian, men from the farms and mines of Mercia, from the downs and fens of Brigland, and from the fishing villages of Venia. The Saesnesi of the Summer Run rode behind their Celwalda, Aellegh, all of them big men, as big as Kenzie, blond and strong, carrying the war axes and broadswords that had made them such fearsome and awe-inspiring enemies before Tiernyn and Elesan made the peace between our two peoples.

I had never seen so many soldiers together at one time. One of Tiernyn's laws stated that every man between the ages of sixteen and forty-five had to train for three months of the year with the army and maintain at least one horse capable of carrying him into battle, but it wasn't until I saw them all together like this that I realized what it meant. Every farmer, every merchant, every herder and miner in Celi could become a soldier on a matter of a few hours' notice.

They had all come when Tiernyn called.

To the outside of the wide column, close to the five captains, rode a small company of mages, who could weave the sunlight into mirrors, as Torey had woven mirrors during the first Maedun invasion. We had learned our lesson well back then. Gentle Tyadda magic could not be used to kill, but it could direct a Maedun warlock's magic back upon himself, and burn him to ashes in a flash of his own reflected blood sorcery.

But no one knew if that same magic could turn Hakkar's blood sorcery back upon him. And we no longer had an enchanter of Donaugh's caliber to fight Hakkar.

The sun was warm on my back, but not warm enough to dispel the chill of apprehension and fear that knotted under my ribs. Whisperer sang softly on my back. All the Rune Blades had been crafted for one purpose only—to defend Skai and Celi. In the hands of my grandmother Kerri, and her father before her, and his mother before him, Whisperer had tasted enemy blood. It seemed anxious and eager to taste Maedun blood in defense of Celi. I was not so eager. I'd had a taste of blood sorcery from Francia. The thought of Hakkar of Maedun's blood sorcery frightened me cold. I couldn't help wondering how much stronger it would be than his aunt's magic.

I glanced at Tiegan, who rode beside me. Nothing showed on his face, but the bond between us shimmered with uneasiness and disquiet. I couldn't tell if it was his or mine. He watched his father, and I watched him. And Kenzie, when he thought I wasn't looking, watched me.

I had the unholy urge to break into hysterical laughter. All of us watching the others, worried about what showed on our faces, hoping none of us looked as apprehensive as we felt. Was this how soldiers always felt?

And at the head of the army, Tiernyn rode alone, his face etched by the weight of his grief for his brother and his concern for the lives of the men he led, and for the country he ruled.

18

We met the Maedun army in a broad valley in the heart of the Dorian peninsula. A small burn wound its way through the lush grass of the valley floor, a thin thread of water that reflected the silver-blue of the sky. They had chosen their site well, and waited for us. They stood on higher ground, and the footing in the valley was firm and solid for both men and horses. The hillside on the other side of the valley was black with the massed Somber Riders. They ranged along the crest of the hill and spilled halfway down the sides, neat ranks of men in long, orderly files. Thousands of them. No flashes of sunlight glinted off bright metal. From here, even shields and swords looked black.

It was still early spring, only a little less than two fortnights since Vernal Equinox, yet the day seemed borrowed from Midsummer. Overhead, the sky arched in an endless blue dome, and small, puffy clouds scudded ahead of a warm wind that smelled of the rich, awakening earth, of new grass and wildflowers, and the sea. The sun was warm, nearly a tangible weight on the skin of my cheeks. From somewhere close by, a skylark filled the air with joyous song, and, in the distance, the plaintive cry of seagulls sounded sweet and clear. It seemed impossible that death would come to so many on such a soft, spring day. How could it happen that those black ranks of Maedun Somber Riders stood on Celae soil when the new life of the country was surging all around us?

Above us, the standards snapped and rippled in the wind off the sea, the colors preternaturally bright under the soft blue of the sky—Tiernyn's red hart leaping across its green field, the white falcon of Skai against its blue background, the white boar of the Summer Run on its field of red, Wenydd's gold mountain cat. Across the valley, only one banner stood in the wind, white on black. I was too far away to make out the device, but I knew it. I had seen it in a badge on Mikal's tunic—Hakkar's white badger on a field of dead black.

I glanced at Tiernyn. The King had walked his horse out ahead of the first ranks and sat with his wrists crossed over the pommel of his saddle as he considered the Maedun army. The years of his Kingship had given him a regal nobility that he wore as naturally as he wore his own skin. In his youth, he'd built his reputation as a clever and canny tactician and strategist. He'd lost little, if any, of that skill. He studied the enemy, his face calm and thoughtful, his eyes shrewd and appraising. Finally, he nodded and turned his horse back. He drew up alongside Tiegan.

"They want us to make the first move," he said. "Draw us down into the valley so they can sweep down on us like wolves on a fold of sheep. Tell the captains to deploy their men along the crest of the hill here, and pass the word that we wait for them. We can afford to wait longer than they can." A spark of his former humor glinted in his eyes. "Our lines of supply are far shorter."

So we waited.

We waited until I had to grind my teeth with effort to prevent myself charging down the hill just to get this *over* with. Which, I suppose, was exactly the reaction Hakkar's army wanted from us.

Then, between the space of one heartbeat and the next, the waiting was over. The dark line across the valley began to move, slowly and ponderously at first, but gaining speed and momentum as they poured down the hillside. They came at us, their ranks neat and precisely straight, each rider moving in unison with the next. The gray-clad warlocks held back, spaced evenly along the hillside. The black ranks of Somber Riders flowed around them as the water of a river flows around a rock in the streambed.

Details stood out with carved, chiseled clarity. I looked up and saw Mikal riding in the center of the first rank. It seemed as if he looked straight at me, and a red ember burned deep in the blackness of his eyes. His lips drew back from his teeth in a grin of feral anticipation, and the blade of the sword he carried absorbed all the light, spilling darkness around him as a broken flask spills wine.

I tore my gaze away from Mikal and looked at the King. Tiernyn raised Kingmaker and held it high above his head. He held the heavy blade steadily. It gleamed in the sun as he watched the approaching Maedun with calm detachment. Then, when the first of the dark ranks were halfway down the hill, Kingmaker flashed down. The companies of archers on the outsides of our ranks readied their deadly little recurved bows, nocking arrows and waiting for the signal from their captains.

Even as the archers raised their bows, the red glow of sorcery grew in the hands of the Maedun warlocks—the magic that could turn our own weapons back upon us. But our mages were ready. The air shimmered as they fashioned mirrors out of woven strands of sunlight and sent them winging swiftly across the valley. The bright shields found their targets and fully half of the warlocks vanished into drifts of floating ash, incinerated by their own reflected blood sorcery.

But the Somber Riders kept coming. I didn't see the signal, but suddenly the sky was dark with arrows as all the Veniani bowmen fired at once. The air rang with the musical sound of their bowstrings. The front rank of the charging Maedun broke as men and horses tumbled under the rain of arrows.

Tiernyn raised his sword again. It slashed down. Our own charge began, and I had no more time to think.

I remember noise—incredible noise. Men shouting and screaming. The wild, ululating war cries of the yrSkai and the yrWenydd shivering the air. The thunder of horses' hooves across soft spring soil. The rattling clash and clangor of weapon meeting weapon or shield. And above it all, the raucous, greedy squawking of the ravens, the carrion eaters waiting eagerly to feast on broken and bleeding flesh.

Terror shuddered along the bond between Tiegan and me. Mine, I think, for he glanced at me across the flying mane of his horse. He gave me a fierce, hard grin, and I suddenly recognized the sensation flashing and leaping under my heart. Not terror. I was mistaken. No, not terror at all, but excitement. The same blood-pounding, breath-quickening rush of exhilaration that looking over a steep, high cliff slams through the body. I found myself laughing aloud as we swept down that hill. I had never felt so alive! Every muscle, every sinew, every nerve fiber of my body vibrated, taut and eager. Whisperer sang in my head, its song wild and high and clear above the cacophony, its music and magic tingling through the blood and bone of my arm and hand. In my hand, each separate ridge of the pommel was sharply and clearly defined.

The Maedun ranks broke and swirled in confusion, and I lost track of everything but guarding Tiegan's left side. Whisperer rose and fell, rose and fell in my hands, chopping, hacking, slicing into black-clad flesh and bone, almost as if the sword itself and not I commanded the arm that wielded it. My horse, superbly trained for this, seemed to read my mind, anticipating the pressure of my knees to guide it. Somehow, I managed to stay hard against Tiegan's side in the right position to guard him as we fought together as one unit.

Two bright flashes in rapid succession startled me, and I looked around quickly in time to see two more gray drifts of ash floating on the breeze. Beyond the drifting clouds of ash, a black mist billowed up from behind the crest of the hill, darkening the sky. It rolled down the gentle slope of the hill against the wind, and settled around the struggling men and horses in the valley. Our mages sent more of their woven sunlight mirrors against it, but they crumbled into useless shards of brilliance that sparked for an instant in the black mist then winked out, swallowed completely by the blood sorcery. One by one, then in droves, the Celae soldiers froze into listless, glazed apathy as the black mist engulfed them.

The air thickened around me as the foul black mist closed

in. It wrapped itself in snaking tendrils around my throat, suffocating and strangling. Cold as lost hope, it fastened itself to my soul, draining my strength and my will, replacing my lifeblood with its own smothering void. I coughed, choking and gagging on the loathsome stuff, tasting death against the back of my tongue. Fingers of mist closed around my heart, squeezing until each labored breath was agony.

But I had fought against Francia's blood magic. I fought against Hakkar's. Lifting Whisperer took a massive effort of will, but I could do it. And I could bring the blade down against the Maedun soldier who lunged at Tiegan's back. Tiegan seemed to move as if he were underwater, but he shook off the cloying, enervating miasma and fought hard, while around us on the battlefield the men of Celi lowered their weapons and sat motionless.

But many of the men of Skai still fought, clustered in a tight defensive circle around Tiernyn. The effort it cost them showed clearly on their faces, but they struggled against the debilitating magic, and Somber Riders fell to their swords.

A wedge of charging Somber Riders swept through the black mist, swords raised, carelessly thrusting aside the milling throng of bespelled Celae soldiers as if they weren't worth the effort it would take to kill them. Mayhaps they weren't. They could offer no resistance. At the apex of the wedge rode Mikal, his eyes gleaming with that eerie red spark, the black sword he carried spilling darkness all around him.

I cried out a warning, and turned to meet them. From the corner of my eye, I saw Tiegan begin to swing around, still moving with painful slowness. My horse stumbled, then went down, its throat torn out by a black sword. I flung myself clear of the tumbling horse and landed with my shoulder tucked, rolling beneath the flying hooves of the Maedun horses. Desperately, I hung on to my sword and tried to duck. I rolled up against something—my dead horse, I think—and curled myself small against it. I wasn't quick enough. Something hard—a Maedun horse's hoof?—clipped against the side of my head, stunning me. The world went dim and vague and far away, and the black mist wrapped itself tightly around my heart.

From then on, I remember only impressions, each as sharp and clear as a fresh painting on a wall, but separate and distinct. I had difficulty connecting them to something that had anything to do with me, or with those I knew and loved. My world shattered before my eyes, and all I could do was huddle against the dead horse's belly and watch helplessly.

. . . Kenzie stared at me, blank and impassive, his greatsword hanging from his limp hand by his leg. No spark of intelligence lit his eyes, and his mouth hung slackly open. Blood dripped into his eye from a wound above his eyebrow, but he made no attempt to wipe it away. It smeared the side of his face, matting the hair by his cheek. The wedge of Somber Riders swerved around him and he disappeared behind a mass of dark figures.

. . . Aellegh fought alone among his bespelled and apathetic Saesnesi warriors, unaffected by the strangling black mist. His face suffused with rage, he stood his ground, one hand swinging his deadly short sword, the other hacking with his Saesnesi war ax. His wheat-blond hair flew wildly about his face, gleaming like gold in the sun.

. . . Brennen urged his horse closer to Tiernyn, his face grim and set, teeth clenched with effort. He swung Bane, our father's sword, and a bright spray of blood gouted from the throat of a black-clad rider. The Maedun bled red as the Celae did.

. . . Fiala struggled to remain at Brennen's side, her blue-black hair matted with blood, her intensely blue eyes glittering with the light of battle-madness. One arm hung limp at her side, ropes of blood congealing along the back of her hand. She controlled her horse only by knee pressure, and if she felt the pain of her wounds, it didn't stop her.

. . . Mikal slashed his way straight toward Tiernyn, the red gleam of his eyes bright and smoldering like a coal in the dark ash of a brazier. His black cloak billowed around his shoulders, the stark white emblem of Hakkar's badger sharply etched against the black fabric.

. . . Tiegan turned slowly and painfully to meet Mikal, his mouth wide in a shout I couldn't hear, his greatsword gleaming as it sliced through the thick miasma of the blood sorcery around him. He spurred his horse forward and threw himself into Mikal's path between our cousin and Tiernyn. Mikal's sword sliced down and under Tiegan's sword. The blade bit deeply into Tiegan's side. Blood poured down onto Tiegan's thigh and the leather of his saddle as Mikal yanked back his sword. Tiegan's eyes went glassy and blank. He slumped forward across the pommel of his saddle, then toppled to the ground and lay in a crumpled heap as Mikal's horse leapt over him toward Tiernyn.

. . . Tiernyn raised the greatsword Kingmaker, grief and rage suffusing his face. He spurred his horse forward recklessly to meet Mikal's charge. Kingmaker glowed faintly amid the smothering mist, but the black scar near the shoulder seemed to absorb the glow and swallow it as Tiernyn swung the blade at Mikal's body. Mikal ducked under the wild swing and brought his sword up to meet Kingmaker. The two swords, brightly glowing blade and lightless black one, met in a blinding and soundless explosion of cold light.

. . . Kingmaker shattered.

. . . Tiernyn stared in horror at the truncated blade. It had broken cleanly along the scar several inches below the handguard. The tip of the blade fell, burying the point into the trampled grass. The horror on Tiernyn's face turned to rage. He snatched the dagger from his belt and lunged at Mikal.

. . . Mikal thrust forward with his sword. The blade slipped easily under Tiernyn's dagger and outstretched arm, and plunged deep into the King's belly. His eyes ablaze with the fire of his rage, Tiernyn dropped Kingmaker's hilt and his dagger, and reached up to grab the blade of Mikal's sword. The edges of the blade cut into his hands, but he held it tight, and Mikal could not yank the sword back out of the King's body.

... Screaming incoherently, her face twisted in fury, Fiala spurred her horse, riding straight at Mikal. She used her sword like a lance. The point entered Mikal's body just above the small of his back, and came out below his collarbone. Mikal screamed in pain. Fiala pulled her sword back, and a gout of blood burst from Mikal's mouth. He and the King fell to the crushed grass together.

19

The King's death shocked me out of my stupor, and I found I could move again. Too numb for grief, or pain, or fear, I crawled on hands and knees to Tiegan, who lay sprawled beneath his horse. The fight had moved swiftly away from us, back through the ranks of the yrSkai, who still battled both Hakkar's spell and the Maedun soldiers. Only the dead surrounded us, still and quiet under the soft spring sky, making a pocket of incongruous peace within the horror of the battlefield. Even the sounds of battle were muted and faint now.

Tiegan lay on his back, open eyes staring up at the endless blue of the sky. No breath stirred in him. He lay so very still and quiet, and somehow diminished, as if the land that had nurtured him and given him life had already begun to take him back into its womb. The breeze gently riffled his hair, which shone bright gold in the sun. A lock had fallen forward across his forehead and lay against his pale skin, curling around to frame one eye.

I knelt beside his shoulder and reached out to brush the stray lock of hair away from his eye. My hand trembled so violently, I had to try twice before I could find the hair. It was like silk against my fingers, but lifeless now, all its resilience gone, as if it had drained into the earth with Tiegan's blood.

Someone was making horrid little raspy sounds of pain, a terrible, gasping keening that tore at my head like claws. It was a long time before I realized it was my own voice. I put up my hand to cover my mouth to stop those appalling noises. Great, shuddering waves of horror flooded through me; I couldn't control the trembling in my limbs. Pain tore through my belly. It felt as if my heart and my guts had been torn physically from my body, leaving a huge, yawning void, black and empty as the pits of Hellas. For a moment, I thought I would die from the intensity of just the pain itself.

Tiegan was dead. My prince was dead, and I still lived. That was wrong. *Wrong.* I should have died with him. I should have given my life to protect him, but I had stayed crouched in a helpless huddle while my prince was cut down. It was *wrong!*

My sword. Where was my sword? I had to avenge him . . .

I stared stupidly at the sword I still held clutched in my right hand and couldn't remember drawing it. Blood smeared the knuckles of my hand, livid against the white of my skin.

But I hadn't sheathed Whisperer since we began our ill-fated charge. I had managed to hold on to it during my tumble from my horse, and even while I crouched, stunned, as the Maedun rode over us.

I looked around frantically, searching for an enemy. But they were gone—out of sight. Even the bespelled Celae soldiers had drifted away. Nothing was left where I knelt beside Tiegan's body but more dead. Brennen was gone, as was Fiala. So was Kenzie. Were they dead? Or just vanished into the confusion?

Gradually, I became aware of Whisperer's song murmuring softly in the back of my mind—a low, keening wail in a mournful minor key. I couldn't tell whether the sword trembled in my hand, or my hand trembled on the hilt.

It didn't matter. Tiegan's blood cried out for revenge. And Whisperer echoed the need.

I looked down at my prince again. His brown-gold eyes stared through me, beyond me into the vast emptiness of the sky. Another wave of pain washed through me, bending me double in agony. Breathing itself was torment. I pressed my forehead to my knees and clenched my teeth to stop the terrible whimpers coming from my throat.

Oh, gods, how could this happen? How could he be taken from me like this? How could it be that I still lived while he lay dead? How could I go on living without him? Without the bond that had been such an integral part of me for most of my life?

I couldn't live now. I had nothing to live for. My soul lay dead on the ground before me, and I could not live without him.

You have a vow to fulfill, Brynda al Keylan. Tiegan's voice murmured softly in my head.

Badly startled, I jerked upright, staring down at him. But he had not moved, nor had he spoken. At least not aloud.

You swore a vow to me in the shrine. Now you must keep it.

"How can I leave you here like this?" I whispered.

You swore a vow to me . . .

"But I didn't know I'd have to leave you to keep it . . ." I reached out again to touch his hair—his beautiful dark gold hair. Lifeless now. As lifeless as his staring eyes. "Tiegan, how can I leave you?"

You swore me a vow . . .

The sword in my hand quivered, and again I felt the stickiness of my blood on the pommel from the nick Tiegan had made in my palm. I laid Whisperer in the grass beside Tiegan and slowly raised my hand to look at my palm. The red line of the small cut just below my little finger was already nearly healed, but it throbbed. Reminding me. Rebuking me for not remembering.

I could hardly see through the tears that welled up in my eyes. "I could not protect you, Tiegan ap Tiernyn," I said softly. "But I swore to protect your son, and I will die before I let anything harm him. This I swear to you again."

Never in my life before had I done anything so difficult as the simple act of getting to my feet beside my prince's body, and I never will again. Every instinct, every ingrained habit screamed at me to stay with him, to follow him to the blessed shores of Annwn. But how could I present myself to the Counter at the Scroll and declare my days counted and totaled when there was a vow I still must fulfill?

But I couldn't leave him like this, lying defenseless on the trampled and bloody grass . . . I fell to my knees again beside him and bent to kiss his pale, chill forehead. I closed his eyes gently and folded his hands on his breast, then pulled the cloak from my shoulders and wrapped it around him.

His bloodstained sword lay some distance away, where it had fallen when Mikal killed him. His wasn't a Rune Blade, but it was good Celae steel, forged in Skai, slaked in the waters of a clear mountain stream. No, not a Rune Blade. He had always expected to inherit Kingmaker one day. And now Kingmaker lay shattered beside the dead King, and the King's son inherited nothing but a place among the dead beneath a sky filled with ravens.

I picked up his sword, carefully cleaned it on my cloak, and laid it beside him. It was all I could do.

"May your soul be brightly shining, Tiegan ap Tiernyn, beloved cousin, so the Duality find you swiftly, and may the Counter at the Scroll be pleased with the glowing tally of your days. Be at peace, my Prince."

Dizzy and giddy, I picked up my sword and got to my feet again. My head pounded and throbbed, and I nearly fell, but caught my balance by using the sword like a walking stick. I looked around. Ten paces away, the King and Mikal lay tangled together in death. Kingmaker's blade stood, point buried in the soil, near Tiernyn's head, as if it marked his place. The hilt with its six inches of blade lay near his outstretched hand. It had broken cleanly along the line of the scar. But no black remained on either piece of the blade. The runes flashed and flared along the blade, but I could not read them. No one can read the runes on a sword not one's own. I knew what they said, though. I'd heard the phrase so often, I could almost trace each letter cut into the blade like facets of a gem.

Take up the Strength of Celi.

But there was no strength left in Celi now. None left in Kingmaker itself.

Donaugh had predicted the sword would let Tiernyn down when his need of it was greatest. His need—the need of all

Celi—had been greatest on this day, and the Kingsword lay broken on the field of our greatest defeat.

A cold, uncanny calm settled over me. I shut out the screaming pain clawing at my belly and chest, shut out the ghastly emptiness left by the severing of the bond. Time enough later to deal with that. Right now, I had tasks to perform.

I went to Tiernyn and gently unfastened his cloak. It was of rich, scarlet wool, embroidered at the hem with gold thread in a pattern that left an intricate network of red harts outlined in gold filigree leaping across the bottom of the fabric. I picked up both pieces of the broken sword and laid them on the cloak. He very seldom wore his crown, but his gold torc gleamed at his throat, the finials shaped like the heads of harts with eyes of bluest topaz. I knelt beside him and unfastened it, then wrapped it along with the two pieces of Kingmaker in the cloak. His grandson would have need of them, and by the torc would the Celae know him when he grew to be a man.

Finally, as a last act of respect and love, I smoothed the matted silver hair back from his forehead and closed his eyes. "May your soul be brightly shining, Tiernyn ap Kian, so that the Duality find you swiftly, and may the Counter at the Scroll be pleased with the golden tally of your days. You accomplished so much for your country in so little time. Be at peace, my King."

Tiegan's horse stood quietly near his body, its reins dangling on the ground. It looked around as I approached, but didn't try to move away as I tied my bundle to the back of its saddle. I had little time left. Hakkar's army might already be riding for Dun Camus. I had no doubts at all that he would want to take the palace as his own, as a symbol of his victory. I had to get to Dun Camus before he did, and get Sheryn away.

I shortened the stirrup straps, then swung into the saddle, taking one last look around the battlefield. Celae dead and Maedun dead lay together on the churned and trampled grass. Already the ravens had descended to take their feast, but there was nothing I could do about that. This place—called Cam Runn for the little burn that threaded through the shallow valley—would forever be burned into the memory of all Celae as a place of infamy.

Hakkar's army would, I thought, stay with the road to Dun Camus. I set out across the fields, riding as swiftly as I could without killing the horse beneath me. One person could surely make better time than a whole army, especially if that army had to pause several times to take care of isolated pockets of resistance. I didn't think that Hakkar would waste his powers on the scattered remnants of our army, if any of them still remained.

I arrived early in the morning, to find Dun Camus nearly deserted. Most of the houses and shops in the town stood abandoned and empty. I didn't know where anyone could find safety from Hakkar's blood sorcery, but I wished the people of Dun Camus what shelter they could find.

News of our defeat had already reached the palace. The small defensive garrison under the command of an aged Lluddor ap Vershad, Fiala's father, remained to guard the palace. Most of the servants had fled with the news of the coming of the Maedun army. Only a few had stayed, those who had nowhere else to go. Lluddor himself opened the gates for me.

"Lady Brynda," he cried in surprise. "But where is Prince Tiegan?"

My face felt made of stone as I dismounted and threw the reins of the horse to him. "Dead," I said shortly.

"Dead? But you live . . . "

"I live because I made a vow to Tiegan."

He nodded, his face grave. Lluddor understood vows. He had been among the first to swear support for Tiernyn, one of the first Companions of the *Corrach* before Tiernyn was raised to be King.

"Where is the lady Sheryn?" I asked.

He gestured with his chin toward the palace. "In the solar, I believe."

I nodded. "Thank you." I started to run up the steps, then turned and looked down at him. "Lluddor, old friend, when the Maedun army arrives, throw open the gates for them. You cannot stand against Hakkar's blood sorcery, and I would not have any more deaths this day."

Shock spread across his face. "Surrender the palace?" he asked, his voice scratchy and hoarse.

"Yes. Surrender the palace. You cannot know the horror of that blood sorcery. It drains the soul . . ." I shuddered. "We may be forced to surrender now, Lluddor, but every Celae soldier who survives this day may live to fight another. There will come a day when we shall have need of them."

For a moment, I thought he would spit in disgust onto the cobblestones at his feet, but he nodded. "I see the wisdom in what you say," he said softly. "You should know that a messenger arrived just before you did. The Maedun are less than two leagues away. They'll probably be here within the hour."

"Oh, gods . . ." I spun and ran up the steps.

The Great Hall was deserted except for one servingwoman who calmly went about the task of replacing the candles in their brackets along the walls. I took the stairs two and three at a time up to the second floor.

Sheryn was not in the solar, nor was she in the quarters she had shared with Tiegan. I ran frantically along the corridor, flinging open doors and calling her name. Not until I came to Tiernyn's chambers did I find her. I called her name again, and heard her answer from within the bedchamber.

She sat on the edge of the bed, her head bowed, holding Ylana's hand in both of hers. The Queen lay fully dressed on the bed, her hair spread like a silver cloud across the embroidered linen of the pillow. Her face was pale as chalk, her lips blue. Even from the doorway, I could tell she was dead.

On their own, my hands clenched into helpless fists by my

sides. But I had no more room in me for added grief. I knew what had killed Ylana. Knew it as surely as I felt the tearing pain of the severed bond in my own chest and belly, in my own spirit. Ylana had followed her king to Annwn as a bhean-coran should. I could feel no pity for Ylana, no sorrow. She had found the peace I could not seek. I envied her the serenity that showed on her face.

Sheryn looked around as I entered. Her eyes were swollen and red, her face stained with her tears. She stared at me uncomprehendingly.

"She was out on the battlement walk every day," she whispered. "Every day after the army left. And I was with her. We waited there. Just waited. For some word of the battle, you understand. But we got no word. Nothing at all. Then two days ago, she gave a great cry and collapsed. I couldn't stop her falling to the stone. We carried her here, and she died just an hour before dawn this morning."

I went to the bed. Sheryn's hands were locked around Ylana's. I had to pry her fingers loose. Shock, fear, and grief widened Sheryn's eyes. I doubted she even realized who I was or what was happening.

"Sheryn, we have to get out of here," I said gently. "The Maedun are coming."

"Yes, I know," she said in a childish, singsong voice, like a small girl. She pulled her hand from mine and smoothed the skirt of her gown. "They're coming, and they're almost here."

"Yes, they're almost here. We have to get away, Sheryn. Now."

She tilted her head and looked up at me. I had seen that expression on the faces of people walking in their sleep. "Tiernyn's dead," she told me gravely. "And Ylana's dead because the breaking of their bond tore her heart out." She frowned as if trying to remember something important. "And Tiegan's dead, too. My husband is dead." She placed her hand over her belly, which was still flat and trim. "My child has no father . . ." She looked up at me, puzzled. "But if Tiegan's dead, how is it you live?"

I went to my knees on the floor before her and put both my hands to her face. "Sheryn, you have to snap out of this," I said forcefully. "Tiegan is dead, yes. He's dead, and the child you carry will be King of Celi. I swore to him that I'd see you safely to your people back in Skai."

She smiled. A brilliant, empty smile. "Yes. My child will be King . . ."

I saw no other means of bringing her out of her daze. I slapped her cheek as hard as I could. The imprint of my hand came up livid red outlined in white on her soft, smooth skin. She drew back, shocked at first, then angry. But life came back to her eyes.

"How *dare* you strike me!" she cried.

"Sheryn, the Maedun are nearly here," I said, deliberately cold and cruel. "If they find you, they will most certainly kill you, and they will kill your child. We must get out of here right now if you are to live to give birth to the child who will be King of Celi. Do you understand me?"

She put both hands to her face and took a deep, shuddering breath. When she dropped her hands, resolve had firmed her face.

"Of course," she said quietly. "Forgive me, Brynda. Your pain must be as deep as mine."

"Go to your chambers and change into something you can ride in. Bring a warm cloak and a weapon if you've got one. I'll meet you in the solar in a few minutes."

She nodded and rose to her feet. I left her in the corridor and ran to my own room. I wanted another cloak, myself. The nights were cold in the mountains of Skai, even in the height of summer.

The windows in my bedchamber faced out across the gates of the palace. I dropped my bundle on my bed and glanced out at the road as I ran to my clothespress. My heart nearly stopped.

The Maedun were already here.

A long column of soldiers moved purposefully up the road through the town. At the head of the column, beneath the white badger banner, rode two people. I didn't recognize the man, but I knew he had to be Hakkar of Maedun, the man who had vowed vengeance on all of Celi for the death of his father, and his grandfather. Beside him rode a woman, her flamboyant red gown and royal blue cloak garishly bright against the unrelieved black of the army behind her. I knew her.

It was Francia.

And I had run out of time.

20

I don't know how long I stared out the window in blank, helpless dismay. All I knew was that I could not take Sheryn out through that throng of Maedun soldiers. Even in the confusion, there would be little chance of slipping past them. And only the gods alone knew what they might do to a pair of women. I'd heard stories about what happened to women who caught the Maedun soldiers' fancy in Isgard, and Falinor, and Saesnes when they invaded. They weren't pretty stories. I didn't want that to happen to me. Or especially to Sheryn.

As I watched, Hakkar and Francia rode into the courtyard. A company of several score soldiers entered behind them and spread quickly around the courtyard. The massive gates swung closed behind them, shutting out the remainder of the Maedun army. They dispersed in an uncannily orderly fashion around the town.

Hakkar dismounted and threw his reins to a stableboy, who crept out to take them. Hakkar stood for a moment, hands on hips, looking at the palace. Even from here, I could see the expression of triumphant satisfaction on his face. After a moment, he turned and helped Francia from her horse, and both of them went up the steps into the Great Hall.

Sheryn flew into my chamber, dressed only in her shift. "They're here, Brynda," she gasped breathlessly. "Oh, gods, they're here already. What shall we do?"

They mustn't find me with Whisperer still strapped to my back. And they especially mustn't find Sheryn here in the family quarters. If they did, she'd be lucky if she lived until nightfall, and her death would be an unpleasantly grisly one.

I took a deep breath to steady myself, and turned to her, already fumbling with the buckles of my sword harness. I tore Whisperer from my back and fell to my knees before my clothespress. "Bring me that bundle on the bed," I said as calmly as I could. "Hurry."

There was nothing useful in the clothespress. I pushed Whisperer in its sheath, harness and all, down to the bottom, then threw in the scarlet bundle Sheryn handed me and covered both with my old clothes. "Rhianna of the Air," I muttered, "if you love us, protect this sword and this torc. Block them with your magic and don't let the Maedun see beyond the old clothes. Oh, please. Please . . . "

It was the best I could do for now. I sprang to my feet and seized Sheryn's hand. Outside, heavy footfalls sounded on the staircase and in the corridor. I snatched a quick glance through the door. A troop of Maedun soldiers filled the corridors. They methodically opened every door, and two or three of them entered each chamber to search it. I had no doubts that they would be anything else but thorough.

I swore and dragged Sheryn over to the door that led out onto the terrace. She protested as I pulled her behind me, but there was a chance we could get down to a room the Maedun had already searched and escape detection that way.

A Maedun soldier stepped out onto the terrace from Tiernyn's solar. I pulled Sheryn down behind a huge tub containing an ornamental tree, and we crouched there, hardly daring to breathe. But no shout of discovery came. When I risked a quick glance around the tub, the terrace was again empty.

We slipped through the solar. Presently, the clatter of booted feet on the main staircase indicated the Maedun soldiers leaving the second floor. I glanced quickly out into the hall. It was empty. Sheryn and I slipped out into the corridor and down the back staircase to the servants' quarters near the kitchen. The kitchen was empty, the fires dead and cold on the hearths.

"Where are we going?" Sheryn demanded in alarm as I dodged into a small room.

I dropped her hand and went to the tall, narrow wardrobe standing against the wall opposite the bed. If my memory was correct, these were Minna's quarters. Her granddaughter was about Sheryn's size. I pawed through the few gowns hanging in the wardrobe and pulled out a dull brown one. Plain and unadorned, it was perfectly suitable for the young granddaughter of a servant. I threw the gown to Sheryn.

"Put that on," I said. "You're about to become a serving girl."

She stared down at the dress in her hands, then glared at me, a spark of fury in her eyes. Her jaw firmed stubbornly. "I am the daughter of a Tyadda Elder, and the wife of the Prince of Celi," she said coldly. "I am *not* a serving girl. I refuse to meet the Maedun dressed as anything but what I am."

"Sheryn," I said softly, "you may be the daughter of a Tyadda Elder, but you are the *widow* of the Prince of Celi, and if we aren't very, very careful, you will be the *dead* widow of the Prince of Celi, and your child will die with you. Put on that gown. Now."

For a moment, I thought she would cry again. But finally, her shoulders straightened, and she did as she was told.

"Take those combs out of your hair," I said. Certainly no servingwoman ever wore gold combs adorned with pearls. "And braid it like a servant. Quickly. We've no time to waste. Just do as I say. One long braid." I rummaged through the wardrobe again. Minna was nearly as tall as I, but at least twice as big through bust, waist, and hips. I found a serviceable-looking gray gown and threw it onto the bed. I tore at the fastenings of my tunic and trews. "The Maedun will be looking for a princess, wearing the fine clothing of a princess. They may not pay any attention to two serving-women. Hurry!"

I wore no shift, but there was no time to look for one. The sound of men shouting came faintly down the corridor. A woman screamed. Someone ran past the door, sobbing. I pulled the gray gown over my head and fastened the draw-string at my throat. The gown hung on me like a tent.

Sheryn finished with her hair. Stripped of all finery, she still looked delicate and fragile. And her hands were far too soft and smooth to be the hands of a servant.

She looked at me, pursed her lips, then went to her knees and searched through a chest at the end of the bed. She came up with a leather belt that looked as if it had once belonged to Ylana, but had been discarded because it had become worn and shabby. Handing me the belt, she crouched down beside me.

"Let me see you," she said. With quick, deft fingers, she arranged the fullness of the fabric around my waist into pleats. She made an adjustment or two and buckled the belt around me, frowning in concentration. "You'll do, I think," she said as she got to her feet. She studied me for a moment. Her hand went to her mouth. "Oh!"

"What's wrong?"

"Your face. . . Your face is all bloody. And so is your hair."

I raised my hand to face. Flakes of dried, crusted blood crumbled under my fingers. The hair above my ear crackled as I ran my fingers through it, stiff with dried blood. It had to be from the wound where the horse's hoof had grazed my head. "Oh, gods."

"Wait here . . . "

Before I could stop her, she spun and flew from the room. I leapt after her, but the kitchen corridor stood empty of soldiers. She was back a moment later, a damp cloth from the kitchen in her hands.

"Don't do that again," I said stiffly.

"Do what?"

"Go running off like that. You could have run straight into a Maedun soldier."

"I looked before I went," she said. "Now bend down and let me see what I can do for that mess on your face."

I looked at her. My exasperation must have shown on my face, but she blithely ignored it. Seeing nothing else for it, I bent and she scrubbed at my face.

"That's a little better," she said at last. "But I can't do much about your hair."

"I can cover it with a kerchief," I said. I knelt by the hearth and scooped up a handful of sooty ash, then rubbed it thoroughly into my hair while Sheryn pawed through the chest again. Francia had seen the color of my hair, and she knew there were very few Celae with this reddish gold hair. When I finished, I turned to Sheryn.

"How is that?" I asked.

She pursed her lips. "It makes your hair an awfully funny color, but I think it should do. Put this on and see how it looks." She handed me a bright yellow kerchief and waited as I tied it around my hair, fastening it at the nape of my neck. "That hides your hair pretty well, I think. I can't tell that it's reddish at all now." She glanced down at my feet and frowned. "Would a servingwoman wear boots?"

I hadn't even thought of that. But the hem of the gown hung nearly to the floor. Mayhaps no one would notice that I wore boots instead of sandals or house shoes.

Sheryn looked down at her own feet, then went to the hearth. She threw the gold combs that had bound back her hair into the cinders, then deliberately scuffed her feet through the soot and ashes. Her delicate little satin slippers no longer looked as if they belonged on a princess. Turning to me, she let her glance move from my head down to my feet. She laughed. It came out hovering on the thin edge of hysterics, but her jaw was firm, and her eyes were clear and steady. "Well, you certainly don't look like the lady Brynda al Keylan anymore," she said breathlessly.

I studied her. She had braided her hair into one long plait that hung over her shoulder. She still looked far too delicate to do the heavy work most serving girls were required to do, but she might pass if no one looked too closely. And as she had said of me, she emphatically did not look like the Princess of Celi anymore. The Maedun thought servants beneath their notice. I prayed that Francia would never take a real look at me. Or Sheryn.

The shouting grew louder. The heavy crack of hardened

leather heels against stone sounded loud in the corridor outside. Someone flung open the door. Two Maedun soldiers
stood there, their faces grim and set. Sheryn gasped in shock
and cringed back against me.

One of the soldiers made an imperious gesture. "Out," he
said. "This way." We didn't have to understand the words. The
gesture was explicit enough. He reached out and grasped
Sheryn's wrist, yanking her out into the corridor. I followed
quickly, and the soldiers herded us to the Great Hall.

Hakkar of Maedun lounged in Tiernyn's high chair on the
dais before the hearth at one end of the room. Francia sat
erect and arrogant on Ylana's chair. A score of black-clad
guards had arranged themselves behind the high chair,
standing with their feet planted wide, hands clasping the
hilts of sheathed swords at their hips. Two men in warlock's
gray flanked Hakkar, their faces calmly impassive.
Tiernyn's Red Hart banner, which had been hanging on the
wall behind his chair, lay crumpled and smoldering in the
hearth. In its place hung Hakkar's white-and-black badger
banner.

For some reason, the desecrated Red Hart banner made
Tiernyn's death and our defeat at Cam Runn immediate and
real. My worst nightmares might conjure up visions of Tiegan
and Tiernyn lying dead on a battlefield, but that small detail—
the stain of char spoiling the leaping outline of the deer on the
field of green—drained the last hope from my heart and filled
my spirit with icy despair.

Those servants who had not fled stood clustered together
near the foot of the dais. There were fewer than a dozen of
them. More than half of them were elderly, men and women
who had been with Tiernyn since he was raised as King of
Celi more than forty years ago. All of them were fiercely loyal
to Tiernyn, but any one of them might accidentally betray
Sheryn and me. I remembered what Kenzie had told me about
the questioning methods of the Maedun, and I prayed none of
them would be interrogated.

Our guards shoved Sheryn and me in with the servants, then stood behind us, their hands on their sword hilts.

Hakkar made an unobtrusive hand signal. One of the warlocks stepped forward, scanning the clustered group of servants.

"Are these all the servants?" he asked. His Celae was thickly accented, almost unintelligible. He received no answer, and repeated the question, raising his voice.

Lloghar ap Rhegar, Tiernyn's bard, stepped forward. He held himself proudly erect. When he spoke, his tone was cold and contemptuous. "These are all that remain," he said. "The rest have fled."

The warlock turned to Hakkar, translating for him. Hakkar said something and the warlock turned back to face us. He made a signal to one of the guards. The guard stepped forward and hit Lloghar in the face hard enough to knock the old man to the floor.

"You will address the Lord Protector of Celi as my lord," the warlock said coldly. "You will remember that, Celae hound."

Lloghar climbed painfully to his feet. He stared at the warlock, but said nothing. The warlock glared, but gave no further signal to the guard, who stepped back.

"We have found your queen dead in her room," the warlock said. "Where is the wife of your dead prince?"

Lloghar stood his ground. "Fled, also," he said. "I saw her ride out yesterday. She went west with three of her personal guards."

The warlock gestured to the guards behind us. One of them shouldered through the servants and seized a young woman by the hair, dragging her out into the space before the dais. He threw her to the floor and stepped back. Sheryn gasped and pressed her hand over her mouth. The woman was Leilia, one of her personal servants.

"You," the warlock said, pointing a bony finger at Leilia. "You were servant to the prince's whore. Where is she?"

Leilia scrambled to her knees. "Gone, my lord," she cried. "She's gone. I haven't seen her for two days."

The warlock pointed at her again. A garish crimson glow surrounded her, twisting around her body, flickering like flame. She screamed in agony and writhed within the seething glare of the blood magic. Francia leaned forward eagerly, watching with avid interest and enjoyment.

"Do you tell the truth?" the warlock demanded.

Leilia convulsed, her body jerking like a woman in a fit. She looked straight at Sheryn, then crumpled into a heap. "I swear," she screamed. "Oh gods, I swear. She's gone!"

The warlock nodded, apparently satisfied. He flicked his hand negligently. The oily red glare around Leilia intensified to terrifying brilliance, then it subsided and was gone. It left behind only a heap of greasy ash.

My stomach roiled with nausea. Sheryn made a sick little sound and hid her face in her hands. Not far from me, someone was violently ill onto the floor.

"There are new rules here now," the warlock said dispassionately. "You will all serve the lord Hakkar as Lord Protector of Celi. If you fail to do your duty, you will be treated the same way as the harlot who served the prince's whore. Leave us now, and go about your duties. Within a sennight, there will be Maedun servants here who will show you the proper way to serve us."

Dun Camus was not large, as palaces go. Tiernyn had not built for luxury and comfort. His palace was smaller and more utilitarian than Gwilyadd's palace in Clendonan or my father's palace in Skai, but there were nooks and crannies where people seldom went, and Sheryn and I had little trouble keeping ourselves out of everyone's way. It didn't take us long to discover that every door was guarded, and nobody, Maedun soldier or Celae servant, passed the sentries without a chit signed by Hakkar himself.

More sentries stood guard over the main gates to the palace, and nothing passed them without a thorough search. The postern gate at the bottom of the kitchen garden had a pair of guards flanking it. Hakkar had wasted no time in making sure that his stolen palace was absolutely secure. And in doing so, he had effectively cut off any route of escape Sheryn and I might have had.

When night fell and the servants began to return to their quarters to sleep, they found themselves dispossessed and Maedun soldiers in possession of their rooms. Left without even a blanket to keep themselves warm, they found corners in the Great Hall and huddled together to sleep.

We didn't go into the Great Hall. Sheryn and I tucked ourselves into a small closet under the back stairs, just off the kitchens, where the cooks stored empty jars and crocks, old flour sacks and boxes. It smelled musty, and the air was full of dust, but it was snug and secure, and reasonably warm. I fell asleep still trying to come up with a feasible plan of escape.

During the night, I awoke to hear a woman's faint sobbing coming from a room not far away. One of the servants, taken against her will to the bed of a Somber Rider. I shuddered, and tried to block out the sound. I lay awake long after the broken sobbing had stopped. The hopeless empty space within me where once my heart had been ached with sharp, piercing agony, and I could find no peace.

Tiegan had known then in the shrine when he made me vow to watch over Sheryn. Even before that, he had mayhaps sensed it that day Kenzie came to Dun Camus, the day Tiegan tried to warn me that Sheryn might need to rely on me someday. Then in the shrine, somehow he had known that he would not return from the battle. It had been plain in his eyes and the bittersweet quality of his smile. Mayhaps he had a touch of the Sight—just enough to warn him before the battle. And he had known, even if I didn't, what his death would do to me. How much easier it would be if I had been able to follow him to Annwn. The pain was so sharp, so clear, and so fresh, I could even find it in me to blame him for causing me this torment.

Sheryn slept only a few feet from me. I could not see her in the dark, but the soft, even sound of her breathing whispered in the silence. She carried the heir to Tiernyn's throne within her belly. She carried the king I had sworn to Tiegan to protect and to see safely to a Tyadda steading deep in the mountains of Skai. Once that task was accomplished, perhaps I might be able to find the peace of Annwn for myself, and meet the Counter at the Scroll with the tally of my days totaled and complete.

I shut away the pain. There would be time enough to give in to it and grieve later.

Sleep was gone for me. I rose and crept out into the deserted corridor. Only a single torch burned in its bracket on the wall, casting flickering shadows along the stone floor.

Two sentries stood, alert and watchful, at the end of the corridor by the kitchen door, just barely within the spill of light from the torch. I ducked back against the wall within the shadow and slipped noiselessly down the corridor to the Great Hall.

A Maedun soldier appeared at the end of the corridor, dragging a woman with him. I slipped quickly into the shadow of a doorway as the soldier pulled the woman past me. She struggled in his grasp, but could not break away. When he paused before the door to one of the small rooms, she wrenched her arm from his grasp and raised her fist as if to strike him.

The blow never landed. In sudden agony, she fell to her knees, writhing in pain, her arms folded across her belly. The soldier stood impassively watching, not touching her, until finally the spasm of pain ended. Gasping, the woman sagged against the wall, still on her knees. The soldier seized her wrist again and dragged her into the room.

I couldn't help her. Not without giving myself away, and leaving Sheryn with no one to help her. My fists clenched into hard knots by my side, I waited to make sure the soldier would not come back out into the corridor, then made my way quietly down the passageway to the Great Hall. I needed to find out how well the palace was guarded.

Fires blazed in the hearths at either end of the Great Hall, casting dancing shadows across the huddled forms of the sleeping servants. The air smelled thick and stale, with an underlying stench of carrion to it. It reminded me of the battle-field and the dead lying waiting for the ravens.

Two more sentries stood at the foot of the staircase leading up to the family quarters on the second floor. More guards stood by the main entrance out into the courtyard. One of the sleeping servants moaned in his sleep, and the guards all turned their heads toward the sound. Very alert, these Maedun soldiers. There was no escape from the palace this way.

I made my way back down the corridor toward the closet beneath the back stairs. The opening to the narrow stairway faced down the corridor, away from the guards at the kitchen door, set in a branch of the corridor that led to the bathhouse. Halfway up the stairs, a landing with a small window faced out onto the back garden. In the gloom outside, I could barely make out the dark silhouettes of two black-clad sentries guarding the postern gate.

Berry bushes and ornamental shrubs grew in curving rows, throwing areas of deep shadow across the garden. Two women alone might be able to slip through those shadows and to the postern gate, especially if one of those women were armed and knew how to use her sword. And we might be able to steal horses out of the stables of the main barracks at the edge of the town.

Not tonight, though. Mayhaps in a few days, when the guards would be a little more complacent. Provided there was no trouble in the interim.

I crept back down the stairs and into the closet. As I was settling down again on my pile of flour sacks, Sheryn's hand came out of the dark and closed around my wrist. Her fingers were cold as the stone of the corridor floor, startling me badly.

"Where have you been?" she whispered shrilly. "I was worried sick."

"It's all right," I said. "I was just reconnoitering. They've set guards at every door, and at every gate. We're going to have to wait a while before we try to escape."

"I'm frightened," she said softly. "It shames me to admit it, but I'm so frightened, I feel sick."

I put my hand over hers. "I'm frightened, too," I said. "But we can't give in to it and let them win."

Her clothing rustled as she sat up. "They've bespelled the servants," she said. "Can you feel it?"

The underlying stench of carrion . . . That's what it was. Hakkar's blood sorcery. And the servants all moved as if they walked in their sleep.

"Yes," I said in surprise. "But I don't feel bespelled."

"Because you've got Tyadda blood," she said. "I can feel it, but I don't think it can affect me. At least not at the level he's spread it here. If anyone tries to raise their hand against a Maedun, the spell punishes them."

"I saw," I said, and told her of the woman in the corridor.

"But we're immune," she whispered, then shuddered. "Brynda, I'm so frightened."

I remembered the battlefield again, and how only some of the yrSkai soldiers were able to continue fighting through that ghastly black mist. Many yrSkai had Tyadda blood in their veins. I nodded slowly. It answered one of my questions. And perhaps it gave me a place to start in planning our escape.

21

A bucket of water, a scrub brush, and a smutch of dirt on my face was a good disguise. I found that I could move with reasonable freedom throughout the palace. If anyone came along, I was merely a scrubwoman on her way to do a chore, and servants are invisible people.

Sheryn kept herself busy in the kitchen garden, or in the kitchen itself, working in the scullery, well out of the way of Francia and Hakkar, and most of the Maedun guards. With her hair braided in a long plait that fell over her shoulder, and wearing the shapeless brown dress, she looked little older than twelve. She even moved like a child rather than a woman grown, and I wondered if she might be using some of her magic to make herself appear so young and completely insignificant.

Late in the afternoon, two days after Hakkar and Francia took up residence in the royal suites, Sheryn wasn't in our little cubbyhole under the stairs when I returned. I made sure no one was looking before I ducked into the closet. My knees ached from kneeling on the cold floors all day, trying to overhear anything helpful.

Sheryn burst into the closet. "Brynda," she cried. "Come quick." She seized my arm and dragged me out into the corridor. "It looks as if they're bringing in some prisoners. Come and see."

I allowed her to pull me after her out the kitchen door into the garden, where she had been working. Her basket of seeds lay on its side in the middle of a row. From the end of the garden by the laundry shed, we could see half of the courtyard.

Mounted Somber Riders flanked a ragged column of thirty or forty Celae men dressed in tattered and dirty uniforms. Most were wounded; all looked exhausted. They stumbled into the courtyard listlessly, as if they neither knew nor cared where they were or what was happening to them. The carrion stench of Hakkar's blood sorcery hung over them like a malevolent miasma. Sheryn clutched my arm and pointed wordlessly.

In the midst of the column of dispirited soldiers, Aellegh and Brennen stood out plainly. They were filthy and battered, and they walked with their heads hanging as lethargically as the other prisoners, but their eyes were watchful and wary. Between them, they supported Kenzie, each with an arm around the blankly staring and staggering Tyr. There was no sign of Fiala among the prisoners.

Some small spark ignited in my chest where before there had been only emptiness. I had given my brother up for dead. I had never expected to see him again, nor even to find out for certain what happened to him. For a moment, there didn't seem to be enough air in the corner of the garden to breathe properly, and my heart beat hard against my ribs.

I glanced from him to Kenzie. So he, too, had survived the battle. The quick surge of relief that shot through my chest at the sight of him surprised me.

Sheryn's fingernails dug into my arm, but I hardly noticed. All my attention was on Brennen. Of all the prisoners, only he and Aellegh seemed to realize where they were. Only the two of them seemed unaffected by Hakkar's spell. Of course, Aellegh's father was Donaugh, and while he had not inherited any of his father's magic, he had certainly inherited a large measure of Tyadda blood. And Brennen and I—our mother was more than half-Tyadda, and our father was one-quarter. If what Sheryn had told me was true, both of them would have a lot of resistance to the spell. Kenzie, of course, being Tyran, had none.

"What are they going to do with them?" Sheryn whispered.

"I don't know," I said. "But I intend to find out."

*   *   *

Sheryn insisted on coming with me. She flatly refused to remain in our cubbyhole while I went to the Great Hall. I was afraid of what might happen if someone recognized her, but she pointed out that, after working in the garden for two days, even her hands didn't look like anything but a servant's hands now—broken fingernails and soil embedded deeply under what was left of them. With dirt on her face where she had wiped away sweat, she said she looked no different from Minna's own granddaughter, who worked in the scullery. And she looked about the same age, too—barely into her teens.

I gave in because it was quicker and easier than arguing with her, and I needed to find out where the prisoners were to be taken, and what was to be done with them. She took a flagon of oil for the lamps, and I carried my bucket as we made our way down the corridor to the Great Hall.

The prisoners huddled together before the dais, where Hakkar sat again on Tiernyn's high chair. Brennen, Kenzie, and Aellegh stood together near the back of the assembled cluster of prisoners. Brennen and Aellegh still supported Kenzie between them as if Kenzie were badly wounded as well as bespelled. Pain and exhaustion marked Brennen's features, and I knew suddenly what he would look like as an old man. He glanced around the Great Hall and for a moment, he looked straight at me. But his expression didn't change. No flicker of recognition crossed his face, or glimmered in his eyes. His glance moved on and he looked back at Hakkar.

Hakkar gestured to one of the two warlocks who stood beside his chair. The warlock stepped down onto the floor and moved among the prisoners, an expression of distaste on his face. He stopped for a moment before each of the prisoners, staring hard at him before moving on to the next. Twice, he gestured to the guards, who pulled the chosen man out of the group.

When he came to Aellegh, the warlock hesitated a long time. He asked a question I couldn't hear. Aellegh turned his head and spit on the floor, but the warlock moved his foot and

Aellegh missed. Not deigning to touch a filthy prisoner, the warlock called a guard. The guard pushed his way through the apathetic prisoners and hit Aellegh hard enough to stagger him. He stumbled away from Kenzie, and Kenzie nearly fell, even with Brennen's arm still around his waist.

The warlock barely glanced at Brennen and Kenzie. He gestured to the guards again. Four of them pulled Brennen, Aellegh, and Kenzie to the opposite side of the room from where the first two prisoners the warlock had separated stood.

Hakkar raised his hand, making a dismissive motion. The guards marched the prisoners out of the Great Hall. When they were gone, only the two the warlock had first chosen, and Brennen, Kenzie, and Aellegh still remained. Their guards dragged the first two prisoners back out into the courtyard. The other four guards took Brennen, Kenzie, and Aellegh through the door that led to the armory. And the cells in the lower level of the palace.

The warlock went back to the dais and he and Hakkar spoke at some length. But I was too far away to hear what they said, and I had no chance to get closer.

Frustration knotted my fists hard enough to dig my nails into my palms. I swore under my breath as Sheryn and I retreated back to the kitchens.

"I can find out what they're going to do with Brennen," Sheryn whispered. "Even a Maedun soldier will talk with a pretty serving girl if she flatters him enough."

"Sheryn, no!" I gasped. "I can't let you—"

"Can you do it?" she demanded. "When was the last time you flirted with anyone?"

Never. While most young women were learning to flirt, I was in the practice field learning to dance with a sword. I had watched women flirting and teasing men, but had never been able to do it myself. It had always struck me as being a colossal waste of time and effort, and for no result.

Sheryn nodded. "I thought so," she said. "Let's see if we can find one of those guards who took them away. If I catch him on duty, I can promise him anything he wants, but he won't be able to do anything until he's off duty. Not unless he wants to lose his head for dereliction of duty." She grinned in smug satisfaction. "And when he's off duty, he won't be able to find me."

"What happens if he does find you?" I asked grimly.

"I'll look like this if he ever sees me again." She indicated the shapeless dress and her dirty face. "I'll be merely another grubby child. He won't recognize me."

"You sound very sure of that."

"I am."

"Your life depends on it, you know."

"I know. But I'll do it for Brennen anyway."

"Sheryn, I'd rather you didn't do this. I'm afraid for you."

She put her hand on my arm. "You'll have to trust me for this, Brynda," she said quietly. "I'm really not completely helpless. Besides, one of us has to do it if we want to help Brennen."

She was right. One of us had to do it. And I didn't have the skills. It had to be her. Finally, I nodded. "I'll meet you back here."

"Thank you," she said simply, then slipped away.

While Sheryn went off to search for the guards who had taken Brennen, Kenzie, and Aellegh away, I carried my bucket up to the second floor to fetch Whisperer from its hiding place. I wanted it near me, where I could keep an eye on it, and if Sheryn and I were to do anything to help the three men, I would need it then.

And it gave me something else to think about while Sheryn was practicing her wiles on the Maedun guards.

The servants were busy lighting the candles and torches in the Great Hall against the coming night. The upstairs corridors were already dim except where the windows let in the last of the daylight. Whisperer still rested in the bottom of my clothespress, I hoped. I shuddered to think what might happen if Hakkar or Francia got their hands on a Rune Blade. While it's true that a Rune Blade will not fight in a hand not born to wield it, who knew what use Hakkar's ghastly blood sorcery might make of it.

They had found a way for Mikal, curse his soul, to use Celae magic. But he had a half measure of Celae blood in his veins—Donaugh's own blood. And perhaps he had inherited a small measure of Donaugh's power with it. We would never know for sure. But if they had needed Mikal to break through the curtain of enchantment, might that mean neither Hakkar nor Francia could make Celae magic work for them?

The door to the solar opened. I dropped to my knees and had my wet brush scrubbing circles on the tile when Hakkar and Francia came out into the corridor.

". . . can't use the magic of this cursed land," Francia was saying. Without sparing me a glance, she raised the hem of her russet-and-orange skirt slightly as she swept past me. "It curdles in your hands and crumbles to nothing. It's useless."

"The man has some magic," Hakkar said. "I want to try. This island is infested by magic, and I mean to eradicate every trace of it before I'm done with it. If we fail with this experiment, we've lost nothing. If we succeed, think of the power for both of us here."

"Gherhad says he's sensed more magic among the servants," Francia said. "Someone was using a little of it just today."

"He's searching for whoever it was?"

"He is. But it was faint, and he's having trouble locating it."

"This cursed island is rotten with that useless magic. There *must* be some way we can make it work for us."

I lost Francia's reply as they stepped into Queen Ylana's chambers. The revelation that one of their warlocks could sense magic being used was not good news. I had the nasty, sinking feeling that it was Sheryn's mild masking spell he might have felt. I'd have to warn her. And quickly. We couldn't risk her being unmasked.

What if the warlock was able to sense the faint shimmer of magic that surrounded Whisperer?

Oh, gods, I couldn't let them find my sword!

I picked up my bucket and slipped into the solar. The terrace outside the tall windows was empty. The sun hung just above the western horizon. The crenellations of the walls and the potted plants and trees cast long shadows across the warm, brown tiles. I set the bucket down and slipped out onto the terrace, making my way from shadow to shadow along the wall until I reached the window to Ylana's chambers.

They had drawn the thick, heavy curtains across the windows, leaving only a narrow gap where a small slice of red torchlight gleamed through to spill along the tiles. By pressing myself up against the glass and cupping my hands around my eyes, I could see a thin wedge of the room inside.

Light came only from two guttering torches standing to either side of a brazier. A man lay bound and gagged on the floor between the torches, curled on his side, his face toward the window and me. A man in warlock's gray knelt behind him, facing the window. Hakkar and Francia stood with their backs to me, looking down at the man.

My stomach contracted in nausea. The man on the floor was Lloghar ap Rhegar, Tiernyn's bard. He moved feebly as the warlock placed both hands around his head, trying to pull away. But the warlock held him in a firm grip.

Hakkar drew a wickedly curved dagger from his belt. He tested the blade with his thumb, then glanced at the warlock. He said something, and the warlock nodded. Lloghar's eyes went wide in terror. His throat muscles worked, but the gag prevented him from crying out.

Francia stepped back and raised the hem of her skirt. Hakkar dropped to his knees and stabbed the dagger into Lloghar's abdomen, ripping the blade viciously upward. As the steaming, glistening entrails tumbled and spilled out onto the floor, Hakkar dropped the dagger and thrust his hands into Lloghar's belly. Lloghar threw his head back in agony. The cords of his neck stood out like steel bands against his pale skin, then vanished as he went limp. His bound limbs twitched, then stilled as the strength drained from his body with his blood.

My stomach spasmed. I clapped both hands over my mouth and gagged, watching in horror as Hakkar, wrist-deep in the entrails of the dying man, threw back his head, his lips moving in a chant I couldn't hear.

A pale, golden mist rose from the tangle of guts around Hakkar's hands. Slowly, it circled his wrists, climbing inexorably along his blood-splashed arms. It began to shimmer, softly at first, with faint, iridescent color barely visible in the gold mist. As it reached his elbows, the colors became brighter, flashing and flaring, blues and greens and bright saffron.

But it never reached his body. It exploded in a bright, glaring flash of light. In bright whorls and sparks, the golden light spun away from Hakkar in what I swear was revulsion. The dissipating magic crackled and popped so loudly, I heard it faintly from outside the closed windows. Then, in a blinding burst of color, it was gone as completely as if it had never been.

My skin crawled, and my very flesh crept. I stumbled back from the window and ran back across the terrace. I didn't make it all the way back to the solar window before I had to stop. Holding on to one of the ornamental trees for support, I bent over and vomited into the deep tub.

"Oh, gods, Lloghar," I muttered, my teeth chattering. He had shown me how to coax simple chords and tunes from a lute when I was only four years old, and with his patience, he had given me the gift of music. "Oh dear gods, my good friend . . . "

I had once heard my grandfather talk about the grisly ritual Hakkar's grandfather the general had perfected. Kian rarely spoke of it, and now I knew why. If I had needed further proof that the Maedun sorcerers were evil, what Hakkar and Francia had done to Lloghar, the gentlest of men, a man who had never hurt anyone his whole life, ended that.

Was that how Mikal had obtained his ability to use Celae magic? Stealing it from another? I shuddered, wondering if Francia had that fate in mind for me when she'd had me kidnapped in Silichia. Then I remembered the strange dream I'd had in the mountains of Isgard, and suddenly the pile of mutilated bodies behind the image of Mikal made sense. He had stolen their magic. He'd been born with a touch of his father's magic, and he'd stolen enough from others, using that horrifying ritual, to make the magic of Celi work for him. It had worked well enough for him to penetrate the curtain of enchantment Donaugh raised around Celi, and it had worked well enough so that his masking spell had fooled even Donaugh.

Only the gods and goddesses knew how that bright Celi magic might mix with the blood magic he and Francia had used. They'd be at war with each other all the time.

Shivering with horror, I stumbled back into the solar.

I was back in the hallway, my head bent over my scrub brush, when Francia and Hakkar came out of Ylana's dayroom. They were both angry. I felt their rage and frustration seething in the air around them, although Francia's frozen porcelain features showed nothing. Hakkar aimed a kick at my bucket, spilling the water all over my knees as he passed. I cowered back against the wall, clutching my scrub brush to my chest, until they had gone back into the solar.

A moment later, Francia came back out into the passageway and went to the door of the chambers she had appropriated as hers—the largest and most luxurious of the guest quarters, where Tiernyn had housed visiting princes and dukes. As she passed me, she snapped her fingers imperiously.

"You, girl," she said, without bothering to look at me. "Come with me."

I scrambled to my feet, keeping my head down, and followed her into the main chamber. She didn't pause, but went straight into the bedchamber and sat on the edge of the bed beside the man who lay there. She put her hand to his forehead, then beckoned to me.

"Clean up this mess." She waved at a chamber pot, a bowl of dirty water, and a pile of bloody bandages, then turned her attention back to the man in the bed.

It was Mikal.

For a moment, I simply stood there, staring. I had been certain he was dead after the terrible wound Fiala had given him. How could he have survived that? Surely the wound had been mortal.

Francia snapped her fingers at me again. "Don't stand there gawking like an idiot, girl. Hurry. Clean up that mess."

I went quickly to the chamber pot, picked it up, and took it out into the hall. I left it by the door and went back to tidy the mess of bloody bandages. Francia still sat on the edge of the bed.

She leaned forward and put her hand to Mikal's shoulder. He pushed her away irritably.

"I finished Healing it this morning," he said, his voice rasping. "Just let me rest. I'll be better in a few days. I just want to rest now."

"Hakkar can't use the Celae magic," Francia said, nearly purring with satisfaction. "He can't take it for himself. That means just you can, my dear son. Think of it. You can use Celae magic. You are the son of the dead King of Celi. Do you think Vanizen will make Hakkar Lord Protector of Celi when he can have you as King of Celi?" She laughed softly and smoothed back his hair again. "Rest well, Mikal. You'll need your strength for your coronation."

I scooped the dirty bandages into the bowl of water and hurried out of the chamber, my hands shaking so badly, I nearly spilled the water. I shoved the chamber pot and the bowl into Tiegan's empty workroom and ran down the back stairs. I crept back into the cubbyhole under the stairs to wait for Sheryn.

I sat in the dark and shivered. I was glad Sheryn wasn't there. I needed time to recover my calm after what I'd seen in Ylana's chambers. And the discovery that Mikal still lived.

He was a Healer. He had the Gift of Healing, inherited through Donaugh from Kian and Kerri. But he didn't yet know how to replenish his strength using the magic in the earth and air around him. Like many self-taught Healers, he used his own strength, and had to spend several days recuperating after Healing.

Sheryn and I had to get out of Dun Camus, and quickly. Once Mikal recovered strength, he would be searching for me again. I couldn't let him find us here.

When my stomach finally stopped cramping with nausea, and I was able to control the shaking of my hands, I realized I had forgotten to retrieve Whisperer from my chambers. But I dared not go back upstairs. Not so soon. And I couldn't bear the thought of passing the door to Ylana's chambers, knowing what lay within.

Sheryn burst into the cupboard, her face pale. "Brynda," she whispered shrilly. "Hakkar thinks Brennen has magic. He wants him brought to him tomorrow at sunset. That guard said Hakkar wants to take his magic."

22

The palace guard changed just before midnight. Sheryn and I sat in our closet, listening, as the new guards marched noisily down the corridor to relieve the sentries standing guard at the kitchen doors. A few moments later, the off-duty men came clattering and laughing down the corridor, and into the rooms assigned to them.

Then we merely waited.

We waited until the last of the night sounds had gone. One of the off-duty soldiers had a woman in his room. Her sobs and his grunts and moans of pleasure went on for an interminably long time while Sheryn and I sat helplessly listening. Beside me, Sheryn trembled, a light, quick quivering that could have been fear or anger, or both.

"Pigs," she whispered once. "All of them. Pigs. Someday, they'll pay for every tear they caused to be shed."

I bit my lip and remained silent. I had thought Mikal paid with his life for Donaugh's death. And Tiernyn's. And Tiegan's. I was wrong. Now, I'd see to it that he *did* pay. But it would not be enough. Nothing could ever be enough, because nothing would bring them back, and nothing could ever ease this bleak, hollow emptiness where once my heart had been. What were a servant's tears to the deaths of those I loved?

As much and mayhaps more . . . a small voice within me whispered. Tiernyn and Tiegan had died in an attempt to protect that same servant woman who sobbed in vain not far from where we sat, listening helplessly.

When silence finally fell over the servants' quarters, we crept out of our little cubbyhole and darted around the corner to the narrow stairway.

The stairway was unlit and darker than the inside of a tin mine. Sheryn hooked her fingers into my belt as we made our way slowly and carefully up the steps. The stone of the wall was rough and cold beneath my fingers as I groped my way upward. The narrow window on the landing halfway up let in nothing but starlight. Moonrise would not be for another hour, and only a thin crescent would be in the skies tonight. That would help to conceal us once we made it outside.

If we made it outside . . .

The fourth riser from the landing was broken. The stone moved under my foot, and I nearly stumbled. Sheryn gasped as I swayed, but I caught my balance again. I muttered at her to be careful, and continued to climb.

A faint gleam of torchlight showed beneath the door at the head of the stairs. If the guards along the upper corridor were dispersed the same way they had been the last time I reconnoitered up here at night, there would be only four of them, two at the door to Tiernyn's chambers where Hakkar slept, and two more guarding the guest quarters where Francia had moved in. Both were down at the far end of the corridor. The only rooms farther along the hall were Ylana's dayroom, where they had murdered Lloghar, and a spare workroom.

Directly across the corridor from the little stairway lay Lloghar's chambers, but they had no direct access to the terrace as his rooms faced out over the stables. My own chambers were next, near this end of the corridor, facing out over the terrace garden above the Great Hall, on the opposite side of the corridor from the stairway where we stood. Between my door and Hakkar's lay Tiernyn's workroom, then Tiegan's workroom, and the guest quarters. If Sheryn and I had any luck at all—if the gods and goddesses watched over us—the guards would not be looking this way. They'd be watching the main staircase from the Great Hall, and not expecting anything from this end of the corridor.

I pressed myself up against the wall and put my hand to the door latch.

"Be careful," Sheryn whispered. She moved quickly to stand beside me, her back hard against the wall.

I nodded, then pulled the door open an inch. Light spilled into the stairwell, flickering faintly along the wooden planking of the landing and casting long shadows along the stone of the walls.

Two torches flared in brackets on the wall, one halfway down the corridor not far from Hakkar's door, the other at the head of the main staircase. The guards were barely more than tall pillars of darkness near the doors, their shadows wavering along the polished tile of the floor. I couldn't make out their faces in the gloom. That could mean they were turned away, looking toward the main staircase. As I watched, one of them stretched and worked his shoulders as if they were stiff, then settled back into his watchful stance.

The stairway door and the door to my chambers were well within the spill of light cast by the torches. But my gown was dark gray and Sheryn's was dull brown. Gods willing, we should blend in with the flickering shadows.

Standing in the doorway wasn't getting us anywhere. "I'll go first," I whispered to Sheryn. "If anything happens, you run straight back down these stairs and into the closet. Understand?"

"Yes," she replied softly. "Be careful."

I dared not use a masking spell to hide my movements. Pressing myself against the wall, I slid across the end of the corridor and ducked down as I passed the window. Moments later, I was deep in the shadow cast by the recessed door to Lloghar's quarters. When I risked a glance down the corridor, the guards hadn't moved. I beckoned to Sheryn.

She moved like a wraith, flitting silently along the wall under the window. I heard nothing, not even the rustle of the fabric of her gown as she tucked herself into the shadow beside me.

The torch set at the head of the main staircase flared, throwing leaping shadows down the corridor. The guards moved restlessly, leaning forward curiously. Sheryn and I darted down the hallway and into my chambers, closing the door silently behind us.

I hadn't realized I'd been holding my breath until I let it out in a long sigh of relief. We moved together through the outer chamber and into my bedroom. Again, we closed the door, and it moved silently on oiled hinges.

Sheryn went quickly to the window and made sure the curtains were tightly drawn across the glass. The room was completely dark. We could see nothing at all. "Can we light a candle?" she asked.

Automatically, I groped along the wall where Whisperer usually hung on its peg. But it wasn't there. My heart nearly stopped in dismay, my mind a sudden blank. I had been so sure it was right there, where I always put it. Where could it be but there? For a moment, I couldn't think.

"Brynda? Can we light a candle?"

"No," I whispered. "If we need to put it out quickly, someone would smell the smoke. Go back to the outer chamber and keep an ear out for someone coming."

I barely heard her move across the floor. I rubbed my sweaty hands down my skirt and forced myself to calm down. Two deep breaths helped.

Where was Whisperer?

Then I remembered. I had thrust it down into my clothespress when I had heard the Maedun approaching the palace. Thrust it deep down into the bottom of the chest, along with Tiernyn's torc and the two pieces of Kingmaker wrapped in his cloak.

How could I have been so stupid as to forget?

I didn't hear Sheryn come back into the room. Her voice at my elbow startled me so badly, I bit my lip to prevent myself crying out.

"Someone's coming," she said softly. "Hurry, Brynda."

I threw myself to my knees beside the press, flung up the lid, and pushed my hand deep into the tangle of old clothing. Whisperer's hilt slid, cold and solid, into the palm of my hand. Sheryn caught at my arm and I lost my grip on the hilt. The sword fell back to the bottom of the press.

"They're coming in *here*!" she cried.

"Quick! Behind the hanging."

I leapt to my feet and seized her hand, dragging her with me. The wall hanging beside the clothespress was heavy, thick with embroidery. Mountains and a river. Skai scenery. It had always helped me overcome my homesickness when I had first come to Dun Camus. Between it and the stone of the wall, there was a space not much deeper than the length of my forearm. Sheryn and I pressed ourselves up against the wall just as the door to the outer chamber opened. The sound of men's voices speaking in guttural Maedun filled the room. Two of them, perhaps. Certainly not more than three.

Moments later, laughing, they came into the inner chamber. Light flooded in with them, trailing the smell of smoke. Even behind the hanging, the brightness hurt my eyes. Two torches, perhaps?

"These quarters should do well for the lord Horbad," one of them said. "Check that desk for anything important before we throw it out."

"I don't see why this couldn't wait until morning," the second one grumbled.

"We're not on duty in the morning, and Lord Hakkar gave the task to us," the first man said reasonably. "Lord Horbad arrives by midmorning. These chambers have to be ready for him. Are you willing to tell Lord Hakkar it can wait?"

The second man grunted, but made no other reply.

Their footsteps rang loudly on the polished tile of the floor. I could see nothing through the dense fabric of the hanging, but by the sound of their voices, I could tell they were over by my desk near the window. A loud, rending crack of shattering wood startled me. They had forced the drawer open. Probably looking for important papers. Well, if they expected to find any royal secrets in my desk, they were to be sorely disappointed.

"Don't forget that chest," one of the men said.

Footsteps crossed the room. As he passed in front of the hanging, the man hesitated.

"I think I've found a mouse," he said.

I looked down. Sheryn's foot protruded beyond the hanging. Cold fear pricked at the back of my neck.

I touched Sheryn's shoulder and pointed down at her foot. She glanced down, and her eyes widened in horror. Then her face firmed, and she took a deep breath. She put her finger to her lips and reached up to tousle her hair around her face. Deliberately, she undid the drawstring at her throat and pulled the neckline of her gown down over one shoulder.

"Stay here," she mouthed at me. "Don't move until you can get your sword."

I shook my head, but she frowned sharply at me. Finally, seeing no other alternative, I nodded and pressed myself farther back against the wall. She moved sideways, away from me, pushed the hanging aside, and stepped out into the room. I held my breath.

Sheryn giggled. "You've found me," she said, her tone flirtatious and sultry. "A poor serving girl can't hide from such clever and handsome officers as you."

Officers! I swore softly under my breath. These two would be a lot more clever than the guards Sheryn had played with to find out where Brennen, Kenzie, and Aellegh were being held. Much more difficult to fool. I swore again, and edged toward the end of the hanging, closer to the clothespress.

She moved to the other side of the room, drawing their attention away from the wall hanging, away from me.

"Such big, strong men, too," she murmured.

One of the men made a startled exclamation of delight. The other laughed. Both of them crossed the room quickly to her. Sheryn's stumbling footsteps and muffled cry of protest came clearly through the hanging.

Moments later, I heard another brief scuffle, then the sound of a body landing on the bed. Sheryn cried out again. One of the men laughed, a particularly nasty sound in the closeness of the bedchamber.

I couldn't bloody *see*! The cursed wall hanging was too

thick. Hardly any light passed through it, and I could see nothing, not even shadows. But I didn't have to see to know what they were doing to Sheryn. They were going to rape her. Rape her with me cowering behind a wall hanging, doing nothing to help her.

Cold, clear rage knotted under my heart. No, by all the gods, they weren't going to rape her. Not if I could do anything about it. I had promised Tiegan I would take care of her. Promised him in the shrine, and promised him again as he lay dead on the trampled grass on the flanks of Cam Runn.

By all the gods, Tiegan, I won't betray my vow to you. I won't let it happen.

I closed my ears to the sounds of struggle on the bed, and edged along the wall until my foot found the bottom of the clothespress. One of the men laughed, but I didn't know whether it was the man grappling in what had been chilling silence with Sheryn on the bed, or the other man simply enjoying the performance. It didn't matter. As long as both men were fully occupied for the moment, it didn't matter at all.

Slowly, careful not to disturb the hanging, I crouched down. With one hand, I pushed the hanging an inch to one side and peered around it.

Sheryn lay on the bed, her skirt thrown up over her head. One of the men stood at the foot of the bed, struggling with one hand to unlace his trews while he tried to hold down her thrashing legs with the other. The other man sat beside Sheryn's shoulders, pinning her hands to the mattress above her head with one hand, the other hand moving across her breasts in a rough, explicit parody of a caress.

I glanced down. Whisperer's hilt lay exposed among a tangle of old tunics. Beneath it, the scarlet of Tiernyn's cloak glowed among the more neutral tones.

Watching the two men, I thrust my hand into the press. Whisperer's hilt slid into the palm of my hand, and the welcome vibrato of the sword sang in my heart. As I pulled it out of the press, the hilt trembled in my hand. I eased the blade out of the scabbard. The sword glowed faintly with its own light, and the runes spilling along the blade glittered sharply and fiercely, like the facets cut into a gemstone.

I am the Voice of Celi. The quiet lyrical chant of the sword echoed in my mind.

I was only fourteen when my grandmother Kerridwen placed the sword in my hands, and I first heard that song. In the ten years since, the song had grown familiar, striking an answering chord in my spirit. I'd heard exhilaration and excitement in that voice as we danced together in the exacting rhythms of the practice sequences. And I'd heard anger and the lust to kill as we fought together on the hillside at Cam Runn. Now I heard blinding rage and an overwhelming need to protect something precious.

Ever after, I was never sure whether I leapt out from behind the hanging on my own, or whether the sword threw me forward. It didn't matter.

Whirling the brightly glowing blade around my head, silently screaming my own battle cry, I lost myself in the passion of the sword. The officer by Sheryn's head had only time to lurch around, his eyes wide and staring, before the blade caught him under the chin. His head hit the wall of the chamber behind him with a wet thud, and a gout of blood burst from his neck, splashing down over the woven rug and the silken coverlet of the bed. His body, still in a stiff, sitting posture, toppled over onto the floor.

The other officer, at a severe disadvantage with his trews down around his knees, fumbled for the sword he had dropped onto the foot of the bed. I was upon him like an avenging fury before he could even extend his hand to grasp at the hilt of his sword. He grunted in pain as Whisperer's blade clove into his spine above his hips. He collapsed across Sheryn's feet.

I stood for a moment, gasping for breath, my sword still held in both hands, hardly able to believe it was all over. Then, calmly and deliberately, I bent down and cleaned Whisperer's blade on the silk of the coverlet.

"Sheryn, it's over," I said, surprised at the composure in my voice.

I pushed the headless body half under the bed, as far as it would go, and sat beside her. Sheryn didn't move. I reached out and pulled the skirt from her face and smoothed it down over her legs. She lay rigid on the bed, staring up at me, her eyes wide in her chalk-pale face. Deep, wracking shudders shook her whole body. She tried to speak, but no words came through her trembling lips. Two tears welled up in her eyes and spilled down her temples to disappear into the soft tangle of dark gold hair above her ears.

"It's over, Sheryn," I murmured soothingly, and brushed the hair from her forehead. "They're both dead. They can't hurt you now."

She nodded, still shuddering. She took a deep, quivering breath and closed her eyes for a moment, visibly pulling herself together. Gradually, her shivering stopped. She sat up, drawing away from me, and pulled the neck of her gown closer around her throat. Her fingers trembled as she knotted the ribbon firmly. A dull red flush crept up her throat to suffuse her cheeks.

"I thought I could handle them," she said remotely, not looking at me. "I thought if I could just divert their attention long enough . . ." Her voice trailed off, and she choked back a sob.

"You did," I said. "It worked. I'm sorry I took so long getting the sword, but it worked. Look. They're both dead."

She shivered again and refused to look at the two sprawled bodies. "It was terrible," she muttered. "I thought I would be sick with revulsion. It was terrible!" She straightened her shoulders and turned her head to stare, first at one body, then at the other. "I'm glad they're dead," she whispered fiercely. "I'm *glad* you killed them! They deserved to die. Pigs, all of them! Pigs!" She shuddered with repugnance.

I grasped her wrists. "Sheryn, enough," I said gently. "We've got to get out of here. We can't let them find us here with two bodies."

She scrambled off the bed, stepping fastidiously over the puddle of blood on the rug. She shook out her skirts and pushed her hair back out of her eyes. When she looked at me again, she was pale, but icily calm.

"I am Tyadda," she said. "And we . . . endure. We still have to get Brennen and Aellegh out of that prison cell. And Kenzie, too. We'd better hurry."

The walls of Dun Camus are blessedly thick. When I peered out into the hallway, the guards at the other end of the corridor still stood quietly, watching the head of the main staircase. Certainly, if they'd heard anything, Sheryn and I would be up to our ears in irate Maedun soldiers by now.

When I came back into the bedchamber, Sheryn was stripping the bloodstained coverlet from the bed. She bundled it up and thrust it into the wardrobe, then stood looking distastefully down at the two bodies.

"We can't leave this mess here for them to find," she said. "They'll have the whole palace up on its ear in no time, and we'll never be able to get Brennen and Kenzie out."

I wasn't about to leave without the bundle wrapped in Tiernyn's cloak. I pulled it out of the clothespress and bound it with two belts, one at each end, so I could sling it over my shoulder like a bedroll. When I was satisfied it was secure, I turned back to the clothespress and pulled out trews, a tunic, a shirt, and a dark blue cloak.

"We can stuff one of them into here," I said, indicating the clothespress. "The other one should fit into the bench under the window in the other room."

Both of us were breathless and smeared with blood by the time we finished, but the bedchamber didn't look quite so much like a charnel house anymore. I changed into shirt, tunic, and trews, and stuffed the bloodstained gray gown into the clothespress on top of the headless Maedun soldier. With Whisperer once again strapped to my back, I felt much better. We weren't defenseless now.

Finding Sheryn something else to wear proved a little more

difficult. None of my gowns would fit her, nor would any of my trews and tunics.

"This is silly," Sheryn said. "This is far too big for me. It would fall off if I tried moving in it." She discarded one of my gowns and turned to me. "We'll have to try getting into my rooms. I have perfectly good riding outfits there. Is the terrace guarded?"

It wasn't. It took less than a quarter of an hour to get into her rooms, find something suitable, and get back to my chambers.

Carrying the bundle containing Tiernyn's torc and the pieces of Kingmaker, I eased open the door into the hallway. The torches in the hallway guttered fitfully, nearly at the point where they needed replacing. The flickering lights threw wavering shadows along the polished tile. At the far end of the corridor, the guards outside Hakkar's door and Francia's door still stood erect and alert, but they weren't looking in this direction. I drew Whisperer, watching the guards.

"Now," I told Sheryn softly.

Small and light on her feet, she was across the hall and into the doorway of the service stairway in a trice. Moments later, I joined her, and we made our way back down the dark stairwell to our little closet.

23

When Tiernyn built Dun Camus as his headquarters, like every other leader anywhere, he knew he needed somewhere to keep people who insisted on breaking the law. The great fortress manses of the continent all contained cells deep underground, some carved right into the living rock on which the fortress stood. But Tiernyn had neither the time nor the material to build deep dungeons when Dun Camus grew from an abandoned tower and curtain wall into the palace of a soldier-king. Nor did he have the inclination. The barracks of his home army contained a few cells where drunk and disorderly soldiers and errant townspeople might contemplate their minor sins for a few days, or a few fortnights, or even a few seasons. For more serious crimes, Tiernyn had built six cells into the palace foundations, beneath the armory and the kitchens. This was where Hakkar was holding Brennen, Aellegh, and Kenzie.

These cells weren't even fully underground. Each of the six cells had a narrow, heavily barred window just below the ceiling that looked out at ground level over the kitchen gardens. The only way they could be reached was from a winding set of stairs that opened off the small armory, and there were only three ways into the armory. One was from the Great Hall, through a small door near the west hearth. One was from the battlements above, and the same staircase led down past the armory into the corridor by the cells. The last entrance was through a small passageway leading off from the kitchen corridor.

Before Hakkar had arrived, the small armory had served only to store old or broken weapons, and as a workroom for the Master-at-Arms, who drew up the work schedules for the palace guard. Mornad was no longer in the palace, and one of

Hakkar's officers and a clerk now used the workroom. I was
sure the officer slept in one of the rooms that had once been
servants' quarters, but I didn't know where the clerk spent his
nights. He would be little more than a servant, and Maedun
servants did not warrant quarters to themselves. He might very
well sleep in the armory workroom to gain a small amount of
privacy. But he was only a clerk. I didn't think I'd have any
problem dealing with him. The difficulty would be in dealing
with him quietly.

What I didn't know, and had no way of finding out, was
how many guards were on duty in the guardroom at the foot of
the winding staircase leading from the armory to the cells. But
that was something I'd have to deal with when I got there. We
had the advantage of surprise. Surely those guards would
never expect to be attacked from behind.

I didn't want to bring Sheryn with me as I crept out into the
passageway leading to the armory, but she insisted. Had there
been a place for her to hide, from which I could be sure I could
collect her once I had freed the men, I would have left her
there despite her protests. But there was no such place, so perforce, she came with me.

The armory was still and quiet, the door to the workroom
tightly closed. I pressed my ear to the smooth wood. From
within the workroom, very faintly, came the soft, buzzing
snores of a man in deep and profound slumber.

Now, if he'd oblige us and stay asleep, mayhaps he'd survive this night.

Torches lit the winding staircase, one just inside the door
on the landing, one just around the first curve below us, out of
sight, and probably one more on the lower landing. I drew
Whisperer and held it carefully upright as we descended the
stone steps. The last thing we needed was the clang of steel on
stone announcing our presence.

The door at the bottom stood wide-open, casting a long
shadow down the corridor. I peered carefully around the corner.

There were four guards, all of them armed with swords and

daggers. Two of them sat at a table in the guardroom, absorbed in a desultory game of dice. One of them leaned against the wall watching the game, his expression bored, his eyes dulled for want of sleep. The last attended a kettle on a small brazier. The kettle whistled cheerfully, and steam redolent of khaf berries billowed from its spout. On the wall just behind the fourth man's shoulder hung a ring of iron keys.

I got that much from one quick glance around the corner. What I didn't get was an idea on how to take out four armed men very quietly. It had to be done very quietly indeed, and quickly, if we didn't want them raising the alarm and alerting every Maedun soldier in the palace.

"How many?" Sheryn whispered.

"Four," I replied. "All armed. And awake, curse them."

"They need a distraction." She stripped out of the shirt of her dark blue riding outfit, leaving her in her sleeveless shift and the divided skirt. "I think a nice little half-drunk serving girl would please them."

I caught her wrist. "Sheryn, no! Remember what nearly happened upstairs—"

I hardly saw her hand move, but suddenly she had a slender, deadly dagger in her left hand. "I'm prepared for them this time," she said, her voice soft but grim. "And you have your sword drawn. Besides, these pigs aren't officers. They won't be nearly as quick to act." She wrenched her wrist out of my grasp and stepped out into the corridor.

Cursing under my breath, I dropped the scarlet bundle and watched her totter across the stones toward the door of the guardroom. She hummed a drunky little tune, giving a perfect imitation of a woman who had sampled far too much wine. The two dice players merely gaped at her. The man who had been leaning against the wall pushed himself slowly away from the cold stones, an expression of sheer delight spreading across his face. Only the man at the brazier reached for a weapon.

Sheryn giggled, and stumbled into the guardroom. Her

dagger went deep into the man's throat. By the time any of the other three realized what had happened, I was there with Whisperer, and the sword made short work of all three.

Sheryn grabbed the keys from their hook and threw them to me. Thrusting Whisperer home in its scabbard on my back, I ran down the corridor. She followed with a torch.

The first cell I opened was empty. Gods, I hadn't realized they were so small! Barely two cloth-yard arrows wide and only a little more than that deep. Brennen, Kenzie, and Aellegh were all men of great size. All three of them would have difficulty lying down without having to tuck up their knees. The only meager attempts at comfort the cell contained were a lumpy straw pallet, a thin blanket, and a slop bucket. I shuddered and closed the door quickly.

Brennen was in the next cell. He was sitting against the back wall, beneath the window, his knees drawn up, and his arms propped on his knees. Until the light from the torch Sheryn carried flooded into the cell, he had been holding his head cradled in his hands. He looked up warily, blinking against the glare.

"Brennen?" I said.

He lurched to his feet, crossed the small cell in two strides, and folded me into his arms. For a moment, he didn't speak. If his throat felt as thick and full as mine, I knew why.

Finally, he raised his hand to stroke my hair. "Oh, gods, Brynda," he whispered. "I thought you were lost, too." His voice sounded rusty and hoarse, as if he hadn't used it for too long.

"We haven't much time," Sheryn said crisply. "Where are Kenzie and Aellegh?"

I broke away from Brennen and ran to the next cell. Aellegh was already near the door, both fists clenched and a look of murder on his face. When he realized who was at his door, his expression went completely blank for a moment, then he grinned widely.

"You are well come here, little cousin," he said. He made a

deep, courtly bow to me. "I regret I have not the amenities to entertain you properly, though."

"You'll forgive me, cousin, if I politely refuse your offer of hospitality," I said breathlessly. "But right now, all I want is for all of us to get out of here."

"A reasonable wish," he said, and stepped out of the cell with alacrity.

I hurried to the next cell and opened the door. Kenzie crouched in the corner of the cell, huddled in upon himself like a child with nightmares. He hardly looked up as we burst into the cell but cringed away from us. The stench I had come to associate with Hakkar's blood magic hung thickly in the air.

Sheryn went to him and put her hand to his forehead. He flinched away and ducked his head down onto his folded arms. The gesture was so unlike the Kenzie I knew, the man who had never hesitated at danger in his life, or never tried to shirk what he knew to be his duty. Something twisted painfully within me.

"He's deeply bespelled," Sheryn said quietly. "He has no Tyadda blood as we do to protect him. He'll need help."

I remembered the hopeless despair I had felt when Francia cast her loathsome spell over me in the small cabin of the ship. Because of my Tyadda blood, I had been able to fight it, but Kenzie was a trueborn Tyran clansman. He had no such protection. And if what he felt were even half as bad as what I'd felt, he must believe he was lost and abandoned in the pits of Hellas.

Brennen and Aellegh each took one of Kenzie's arms and hoisted him to his feet. His head hung dispiritedly, but his feet moved as the two men urged him out into the corridor.

We made our way quickly back to the winding staircase. I didn't miss Aellegh's expression of approval as he glanced into the guardroom at the four dead guards. Sheryn picked up her shirt, and I scooped up the bundle containing the pieces of Kingmaker and Tiernyn's torc, tossing it over my shoulder.

The clerk still made his contented little snores behind the

closed door of the workroom. For a heartbeat, I considered dispatching him, then changed my mind. He was going to have a difficult time explaining first to his officer, then to Hakkar, how he had let three prisoners get past him in the middle of the night, leaving four dead guards. I had no doubts that Hakkar would have a much more fitting punishment for him than any I could mete out.

Brennen and I took care of the two guards by the kitchen door by the simple expedient of leaving Kenzie, Sheryn, and Aellegh in the shadows and marching up to them as if we had a perfect right to be there. When they challenged us, I drew Whisperer and ran one of them through while Brennen neatly snapped the other's neck. We could never have crept past them without them seeing us, and this had the immediate efficiency of direct simplicity.

It worked just as well on the guards at the postern gate. Hakkar might have to teach his guards that enemies do not always sneak through shadows like thieves in the night. Or that not all women were good only for bedding and breeding.

No lights burned in the town beyond the walls. There were shadows enough to hide a small army, let alone five people. All we had to do was stay out of the way of any foot patrols.

"Now what we need are horses," Brennen said. "The main stables by the paddocks?"

"No," Sheryn said. She put her hand to Kenzie's forehead again and grimaced. "First the shrine."

"The shrine?" I couldn't hide my startled shock. "We've no time for that."

"We must make time then," she said. "If we don't remove this spell from him, he'll betray us to the Maedun first chance he gets. He won't be able to prevent himself. Either we do this, or we leave him behind."

Kenzie had not deserted me in Laringras, not even when I so richly deserved it. I couldn't abandon him now. I nodded. "Then we go to the shrine."

*   *   *

The streets of the town were deserted. No lights showed anywhere. We had only the crescent moon to light our way, but it provided deep shadows to hide us as we moved quickly through the streets.

The shrine on its promontory above the river was also deserted. Something about it looked different, but I didn't realize what it was until I noticed that all the ivy had been torn from the oak trees and lay in crumpled, drying heaps beneath the spreading boughs. Inside, the desecration was more marked. The stone bowl lay broken on the floor beside the altar, small wisps of dried petals clinging to its curved sides. The shredded remains of the decorated ivy hoop symbolizing the Unbroken Circle of birth, life, death, and rebirth had been scattered and ground underfoot. The Maedun had done their best to evict the Duality from this shrine, but they were fools. They didn't know our gods and goddesses were so much more than the symbols that represented them. As long as one oak tree remained on Celi, or as long as one leaf of ivy grew in a shaded glen, or one mountain still reached upward to the sky, the Duality would be here, as would all the seven gods and goddesses.

Aellegh and Brennen lowered Kenzie to the floor at the foot of the altar. Pliant and acquiescent as a sleepy child, he sat cross-legged, his hands in his lap, his eyes half-closed. Sheryn knelt before him and put her hands to either side of his face so she could look deep into his eyes. The line of her mouth lengthened in concern and she dropped one hand to the soft curve of her belly.

"I think we can do this," she said quietly. "We can make him one of us. The Tyadda have a ceremony . . . We've only used it mayhaps four times in the last century, but I think we can make it work. Especially here. It will make him as immune to Hakkar's spell as we are."

"How can we do that?" Aellegh asked.

Sheryn looked at each of us in turn. "Every one of you

has a share of Tyadda blood, and I am trueborn. We have to . . . adopt him. It involves using magic to make him a part of us."

Brennen frowned in concern. "I've heard of that," he said. "You're with child already, Sheryn. Will this be dangerous for the child?"

Sheryn touched her belly again hesitantly. "I don't think so," she said. "If anything, what might happen is that Kenzie will be blood-bonded with my son. But we have to get that nastiness out of his spirit first." She looked at me. "Can you do it? Can you use your Healer's Gift to rid him of it?"

The hair on the back of my neck rose. My Gift was small, barely enough to stop bleeding. I had never tried to go in to Heal a spirit before. Torey could have done it. So could Donaugh, even though he had no Healer's Gift. My grandfather Kian had done it once to save my grandmother. But I? Could I do it? And could I do it without becoming lost in Kenzie's spirit?

"I don't know," I whispered.

"You've Healed him before," Sheryn said. "You must be familiar with his patterns now."

"But that was only for a simple sword cut. Nothing like this."

"You're his only chance," she said. "I can do the ceremony. I have magic enough for that. But I have no Gift at all for Healing."

"I—I don't know," I said again. "I don't know if I have the strength to do it."

She said nothing, but knelt there, watching me. I looked at Kenzie. He sat staring blankly at the wall behind me, vacant eyes wide in the dimness of the shrine's interior. He had not even will enough of his own to ask me for help.

I went to my knees beside Sheryn. She moved aside, and I put the palms of my hands against Kenzie's temples. Concentrating, I gathered my Gift around me. For some reason, it seemed stronger here in the shrine of the Duality, with the threads and ribbons of power swirling about me in the ground beneath me, in the air around me. I looked deep into Kenzie's eyes, and projected my Gift into him.

. . . And met blackness. The same thick, dark mist that had surrounded us on the field of Cam Runn. It surged outward, seized me, and tried to drown me, too, in its darkness. I fought it, but it was like wrestling with the night itself. Smothering, hungry, clutching, it was all around me. I could not find anything to hold on to. It slipped through my fingers like quicksilver, only to wind tendrils of itself around my throat. I tore away wisps of it, but could not loosen its hold, neither on me, nor on Kenzie. Choking and gagging on the foul stuff filling my nose and mouth, I struggled to breathe. I could not cry out, could not break away from the link with Kenzie that lashed me to the dark and formless enemy.

I was trapped in the empty blackness within Kenzie's spirit. Someone sobbed harshly. It might have been me. I couldn't tell.

"This is magic of the dark," Donaugh's voice whispered behind me. His hands came down on my shoulders, and the warmth of his presence lent me strength. *"Light will banish it. You know how to shatter this darkness, child. Use the light of earth and air magic."* An image of Whisperer's glowing blade built in my mind.

But I could not tear my hands from Kenzie's head to reach for the hilt at my left shoulder. My strength ebbed quickly. I would not be able to fight much longer. In despair, I felt the sense of triumph throbbing and pulsing through the black, formless entity invading him.

Then, in a flash of lucid understanding, I knew what I had to do. As the last of my strength drained into the darkness, I grasped the image of the sword. I saw the silver chasing of its hilt fitted comfortably and snugly into my hands, saw the polished, graceful blade with its glittering runes spilling down the center. I made it glow with that radiant brilliance only a Rune Blade is capable of. Light in a burst of color sprayed out to slice the darkness to shreds and tatters.

Terror and rage suffused me. Not mine. Not Kenzie's. It emanated from the dark mist itself. In one last burst of passionate fury, the mist blew apart, fragments raining like splinters of rock around me. Then even the shreds evaporated.

"You've won, child. Your magic is strengthening, as I thought." The pressure of Donaugh's hands on my shoulder increased briefly, then was gone.

Sweat pouring down my forehead and into my eyes, I turned. But Donaugh was not there. No one stood behind me but Brennen, and he was too far away to have touched me.

"Stay with him, Brynda," Sheryn said softly. She moved quickly to stand behind me and placed her hands on Kenzie's head. "Keep him tranced if you can. It will make him more open to the magic. Brennen, Aellegh, we'll need all of us for this. Stand behind him. Put your hands on his shoulders. Quickly."

Once again, Kenzie's spirit engulfed me, but this time it was clean and pure as a Skai mountain meadow, or the forest after a rain. I found I could take his spirit into my hands as if it were a crystal globe, glowing like a cabochon gem. My spirit merged with his, and I had the strange feeling of seeing everything through his eyes. The sensation startled me, and I nearly lost the connection.

Sheryn's voice above me sounded hollow and far away, as if it echoed through a vast distance. "Powers of Celi, we come to you as supplicants. This man, Kenzie dav Aidan of Tyra, is not of our blood, but he also is one of your children, born in the mountains of Tyra. We wish to make him one with us that he may have the protection you grant us from the darkness."

No voice answered her, but a limitless *presence* filled the shrine around us—warm and comforting and accepting. Kenzie stirred beneath my hands, and I tightened my hold on his temples. His eyes, wide and brilliant, stared into mine, and I lost myself, becoming one with him.

Men's voices, blended into a quiet chorus, followed the

softer feminine voice that led them. "From me to you, Kenzie dav Aidan, man of Tyra. My blood to yours. My spirit to yours. My soul to yours. Flesh to flesh, blood to blood, bone to bone. Be born of my seed."

Sheryn pressed her hands to the top of Kenzie's head, fingers curling in his bright hair. "From me to you, Kenzie dav Aidan, man of Tyra. My blood to yours. My spirit to yours. My soul to yours. Flesh to flesh, blood to blood, bone to bone. Be born of my body."

Energy pulsed and flowed into Kenzie's body, and I felt it as surely as if it were my own body. It coursed through his veins—our veins—and along every nerve fiber like music thrumming along a harp string. The singing energy filled him, seeped into every muscle, every sinew, every tissue of his body. It surged up, then sparked from him to Sheryn.

Kenzie was drawn into her, as was I, entangled inextricably with him. We became part of her, sharing her body and her spirit and her soul in the special and unique way a child shares with his mother. The energy became infused with a deep and abiding love, a soaring joy. It grew in him—in us—quickening as beautifully and surely as a child quickens beneath his mother's heart.

Then even as a child must leave the womb and be parted from its mother, Kenzie moved away. The sense of loss was devastating. One of us cried out, but I have no idea which. I closed my eyes in despair.

And when I opened them, I was once more separate and apart from Kenzie, back in my own body. He sat staring up at Sheryn, tears in his eyes. But his eyes were clear and alert, and he was Kenzie again. Then, like a newborn babe, forced against its will into the harsh, unfriendly world, he bent his head, covered his face with his hands, and wept.

Limp from the effort, Sheryn reached out to him again. "Arise, Kenzie dav Aidan," she said softly. "Child of Nemeara."

Brennen caught her as she sagged in exhaustion and picked her up as easily as if she had been a ten-year-old child.

"*Now* the horses," Aellegh murmured.

My grandfather Kian was right when he called the Maedun so arrogant, it sometimes made them stupid. They were so sure that nothing or no one could withstand Hakkar's spell that they posted no guards by the stables. Less than a quarter of an hour later, Kenzie and Brennen had four horses saddled and ready.

"Only four?" I asked.

"I shall not be going with you," Aellegh said. "My wife and children are still in the Summer Run. I must go back to find them, and I go on foot." He clasped hands first with Brennen, then Kenzie, and turned to Sheryn. "You are in good hands, my lady Sheryn," he said quietly. "Gods protect all of you on your journey."

"And you on yours," Sheryn said. "Thank you, my lord Celwalda."

Aellegh put his hands on my shoulders and bent to kiss my forehead. "Gods and goddesses be with you, little cousin," he said softly. Then he turned and set off at that mile-eating trot the Saesnesi could keep up for leagues at a time.

"Gods and goddesses be with you, too," I murmured, then mounted my horse. I knew I would never see him again.

We forded the Camus and set off northwest, toward the Wysg River and the track toward Cloudbearer near where Sheryn's people lived.

PART

3

Exile

24

Dawn found us better than four leagues northwest of Dun Camus, in a small forest bordering the open meadows of the farmland stretching along the River Wysg. We were only a league or two south of Craigh na Drill and Brae Drill where Tiernyn had defeated the Saesnesi all those years ago. The narrow track we followed was little more than a footpath along the rivercourse, used by farmers and cows. We had seen no signs of people as we traveled. Twice we passed farmsteads that looked deserted. No smoke issued from the chimneys of the thatched farm cottages, but cattle lowed from the byre yards and paddocks.

The farmers could have fled before the Maedun. Or they could be bespelled. The characteristic stench of Hakkar's blood magic hung faintly over the farmsteads.

"Hakkar's spell," I said softly as we stood hidden in the trees near the second farmstead. "Can't you smell it? Like a charnel house."

"You can smell it?" Sheryn asked, surprised.

"Yes. Can't you?"

"No," she said. "I smell nothing out of the ordinary."

"He'll enslave the whole of the island," Kenzie said. "As they did Isgard and Falinor and Saesnes."

"It's spreading from Dun Camus," I said. "Soon there'll be none who can stand against them."

"Except the Tyadda," Sheryn said grimly. "And those who have Tyadda blood."

We gave the farmstead a wide berth, and moved on.

We spoke very little, each of us absorbed in our own thoughts. Brennen rode in an abiding silence, deep and brooding. He had not spoken since we bade farewell to Aellegh by the stables. The air between us was thick with the questions I didn't dare ask because I feared to hear the answers. But even had I wanted to ask, Brennen had insulated himself with the heavy silence, discouraging any questions.

Just before the sun rose, we found a sheltered place well off the track amid a copse of birch, where we could sleep for a while and rest until nightfall. We were all too tired to eat, and we had to make cold camp because we didn't want the smoke from a fire to betray our presence. Kenzie gave in quickly enough to Brennen's insistence that he would take the first watch and waken Kenzie in two hours.

I helped Sheryn prepare a pallet of fresh-cut bracken for her, then curled down with my cloak around me in a mossy hollow near a fallen tree, using the scarlet bundle of Tiernyn's cloak as a pillow. The hard outlines of the torc and the pieces of Kingmaker through the layers of fabric were somehow comforting.

I awoke suddenly with the sun shining directly into my eyes through the new leaves on the birch trees, and sat up with a start. It was well past time that Brennen should have wakened Kenzie for his turn at guard duty, but he sat hunched over beneath a tree, staring out over the treetops at the clouds puffing across the sky. I left my hollow and went to sit beside him.

"You should be resting now," I said.

He barely glanced at me. "I'm not tired."

"Mayhaps not tired," I said gently. "But certainly exhausted."

He turned to look at me. In the harsh sunlight, I saw what I had not been able to see in the dark of night, or under the feeble glow of torchlight. The stubble of new beard could not hide the fact that his gaunt face was lined with grief and fatigue. The skin under his eyes looked bruised. He gave all the appearances of a defeated man. My brother had always been an indomitable spirit. This new facet of his character frightened me. It was so unlike him.

"Father's dead," he said bluntly. "And so, I would imagine, is Mother."

The news was not unexpected, but still my breath caught in my throat, and my heart kicked against my ribs. For a moment, the backs of my eyes stung, but I blinked and my vision cleared. I could not allow my personal grief to distract me from my purpose. When Sheryn was safe among her people, there would be time enough for grief. "Did a messenger from Skai find you?" I asked.

He shook his head. "No," he said. "Bane told me. All I know for sure is that Father died fighting."

Bane was Father's sword—his Rune Blade, inherited from Prince Kyffen, and all the princes of Skai before Kyffen. Keylan, Prince of Skai, had carried it from the day he turned sixteen until three years ago, when he had handed it over with due ceremony to Brennen as heir to the torc and coronet of Skai because his hands had grown gnarled with the swelling sickness, and gripping a sword hilt was too painful. But Brennen had not been invested as Prince of Skai, so Bane was still bonded with Father. Brennen had enough magic to resonate with the sword. He would have enough to sense from the sword when Father died. And when Father died, the breaking of the bond would kill Mother as surely as the breaking of the bond with Tiernyn had killed Ylana. As the breaking of my bond with Tiegan should have killed me, were it not for this vow.

I could not weep. I had already spent all my tears weeping for Tiegan. I had none left in me. I wondered if I had any comfort left to offer Brennen.

Knowing what worry would be first in his mind, I said, "Then you have no word of Mai and the children?"

A spasm of agony crossed his face. "No," he whispered hoarsely. "Nothing."

My belly knotted as I thought of his daughter Lisle, and the two boys, Eryd and Gareth, in the hands of the Somber Riders. Lisle was only eleven, barely on the threshold of womanhood, and the two boys were seven and three. I reached out to touch Brennen's arm. I could not offer him false hope, but what little I had was real enough.

"Rhan will be in charge of defending Dun Eidon," I said. "He's a good man. A good strategist and an even better tactician. And Hakkar has not gone to Skai. Rhan knows how to combat the warlocks, and he has enchanters who know how to weave the sunlight into mirrors. He and his soldiers wouldn't have to deal with Hakkar's blood magic."

"And Skai is mountainous land. I know all that, but it doesn't help." He dropped his head into his cupped hands. "Gods in the circle, Bryn. I should be there with Mai and the children. They need me."

I couldn't answer that. He was right. But we needed him, too. Sheryn needed more than my sword arm to defend her. She carried the future of Celi within her womb. Right now, she was more important than any of us.

"Fiala's dead," he said tiredly, his voice muffled by his hands. "Did you know that?"

I put my hand to his shoulder. His muscles were so tight and rigid, they felt as if they were carved from oak. "I feared she was," I said. "Or she would have been with you."

"She died taking a sword blow that was meant for me." He raised his head and looked at me, his eyes red. "I would have died in her place. She was like my second soul."

That bleak, empty place within me that had once contained the bond with Tiegan, wrenched with renewed pain. I put my hand to my chest to still it and took a deep breath. "She would have died if you did," I said. "Believe me, Brennen, she's far happier now in Annwn, knowing you still live." My voice sounded raw and rasping even to me.

He scrubbed his hands over his face and looked up through the canopy of leaves at the clouds again. "I know you mean that as comfort," he said. "But it doesn't help me much right now."

"Nothing can," I said simply. "I know the pain of a broken bond."

"But you have your vow." He looked at me, frowning, his eyes troubled.

"Yes. For now, I have my vow. And when I see that through, I can join Tiegan without shame."

He reached out and grasped my arm tightly enough to hurt. "You can't leave me alone, Brynda," he said fiercely. "Not you, too."

"I may not have much choice," I said.

"We all choose whether we live or die," he said. "Except mayhaps in battle."

"We shall see," I said noncommittally.

He accepted that. He had little choice. We sat quietly together for a few moments, each with our own thoughts, taking what comfort we could from the other's company. Finally, he drew in a deep breath and let it out very slowly.

"I lost Bane," he said. He closed his eyes, and fresh pain etched lines around his eyes. "I'm the only Prince of Skai ever to lose his sword. The gods and goddesses will never forgive me for that."

My first frightened thought was that now Hakkar might have a Rune Blade, but Brennen continued almost matter-of-factly, his voice a dispassionate monotone.

"It was when the Maedun took us, Kenzie, Aellegh, and me. Kenzie had almost recovered from that horrid black mist spell by then. We were fighting by a small stream. Fiala died there when the Maedun overwhelmed us by sheer force of numbers. I dropped Bane into the water when they killed my horse and took me prisoner."

"Did any of the Maedun fetch Bane from the water?" I asked.

He shook his head. "Not as far as I know," he said. "It should still be lying there." He smiled crookedly. "At least we know it won't rust. Rune Blades don't."

Rune Blades also had the unique ability to find their way back to the hands of the men who were born to carry them. No one knew how they did it, but Kingmaker had found Kian, and Kian had brought the sword home to Celi for Tiernyn. It was not beyond the realm of possibility that Bane would find its way back to Brennen. Or to Eryd. It had happened before; it would certainly happen again. Wyfydd Smith was jealous of his swords. He seldom allowed them to fall into the wrong hands, and a Rune Blade won't fight for a man not born to wield it.

"It's not lost," I said. "Wyfydd Smith himself built that sword. He gave it magic enough to find you again."

He gave a humorless grunt of laughter. "And better in the water than in Hakkar's hands," he said. "It doesn't help much."

"Far better," I said. Then, with all the calm practicality I could muster, I said, "And we must find new swords for you and Kenzie. You'll both need them before this journey is finished, I think."

"I'll stay with you until we get Sheryn to her people," he said. "Then I must go to Dun Eidon. I have to find out what's happened to Mai and the children."

"And right now, you have to sleep," I said. "If you're to be any use to Sheryn as a protector, you need to be rested and fresh."

He nodded. "Mayhaps you're right."

I glanced up at the sky. It was only a little past midmorning. "You sleep," I said. "I'll keep watch for now, and I'll waken Kenzie at noon."

He gave me another crooked smile. "I might even be able to sleep now," he said. He reached out and caught my arm again, a gentler grip this time. "Thank you, *cariad*."

He hadn't called me that for a long time. It reminded me of better times, and I didn't want to think about that right now.

Toward noon, Kenzie roused himself just as I was beginning to think about wakening him for guard duty. He stretched, then crossed the small clearing to where I sat. Once again, he moved with that light, springing step I had become accustomed to on the continent, lithe and graceful as a northern silver wolf. No trace remained in his face of the dulling lethargy of Hakkar's spell.

He took a seat beside me and glanced over his shoulder at Sheryn. She had hardly moved since dawn, deeply immersed in the sleep of exhaustion. He plucked a grass stem and twirled it between his fingers, watching the slender stalk blur in a circle about the ends of his fingers.

"I fancy the Maedun will have found the mess we left behind us," he said at last. "Probably about dawn."

We had left behind ten Maedun corpses—two in my chambers, four in the cells guardroom, two by the kitchen doors, and two more at the postern gate. Quite a bit of *mess*, as he put it. I thought briefly of the clerk in the armory workroom. He was very likely wishing devoutly he were somewhere else and someone else at this moment. "They'll be after us now," I said. "We'll have to leave here soon."

He looked again at Sheryn. "The lady needs more rest," he said. He took a deep breath. "It was powerful magic she worked last night."

I drew my knees up and rested my folded arms on them. The memory of that odd blending with him, as if I shared his spirit and became part of everything he was, or would be, or wished to be, was too intimate a sharing to mention. I wanted to forget the experience, but could no more put it out of my mind than I could forget who *I* was.

"Very powerful," I said.

He cleared his throat, dusky color suffusing his throat and cheeks. "I don't understand what you did—what all four of you did *to* me last night, but I know what you did *for* me. And I'm deeply grateful."

"We couldn't leave you there." I looked at him and realized the painful color in his face wasn't embarrassment. It was shame. Tyran clansmen are men who wear their pride like badges, and I had cause to know that pride could make them stiffly obstinate. Kenzie's pride had taken a deep blow from the dehumanizing blood sorcery Hakkar had wrapped around his soul. He would accept no excuses for his inability to overcome the spell by himself. The spell had left him completely unmanned, and that would take a long time to heal in him. What he would find even more inexcusable was the way the spell could have made him betray friends—kinsmen.

"You should have," he said. "I would have betrayed you first chance I had. Better I should have fallen on my sword than betray friends." The corners of his mouth turned down in a bitter, self-mocking smile. "Had I a sword to fall on, that is."

"You can't blame yourself for falling prey to the same spell that twenty out of twenty-one of our own soldiers fell to," I said mildly enough. "If you're looking for someone to blame, lay it at Hakkar's feet. You won't fall under the spell again." I climbed wearily to my feet. "We'd best be on our way. Wake Brennen. I'll waken Sheryn."

The day was warm. We kept to the small path along the river, away from the main track. I was tired. I wasn't quite asleep, but I certainly wasn't awake and alert. The changing pattern of light and shadow as the horse passed beneath the alders and willows lining the path was hypnotic. Sunlight played on the river, reflecting scattered shards of light that glittered and sparked and swirled . . .

. . . *The water in the bowl swirled and shimmered, revealing an amorphous, glowing mass, but no images formed in the iridescent mist. The faltering magic revealed no shape or substance to the prey. The glow was the residue of magic, and within it lay the quarry. The formless mist offered no revelation of which direction it came from, neither north nor south, east nor west. Nor did it give any sense of distance—merely a* not here *indication.*

The woman leaned forward, peering intently into the bowl. In the flickering light of the torch, the alabaster perfection of her face was strained and anxious. She clutched a carved stone symbol in her hand, the gold chain it dangled from twisting

*against the pale skin of her throat. The strange symbol glowed
a faint, unpleasant acid green between her pale fingers.*

"Where is she?" *she whispered.* "Where have they gone?"
She glanced down at the glowing stone in her hand. "They
used strong magic. Surely you can find where that magic is.
You must have that magic for yourself. Where are they?"

*The glowing mist swirling in the bowl illuminated the
unhealthy pallor of the man's face, accentuating it as he
frowned down at the glimmering water. The slow, labored
movement of his hands above the bowl made his weakness
glaringly apparent.*

*He put one hand to his head as if to ease an ache behind
his temples.* "They're masked," *he said irritably.* "Something
is masking the scrying bowl. I haven't enough strength yet to
break through it."

*He sat back on his heels, then looked up—and looked
straight into my eyes where I stood behind the woman. The
hard glitter of rage sparked in his eyes.*

"So, we are still linked, dear cousin," *he said softly.*
"Where are you?"

I stepped back, startled and frightened.

He lurched into a crouch, reaching toward me. "Where are
you?" *he shouted.* "Show me where you are!"

I shook my head and tried to run . . .

. . . And came to myself, sitting on the grass beside the
river, the hard sparkle of the sunlight off the water burning
into my eyes. Sheryn sat her horse, looking down at me
expressionlessly, her face dulled with fatigue. Kenzie knelt
beside me, his mouth twisted in concern.

"You fell from your horse," he said. "Are you all right?"

I looked up at him, my mouth dry, my heart hammering
against my ribs. "They're scrying for us," I said. "They found
the traces of the magic we worked in the shrine, and they're
scrying for us."

The skin around Brennen's mouth paled and tightened.
"Have they found us?"

I shook my head. "Not yet. Mikal isn't strong enough yet. But he will be. We've got to get to the mountains before he can find us."

Kenzie caught my hand and pulled me to my feet. As I mounted my horse, I found myself wondering about the link with Mikal. Always before when I had known he searched, I had been asleep, and seen him only in a dream. This time, I had been awake—groggy, but awake.

The link had strengthened. But whether that would make it easier for him to find me, or for me to avoid him, I didn't know.

25

Kenzie noticed the ravens first and drew his horse to a stop. The day was getting on for evening, and the sun had already touched the tops of the trees to the west. Turning in his saddle to look at me over his shoulder, he pointed upward. Above the trees ahead of us, a flock of ravens circled against the bleached blue of the early-evening sky. I reined in beside him, watching the ravens.

"What is it?" Sheryn asked.

Kenzie made a sharp gesture to quiet her, frowning and listening intently. Then I heard it, too. Faint with distance, but distinct and unmistakable came the sound of men shouting, and the rattle of weapon against weapon.

"What is it?" Sheryn asked again.

"Fighting," I said. "Not that far ahead of us."

Kenzie cocked his head to one side, his eyes going unfocused as he listened. "Not a big battle," he said softly. "Probably not more than a dozen or so men."

In the distance, a horse screamed in mortal agony. My horse danced restively beneath me, whickering nervously. I soothed it and reached up to touch the Whisperer's hilt behind my left shoulder.

"How far ahead?" Sheryn asked.

"Hard to tell," Brennen said. "Brynda, take Sheryn into the trees. Kenzie and I will scout ahead—"

"No," Sheryn said sharply. "Let her go with Kenzie. You stay here with me." Brennen and Kenzie both started to protest, but she cut them off. "She has a sword. Better she goes and you stay with me."

Brennen hesitated, then nodded. "Signal us when it's clear," he said.

"When you hear a fox bark three times," Kenzie said.

Brennen nodded again. He gathered up the reins of my horse and Kenzie's as we dismounted. I checked the scarlet bundle tied to the back of my saddle to make sure it was secure, then nodded to Brennen. He waited for Sheryn to urge her horse off the track, and followed, leading the other two horses into the forest. In moments, the trees had swallowed them up.

Kenzie and I set off on foot through the trees toward the sound of fighting. The soft greens, blues, and grays of his plaid and kilt blended well with the leaves on the trees and the bracken and low shrubs growing thickly between the tree trunks. He moved through the forest like a wraith, so quietly I couldn't hear his footfalls. Twigs snapped and old leaves rustled beneath my own feet as I ran to keep up with him. Ahead of us, the shouts and screams of men became more clear. A moment later, an ominous silence fell.

The trees thinned. Kenzie ducked behind the trunk of an old oak, its lower branches choked with mistletoe and ivy. He put out his hand to caution me. What I had thought was a clearing was a wide track cut through the forest. I hadn't realized we were so close to the main road leading into the northern pass. Trying to control my panting breath, I fell to my knees behind a screen of flowering berry bushes and reached out to push a branch aside so I could see.

We were too late. The battle was over. Kenzie swore vehemently under his breath, and his clenched fist beat silently against his thigh.

I counted five Celae soldiers lying in the dust of the track and the trampled grass along the verge, their swords strewn beside them. At least eight black-clad corpses lay among them. Two of the fallen Celae soldiers wore the white falcon badge of Skai on the shoulders of their tunics. The other three wore Tiernyn's red hart.

Nine Somber Riders, swords drawn, walked among the dead. Standing quietly beside his horse near the verge of the road, a gray-clad warlock watched impassively. Not more than

ten paces from where we stood hidden, one of the Celae soldiers—one wearing the white falcon of Skai—moaned and
groped at his bleeding thigh. A Somber Rider raised his sword
and stabbed it down into the soldier's belly. The soldier
grunted, then lay still.

On the other side of the road, another Somber Rider
appeared to find another Celae who still breathed. As he raised
his sword, Kenzie swore aloud.

"That's quite enough of that, I think," he said.

He burst out onto the verge of the track. Kilts flying, he
leapt over the body of a dead Somber Rider and bent low to
scoop up the sword of the fallen yrSkai soldier. Caught
unaware, the Somber Riders had barely time to turn before
Kenzie was upon them. The Maedun with the raised sword
gaped over his shoulder, his sword still poised above the Celae
soldier. Roaring a Tyran war cry, his kilt flaring with the force
of his swing, Kenzie brought the sword across in a deadly two-
handed slice that nearly cut the man in two.

Whisperer's voice screamed in my head, a high, clear note
demanding vengeance. I don't recall drawing it, but almost
without transition, found myself in the verge of the track,
Whisperer's hilt held snug in my hands. A startled face, black-
eyed and black-haired, swirled into my field of vision, then
vanished in a spray of blood as I swept my sword around.

Only a pace or two from me, the warlock, badly startled but
quick thinking, brought his hands together before him. I saw a
dull red glow form between his spread fingers. A thin thread of
black mist wavered above the sullen red globe.

Blood magic! The magic that turned an enemy's own
weapons back against him.

I had no talent to weave sunlight into a mirror. But
Whisperer's blade glowed with its own brilliance as I swung
it. The half-formed globe of blood magic melted like a
snowflake on a hearthstone as Whisperer bit deeply into the
warlock's belly. He crumpled to the ground like a heap of
empty sacking.

A moment later, I was back to back with Kenzie in the middle of the track. I was only subliminally aware of his presence as he swept his sword into the mass of Somber Riders surrounding us. I felt the blade of my own sword bite into flesh and bone, then dodged to one side as another Somber Rider leapt at me from my left. The blade of the black sword in his hand whistled as he swung it, gleaming dully in the fading light. I swept my sword backhand. The blade caught on the shoulder of the black sword, just below the crosspiece of the hilt. The shock of the impact shivered all the way up my arm to my shoulder. The black sword spun out of the Somber Rider's hand. The Rider staggered sideways, and Kenzie ran him through.

Something tugged at my cloak. I spun around and caught a glimpse of a black sword as it tore through the fabric. Fierce black eyes stared into mine as the Somber Rider struggled to free the sword from the folds of my cloak. I brought my sword up in a short, sharp thrust, and opened his belly for him.

I realized I had lost track of Kenzie. Instinctively, I leapt back, then caught a glimpse of the swirling color of his plaid. He ducked under a flashing black blade, then buried the edge of his sword in the notch of the Rider's shoulder as the momentum of the wild swing carried the man past him. He glanced at me, gave me a fierce, hard grin, his green eyes alight with the glow of battle, then turned to meet another Rider.

Someone's hands closed about my throat from behind. I nearly dropped my sword as the Rider dragged me backward, twisting as we fell. We hit the ground together, the Rider on top of me. Most of my breath burst from my chest, and the grip on my throat tightened inexorably. My vision blurred and darkened. I tried to lift my sword, but my arm felt as if it belonged to someone else.

The Somber Rider went suddenly limp. Gasping for breath, I rolled out from beneath the body. A hand caught mine and hauled me to my feet. Kenzie stood grinning fiercely at me.

"My turn, aye?" he said, then spun away to meet another Rider.

I had no time to thank him before another Somber Rider descended upon me, and I raised Whisperer to meet him.

"Brynda! Your back!"

Brennen's voice rising above the tumult startled me. I leapt back and spun around in time to see him snatch up the sword from the limp hand of a fallen yrSkai soldier. In the same movement, he thrust the sword through the Somber Rider who had been ready to stab me in the back.

Sheryn screamed.

I saw the Rider running at Brennen's back, his sword held like a lance, but I could not break away. The Rider Brennen fought pushed him inexorably back toward the charging Maedun.

Screaming incoherently, Sheryn launched herself at the attacking Rider, her dagger clutched in her fist. She leapt onto his back, clinging like a cat, and brought the dagger down again and again into the Rider's chest. He twisted as he fell, trapping her beneath him.

Sheryn struggled to free herself, but the Rider was easily twice as big as she, and lay sprawled across her legs and hips. Another Rider spun away from his attack on Kenzie and raised his sword to bring it down across her neck.

Time slowed for me. I swore, and leapt toward Sheryn. Even as the black sword began its downward sweep, I lunged out. Whisperer's blade met the black sword with a clashing slither. The Rider's sword slammed into the bloodied dust of the track a bare handspan from Sheryn's head. An instant later, Brennen's sword split the man's head from crown to the bridge of his nose.

I turned to meet another enemy, but found none. Black-clad bodies littered the track and the grassy verge, none of them moving. Kenzie stood leaning on his sword, breathing in deep, heaving gulps of air. Blood from a cut above his eye smeared his face, and more blood had congealed along his left arm, soaking the sleeve of his shirt. He straightened slowly and drew his forearm across his sweaty forehead, leaving another smear of blood above his eyebrows. He sheathed the sword on his back and used his foot to push one of the dead Riders out of his way as he made his way across the track to the Celae soldier he had leapt out into the track to save.

He knelt beside the man and put his hand to the still throat. He didn't have to say anything. I read it in his expression. The soldier was dead, too. Kenzie climbed wearily to his feet and crossed the track to us.

Brennen had pulled the dead Rider off Sheryn and was on his knees, holding her in his arms. Her eyes were wide in her chalk-pale face, but she was calm. I sat on my heels beside her.

"Are you all right?" I asked.

She nodded and held up her right hand. Blood flowed from a deep slice below the second knuckle of her first two fingers. "I've cut my hand," she said. "But that's all. It hardly hurts at all."

"Let me see it," I said, reaching for her hand.

She pulled it away. "It's only a little cut," she said. "You'd best see to Kenzie first."

"I'm all right," Kenzie said, still breathing hard. He crouched to sit on his heels beside Brennen. "What I'd like to know is why you showed up when you did. I thought I said to wait for the call of a fox, didn't I?"

Brennen grinned. "You did," he said. "But when we heard the tumult start up again, we thought you might need help."

"Aye, well, I suppose we did need a wee bit of help," Kenzie said. "For that, thank you."

A spurt of anger caught at my throat. I snatched at Sheryn's hand and gathered the threads of magic around me. In a moment, the bleeding had stopped, and the edges of the cut had come together in a narrow scar. "You could have been killed," I said, anger grating in my voice. "Don't ever do that again. You stay hidden when there's danger—"

"Was I supposed to let that Somber Rider kill Brennen?" Sheryn demanded. She closed her fist and yanked her hand out of mine. "I did what I had to do. Stop treating me as if I were made of cut crystal and might shatter at the slightest jar."

"What if you had lost the baby?"

She put her hand to her belly. "The child is safe. I made sure he was protected. I have enough magic for that."

Brennen got to his feet and helped Sheryn up. "No sense in arguing about what's done," he said wearily. "We need to move on, and quickly."

"We'll bury our men first," I said.

Kenzie reached out and caught my arm. "I know it grates," he said gently, "but we canna bury them. If the Maedun find them here among their own dead, they might think they all killed each other. If there's no trace of Celae bodies, they'll know someone else killed these men, and they'll be looking all the harder for us."

He was right. As much as it pained me to admit it, he was right. We had to content ourselves with prayers for the dead, and our thanks to them for the use of their weapons, and for the cloak of deep, Skai blue that Brennen took. Before we left them, we wove five small ivy hoops for them, representing the Unbroken Circle of birth, life, death, and rebirth, and hung them high in the branches of the oak tree among the mistletoe growths.

Oddly enough, it was the Maedun themselves who obliquely provided us with all the supplies we needed for our journey. We had, of course, left Dun Camus with nothing but what we wore and the bundle I carried. We had no food, although we had managed to find a few edible roots to break our fast when we awoke that afternoon.

We traveled hungry until just before dawn, when we found another deserted farmstead. No lights showed in the small windows, and no smoke climbed into the sky from the chimney. Kenzie and I left Brennen to guard Sheryn, and we crept quietly into the farmyard.

A few anxious dairy cattle had gathered by the byre. They obviously had not been milked last evening, nor had they been milked this morning, even though every good farmer milked his cows just before dawn. Several chickens scratched in the dirt near a garden patch, and a rusty red cock with an iridescent neck ruff crowed from the top of the paddock fence. But we saw no sign of the farmer or his family.

"They've fled before the Maedun, I fancy," Kenzie said softly, as we watched from our hiding place behind a tangle of morning glory by the garden fence. "I hope they find shelter somewhere safe."

I nodded in agreement, but said nothing.

We waited for nearly an hour in silence, watching, until the sun was well up in the sky, long past the time the farmer and his family should have been out attending to the animals and the garden. But no one appeared.

When it was finally apparent that no one would come out of the house, I got to my feet. "Let's see what they've left behind besides the animals," I said. "At least we can be sure of fresh milk and eggs for our dinner."

I had feared we would find the farmer and his family slaughtered within the house, but it was as clean and tidy as if the goodwife had just finished her housekeeping chores for the day. And it was completely deserted.

The house was a typical farmhouse. It contained only one large room, a hearth and kitchen area at one end, and a loft containing box beds with straw mattresses at the other. Beneath the loft, in a space just barely high enough for a tall man to stand erect, was a worktable covered with bits and pieces of a leather harness the farmer must have been working on before they fled. Beside it stood a spinning wheel, the spindle half-full of newly spun wool. Two small windows, one in the kitchen area and one near the worktable, were covered with oiled parchment, letting pale, golden light spill into the house.

The family had left nearly everything. We feasted that morning on flat bread, cheese, milk, eggs, and a fat hen. We found blankets for bedrolls, some thin, strong rope for snares, sturdy and easily carried light kettles and pots, and even tin cups and utensils enough for all of us. Sheryn triumphantly displayed a bobbin of fishing line and two or three hooks she had found in the kitchen area.

We put together packs of flour, tea, and cheese to take with us, and boiled all the eggs we had not eaten for our meal so they would travel more safely. Sheryn insisted on packing up some spare clothing, a gown that might fit her, two shirts, and a dark woolen skirt. I rolled them into the blankets to carry behind my saddle.

"You never know when we might need them," she said. She looked longingly at the loft. "Can we sleep here today?"

"I wish we could," Brennen said. "But if the Maedun happen past and find us, we'd stand little chance against them."

"I *hate* sleeping on the ground," Sheryn said. But she gathered her bedroll together and followed Kenzie out to where we had left the horses.

We slept that day in a secluded spot in the forest, far from the main track and the narrow path following the river. But this day, thanks to the blankets we had found, we slept more comfortably and warmly than we had the previous day. No sense of Mikal's presence or dreams of his scrying for us disturbed my sleep.

We rose in the early afternoon and continued our journey. That night, we lost one of the horses, and we very nearly lost Sheryn.

We rode single file along the path by the river at a slow walk. Traveling by night as we were, we necessarily had to move slowly and carefully. We had not even the thin crescent of moon in the sky now to light our way. The river here was narrower, the current swifter. The spring snowmelt from the mountains had filled it until it lapped at the grass along the verge of the path at the horses' feet. As the night wore on, it became more and more difficult to remain alert.

Kenzie rode at the head of our file, with Sheryn behind him. I rode behind Sheryn, and Brennen followed me. The night was filled with the sound of small frogs and crickets chirping, and the slow, steady clop of the horses' hooves on the moist dirt of the path acted as a powerful soporific. With my cloak gathered closely around me for warmth, I was nearly asleep, nodding in the saddle.

Sheryn must have been as close to sleep as I was, neither of us paying any attention to where our horses went, nor to their footing on the path. Kenzie's sudden warning shout startled me wide-awake, but not in time to help Sheryn.

The lip of the path beneath her horse's feet crumbled. Sheryn cried out in alarm. The horse plunged and scrabbled for balance, but could not prevent itself from tumbling into the river, taking her with it. Both of them disappeared beneath the bubbling surface of the water.

Ripping off my cloak, I dived straight from the saddle into the river. The cold water took my breath away as it closed over my head. When I surfaced, there was no sign of Sheryn. I shouted her name, and heard a faint cry in reply. Striking out strongly downriver, I tried to steer myself toward the sound of her voice.

The tips of my fingers brushed against the fabric of her gown. I lunged closer and wrapped my hands into the thick, heavy linen. She reached out for me, clutching at my tunic, and pulled both of us under.

Coughing and sputtering, I fought my way back to the surface, dragging her with me.

"Let go of me," I shouted into her ear. "Let go, or we'll both drown. Let go! I've got you. I won't let you go."

She had the presence of mind to listen. Gasping, she loosed her grip on my tunic. I felt her relax, and turned her so that I could grasp her under the arms and pull the back of her head up against my shoulder. The current swept us around a curve, and something hard banged against my back. Wet grass trailed across my face.

We had been thrust against the riverbank, but the water was too deep. I could not find the bottom with my feet. Frantically, I seized a handful of the long grass. Part of it tore away from the wet earth, but the rest of it held. Sheryn lay limp against me, not moving.

Someone's hand closed firmly over mine. "I have you, lass," Kenzie's voice said calmly above me. "Hang on to her."

Brennen reached down over my shoulder and grabbed Sheryn's hands. I let go of her, and he dragged her out of the water. I turned and reached up with my free hand. Kenzie seized it, and pulled me out of the water in one quick, smooth motion. I lay on the grass beside him for a moment, gasping for air and spewing out the muddy river water I had swallowed.

Sheryn huddled in Brennen's arms, coughing and shivering. He had wrapped his cloak around her, but her wet clothing would quickly rob her body of any warmth the river had left her.

"We need to find shelter," Kenzie said. "We'll have to risk a fire or the both of you will freeze. We won't be able to go on until you warm up again."

I nodded, still unable to speak. Finally, I managed to sit up and push the wet hair out of my eyes. Whisperer's hilt banged against the side of my head, and I nearly cried out with relief. I had thought for certain I had lost it.

"The horse is gone," Brennen said. "Sheryn will have to ride with one of us."

"Better the horse than the lady," Kenzie said. "We might find shelter in yon wood. If our fire is only a small one, the trees should hide it well enough."

While Kenzie and Brennen gathered dry wood and made the fire, I used my Healer's Gift to examine Sheryn. As far as I could tell, the child she carried was still safe and secure within her womb. And except for a deep chill, Sheryn herself had suffered no ill effects from the plunge into the icy water.

I helped her out of her wet clothes and into the homespun gown she had taken from the farmstead. It was too big for her, but it was warm and dry. She still shivered, so I got two blankets wrapped firmly around her, then stripped out of my own soaking clothes. One of the shirts fit, and the skirt was almost long enough to reach my ankles. I felt immediately warmer once I had changed. My cloak was dry, and warm as any blanket. I spread our things out on bushes, and went to sit beside Sheryn.

Her hair straggled down across her forehead and cheeks, and her face was pale in the faint starlight. She held the blankets tightly under her chin, her fists knotted in the fabric.

"I hate this," she said fiercely, her voice quivering from both rage and the chill. "I *hate* this! I want my dayroom and my fire and my good bed. And I want my women bringing me hot tea and small cakes. I don't want to have to think about anything but what we'll name the child, and making little nightgowns for him. I don't want to go haring off through the night anymore."

Kenzie had a kettle of water set to boil on the fire. As he made the tea, Brennen came to sit down beside us. Sheryn turned to him and pressed herself into his arms, her face buried in the hollow of his shoulder.

"I want to go home," she sobbed. "I just want to go *home!*"

He smoothed the hair back from her forehead. "We're going home," he said softly. "We'll be there as soon as we can."

Kenzie came over with a tin cup of tea and handed it to Sheryn. "We can grant one of your wishes, my lady," he said. "I think there'll be no more night traveling. It's too dangerous with no moon to light the way."

Sheryn took the cup, wrapping both her hands around it. "I'm sorry," she said in a small, scratchy voice. "I know we have to run. But I'm just so weary and so cold . . . "

Kenzie got up and poured another cup of tea to bring to me. I sat there, staring down into the cup, letting the heat seep into my hands, and down into the rest of my body. I was so tired, I felt dizzy. My ears buzzed.

The surface of the tea in the cup shimmered, and an image formed in it. Mikal glared up at me, his lips skinned back from his teeth in a primitive, wolfish grin.

"There you are, dear cousin," he whispered. "I've found you at last. All of you! Where are you?"

I cried out and flung the cup away. The tea sizzled as it hit the fire. I felt Mikal's rage as the link between us shattered.

But that momentary link had told me that he was no longer in Dun Camus. I had caught a glimpse of trees and sky behind him as his image swirled across the surface of the steaming tea. He had left the palace and was on the road, following us.

26

We made better time the next day. We kept to the small path along the river's edge. Once, I caught a glimpse of a farm family working in a field, but they didn't look up. At this distance, I couldn't tell if they were bespelled. And Maedun invasion or no, the dairy cattle needed caring for, and the crops needed tending.

We stopped only enough to rest the horses and take a few small meals. That night, we camped near a spring in sight of the foothills, rising like pleated green fabric toward the skirts of the soaring, gray crags of the Spine of Celi.

Our fire was small. I sat watching the hot black shadows chase glowing red across the coals in an ever-changing pattern of light and dark, and tried to empty my mind. But every time I closed my eyes, I saw a flash of those cold, black eyes before me. They glittered with a light that was not quite sane. My belly rolled uneasily, threatening rebellion. The two magics warring within Mikal had completely unbalanced him. I'd felt it when he looked up and stared straight into my eyes. Whatever his purpose had been when he set out after us, now it was simply the delight he would take in our deaths.

Across the fire from me, Sheryn sat staring down into the tin cup she held on her knees, her hair spilling in a heavy curtain of shining gold across her face. The dim glow of the fire limned one perfect cheekbone, but left her eyes as unreadable black pools. Next to her, to my left, Brennen, wrapped in his dark blue cloak, nearly faded into the shadows behind him. He, too, watched the fire, but I could not read his expression. To my right, Kenzie sat in silence. The glow of the fire picked out the faintly gleaming silver of his plaid pin, turning the intricate knotwork design on it into darkly etched lines against the glimmer of the silver. The firelight, even faint as it was, turned his hair to molten copper, and when he lifted a hand to push a stray lock of hair back from his eyes, I caught the muted spark of the emerald in his ear.

I shuddered. I had dreamed this. I had dreamed this circle around a small campfire, but in the dream the rest of my family had been here. Now, they were dead. My parents. Donaugh. King Tiernyn and Queen Ylana. Tiegan. Pain clutched at my heart, threatening to squeeze it dry. *Oh, gods, Tiegan* . . . All that was left of him was the tiny spark of life glowing beneath Sheryn's heart, deep in her womb. The child I had sworn to protect, even at the cost of my life.

And what of Mai and the children? In the dream, the fire-light had washed their faces, too, with stark, bloody color. We'd had no word of Skai before we fled Dun Camus, and no way now of sending or receiving news.

I glanced at Brennen, sitting so insular and quiet, wrapped in his cloak. He watched the fire, a frown drawing his brows together, his expression remote. I could almost feel his pain, his urgent need to go to his family. But he, like me, had placed service to his king before his own needs. I glanced again at Sheryn. Service to a king yet unborn.

Weariness washed over me, and something stung the backs of my eyes. Why had this happened to us? How had we allowed this to happen? I wanted everything to be the way it was before . . .

By my knee, Whisperer's soft, chiming tone murmured quietly. I put my hand down, let my fingers close around the rippled ivory and silver of the hilt. It was warm against my skin, almost alive. The hilt and my hand had recognized each other the first time my grandmother placed the sword in my possession. We were made for each other, and both of us knew it, Whisperer and I. She served me as well as she had served my grandmother. And she comforted me in my need.

Beside the sword, the scarlet bundle of Tiernyn's cloak brushed softly against the backs of my fingers. I think Sheryn recognized Tiernyn's cloak. She had asked about it only once, demanding to know what it was I carried so carefully. I had answered simply, "Your son's heritage." She had not replied, but she had asked no further about it.

Overhead, the last of the light leached from the sky, and the stars glimmered faintly behind a thin veil of nearly transparent cloud. In the dying fire, light and shadow chased each other, shimmering in the night. I watched, my hand clutching Whisperer's hilt as if it were another hand. But the threads binding me to the sword thrummed differently now, a minor key melody shot through with grief and loss. Half the harmonic was gone because Tiegan was gone. The sword's song was incomplete. I was incomplete.

I sensed someone looking at me and glanced up to meet Sheryn's eyes across the circle of throbbing light. She did not smile, did not acknowledge in any way that we shared anything but a wary mutual respect. Then I realized that part of the song I heard was coming from her. She hummed a hauntingly familiar melody, one I knew, but couldn't place.

Holding her tin cup cradled between her hands, she rose and began to dance to the tune. The kilted-up hem of her gown caressed the tops of her bare feet, brushing against the carpet of last year's leaves and this year's spring grasses in the small clearing. She didn't look up. Instead, she gazed down into the cup held lovingly in her hands. She danced alone, swaying gracefully to the cadence of her own music.

Then I knew what the tune was, what the dance was. I had lost track of the seasons, and tonight marked the turn of the season from early spring to late spring. Tonight was Beltane Eve, the night—the only night of the year—when the Duality split into its separate male and female components to couple as man and woman and ensure a plentiful bounty from field and forest, sea and river. Tonight, all over Celi, great fires should have been lit in oak groves on the flanks of mountains in the west, or on hillsides in the east, in tribute to the Duality. Tonight, the air should have been full of the music of pipe and flute, harp and chime as the men and women of the island danced around the fires in the celebration of new life.

But no fires were lit this night. The darkness of the Maedun invasion had settled like a cloak over the island. Celi's king was dead, her people strangling under the Maedun grip. The song Sheryn sang reflected that sorrow. She had slowed the tempo of the music, usually so sprightly and joyful, to the cadence of a dirge, and moved it into a melancholy, minor key. Her dance was a mourning ritual rather than a celebration.

"I dance for the lost ones," she murmured. "I dance to tell the gods we don't forget."

My cup sat on the soft ground by my hip, still half-full of springwater. I groped for it, then climbed to my feet, the rough surface of the cup harsh against the palms of my hands, not at all like the smoothly carved wooden goblets chased with silver I was used to on Beltane Eve. As if of their own accord, my feet found the tempo of the music and began moving. I loosened my hair until it fell forward across my cheeks. Then the music took me, and it didn't matter at all that I was dressed in an old, wrinkled shirt and tunic and stained trews instead of the proper short, white tunic, or that the texture of the cup between my hands was wrong. I danced to honor the Duality, because tonight I represented the female half of the deity, and this night belonged to the Duality.

Brennen rose to his feet and shed his cloak and boots. He placed his sword carefully on top of his cloak, and stepped into the circle. A trace of wetness gleamed on his cheekbones beneath his eyes, and I knew he thought of Mai, and how for twelve years he had shared this night with only her. Their son Gareth was a child of Beltane, conceived on the soft spring grasses outside the oak grove on the flank of Dun Eidon's mountain, doubly blessed to claim a god as father and a goddess as mother.

Finally, Kenzie stood. He unclasped the silver plaid brooch and folded the plaid before he put it onto the weathered log he had been using as a seat. His white shirt gleamed in the faint glow of the fire. He moved into the circle, graceful and lithe for all his size.

We circled the fire, the four of us, our feet moving in cadence to Sheryn's singing. Then Kenzie took up the wordless tune. His rich baritone blended with Sheryn's soprano and gave the melody a haunting beauty I'd never known before.

Sheryn swayed like a willow in the breeze, then stopped before Brennen and held up her cup. "Mead, my lord?" she whispered.

Brennen froze into immobility, his body stiff suddenly, and awkward. His face was as rigid as his body, and he hesitated. For a moment, I thought he might turn away, then he reached out and took the cup from her.

"Your gift honors me, my lady," he said hoarsely. He raised the cup to his lips and drained it, then tossed the cup back toward our saddle packs. Sheryn took his hands and they began to dance together. I closed my eyes and turned away from the pain in his face.

I watched Kenzie for a moment as he danced, eyes closed, lost in the music of his own making. My heart thudded hard in my chest, surprising me, as I moved to intercept him. Sensing my presence, he opened his eyes and looked down at me, startled.

I held up the cup of springwater. "Mead, my lord?"

Something flickered in his eyes, something the half-dark masked. It could have been amusement. Or gentle mockery. I couldn't tell. But he smiled.

"Ye dinna have to do this, lass," he said softly.

My hands trembled on the cup. "It's Beltane Eve," I said, hating to hear the quaver in my voice. "I would honor the god and the goddess. Mead, my lord?"

He bowed, unsmiling now. "Your gift honors me, my lady," he said. He took the cup from me and drained it. Then he took my hands and bent to kiss me. To my everlasting chagrin, I burst into tears. He gathered me into his arms and carried me to a shadowed place beneath the oaks and elms. All I could do was sob blindly against his chest as he sat, holding me on his lap. His big hand smoothed my hair back, and he spoke to me kindly, as one might to a sick child. I couldn't understand the words, but the tone was soothing and gentle, and there was a world of comfort there in the circle of his strong arms.

Finally, empty of tears at last, I drew away and looked up at him. The shine of tears gleamed on his cheeks, too. I reached up and touched them, then lost myself again as he bent his head and took my mouth with his.

I hadn't thought a man so big could be so gentle, nor that hands so large could move so delicately across a woman's body. He drew a response from me that I hadn't thought I was able to give him, first from my body, then from my mind, and at last from my spirit. It was at first tender and sweet, then quickly flared to passion.

There on the soft, spring grass under the oaks and elms, we merged again into one being. But this was a different blending from the one we shared in the shrine back in Dun Camus. I had no sense of losing myself in his spirit. He was Kenzie, and I was Brynda, and I never lost track of that. But the joining of the two into Kenzie-and-Brynda was powerful and sweet, and somehow perfectly fitting and right. Somewhere in the void left by the severing of the bond with Tiegan, a small, fragile thread of joy came to life and glowed softly against the empty darkness.

Finally, as the passion ebbed and I became aware of myself as just Brynda again, he held me and I held him. Above us, the stars moved across the sky. The Huntress Star sought the new, dark moon, and I watched it, listening to the slow, steady, reassuring beating of Kenzie's heart beneath my cheek.

"Brynda . . ." He put his hand up to stroke my hair. "Ye dinna have to answer this, but it needs saying." He hesitated and when he continued, his voice was hoarse and strained. "Brynda, my soul is cupped within the palm of your hand."

I closed my eyes in pain and bit my lip. I had no answer for him. It wasn't so much that his soul could find no shelter within my heart or my hands, but I had no heart left to shelter any man's soul. The thing that beat within my chest was nothing but an empty cinder, dry and sere and burnt, torn and shattered by the broken bond.

I tried to speak, but no words came. He bowed his head and pressed his cheek to the back of my hand. "I know," he said softly. "I'm a man with a shame on him. I canna blame you if you didna want me."

Again, his voice was oddly hoarse, and I knew how much his declaration has cost him, how fiercely his own pride constrained him. "It's not that," I said quickly. I brushed a lock of hair back from his cheek. "Never that, Kenzie. And nobody can blame you for falling under Hakkar's spell. I don't. Believe me, I don't. It's just—I have nothing to give you back."

He was quiet for a moment. "Thank you," he said. Then he raised his head and kissed my forehead. "I think I understand," he whispered. "Your grief is too deep and new to accept this. But grief fades with time. When it does, I wanted you to know that I'll be close by."

I propped myself up on my elbow and looked down at him. His tangled hair shadowed his face and eyes, but the clean lines of his nose and cheekbone gleamed faintly in the starlight.

"You honor me," I said at last. "Once we've seen Sheryn safe to her people, it will be something I'll have to think about."

He put up his hand and traced the outline of my mouth. "Think well, sweetheart," he said softly. "Tiegan made you take that vow for two reasons. Besides wanting you to keep Sheryn safe, he wanted to keep you safe, too. That will be something you'll want to think about, too. He wanted you alive. And safe."

* * *

The foothills bordering the Spine of Celi began to rise around us early the next afternoon. The land became more rocky and the forests thicker. We had left behind the rolling Mercian meadowlands and their parklike woods, and every hour took us closer to the towering crags.

We held the horses to a walk by necessity, but the sense of urgency quivering in my belly made me want to whip them to a gallop. Not that many leagues behind us, Mikal led a troop of Somber Riders in search of us. But with both Sheryn and me working small masking spells, he might have lost our exact whereabouts. I had seen nothing further after that one terrifying moment while I sat shivering by the small fire. I had let down my guard, and he had penetrated it easily. Too easily. I hoped that didn't mean he was growing stronger.

We rode single file, Kenzie in the lead, me to the end of our small line. His bright hair caught the dappled light spilling through the leaves and gleamed like polished copper. The muted blues, grays, and greens of his kilt and plaid seemed to be a part of the forest itself. He looked relaxed, one hand on his hip, but the constant movement of his head as he scanned the woods to either side and ahead betrayed his tension.

Between Kenzie and me, Brennen rode with Sheryn clinging to him behind his saddle. Her eyes were closed in her pale face, and she leaned forward against him, her cheek pressed into the hollow of his spine between his shoulder blades. The pallor of her face against the deep blue of his cloak worried me. She had not fully recovered from the spill into the river, and I knew she had not been sleeping well with the discomfort of the cold camps. Nor had she been eating very much. She made little mention of her discomfort, though, after that one outburst the night before last after we pulled her from the river, and protested when Brennen suggested stopping more often so she could rest.

I had to admit that she surprised me. She was made of sterner stuff than I had given her credit for. She was, after all, Tyadda, and as she had said herself, the Tyadda endure.

The spring sunshine was warm on my back, and the air was full of the scent of new spring growth and moist soil. Beneath the hooves of the horses, young grass sprang enthusiastically from pockets of soil between the river stones, and creamy white clumps of starflower and Beltane apple flared among the pale green fronds of young bracken. Around us, the air rang with birdsong as all the sweet singers called to mates with little regard for the troubles of four humans plodding through their midst. I looked up and caught the impudent eye of a robin, his rusty red breast plumped out in self-satisfied pride as he poured out his heart in extravagant song to a female in her modest brown plumage.

Kenzie drew his horse to an abrupt halt, leaning forward to peer intently through the trees ahead. I reined in beside Brennen and Sheryn, trying to see through the thick foliage. For a moment, I saw nothing but trees, then I realized the trees thinned to a clearing less than a furlong ahead. We were downwind of the clearing and the unmistakable scent of woodsmoke drifted faintly on the air.

"There's a village up ahead," Kenzie said quietly. "Or what's left of a village . . ." His voice trailed off as the subtle underlying stench of death and decay reached us. He glanced at me, then at Brennen, frowning.

Sheryn raised her head. Her eyes looked blurred and unfocused for a moment, then sharpened as she realized what she smelled. "Somber Riders?" she asked.

"I wouldna be surprised," Kenzie said. He looked at Brennen. "Mayhaps you should stay here with the lady Sheryn while Brynda and I see if they left anything salvageable."

The line of Sheryn's mouth lengthened grimly. "You needn't try to spare my sensibilities," she said, a touch of anger in her voice. "I've seen what Somber Riders can do."

So had I. But what we found in that village sickened me. I'd heard tales of how the Saesnesi raiders raged through the land before Tiernyn defeated them at Brae Drill and made peace with the Saesnesi Celwalda Elesan. There were many stories of how they'd left whole villages sacked and burned, the inhabitants slaughtered like sheep. But surely no Saesnesi ever hung men and women from their own doors and skinned them, or nailed infants to trees. Here, no birds sang. Even the small predators were absent, driven off by the stench of blood magic. My stomach rolled uneasily, and I had to look away.

The village was not large—only five or six stone-built houses with roofs that had been thatch before the Somber Riders arrived and burned them. The houses stood in a rough circle around an open square centered around a public well. The people who had lived here had probably been hunters. But there were no people left now. Not alive.

"Not enough corpses to be everyone who lived here," Brennen said, his voice tight and raw in the unnatural silence. "Some of them must have escaped into the mountains."

The nauseating reek of blood magic swirled thickly in the air. It seemed to be stronger to my left. I dismounted and made my way carefully across the littered square, steeling myself against the sight of bloody, flayed corpses. Only once before had I smelled that stench as strongly as I smelled it now, and that was on the terrace of Dun Camus, outside Ylana's day-room.

The body of a woman lay in the dirt between two of the burned-out houses. She wore the pale cream robes of a holy woman. A village this size wouldn't have a shrine attended to by a High Priest and Priestess and twelve priests and priestesses, but even a small shrine always had at least one holy man or holy woman to see to the needs of the people. And very often, the attendant had some magic.

The holy woman lay on her side, her hands and feet bound. Even in death, an expression of terror distorted her face. A yawning rip opened her belly, and her guts lay spilled around her in an obscene tangle in the dirt.

The breath went out of me as if someone had buried his fist in my belly. I turned away to find Kenzie beside me, staring in horror at the corpse.

"Hellas-birthing," he muttered. "What is *that?*"

"Mikal," I said softly. "He stole her magic." I looked up at the mountains rising steeply to the west. "He's not far away right now, and he's between us and the mountains."

27

Kenzie stared at me for a moment, then looked at the mountains.
"How could he get here so quickly?" he asked. "How could he
be ahead of us?"

My shoulder muscles went abruptly slack, as if the weight
of my arms were too much for them to bear. I felt ancient and
weary and listless. "We followed the river, every twist and
turn," I said. "He took the road, and it's straight as the flight
of an arrow. We haven't been moving very fast because we've
been traveling mostly at night. If you don't care about
whether or not you kill your horses, or if you can get fresh
horses every few leagues, you can get here in two days easily
from Dun Camus. He's waiting for us out there. I know it."

He swore, then sighed. "Aye, well, we'll just have to make
the best of it," he said. "We're not beaten yet. Nor taken,
either."

I knelt beside the holy woman and cut the ropes binding
her wrists and ankles, then pulled the folds of her robe around
her to hide the terrible wound in her belly. There was no way
of telling how much magic she had given up to Mikal, or how
strong it made him now. The chilling mutilation of the other
corpses in the village made obscene sense, too. He had
strengthened his Celae magic by stealing what magic this
woman had. And he had strengthened his blood sorcery by the
slaughter of the village people. We were in the spreading
skirts of the Spine of Celi. Maedun blood sorcery worked
poorly in any mountainous region because the mountains have
always been sacred to the gods and goddesses. Their light and
power overcame it.

When I had seen Mikal in my dreams, Francia had been
with him. Was she with him now, and had she been in this village? She could not use Celae magic, but she certainly could

wield blood sorcery. This much slaughter, this much terror and spilled blood would certainly make her powerful enough to work her own spells, mayhaps even this close to the mountains.

I shuddered when I tried to reckon up how it might affect Mikal—how much more powerful he might be now.

When Kenzie and I got back to the square, Sheryn knelt beneath the oak tree by the well, holding the dead infant. She had found a small scrap of blanket to wrap it, and she crooned a lullaby in a soft, quavering voice. As Kenzie and I approached, she laid the tiny corpse gently on the ground and got to her feet. She went quickly to Brennen, huddling against him, shivering. She was even paler than usual as she looked around her. She glanced at me, then at Kenzie, her eyes wide and dark with shock.

"We have to bury them," she said. "We owe them at least that much. We can't leave them here for the animals."

"No animal will come near this village," I said. "The stench of Maedun blood sorcery will keep them away forever."

"Sheryn's right," Brennen said. "We have to bury them. We can't leave them like this."

"Do we have the time?" Kenzie asked. "The Maedun might return."

"Would you leave your people?" Sheryn asked fiercely, glaring at him. "We had to leave those soldiers unburied, but we can't leave these people unburied here. I won't. Not the children . . ."

"Mikal won't come back," I said. "Not here. He'll be waiting for us when we reach the main road through the pass."

"Can we avoid the road?" Kenzie said. "Surely there are more small trails like the one we've been following that go through the mountains."

Brennen looked up at the soaring crags and swore softly, his face bleak. "There's no other way through the Spine," he said. "There are hundreds of tracks leading into the Spine, but fewer than half a dozen roads through it. Not if we're using the horses. If we don't want to travel fifteen leagues south to the main road, we have to take that pass."

"Then we'll bury these people and see if we can come up with an idea how to get past him," Kenzie said.

It took the better part of the afternoon to dig the trench and gather stones for the cairn. Sheryn found more scraps of blanket in the roofless houses and wrapped the small corpses, while Kenzie and I cut down the adults and wrapped them for burial. By the time we set the last stone on the long cairn, dusk had begun to leach the color from the sky. Brennen straightened and wiped the sweat from his forehead with the sleeve of his shirt.

"We'll find somewhere close by to stay for the night," he said. He glanced around at the ruined village and grimaced. "But not here. Up there on the hillside in the trees, I think."

We found a sheltered hollow beneath a rocky overhang deep in the forest above the village, and made camp for the night. A small spring bubbled out of the rock and filled the air with the music of falling water as the outflow trickled over the mossy lip of the basin. Like many springs in the mountains, this one was sacred to Adriel of the Waters. So many years ago that now the outline was little more than shadows in the rock, someone had carved a representation of Adriel's enchanted ewer deep into the stone face of the cliff above the bowl of the spring. The water was not much more than elbow-deep, and was so clear, every tiny pebble, every pale gold grain of sand in the gravelly bottom of the basin stood out distinctly. Tonight, we would sleep under the protection of the goddess who was at the same time one of the most gentle of all the seven gods and goddesses, and the most savage.

I glanced across the fire at Brennen and Sheryn. He sat with his back to the wall not far from the spring, and Sheryn sat beside him. She had been keeping herself as close as possible to him since Beltane morning, and I could tell it made him uncomfortable. I knew his presence gave her a more secure feeling of safety than mine, but I wasn't sure I liked where this swiftly developing dependence on him might be leading. From the strained expression around Brennen's eyes, he didn't, either.

Kenzie had snared a rabbit, and it crackled and spit on a stick over the fire. I made flat cakes, but without much enthusiasm. I had no appetite, not after seeing what lay in that village. I doubted any of the others felt much like eating, either. But we went through the empty motions of preparing a meal.

I thought of Mikal, now ahead of us, lying in wait like a spider in its web. But where exactly was he hiding? I looked up, but the trees and darkness hid the mountains. Even if it had been daylight, I couldn't have seen the pass. From where the devastated village sat, the Spine of Celi looked to be a solid wall of trees, rock and snowcapped peaks. The pass opened unexpectedly only as the road curved around the shoulder of the mountain at whose feet we now camped.

The meal was a silent one. I helped Kenzie pack up the leftover food while Sheryn wrapped herself in her blankets and prepared for sleep. I noticed Brennen carefully waited until she was settled, then spread his blankets on the opposite side of the fire. I also noticed the corners of Kenzie's mouth twitch as he watched, but he, like I, said nothing. He looked up and caught my eye, and shrugged.

"She's with child," he said. "She needs a man's arm to lean on, and he's more suitable than I."

"He's married," I said shortly.

He raised an eyebrow, but said no more.

I wrapped the last of the flat cakes in a cloth. They'd do for breaking our fast in the morning, along with the rabbit.

"Get some rest," I told Kenzie. "I'll take first watch tonight. I need to do some thinking anyway."

He got to his feet and stretched mightily. "Wake me in two hours, then," he said. He unpinned his plaid and swirled it around himself in a deft and practiced motion, then lay down not far from Brennen. In moments, the rhythm of his breathing lengthened into the slow, calm cadence of deep slumber.

I sat for a long time with my back to the fire, watching the slow, majestic wheel of the stars around the pin of the Nail Star. Gradually, I came to a decision.

I pulled a branch from the fire and took it over to the basin of the spring. Carefully, I reached out and traced the outline of the enchanted ewer with a fingertip. My makeshift torch burned with a small, sullen flame, and gave barely enough light to glimmer on the surface of the water. I thrust the end of the branch into a crevice above the basin and looked down into the water.

The surface rippled fitfully with the water bubbling into the basin from below, never still. The restless water caught the torchlight and reflected it back in dancing sparks of red and gold. I looked down into the flashing ripples but could see nothing beneath the surface.

Ever since Banhapetsut, I'd known when Mikal was scrying for me, first in my dreams, then finally when I was awake. Both times he'd broken through to me, I'd been looking into a liquid—the sparking water of the river, then into the steaming tea in my cup. I had never tried scrying. With my meager gift for magic, it had never occurred to me that I might be able to do it. But there was a definite link between Mikal and me, one that seemed to be growing stronger all the time.

I leaned over the basin. Shards of my own reflection peered back up at me. My eyes held no color, just shadow, and my hair blended with the wavering reflection of the flame from the torch.

"Mikal?" I whispered the name softly, and my breath shimmered on the water. "Mikal? Where are you?"

He sat before a fire, legs outstretched, his hands clasped together between his knees as he stared down into the leaping flames. Around him, the shadowy figures of men moved like wraiths, drifting in and out of the spill of light cast by the fire. He, like the other men, was dressed entirely in black, so that his body and his black hair blended with the darkness behind him, leaving his face a pale oval seemingly floating disembodied in the air. Firelight cast a rosy glow across his cheeks, giving unnatural color to his skin, a false illusion of robust health. Across the fire from him, Francia sat huddled in her cloak, her eyes closed, her perfect face still and quiet in the night.

I moved closer to Mikal and reached out to touch his shoulder. He shivered, but he didn't look up. Incredibly, he didn't seem to sense my presence. I stepped around him, between him and the fire. He raised his head and looked straight into my eyes.

In one endless instant, I saw all that had made him what he was. I saw how his own mother had twisted him and turned him into a weapon aimed straight at the heart of Celi. There in his eyes was every small, thoughtless cruelty she'd inflicted upon him, every uncaring or scathing remark she'd ever made to him, every instance when she'd withheld the love he should have been able to expect from his own mother. She'd raised him with one purpose, and only one purpose—to be her instrument of revenge on both Donaugh and Tiernyn for the humiliation she'd suffered at their hands. She had shaped him as a fletcher shapes an arrow, using his love for her as a tool. Even now, the pain of his inability to please her lurked in his face, in the corners of his mouth, in the permanent furrow between the dark eyebrows.

What surprised me was the idea I could pity the bewildered, lost child he had once been.

As I watched, I saw something else in him—the two incompatible magics warring within him. Gentle Tyadda magic would not let itself be used to kill, yet he used it to scry for me, knowing he would kill me if he caught me. The fetid reek of the Maedun blood sorcery wrapped the bright glow of the Tyadda magic as strands of a spiderweb wrap a fly, trying to extinguish it and strangle it. But the brilliance of Tyadda magic melted the blood sorcery so that Mikal constantly had to renew both, struggling to keep them separate. The conflict had completely unbalanced him. I'd seen it first in the swirling surface of the hot tea, and now I saw it again, far more clearly this time. His eyes glittered with an insane light. He was quite mad. Whatever his purpose had been when he set out after us, now it was simply the delight he'd take in our deaths.

I drew back, trying to get an idea of where they were camped. I saw only mountains around the small fire. They glowed softly in the night with their own faint luminescence, shimmering as if they breathed in the night. But I could get no sense of location. The camp could have been one league from our own, or thirty.

Across the fire from Mikal, Francia stirred. The hard, dark aura of blood sorcery surrounded her like a veil, brittle as her expression. She shivered and drew her cloak more snugly about her shoulders.

"These mountains watch us like a snake watches a bird," she said. "Can't you feel it?"

He shrugged. "I feel the magic in them," he said. "They're only mountains, Mother."

"They watch us," she insisted. She glanced around. Only the slightest movement of her eyebrows toward the bridge of her nose signaled her uneasiness. "Or something watches us. Can't you feel it?"

He cocked his head to one side, then grinned that same wolfish, skinned-back smile I had seen in the cup. He looked up at me again. This time, he saw me. His eyes glittered, and he lunged forward. His fingers wrapped around my wrist, so cold they burned.

"Don't run away, dear cousin," he said softly. "Show me where you are before you go. I've been searching for you."

My heart hammered in my chest and I leapt back. My wrist seemed to pass right through his fingers as I yanked my hand

*away. He got to his feet, advancing on me slowly. I cried out,
and turned to run.*

I jumped back from the edge of the spring, my heart still
thudding against my ribs. My wrist hurt. I looked down at
it and went cold. Four parallel welts striped my arm, blistered and red, exactly where Mikal's fingers had touched. I
put my hand over the welts, then plunged both hands into
the cold water in the basin. The pain faded, and gradually,
my heartbeat slowed to normal. I closed my eyes and sank
back onto my knees.

He had frightened me badly, leaping at me like that. But I
had accomplished my purpose. As I had turned to run from
him, I saw the curve of the river and the corresponding twist in
the road as they bent around the flank of the mountain below
the ancient landslip known as Gerieg's Ladder. I knew the
spot. It lay a little less than a league from the village. And it
was almost in the angle formed by the intersection of the road
and the small, hidden trail that skirted the eastern edge of the
tumbled scree and led to Donaugh's lodge high in its hanging
valley.

Mikal would know that road. He had followed me there
when he murdered Donaugh. And Francia herself might
remember it, too. Donaugh had taken her there to birth Mikal.
They were covering all their bets, and making sure all our
escape routes were closed.

But now I knew exactly where Mikal lay waiting for us,
exactly where he planned to set up his ambush.

I thought about that for a while, frowning into the dark.
Presently, the germ of an idea began to form.

28

"Are you mad?" Kenzie demanded.

I didn't look up at him. Instead, I paid meticulous attention to unfastening the scarlet bundle of Tiernyn's cloak from the back of my saddle. He stepped around to the right side of my horse and glared at me across the saddle.

"Have you quite lost your mind?" he asked far too loudly.

I glanced apprehensively over to where Brennen and Sheryn were readying his horse for starting out. They didn't look our way. "Keep your voice down," I said. "I don't want Brennen to hear this."

He made an open-handed gesture of appeal to all the seven gods and goddesses, glancing skyward, the picture of a man provoked beyond all patience. "She doesn't want Brennen to hear," he said to nobody in particular. But he lowered his voice and said it more quietly. He glared at me again. "I can't say that surprises me." Even his softened tone couldn't hide the sarcasm in his voice. "He'd be well within his rights as head of the family to take you over his knee and wallop some sense into you."

It was my turn to glare. "Have you any better ideas?"

He opened his mouth to speak, but no words came out, so he shut his mouth again and made an exasperated noise in the back of his throat. "No," he said at last. "But I couldn't come up with a worse one without several hours' thinking on it." He reached out and caught my wrist. His hand closed around the blistered welts, and I winced. Startled, he looked down at the four red marks. "What on earth did you do to that?"

"I burned it last night." I tried to pull my hand away, but he held tightly to it and examined the burns.

"That happened while you were scrying for him, didn't it?" he said. "When you said he reached out and grabbed you."

"Yes," I said shortly. "You should know that if you're injured while you're dreaming true, the injury stays with you on waking."

"You weren't dreaming true. You were scrying."

"There isn't much difference."

"Brynda, you can't do this. I forbid it."

I yanked my hand away and stiffened. "And just who are you to forbid me to do anything?" I asked coldly.

His reply showed in his eyes. "*I'm the man whose soul you hold in your hands.*" But he shut his teeth on the words and didn't say them. Instead, they hung in the air between us, unsaid, but as clear and distinct as if he had shouted them out. Heat climbed in my cheeks, and I dropped my gaze to the knotted thongs holding the scarlet bundle to the back of my saddle.

"Someone has to do it," I said in a low voice. "It will give you, Brennen, and Sheryn a chance to get past Mikal and onto the track to Donaugh's lodge. There's a small trail leading from there deeper into the mountains, and you shouldn't have any trouble finding Sheryn's people."

He caught my hand again, careful this time of the welts on my wrist. "It's insane," he said more quietly. "You can't go haring off through the midst of those Somber Riders. They'll kill you."

"Not necessarily," I said. "I should be able to catch them by surprise. They'll chase me and—"

"And kill you," he said flatly.

I looked up and met his eyes. They were a true, clear green in the early-morning sunshine, lit from behind with his anger. And his fear for me. I reached up and unwrapped his fingers gently from my other hand. "They might," I said with far more calm than I felt. "But Sheryn will be safe, and that's all that counts." I pulled the bundle off my saddle and held it out to him. "When she's with her people again, would you see this gets to the Dance of Nemeara? There's something inside for Sheryn's son, and the other things need to be placed on the altar in the middle of the Dance. You'll know which is which."

He pushed the bundle away. "You'll take it there yourself," he said.

"Kenzie, this is very important to me. Almost as important as making sure Sheryn gets home to her family again. Think of it as seeing Tiernyn home."

There was no more binding obligation one could place upon a Tyran clansman than to charge him with seeing a friend or a kinsman home. In Tyra, the bundle I handed to Kenzie would have contained a clansman's heart, his earring, and his braid. We did things differently in Celi, but the obligation was the same.

Kenzie looked at me for a long time, his mouth drawn into a thin, grim line. Finally, he nodded reluctantly. "I'll hold it for you, then," he said quietly. "Until you can claim it back from me to see him properly home yourself as is fitting."

"Thank you." I waited until he had tied the bundle to the back of his own saddle. "Now, we'd better tell Brennen what I'm going to do."

Brennen didn't like the idea any better than Kenzie, but he couldn't come up with a better one to get past Mikal's ambush. Sheryn said nothing, but watched me with a decidedly speculative expression in her eyes.

I took a deep breath. "Well, then, if nobody has a better idea, we'll do it my way," I said. "Once the Maedun are out of the way, you take the track leading to Donaugh's lodge. I'll join you there as soon as I can. I'll come up from the other side of Gerieg's Ladder."

"Brynda—" Brennen reached out to me, then dropped his hand and shook his head. "Never mind. Just make sure you're careful."

"Very careful," I said. I handed the reins of my horse to Sheryn. "You'd better ride this," I told her. "I'm going on foot. Horses make too much noise in the forest."

She took the reins, then reached out to touch my hand. "Good speed," she said softly.

I looked down at her hand on mine, then into her eyes. She smiled, and for the first time, the smile contained real affection. I smiled back.

"Give me about an hour," I said. "That should give me enough time to distract them and get them away from the track to Donaugh's lodge."

Kenzie stepped forward and seized my shoulders. Before I could protest, he kissed me. Hard. "Duality be with you, Brynda," he said softly when he let me go.

I made my way back down the side of the mountain to the ruined village. The little trail we had been following along the bank of the river ended there. Just a few paces beyond the village lay the main track leading to the pass. I checked to make sure no one was in sight, then crossed it and ducked into the trees on the other side, well above the river and the track.

To my right, the side of the mountain rose steeply. The forest was fairly open here, but filled with rocks and hollows, and the occasional fallen tree, all covered thickly with moss. I had to move more slowly than I wanted to. It would be too easy to slip and break an ankle if I was careless. I stayed a little more than twenty paces into the forest, paralleling the track.

Halfway between the village and the place where Mikal had made his camp, something caught my eye. Something not quite right about the shape of the shadows beneath the trees overhanging the track. I dropped to my knees behind a boulder and peered over it, trying to discern what had caught my attention.

Gradually, I made out the figure of a man on horseback deep in the shadows below me. I wouldn't have seen him if he hadn't turned his head slightly. The movement caught my eye, causing the sentry to separate from the shadowy background around him. Both man and horse stood with preternatural stillness. They could easily have been carved from black, unpolished wood. The man was dressed entirely in black, and leaned forward across the pommel of his saddle with intense concentration, watching the track.

I crept away from the boulder and deeper into the forest. Ten minutes later, within shouting distance of the first Rider, I passed another lookout watching the road, tensely alert. He, too, blended in with the shadows under the trees. I watched him for a moment or two. Right then, I would have traded Whisperer for a good Veniani recurved bow and some arrows.

I moved cautiously past him. A few minutes later, I was on the shoulder of the mountain above Mikal's camp.

He had chosen a good place to camp, sheltered by a low cliff and surrounded by oak and elm trees. A few horses, saddled and ready to move at a moment's notice, stood picketed between the camp and the road, but I saw no one around the fire. Only a few paces beyond their campsite, a narrow path branched off, leading up the mountain—the trail to Donaugh's lodge.

I crossed the path well above the campsite, keeping a sharp eye out for more sentries. But I saw none. Mayhaps Mikal thought it useless to post sentries here. I hoped so, anyway.

The tumbled rock of Gerieg's Ladder spilled down the side of the mountain at a precipitous angle. Slabs of shale, treacherously unstable and slippery, clung precariously to the slope. At the far edge, the scar was raw and fresh where part of the old landslip had let go last autumn. Dry, dead trees, uprooted in that recent slide, thrust out of the shattered rock. Their crumbling roots cast twisted shadows along the rock and provided safe refuge for hundreds of birds' nests. The animals avoided the area. It was dangerous. Every year, more rocks slid down to block the road, or fall into the river below.

The whole thing was a little more than 150 paces wide at the foot, narrowing to only a few paces at the top. The center bulged slightly, creating a small hill on the side of the mountain. New trees, mostly pine and spruce, grew at the far edge of the fall, their trunks twisting and bending around the boul-

ders piled around them. Here and there across the slope, a few
low bushes clung determinedly to small pockets of soil amid
the tumble of gray, slippery rock.

This seemed like the best place to create my diversion.
Keeping in the shelter of the low bushes, I stepped out onto the
broken scree, placing my feet carefully. One misstep could
dislodge the rocks and send them down onto the road, and
mayhaps take me with them.

Halfway across, I knelt behind the shelter of a tangle of
roots and wiped the sweat from my eyes. I glanced at the sun.
Almost an hour since I had left Brennen, Sheryn, and Kenzie
in the village. Almost time to move.

I waited until I caught my breath before moving out from
behind the shelter of the crumbling roots, out onto the bare
scree below the bushes. Dropping onto all fours, I dug my foot
under a loose rock a little bigger than my head, then pushed. It
came loose more easily than I had thought it would, and I
nearly fell as it bounded away down the steep slope. Other
rocks let go as the first one bounced down to the road, making
a loud, rumbling clatter that was all I could have wished for as
a diversion.

On the road, someone shouted. A rider burst out of the trees
by Mikal's campsite, and stared up at me. Outlined clearly
against the rock behind me, I was completely visible. He
pointed at me, and shouted something back over his shoulder.
Moments later, dozens of Somber Riders filled the road below.
I began scrambling for the far side of the landslip.

Bunched together, the Somber Riders spurred their horses
along the road below me. I snatched a quick glance over my
shoulder. My heart nearly stopped beating.

Francia had come out onto the road. There was a man
beside her. I couldn't tell if it was Mikal, but I had no reason
to doubt it was he. But it was Francia who seized my attention.
She held her hands out in front of her as she urged her horse
along the track. A glowing globe of sullen red formed between
her hands. She drew her arm back and threw it at me. Sizzling

and crackling, leaving a thin trail of smoke and burning air behind it, the ball of blood magic whirled through the air straight for my head.

I rose to my feet and scrambled recklessly for the far side of the landslip, not caring if I dislodged more stones. The searing heat of the deadly globe scorched my arm as it passed.

The ball splashed into the rock just above and behind me, and exploded in a burst of liquid fire. The whole of the mountain seemed to shiver around me as it absorbed the fury of the blood magic. A drop of the liquid fire landed on the back of my right hand, and burned instantly down to the bone. I cried out with the pain, but couldn't stop to look at it.

Gerieg's Ladder was unstable to begin with. It would take less than the impact of Francia's blood sorcery to set off another landslip. Exposed on the face of the broken scree, I was in mortal danger, not only from the Maedun's weapons and Francia's sorcery. If the rock started to slide, I would be buried under half the mountain. I scrabbled recklessly across the rock, aiming for the tenuous shelter of the trees on the other side.

The rock began to move beneath my feet. Desperately, I threw myself forward and managed to reach one of the young pines growing on the edge of the landslip.

Behind me, the whole landslip let go. I wrapped my arms and legs around the stem of the pine and pressed my cheek against the rough bark. A rumble like a hundred hundred thunderstorms filled the valley, reverberating off the mountains and bouncing back until the world shivered and trembled. Sound battered against me, tangible as the stone that poured like liquid down the slope. I thought I heard the screams of men and horses through the thunder, but I wasn't sure. A choking cloud of dust billowed into the air, and I couldn't breathe. Coughing and gagging, I closed my eyes and tried to press myself right into the tree.

Then the tree began to tilt. Slowly at first, then more rapidly, it bent forward, toppling with incongruous gentleness down the slope, as the rocks and dirt around its roots slid down onto the road a hundred paces below. It hit the ground with a jarring thud that nearly dislodged me. Still clinging blindly to the trunk, I waited to die under a crushing tumble of rock.

Something crashed through the branches and slammed into my right arm just below my elbow, then bounced away. It vaguely surprised me that my arm didn't hurt, then I realized that I couldn't tell whether it was still wrapped around the tree trunk or not. The whole arm was numb from the shoulder down.

After what seemed like several lifetimes, the noise stopped. Somewhere, something fell with a final rattle and slither and an eerie, ringing silence descended. The stench of blood magic threaded through the moist smell of raw earth and torn vegetation. Dust still filled the air, choking me, coating my teeth and tongue like fine powder, but I didn't think I was dead. Not yet.

I waited a long time before I dared open my eyes. I clung head down to the pine, which lay on its side, pointed down the slope. There was a space easily the length of two cloth-yard arrows between me and the raw earth below me. At the foot of the landslip, the road was gone, buried under a pile of rocks that would have been at least a manheight deep. There was no trace of the troop of Somber Riders.

Turning my head made me dizzy. I tried to see the place where Mikal and Francia had been, but could see nothing through the thick haze of dust hanging over the new, raw fall of rock. I thought it might be too much to ask that they, too, had been swept down into the river by the slide.

I rested my cheek against the bark of the tree again and closed my eyes. My right arm hurt badly enough to send curls of nausea churning in my belly. I decided I liked it better when it was numb. My head ached as if it had been torn in two and hammered back together with a dozen horseshoe nails. I don't think I could have moved right then if Francia, Mikal, and Hakkar himself had been standing beside my tree, all of them holding those horrifying globes of blood magic in their hands.

If I wanted to get to Donaugh's lodge and find Brennen, Sheryn, and Kenzie, I had to move. But it seemed too much trouble right then. My whole body hurt. It was much simpler and easier to stay where I was.

I looked down at my right arm. It dangled uselessly from my shoulder. The shredded sleeve of my shirt exposed raw, bleeding skin that was turning the same color as ripe eggplant where it wasn't torn. From the elbow down, the arm was swollen into a travesty of a human limb. My fingers wouldn't move when I tried to make a fist. Broken, probably, I thought remotely. That would make it difficult to use my sword if I needed it.

A wave of dizziness and nausea flooded through me, and I had to put my head back down onto the trunk. I couldn't work up the energy to worry about my arm. Then I thought of Francia and Mikal. If they had survived the rock slide—and they quite probably had—they would be looking for me even now.

Below me, someone spoke. "Are you planning on staying in that tree for the rest of the day? Or do you want some help getting down?"

I nearly lost my grip on the tree as I snapped my head up and stared down stupidly into Kenzie's face as he stood right below me. I quite literally fell into his arms.

29

By the time Kenzie had bound my arm and given me a drink of water from the flask he carried at his belt, I began to feel more human. I had almost decided I was going to live after all. He moistened a scrap torn from my shredded sleeve and dabbed at a cut on my forehead.

"I can't tell whether your arm's broken or just badly bruised," he said as he worked. He tilted the flask, poured more water on the bloodstained rag, and gently cleaned around the cut. "Can you move your hand?"

I tried flexing my fingers. They twitched, but didn't form the fist I'd been trying to make. "It feels a bit better now than it did a while ago," I said. Other than the cut on my forehead, my arm, the blood sorcery burn on the back of my hand, the grazed skin on my cheek from the rough bark of the tree, and a spectacular collection of bruises, I was remarkably undamaged. But I felt as if I had been rolled down a hill inside a barrel.

"Do you think you could try Healing the arm?" he asked.

I shook my head. "I can't Heal myself," I said. "I know my grandfather could, but I never could."

"Aye, well, we'll have to find some aspen gall or willow bark later and make a tea for you." He put away his water bottle. "If I'd known you were planning on bringing the whole bluidy side of the mountain down on yourself and those Maedun, I never would have let you go haring off like that," he said. "Gods in the circle, Brynda, you frightened me out of half my life."

"It worked, didn't it?" I asked.

He gave a humorless grunt of laughter. "Oh, aye, it worked very well. Almost too well." He nodded toward the cliff towering above our heads. "I was up there, just at the other edge of the landslip. When I saw the rocks start moving, with you still out there in the middle of it all, I thought my heart would stop."

"Did the rocks get all the Maedun?"

"All but two or three," he said. "It was hard to tell with all the dust, but I think the few at the end of the file managed to get out of the way in time."

"And Mikal? And Francia? They were just barely at the east end of the landslip."

"Then they got away, too," he said. "I saw four riders going back down the road in a flaming hurry."

My heart kicked against my ribs painfully. "Where are Brennen and Sheryn?"

"Halfway to the lodge by now, I should think," he said. "I left them well onto the path, and they were riding as fast as they could with two of them on the horse."

"With two of them on the horse? I thought Sheryn was riding my horse."

"She insisted I take it with me," he said.

I stared at him in horror. "Kenzie, Mikal, and Francia will be after them now. They'll see the tracks in the dirt and follow them. How could you leave Sheryn with just Brennen to guard her? After all this, how could you—"

"Brynda, hush," he said gently. "Sheryn as much as ordered me to come back after you to see if you needed help. She's just a wee bit of a thing, but I fancy she could make a man's life a living misery if she put her mind to it. I decided I'd rather have you thumping me around the ears than incur her wrath."

"I saw two sentries on the road—"

He shrugged negligently. "We saw them before they saw us," he said. "They'll no be bothering anyone again."

"We have to go after Sheryn and Brennen," I said. "We have to get to them before Mikal and Francia do."

I tried to get to my feet, but my knees buckled under me, dumping me back onto the torn earth beneath the toppled tree.

Kenzie took my left hand and pulled me to my feet. After a few moments, my knees firmed under me, and I didn't think I'd crumple again.

"The horses are at the top of the cliff," he said, steadying me. "It's a rough scramble. D'ye think you're ready for it?"

I was about as ready to claw my way up the cliff as I was ready to take wing and fly to the top. But there was no help for it. We had to go now. Every minute we wasted waiting for me to regain strength might be a minute too late to help Brennen and Sheryn if Mikal and Francia caught up with them.

A little way to the west of the landslip, the cliff gentled until it was merely a steeply angled slope. My right arm was useless, but Kenzie managed to haul me up bodily, hanging on to my left hand with his right, and using his own left hand to grab on to trees and bushes to pull himself up the slope. At the top, both of us had to rest, panting to catch our breath.

He had left the horses not far from the lip of the cliff. They stood waiting, docile, reins dangling on the ground. The scarlet bundle of Tiernyn's cloak now sat secured to the back of my saddle. I ran my fingers gently across the rich wool, then grasped the pommel and swung myself up into the saddle.

The ground beneath the trees was rough, but the horses managed to pick their way easily enough across it. There was no path, but the trees were well spaced. It took us ten minutes to reach the path, where we could let the horses break into a canter. The jarring caused my arm to pulse with pain, but I gritted my teeth against it and tried to ignore it, thinking of Mikal and Francia close behind Brennen and Sheryn.

The Maedun had been through before us. The marks of four horses moving swiftly were plain on the soft dirt of the track. I looked up, but could see nothing through the trees. Donaugh's lodge was still a good two leagues away.

We'd covered less than a league when I felt the bundle tied to my saddle begin to slip. I looped my reins around the pommel and reached around behind me. It felt as if the torc had worked its way to the end of the cylindrical bundle, unbalancing it. It bounced unevenly against the back of the horse, throwing it off stride.

There was no time to stop and secure it again. I pulled at it, and the thongs holding it to the back of the saddle let go. Without stopping, I slung the bundle around my shoulder by the belts I'd used as straps. It was heavy, but the strap across my chest held it firmly snugged against my right hip. The horse's stride smoothed back to an even canter without the irritation of the bundle thumping against its back.

We heard the fighting before we came careering out of the trees and into the meadow by the garden.

I saw everything as if in a sudden, blinding flash of lightning. The colors were unnaturally bright, every detail outlined with exquisite precision. Near the outer edge of the garden, two black-clad figures lay sprawled in the vivid green of the grass, either dead or mortally wounded, the red of their blood brilliant in the sun. Beyond them, Brennen and Mikal circled each other warily. Brennen's sword flicked with light as he lifted it. Mikal's black sword swallowed the light around it and spilled darkness as a broken ewer spills water. Not more than a few paces from Brennen and Mikal, Sheryn knelt in the grass near the edge of the drop-off to the river a dizzying distance below. She was close enough to them that she had to scrabble sideways as Mikal lunged at Brennen and Brennen dodged under the vicious arc of the black blade.

Francia stood near the horses, her porcelain face betraying no emotions, but she leaned forward intensely, her body taut and rigid as she watched Brennen and Mikal. And, over near the white stone wall around the house, beneath the blossoms of the fruit trees, lay three stone cairns, hoops of ivy twisted with the red of poppy and the yellow of iris, fresh and bright against the gray stone.

Kenzie was a length ahead of me as the horses burst out into the small meadow. He pulled his horse to a sliding halt and threw himself to the ground, drawing his sword in the same smooth motion. At almost the same instant, Mikal blocked Brennen's thrust and plunged his sword into Brennen's body. My brother staggered to his knees and dropped his sword. Then he toppled to his side and lay still.

Mikal spun away from Brennen's body and turned on Sheryn, his sword raised for the killing blow, his lips skinned back from his teeth in that same wolfish grin I had seen in my scrying. Sheryn screamed, but she could move no farther back, trapped between him and the edge of the deep gorge. Kenzie shrieked out a wild Tyran war cry, his sword clutched in both hands as he ran diagonally across the meadow to intercept Mikal before he could reach Sheryn.

I don't remember dismounting, but I found myself running across the grass toward Sheryn. My right arm flapped and dangled uselessly as I ran. I tried to pull Whisperer from its scabbard with my left hand. But the sword was set across my back to draw right-handed. I tugged at the hilt, but it would not move.

The sudden stench of blood magic filled the air. The nauseating reek of carrion nearly choked me.

Francia! I had forgotten Francia!

Stumbling, I swung around. She stood by the horses, her hands held out before her. Between them, a small globe of blood sorcery formed slowly, glowing that same sullen red as before and trailing tendrils of black mist. Trapped between the overpowering need to help Sheryn and horror with the knowledge of what that blood sorcery could do, I hesitated for one fatal instant. Francia threw the fiery globe straight at Kenzie.

Kenzie glanced over his shoulder, his face white with strain and tension. As Francia threw the ball of blood sorcery, he dropped his sword and flung himself toward Sheryn, his arms outstretched, trying to sweep her out of the way. Uncaring and unseeing, his black sword clutched in both hands, Mikal lunged after Kenzie, directly into the path of the flaming ball.

The sizzling globe hit the ground at Mikal's feet and

exploded in a blinding sheet of flame and a smothering billow of black mist. Only faintly visible through the mist, Mikal threw up his arms, his sword flying from his hand, and fell forward into the midst of the searing blaze. I couldn't be sure if Kenzie had reached Sheryn or not. I could see nothing through the smothering cloud of black mist and raging flame.

Seconds later, the mist and the glare faded. Where there had been a grassy lip to the drop-off, there was now only a raw, torn crater. No trace remained of Sheryn or Kenzie. Nor of Mikal.

For a stunned instant, I could only stare in horror at the empty place at the edge of the gorge. Slowly, I turned to look at Francia. She stood watching me, her perfect face completely expressionless. But her hands worked before her, trying to form another ball of blood sorcery. The red glow wavered between her palms, then faded with a wet hiss.

Sudden realization burst in me. She had no more power. She had used it up, first with that bolt of blood sorcery she had thrown at me on the landslip, then with the weaker one that blasted Kenzie and Sheryn off the cliff. The mountains had robbed her magic of all potency.

Cold, clear rage burst through my chest, driving out coherent thought. The only thing left in my mind was revenge—the need to kill her, to make her pay.

I launched myself at her across the grass. She spun away, trying to reach the horses, but I caught one of her sleeves. Screaming, she swung her other arm, and her fist slammed into my right arm, just below the elbow. A blinding white lance of pain shot up my arm, forcing all the breath out of my body. I let go of her sleeve, gasping, hardly able to see. She leapt at me, her clawed fingers reaching for my eyes.

Those fingernails were like talons. I managed to get my hand up. My forearm blocked her hands, knocking them back, and my hand clutched at her face. The skin of her cheek tore like parchment under my fingers, shredding into brittle strips. But there was no blood. I backed away in horror.

Shrieking, Francia spun away, her hands covering her face. When she turned back an instant later, snarling, she held a slender, deadly stiletto. Without conscious thought, I grabbed the strap of the scarlet bundle, lifted it above my head, and swung it backhand at her. The end of the roll caught her just below her breasts. She staggered back, tearing the strap out of my hands. Oddly enough, the scarlet roll of Tiernyn's cloak stayed suspended from her body, as if it were glued there.

The snarl disappeared from her torn face, and the glitter of rage faded from her black eyes. She dropped the stiletto and slowly put both hands to the scarlet wool, staring down at it in puzzled awe. A strange, listening expression spread over her face as she tugged at the bundle, but it didn't move. She could not dislodge it. Then, like a woman in a shrine paying tribute to the gods and goddesses, she went to one knee, her hands still moving ineffectually across the wool. Her face went slack, her eyes staring, and she fell onto her side.

Gasping for breath, my arm throbbing as if it had been thrust into a fire, I fell to my knees beside her. She was quite dead, and I couldn't understand why. I reached for the bundle, and had to tug it with all my strength to pull it away from her.

Then I saw what had killed her. The broken end of Kingmaker had gone right through the fabric of the cloak to bury its point in Francia's heart. Tiernyn had taken his revenge even from Annwn.

I walked over to the edge of the cliff, grief squeezing my heart until I could not breathe without pain. Far down the slope, a smudge of black that might have been Mikal lay amid a welter of broken bushes. There was no sign of Sheryn or Kenzie on the steep, rocky side of the gorge below my feet. I called out, my voice cracked and hoarse. But there was no reply. Nothing moved on the slope. I saw nothing that might have been the flutter of Kenzie's plaid, or Sheryn's gown.

They were gone.

They were gone, and I had broken my solemn vow, help-less at the end against Francia's blood sorcery. I had let her kill Sheryn because I wasn't quick enough to stop it.

A raw, tearing sob clawed at my throat. *Oh, Tiegan, forgive me. I failed you. Forgive me. Oh, gods . . . Everything is lost. Lost . . . Oh, gods, Tiegan . . .*

Kenzie was gone. How could all his vitality and strength be gone like that, swept away with no trace remaining? I stood staring down at the river, only a bright thread of silver far below me.

Numbly, I turned away and went to Brennen. He lay on his belly in the grass, one arm folded beneath his forehead, the other stretched out before him, his curled fingers only inches from the hilt of his sword. Tears blurred my vision as I fell to my knees beside him. I sat back on my heels, my hand over my mouth, staring down at my brother and rock-ing slowly in my grief. I couldn't bring myself to touch him, to feel the utter stillness of death in him.

Something scrabbled at the edge of the cliff behind me, startling me. I spun around, my heart leaping into my throat.

A man's arm appeared at the edge of the cliff, the battered hand clutching at a clump of grass. Then his head rose above the raw and torn crater. Black hair, black as pitch.

Mikal!

I scrambled to my feet. Slowly, carefully, I reached up and grasped Whisperer's hilt. It came out of the scabbard unevenly, catching once. I let it fall back an inch, then pulled it again, and it slid out smoothly enough. Mikal crawled up onto the grass on hands and knees, then, like a grotesque infant just learning to creep, pushed himself back into a sitting position, one leg bent, the other sprawled straight before him. He looked up at me as I approached, Whisperer's hilt snug in the palm of my left hand. No fear marked his face. His widened eyes stared blindly up at me. Coldly and calmly, I raised Whisperer for the final, killing stroke.

Mikal whimpered. He stared, not at me, but over my shoulder. He raised his bleeding hands, holding one within the other. "Look," he murmured. "I've hurt myself."

Someone trod softly in the grass behind me. A gentle hand closed over mine on the hilt of the sword. "You can't kill a child, my lady," a man's voice said softly. "Nor will I allow you to become a kinslayer."

Beyond surprise, I let go of Whisperer's hilt and turned. The man who stood behind me lowered my sword and laid it carefully on the grass. He was tall and very slender, almost delicate. His silver hair was still streaked with the dark gold of his youth, and his golden brown eyes held all the compassion in the world.

"We'll take care of him now," he said. "You needn't ever worry about him again."

I nodded dumbly, too numb to speak. Behind him, a woman knelt by Brennen's side. She had turned him onto his back, and her hands moved over his body with deft and tender delicacy.

Tyadda. They were Tyadda. I looked over at the three cairns standing below the fruit trees. Of course they were here. Who else would have buried Donaugh, Llyr, and Gwyn, and kept the hoops on their graves so fresh?

Sheryn's people had come for her. They had come, but they were too late. Far too late.

The woman looked up at me, smiling. "He lives, my lady," she said softly. As if to prove the truth of her words, Brennen groaned and raised one hand to his forehead.

"My wife is a Healer," the man said. "You need attending, too, my lady."

I nodded, still unable to think of anything intelligent to say.

A young man I hadn't noticed before walked past me to the edge of the cliff. He stood for a moment, then crouched, reaching down. "Do you need a hand?" he asked.

"Please," Kenzie's voice said. "It would be most appreciated indeed."

Moments later, he came scrambling up over the edge of the

cliff, his face scratched and bruised, smeared with dirt and splotched with blisters from the exploding globe of blood sorcery. The young man had a strong hold on one of his hands. His other arm was snugged tightly around Sheryn's waist. She clung to him, dirty and tattered, but obviously alive. Her eyes widened in surprise as she saw who stood beside me, and an expression of joyous relief spread across her face.

As soon as her feet were firmly on the ground, she broke away from Kenzie and flung herself at the Tyadda man with a sharp, heartfelt cry.

"Father," she cried. "I knew you'd come for me. I called and called . . . "

He folded her into his arms, and she sobbed brokenly against his chest.

I stared at Kenzie, then at Sheryn, then sat down suddenly in the grass when my knees refused to hold me up any longer.

30

Brennen left the small lodge in the hanging valley first. Sheryn's mother had completely Healed his wound, and with Sheryn safe, his only thoughts were for his wife and children. He bade us good-bye shortly after dawn of the fourth day.

Sheryn ran after him as he walked toward the door. She seized his arm. "You can't go," she cried. "I need you, Brennen."

Brennen took her hand and lifted it gently from his arm. "Sheryn, I can't—"

She clutched at the front of his tunic. "My husband is dead," she said fiercely. "Your wife is dead. We're alive. The dead don't need you. You must serve the living—"

Her father put his hand to her shoulder. "The Prince of Skai is not for you, Sheryn," he said softly. "Let him go where he must go."

She let her hands fall to her sides, her face filled with her shattered hope, her eyes wet. Brennen put one hand to her cheek, then turned and left quickly.

Kenzie and I set out the next morning. But before we left, I gave Sheryn's father Tiernyn's torc, charging him to hold it safe until her son reached an age to wear it. He took it solemnly and promised me. I was content that he would discharge his duty most properly.

We left the safety of the high country passes and descended to the narrow, green coastal plain. Cloudbearer loomed ahead of us, standing alone against the sky, the foot of the mountain nearly in the waters of the Western Sea. The mountain shouldered the clouds, an almost perfectly symmetrical cone, snow-capped and shrouded in mist, majestic in its lonely grandeur.

Just before sunset, we rounded the green flank of the mountain and came upon the Dance of Nemeara.

Beyond the cliffs at the edge of the flat expanse where the Dance stood, a Tyran ship lay at anchor in the shelter of a small cove. It hardly surprised me at all to see it. Kenzie had been so sure it would be there, I took its presence for granted. He, at least, would be well away from Hakkar's grim and bloody march through Skai.

Kenzie pointed to the ship. "See?" he said. "Did I no tell ye it'd be there?"

"You did," I said, and smiled faintly. "Have you developed the Sight then?"

He laughed softly. "I? Hardly. But did ye no think your grandfather wouldna have contingency plans for just about any event? There'll be Tyran ships everywhere along the coast about now, I should think, looking for survivors. This is one of many."

Just as we dismounted a hundred paces from the outer ring of the Dance, the sun sank into the sea, leaving us in that mystic, transitional time between sunset and dusk when the sky was still streaked with light and color. Bands of red and orange flamed in the west, illuminating the triple ring of standing stones. The imposing menhirs of the outer ring stood starkly black against the luminescent sky, crowned in pairs by massive lintels to form trilithons. The middle ring of stones bulked slightly smaller, gracefully joined all round by capstones, polished like jet to reflect the incandescent sky. The inner ring, standing alone without lintels, was not really a ring at all, but a horseshoe of seven menhirs enclosing a low altar stone that reflected the burning sky like a mirror—a jewel cradled safe in cupped and loving hands.

Silhouetted against the sunset, the Dance was a place of immense power. The energy of the place tingled against my skin, surprising me. I felt the force of the Dance far more strongly now than I had all those years ago when Donaugh first brought me here. Now it was like the music of a plucked

harp string, vibrating in my blood and along my nerves. Music
and magic, the very soul of the Dance, thrummed in my body
and quickened my breath. On my back, Whisperer crooned
softly in harmony with the song of the Dance.

I stood by my horse for a long time, merely watching the
play of color and shadow through the stones. Then, I thought I
saw something move deep within the center, near the altar
stone. But there was nothing there when I squinted against the
fading sunset. A shadow. No more.

"When you're done, we'll signal the ship," Kenzie said.
"They'll send a boat for us."

I looked at the ship, then at the Dance. "I belong here in
Skai," I said softly.

He reached out and caught my wrist. "You belong where
you'll live to do some good for Skai," he said. "Not spilling
your blood needlessly and to no avail."

I pulled my arm gently from his grasp. Turning back to my
horse, I unfastened the straps holding the scarlet bundle to the
back of my saddle. It was heavy with the weight of the grief of
all Celi. I held it with both arms, cradled against my chest.

"Will you come with me?" I asked him.

He stood looking at the Dance, a remote and thoughtful
expression on his face. "No," he said slowly. "I dinna think so.
It's no place for me tonight, I think. I'll wait here with the
horses until you're finished."

I glanced from him to the Dance. It wasn't exactly a forbidding place, but there was something about it that made me
draw in a quick, nervous breath. I couldn't blame Kenzie for
not wanting to go in there. I didn't really want to go myself.
But I still had one last task that I must perform before I was
free to go my own way.

Holding the bundle against me as if it were my only protection, I made my way slowly across the dew-wet grass to the
gateway trilithon. A soft breeze ruffled my hair, bringing with
it the scent of the sea and the delicate perfume of flowering
thornbushes.

The breeze died away as I stepped between the two massive stones and into the Dance itself. The evening became suddenly hushed and quiet as a shrine. The texture of the air around me seemed to change, as if the Dance were a place apart from the rest of the world, and untroubled by the turmoil of the land. I fancied I could hear the soft grasses crushing beneath the weight of my feet.

Long shadows marked the grass in the center, falling across the altar stone, leaving half the Dance in darkness. I stepped forward to the altar and went to my knees before it. Carefully, I placed the bundle on the ground and unwrapped the two pieces of Kingmaker. One piece at a time, I laid the sword on the altar stone. A last ray of the dying sun caught the gem on the pommel and sent a shimmer of light and color swirling across the seven inner megaliths. I shivered, but not from cold.

"Myrddin, Guardian of this Dance, I bring you the sword of King Tiernyn of Celi," I murmured. "I bring you Kingmaker . . ." My voice broke, and I could not continue. I bent forward and placed my forehead against the cool, smooth stone of the altar, closing my eyes against the tears that stung under my lids. I sensed rather than saw the light die around me.

This place was the heart of Celi, its very soul. Everything my prince Tiegan believed in so fervently, everything he and Tiernyn died for was represented here. All hopes for the child growing in Sheryn's womb were centered here. And from here, I would go out to earn my place at Tiegan's side in Annwn.

A sound just below the threshold of hearing broke the stillness. Something moved with a rustle just barely audible in the night. I lurched around, startled.

A man glided silently as a shadow between the two uprights of the gateway trilithon and across the grass toward me. He moved easily, and so smoothly that the grass seemed hardly to bend beneath his feet. He wore a long robe, pale in the deepening night, girdled by something that glinted like gold. His hair and beard, silver as the moon itself, framed a face carved into austere planes and hollows, the eyes shadowed by silver eyebrows. He gave the impression of vast age and wisdom, but moved with the lithe grace of a youth. I drew back as he approached the altar, but he held out his hand in welcome to me, and smiled.

"Brynda al Keylan, you have brought Kingmaker home," he said. "For this we thank you."

"The sword shattered when our need of it was greatest," I whispered. "It was made to defend Celi, but when we needed it most, it broke in two."

Myrddin nodded. "I could not prevent it," he said. "Tiernyn Firstborn himself put the scars on the blade."

"He thought he was doing the best thing for Celi," I said.

"Aye, he did. And he gave Celi nearly forty years of peace. Forty years of working together. He paid a high price, but his work will never be forgotten. Never again will Celi be only a collection of provinces. It is now a nation."

"A defeated nation," I said bitterly. "The Madeun hold our island, Myrddin. How can we ever again be a nation under them?"

Myrddin smiled. A gentle smile. "Even now, child," he said. "Celi will always be united, a nation unto itself. Tiernyn Firstborn laid the foundation. Others will build on it. The Maedun will not always hold this land. The Maedun themselves have predicted one of Tiernyn's line will defeat them."

I glanced at the broken sword. "But not with Kingmaker," I said, still bitter.

"No." Myrddin shook his head. "Not with Kingmaker. But you may be assured that another king will hold the sword one day. And in the meantime, there are other swords besides Kingmaker."

I remembered the stories of the last Maedun invasion and how that when defeat seemed inevitable, Donaugh had been given two swords forged by Wyfydd Smith himself, in the presence of all the seven gods and goddesses. "Heartfire and Soulshadow . . ." I murmured.

"Of course. Celi will be free again, child. You are the seed of the man who returned the sword to this island. By the Maedun's own prophecy, they will not endure forever. Your line will prove the accuracy of that prophecy. You know this as well as you know your father's name."

He stretched out his hand toward the altar. A bright flare of light flashed around the broken sword. Tongues of coruscating colors sparked around the Dance, painting the stones in bright swirls of green and amber and blue. The colors of life. The colors of Celi itself. The brilliant, burning light intensified until I had to close my eyes against it.

The light died as suddenly as it had come, leaving bright whorls of color dancing behind my eyelids. And a dazzling image of a sword, whole and complete, lying on the black stone of the altar.

When I opened my eyes, Kingmaker was gone. As was Myrddin. I was alone in the hushed and silent Dance.

I reached out to touch the empty altar. It was cold and smooth beneath the pads of my fingers. No trace remained of Kingmaker, nor was there any residual heat from the bright flare of Myrddin's fire.

The moon lifted above the shoulder of Cloudbearer, washing silver along the stones of the Dance. The shadows played strange tricks on my eyes. For a moment, I thought I saw the figures of men and women carved in bas-relief into the tall stones of the inner horseshoe, carved with such clarity and precision, the figures seemed alive, breathing like real men and women. Startled at first, then frightened, I realized they *were* men and women.

And I recognized them.

Rhianna of the Air, her long, moon-silvered hair floating like a veil about her body. Cernos of the Forest, with the tall rack of stately antlers rising from his brow. Adriel of the Waters, carrying her enchanted ewer. Gerieg of the Crags, with the mighty hammer he used to smite the crags and shake the ground, spilling great landslips down the crags. Beodun of the Fires, carrying in one hand the lamp of benevolent fire and in the other, the lightning bolt of wildfire. Sandor of the Plain, his hair blowing like prairie grass around his face. And the *darlai*, the Spirit of the Land, the Mother of All, smiling at me with compassion and tenderness.

Too awed to be frightened now, I climbed slowly to my feet, staring at the gods and goddesses. The *darlai* stepped out of her place in the center of the horseshoe and came forward to face me across the low altar. Her dark hair was liberally streaked with silver and hung down around her shoulders. She was not young, but her face held kindness and love, and I felt as if it were all for me right now. In her hands, she held a small globe that glowed with the soft, opalescent colors of mist in sunshine.

"Brynda, child," she said softly. "I have a gift for you. Hold out your hands."

Obediently, I held out my hands, cupped together like a child expecting a Winter Solstice treat. I noticed with remote detachment that they trembled, but I could do nothing about it.

"Is it magic you have for me, Lady?" I asked. "I don't know if I want magic . . ."

She smiled. "It *is* magic," she said. "Of a sort, at any rate. Not the same magic as I gifted Donaugh Secondborn with, but magic you might want to use." She placed the softly glowing globe into my hands.

Warmth ran up my arms and into my body, melting the ice around my belly. Gently, it filled the empty place where once my heart had been, and soothed the raw, gaping wounds that the breaking of my bond with Tiegan had torn in my spirit.

"The healing power is there, child," she said gently. "If you want to use it. You needn't take if it you truly do not want it."

I looked down at the globe in my hands. Its warmth penetrated my whole body, easing the chill of emptiness and loneliness. I drew in a breath so deep it hurt my chest, and looked back in wonder at the *darlai*.

"I offer you no substitutes for what you've lost, child," she said, compassion lilting richly in her voice. "I know well nothing can take the place of what is now gone. What I offer you is a choice. There is still much for you out there. You may choose whether you will take it or not of your free will."

The globe in my hands melted and flowed away like water, leaving only a delicate, residual glimmer on the palms of my hands. But I still felt its presence wrapping my spirit in healing warmth. When I looked up again, only the tall, stark megaliths surrounded me.

Something tingled in my chest. It had been so long since I felt it, I nearly didn't recognize it for what it was.

The bond!

I spun around, half-expecting to see Tiegan standing between the trilithons, come to take me with him. But of course, Tiegan was not there. Nor would he ever be there for me again. I nearly cried out with the sharp pain of my disappointment.

But that tingle stirred in my chest again. I looked up, and saw the distant figure of Kenzie, standing by the horses. Framed by the massive trilithon, he seemed to be as firm and solid as the megaliths themselves.

I put my hand over my heart. Beneath my palm, the steady beat quickened as I examined the sensations opening within me as I watched Kenzie.

No. Not a bond. Not exactly. But something very like it. Very similar, but unlike anything I had experienced before. Whatever it was, the sight of Kenzie's lonely figure strengthened it immeasurably.

Whisperer vibrated softly against my spine. But its song wasn't a song of revenge. Something more gentle. I listened intently, then finally realized what it was. A song of life. Mayhaps of love.

I watched Kenzie. He stood stiffly in the brilliant moonlight, merely a dark shadow against the silvered glass. He looked toward the Dance, his stance betraying his fear. But it was not fear for himself. His concern was all for me.

The healing power is there, child. The words of the *darlai* echoed in my mind. *If you want to use it. You needn't take it if you truly do not want it.*

Then I knew what the magic the *darlai* offered me was. Life. The magic of life and love and a chance at happiness.

Did I want it? More exactly, did I want to bind myself to Kenzie? A love bond this time, not the bond of prince and bheancoran.

Before I realized it, I was out of the Dance, walking swiftly across the grass toward Kenzie. And by the time I reached him, I was running. He came forward swiftly and caught me in his arms, folding me protectively against his chest, his cheek pressed against my hair, and he was saying my name over and over again, just as I was saying his.

I don't know how long we stood there, simply holding each other. But finally, we stepped away and gathered the reins to our horses. Behind us, the Dance stood silent and empty again as we made our way down to the shore and the Tyran ship that awaited us.

The Song of the Swords

Armorer to gods and kings,
Wyfydd's magic hammer sings.
Music in its ringing tone,
Weaponry for kings alone.
He who forged the sword of Brand,
Myrddin blessed it to his hand.
By iron, fire, wind, and word,
Wyfydd crafts the mystic sword.
Blades to fill a kingly need.
Royal blood and royal breed.
Wyfydd made and Myrddin blessed,
Hilt and blade wrought for the best.
He alone its mettle test.
In but one hand each sword shall rest.

Twin the swords that Wyfydd wrought.
Cold iron fired to searing hot.
Two swords both alike he made.
Two split from a single blade.
Made them for the King's own seed.
Royal blood and royal breed.
Wind and water, fire and earth
Forged the blades and gave them birth.
Music to the blades he gave,
With magic did the hilts engrave.
Only one hand for each hilt,
One to raise each sword he built.
Forged by fire, quenched by flood.
Two lives but a single blood.
Two conceived and born as one.
Two that were as one begun.
Two sons from a single seed.
Royal blood and royal breed.

Only seed of kings may lift
Wyfydd's sword, take Myrddin's gift.

My Lord, the battle has been lost.
Dire the day and high the cost.
My Lord the King lies cold and dead.
Lies the crown not on his head.
When blood-red rose the sun at dawn,
From his throat the torc was gone.
Mikal's sword his life did take.
Cam Runn's flank his blood did slake.
Where now the hands and where the sword
To stem the tide of darkness' horde?
Forgotten now lie Wyfydd's blades,
Side by side the swords he made.
Waiting for the King's own seed.
Royal blood and royal breed.
Hands to grasp and hands to lift,
Hands to take up Myrddin's gift.
Twin the blades and twin the hands,
Raised to hold a restless land.
Two swords standing side by side,
Pledged to hold back chaos' tide.
One the ruler, one the seer,
Holding steadfast, holding clear.

Where the seed that scattered far,
Blown upon the winds of war?
Hidden long by Myrddin's spell,
Enchanted now 'til blood will tell.
Royal spirit, royal need.
Royal blood and royal seed
Seeks to meet a kingly test.
Rise it will to take the quest . . .

Enter a New World

THE WESTERN KING • Ann Marston

BOOK TWO OF THE RUNE BLADE TRILOGY

Guarded by the tradition of the past and threatened by the
danger of the present, a warrior — as beautiful as she is
fierce — must struggle between two warring clans who were
one people once.

Also available, *Kingmaker's Sword*

FORTRESS IN THE EYE OF TIME • C. J. Cherryh

THREE TIME HUGO-AWARD WINNING AUTHOR

Deep in an abandoned, shattered castle, an old man of the
Old Magic mutters words almost forgotten. With the most
wondrous of spells, he calls forth a Shaping, in the form of
a young man to be sent east to right the wrongs of a long-
forgotten wizard-war, and alter the destiny of a land.

THE HEDGE OF MIST • Patricia Kennealy-Morrison

THE FINAL VOLUME OF THE TALES OF ARTHUR TRILOGY

Morrison's amazing canvas of Keltia holds the great and epic
themes of classic fantasy — Arthur, Gweniver, Morgan, Merlynn,
the magic of Sidhe-folk, and the Sword from the Stone. Here,
with Taliesin's voice and harp to tell of it, she forges a story with
the timelessness of a once and future tale. *(Hardcover)*

Fantasy from ▟ HarperPrism

DRAGONCHARM
• Graham Edwards

IN THE EPIC TRADITION OF ANNE McCAFFREY'S PERN NOVELS

An ancient prophecy decreed that one day dragon would battle dragon, until none were left in the world. Now it is coming true.

EYE OF THE SERPENT
• Robert N. Charrette

SECOND OF THE AELWYN CHRONICLES

When a holy war breaks out, Yan, a mere apprentice mixing herbs in a backwater town, is called upon to create a spell that can save the land . . . and the life of his beloved Teletha.

Also available, Timespell